12/02

# THE
# PRIZE
## IN THE
# GAME

Tor Books by Jo Walton

# THE
# PRIZE
## IN THE
# GAME

## JO WALTON

A TOM DOHERTY ASSOCIATES BOOK

NEW YORK

THE PRIZE IN THE GAME

Copyright © 2002 by Jo Walton

All rights reserved, including the right to reproduce this book, or portions thereof, in any form.

This book is printed on acid-free paper.

Edited by Patrick Nielsen Hayden

A Tor Book
Published by Tom Doherty Associates, LLC
175 Fifth Avenue
New York, NY 10010

www.tor.com

Tor® is a registered trademark of Tom Doherty Associates, LLC.

Library of Congress Cataloging-in-Publication Data

Walton, Jo.
    The prize in the game / by Jo Walton.—1st ed.
      p. cm.
    "A Tom Doherty Associates book."
    ISBN 0-765-30263-2 (acid-free paper)
    1. Friendship—Fiction.  2. Goddesses—Fiction.  3. Islands—Fiction.
  I. Title.

  PR6073.A448 P75   2002
  823'.92—dc21

                                                          2002020465

First Edition: December 2002

Printed in the United States of America

0  9  8  7  6  5  4  3  2  1

# DEDICATION AND ACKNOWLEDGMENTS

*This is for Kate Nepveu, for asking the right question.*

I'd like to thank Emmet O'Brien, Lucy Kemnitzer, David Goldfarb, Mary Lace, Carl Dersham, Edward Shoenfeld, Janet Kegg and David Starr for reading this novel in manuscript.

Additional thanks to Patrick Nielsen Hayden and Fred Herman for being wonderful to me about Chapter 31, Sasha Walton for being forbearing and helpful when I was stuck, and Emmet O'Brien (again and always) for synergistic idea bouncing.

When you light a candle, it casts light and shadows in both directions. It is the same with telling a story. This novel is set in the same world as *The King's Peace* and *The King's Name*. Most of it takes place during the first few paragraphs of Chapter 12 of *The King's Peace*. It is not necessary to have read that book before reading this one, it shouldn't do any harm either way. The characters in this story who appear in that one do so before their appearance there. The illumination and the shadows will fall in both directions just the same.

When I was first doing research on the Celts, years ago, I found the Horslips album *The Tain* remarkably inspiring. It continues to be an influence. My whole conception of Darag and Ferdia and their relationship in this novel would be very different without that music.

There is a reconstructed dun much like the ones in this story at Castell Henleys in West Wales, not terribly far from Cardigan.

The poem at the end of section 7 was first published in my collection *Muses and Lurkers*, Rune Press, 2001.

I have been a prize in a game
I have been a queen on a hill
From far and far they flocked to see me.

White am I, among the shadows,
My shoulder is noted for its fairness
The two best men in all the world have loved me.

My crown is of apple, bough and blossom.
They wear my favor but my arms are empty.
The boat drifts heedless down the dark stream.

# 1

# TAKING UP ARMS

# — 1 —

## (CONAL)

My parents are always fighting," Elenn said.
Conal looked at her. She really was a distractingly beautiful
girl. He had thought so even when she had first arrived in the king's hall,
wet and bedraggled, with her huge-eyed little sister standing beside her.

Here in the sunny orchard with the blossoms around her she was the
loveliest thing he had ever seen. His father, the poet Amagien, had already
written about her looks in extravagant terms. But it was very hard to look
at her and deny that her hair was reminiscent of black night or her eyes
of stars. She looked like Nive herself come down to walk among men for
a season. It was a pity she didn't have wit to match her looks. All she
seemed to care about was having everyone adore her. This was the first
time she had said something that wasn't directly about her, and even this
wasn't far away. "Always?" he asked.

"All the time," she confirmed, smiling a little as if she could see
something Conal couldn't.

"What about?" he asked, mildly interested despite himself. He knew
she was walking with him only because Ferdia and Darag couldn't be
found and she didn't want to walk alone.

"Everything," she said. "Anything at all. What weapons the three of
us should be taught. What color my sister should wear for the Feast of
Bel. What crops the farmers should plant and in which fields. Whether
the hall needs new rushes yet. If we are to go to war with Muin this
summer. If my brother should marry Atha ap Gren. Who is the father of
the white cat's kittens."

Conal swallowed hard. He was glad they were alone. He knew that
if anyone were to catch his eye at that moment, even Darag, he wouldn't
be able to keep himself from laughing aloud. Elenn looked as serious and
as beautiful as ever. In the month she had been at Ardmachan she had
already reproached him for laughing at her at least a dozen times. "Some
of those matters are of great import, and others are very trivial," he said
as calmly as possible.

"I know," Elenn said composedly. "Sometimes they will fight about
whether this is the way a king should behave."

"My uncle Conary would say that it is not," Conal said definitely. He
had heard Conary's lectures on kingship often enough. They were always

made to all the royal kin, though it was Darag he always looked at, and Darag whose questions were answered first.

"My parents have very different ideas about kingship from King Conary," Elenn said, looking up at him under her lashes in a way he would have found enchanting if he could have believed for a minute that she liked him.

"Which of your parents is the king of Connat anyway?" he asked, realizing that he did not know for sure. "I think I have always heard them mentioned together."

"Both of them are of the royal kin," Elenn said. "My mother, Maga, is the daughter of the last king, Arcon. My father, Allel, is her cousin. When the kindred came to choose, many of them wanted Maga, for her wisdom, and others Allel, who was reknown as a warleader when he was young. So it was agreed that they should marry and give each other the benefit of their skills."

"And they've been arguing ever since?" Conal asked.

"Oh, yes," Elenn said. They were almost through the orchard. Conal could already see the oak tree his grandfather used for a school. Emer was there already, pulling a flower apart intently. Leary and Nid were playing fidchell with leaves in the dust. There was no sign of Darag, or Ferdia and Laig, or of Inis himself. "I think marriage of cousins is very wrong, do not you? I think marriages work better when people know each other much less well to begin with."

"No doubt," Conal said politely. Then he thought of his own parents, who had known each other since his father had been fostered here as a boy. "Definitely. But as for your parents, which of them holds the kingship from the land?" he asked. "Only one person can hold it, that I'm sure about." They passed the last of the apple trees and slowed their steps to salute the trees as they passed through the grove.

"My mother does," Elenn said, bowing to the birch tree. "But it is something else they argue about incessantly. My father says that the kingdom would be nothing if not for his leading armies, and my mother says it would be nothing if not for her alliances."

"Are those two paths?" Inis asked.

Conal jumped and Elenn gave a little squeal. His grandfather had a habit of doing that and it never failed to disconcert him. Conal tried to be aware of people and movement. Inis was the only person who had managed to surprise him in half a year, but he managed it almost every time. He strove not to let his surprise show on his face or in his movements. Most of a year ago, he had asked Inis for advice on how to deal with Darag, and Inis had told him that he had already learned how. That meant his way of taking things lightly and not showing when he was wounded. He had learned that from his father's constant prodding, not from Darag. He had a shrewd idea that Inis knew that, too. Now he tried to keep his reactions to himself as much as he could, while smiling and speaking airily. He bent his mind to what Inis had said as if it were a riddle he was using to teach them. Were Maga's alliances and Allel's war-leading two paths?

"I think you mean that Connat needs both their strengths to be strong, Grandfather," he said, phrasing his answer carefully.

Inis looked pleased and began to walk with them towards the others. "Do you see it, girl?" he asked Elenn. She raised her chin affirmatively, but Conal didn't think there was room for much thought behind her pretty face.

"Where are Ferdia and Darag?" she asked.

Most of a month in Oriel and she hadn't learned yet not to ask Inis questions. Not to mention how much that one gave away. Even the order of names revealed her hidden preference, Conal would guess. Elenn had spent most of the month letting Ferdia and Darag act as rivals for her favors, offering each of them the hero's portion in turn, with an occasional shred of meat thrown to Leary and Conal. She hadn't managed to spoil the friendship between Darag and Ferdia. There was no friendship between them and Conal to spoil, even if he had cared, but he hated to watch what it was doing to Leary.

Conal had originally thought it might be a good thing for the two princesses of Connat to be fostered with them for a while. He remembered the time he had spent at Cruachan fondly. But he had forgotten the great distance that stretched between eight and seventeen. He would have begged his uncle not to invite them if he had guessed how disruptive rivalry for a beautiful girl could be. Conal realized that Elenn's question had fallen into silence, which meant that his grandfather was looking for the answer across the worlds. Conal turned to him in concern, just in time to see the emptiness in Inis's face before he spoke.

"Acting on what I taught you this morning," Inis said. His voice sounded different, full of the echoes that meant he was speaking from the depths of his oracle-knowledge. His eyes met Conal's without recognition for a moment.

Conal felt disgusted with Elenn for pushing his grandfather away from sanity. Then he took in what Inis had said, so suddenly that his head spun. "This morning we were learning how to recognize a fortunate day," he said.

"And you said that all days were fortunate, but there is an art to telling for what they are fortunate, for some day fortunate for one thing might be unfortunate for another," recited Elenn in a monotone as they came up to the oak tree where the others were sitting.

"And you read the signs for today and said that it would be a good day for a great warrior to take up arms for the first time," Emer said enthusiastically, jumping up and taking Inis's arm. "Sit down now, sir, and teach us how to read the signs. I could almost see it, but not quite."

Inis blinked at the girl, rubbed his eyes and sighed. "You would have made a fine oracle-priest," he said.

Emer looked down, smiling.

"I have to go," Conal said. It had never occurred to him that Darag would have acted on Inis's divination. They were seventeen; it would be a year before any of them could take up arms. A year, which Conal had been counting off by months and days. How could anyone . . . how could Darag and Ferdia and Laig have gone off to defy that? He felt stricken. They all spent as much time as they could practicing, but even so, they would not be ready to take up arms until they were eighteen, six threes of years, nobody was. It was a law of Oriel, of the whole island of Tir Isarnagiri, of the whole world as far as Conal knew.

"I must go too," Elenn said.

"We must all go," Inis said, sounding as if he knew where he was again. "I have acted without thought." He hesitated, looking from Emer to Conal, then he sighed. "Come back to the dun, we must see the king."

"What? All of us? Why?" Nid looked up from her game for the first time, pushing her hair out of her eyes.

"Darag has gone to take up arms," Elenn explained to them.

Nid and Leary exchanged a startled glance, then got to their feet as Inis gestured to them. Then, without looking, he put out his hands and held back Emer and Conal, one on each side of him, and let the others go ahead. Leary and Nid at once flanked Elenn, one on each side, Leary offering her shy compliments. She did not so much as glance back at Conal.

Inis sighed again as he held Conal back. "I did wrong, but I could not have done other; so I did in all the worlds."

"You said in 'all the worlds,' ap Fathag," Emer said. "I don't understand how it would be possible to know without looking into every world there is."

Conal grinned at her behind Inis's back. That was the way to ask Inis questions if you wanted information out of him. Conal hadn't taken much notice of Emer before. She was a year younger than the rest of them, only sixteen. She'd just gone through a growing spurt and seemed all eyes and legs. She hadn't caused disruption among the rest of them the way her sister had. He'd been concentrating on Elenn, and Darag, of course. But now it seemed that unlike her beautiful sister, Emer had more wit than hair.

"Some events have such weight that they cannot be changed," Inis said. "Most times we are free to choose, and if folk choose the same in other worlds, it is because they are much the same folk and so choice arises. But some things touch the way the worlds are held together and with them, it feels like choice but is not."

Conal frowned, wishing this riddle made sense. Emer drew breath to speak, let it out, drew it in again. "I don't think I can tell the difference between those events and any others," she said.

Inis laughed, the laugh Conal's mother Finca called his cracked cackle. Elenn and the others ahead turned to look, but Conal gestured them on and they started walking again.

"If I cannot tell after all these years of looking across the worlds, then how can you hope to, child?" he asked. "Being able to tell is part of what an oracle-priest must know. I cannot tell until afterwards, and that is only the second such time in my life."

"It would be very interesting to know the other time," Conal said.

Inis grinned at him, looking almost like any old man, except for the way his head was shaved in the front and the brightly colored shawl that would have marked him as an oracle-priest however sane he seemed. "It was when I got Conary on King Nessa," he said.

It was such an ancient scandal, from so long before Conal was born, that he was surprised to see Emer look shocked. Maybe it wasn't well known in Connat. Conal's parents didn't like to talk about it, but all the same, he had known since he was five years old.

"If only two events in all your length of life have been of such stature as to hold across all the worlds, then maybe there will be none in mine," Emer said.

"Such are lucky folk," Inis said. "And such are most folk, truth told. But I do not think either of you are so lucky."

"I know better than to ask," Conal said, looking ahead through the trees to where Elenn inclined towards Leary. They were holding hands. Nid had gone a little way ahead. "You know, Grandfather, though my mind is quick for the branches of learning, and though I love you, I hate learning from you. I have always learned songs and figuring fast enough, but this Oak Knowledge of learning to read luck and the way of other worlds makes my skin crawl. I don't even like thinking about it."

"You know the story of Curog the Oracle-priest?" Inis asked. "He prophesied that a certain lady would win the love of a certain lord. When the lord died, the lady came to him and reproached him for being wrong, for he had never loved her. Then Curog said that in the worlds he could see, where he had not spoken, she had acted to win his love and won it, but in our world, she had been sure she would win it without acting, and so nothing came of it."

Inis said no more. Conal glanced at Emer, who was frowning at nothing. They walked in silence for a while. Conal started running through arguments he would make to Conary. It was hideously unfair to let Darag and Ferdia take up arms early and on a fortunate day, and not the rest of them. But Conary always favored Darag of all his nephews. There were good reasons for that, of course. Though Conal was good, Darag was better. But Conal was sure that if he put in more effort, more time practicing, building up his strength, he would eventually catch up and even overtake Darag. Being strong and fast as a boy was nothing, what counted was when you were men. Even his father said so. If Darag had taken up arms today, then Conal would do the same, that's all there was to it. Anything else was unthinkable.

When they came out of the orchard, Elenn, Leary, and Nid were waiting for them at the foot of the mound. Nid was swinging on the gate. The bottom palisade was no ring of sharpened stakes but a tall fence of strong bog-oak, the oak that could break an iron ax. No enemies had ever breached it. No enemies were expected today however, which was fortunate as there was nobody guarding the lower gate.

"We thought we'd wait for you slowpokes," Leary said, sticking out his tongue at Conal. Conal smiled as if amused at how childish boys of seventeen could be, hiding all the pain. Leary had been his friend. They had always practiced together, each of them hoping to become as good as Darag. Now Leary hardly spoke to him except to jibe.

"It is unkind to mock my old bones, Grandson," Inis said sharply. Leary jumped. He was used to the old man not paying any attention. Conal kept his face still, to show nothing.

Inis let go of Conal's arm, and then, a moment later, Emer's. He led a brisk pace past the stables and up the hill towards the dun. Here, where Conal would have guessed he'd want support, he decided to do without it. The rest of them followed him in a straggle, Conal first, quickening his pace, and Emer beside him. "I didn't know Leary was ap Fathag's grandson as well," Emer said quietly.

"You're getting really good at not asking questions," Conal said and smiled at her. This time, she smiled back, shyly, not at all like her sister. "But it's all right to ask me. Inis had four children. My mother, Leary's mother and Darag's mother by his wife, and Conary by King Nessa as he just told us."

"I had heard before," Emer said even more quietly. "Do you think he told us that last story to stop us asking questions?"

"Yes," Conal said. "Or maybe to tell us he isn't infallible, or that oracle-talent isn't infallible. He hates being asked questions. He can't help but look then, and he prefers to look in his own time."

"Can you see across the worlds?" Emer murmured. Conal had to lean close to hear her.

"Of course not!" he said quickly, surprised she would ask. "I'm not an oracle-priest, and you must have heard me saying just now how I hate to think about those things."

"That's what made me wonder whether you could," she said.

"Can you?" he asked.

Emer shook her head. "Sometimes when I talk to ap Fathag, or to ap Fial at home, I can almost see how to do it. They say I could learn. But I don't want to. Like you, I'd rather not know what might happen already. You know what ap Fathag said when I asked him whether I really would marry Darag the way my mother wants?"

"Your mother might want it, but it will be up to Conary just as much," Conal said.

"I know," Emer said. "I don't want to. He's in love with Elenn."

"Marriage is nothing to do with love," Conal said.

"I know that, too," Emer said. "But anyway, when I asked your grandfather, he said 'Often enough you do.' That's just so horrible. Even if I don't, even if I manage to get out of it, often enough other ones of me didn't and have to marry him. Ugh. I'd much rather not know that."

Inis was at the top gates, speaking to the guard, and they were almost on him. Conal was intrigued enough to stop. "Ugh? You don't like Darag?"

"He's horrible. I hate him," Emer said in a whisper. Then she went on, almost running to catch up with Inis. Conal followed more slowly, trying to smooth out the frown that wanted to come down between his eyes.

# —2—

## (ELENN)

Elenn smiled at Leary, but it wasn't any fun—he was too besotted, there was no challenge there at all. He would have done anything for her, but it didn't matter. Besides, he might be King Conary's nephew but he wasn't anybody really. Nobody thought he might be the next king of anywhere. Dear Ferdia was almost sure to be the next king of Lagin. As for Oriel, it was bound to be Darag or Conal. Her mother had told her before she left home that it would almost certainly be Darag. That didn't mean it wasn't worth being nice to Conal in case, Maga had added. As if Elenn would ever be mean to people just because they weren't important. That wasn't the same as not worth bothering with. She smiled at Leary again and looked up at him through her lashes. It was amazing how easy it was.

Maga had told her a lot of things about how to act with men, but she had never had a chance to try them out until she came to Ardmachan. Back at Cruachan, everyone knew her, and what was more, everyone had seen Maga. Next to Maga, Elenn thought, she barely counted as prettier than Emer. Away from Maga, it was a completely different story. Amagien ap Ross had written a poem saying she was one of the three most beautiful women in the island of Tir Isarnagiri. That made her feel quite shaken and all excited deep inside, but she knew how to act. Alone with Emer at night she had laughed and recited the poem over, but in front of everyone she sat listening to it being sung as if it were nothing unusual. But it was, it was very unusual for such a poem to be written about a seventeen-year-old girl who was away from home for the first time in her life and enjoying every minute of it.

It was strange that Amagien was Conal's father. It was hard to imagine two people more different. Amagien was so emotional and Conal was so driven. Conal was so handsome, too, like ap Fathag, even though ap Fathag was so old. Amagien wasn't at all handsome. But he had good manners, unlike his son. She could have liked Conal, except that he didn't like her. He tried not to show it, but he didn't. He was too clever. She thought maybe sometimes he could see what she was doing and laughing at it, or even disapproving of it. She'd have to try harder with him, she could see that. He thought too much.

The one she really liked was Ferdia. He was the one she was going to ask her mother if she could marry. Then Maga would fix it. Emer could have Darag if she wanted; Maga thought that was a good idea anyway. Maga was good at that sort of thing. Elenn liked Darag, but he scared her sometimes. Darag was wild. He might be the strongest and the best fighter, but Ferdia was taller and gentler. She had the feeling he would have been kind to her even if she hadn't been beautiful. He was kind to Emer. Darag and Conal had hardly noticed that Emer existed. In some ways it was really nice that she was the important one, that nobody cared about Emer here. But it was wrong even so. Elenn was so used to being compared to her sister. And she had to share a room with her, she had to hear Emer's views on everything. In front of everyone, Emer was quiet, the way Maga had told them to be. But get her alone and she wanted to share what she thought. So Elenn couldn't forget about her. And if she was going to have to care about her, then everyone else ought to.

She looked to see where Emer had got to. She had been walking with ap Fathag and Conal, which was all right, but now ap Fathag had gone on ahead and she seemed to be talking intently to Conal. That wasn't all right. It especially wasn't when Conal paused to hear what Emer was saying. Elenn just knew they were talking about her. She couldn't catch up to them either, because she had to walk with Leary and pretend to be paying attention to what he was saying. What was he saying anyway? She listened for a moment.

"Nobody takes up arms until they are eighteen, which won't be until next spring," he was saying. Leary had been talking about Darag and Ferdia being wrong all the way from the grove. Well, Elenn thought it was wrong, too, but she wasn't going to bore anyone with it. She closed her ears again, which was a useful skill sometimes. Sometimes what a queen has to do is just sit and smile and look beautiful. Maga had told her that, though Maga wasn't a queen of course, but a king. A king needs different skills. But Elenn wasn't going to be a king, and she was glad. Being a king would be boring and you'd have to listen to people going on and on all the time. A queen had a lot of work to do with organizing food and supplies for everyone and being gracious, but no fighting.

Not that Maga did any fighting, she hadn't for years. But she might have to if there was an invasion. No fighting, no being forced to do more than pretend to listen to boring people, and no talking to the gods. Talking to the gods was scary. Let her brother Mingor be the king, she'd be a queen and make a good alliance for Connat. If Ferdia were king of Lagin, he'd make a very good alliance indeed.

They had reached the top of the mound. It was strange how familiar with Ardmachan she had become in the month she'd been here. At first it had seemed huge and frightening. There was the wall at the bottom, and another wall at the top, and then three big halls inside, as well as the ordinary buildings. Everything was inside here, except things that couldn't be on top of a hill, like the well and the smithy.

Elenn smiled at the guards on the gate as she went through. She always did. It wasn't any trouble, and it made them like her, and things were always easier if people liked her. She knew one of these guards. He was Casmal, who taught them spear-throwing. He looked worried, and she wondered what ap Fathag had said to him. She gave him a special smile, then hurried after Leary and the others.

Nid gave her a strange look as she caught up. Elenn didn't understand Nid very well. She was a girl, but she wasn't at all beautiful, not even as pretty as Emer. That wasn't strange, but Elenn couldn't understand why Nid didn't care about it. She wore long brown straight shifts and saved embroidered overdresses only for special days. She kept her hair tied on top of her head almost all the time. All she wanted to do was be a charioteer. Finca, Conal's mother, who taught them chariot-fighting, said that Nid would probably be very good at it. She was good with ponies and she wasn't going to be heavy, which was important for a charioteer. Finca said Emer would as well, and Elenn, too, if she would only try harder. Lots of the best charioteers were women. Darag's mother Dechtir had been Conary's charioteer before she was killed. There were songs about her.

But Elenn didn't want to be a charioteer at all. She just wanted to know how to fight well enough to defend herself, that was all. She didn't need to be a champion. She was going to be a queen. Her king would have a whole hall of champions to defend her honor. Like Maga. If anyone insulted her, she could just raise a finger and everyone in the hall would be begging to be chosen as her champion and she'd choose the best one and they'd always win. That was better than fighting for yourself. Maga had explained that to her years ago. Nice as it was to be away from her for a while, Maga made a lot of sense about that sort of thing.

Ap Fathag charged straight past the Speckled Hall, which was a huge storehouse for supplies, with a special room where weapons were left when people were in the dun and didn't need them. He marched right into the Red Hall, which was the king's. Emer and Conal followed close behind, and Leary, Nid, and Elenn a little behind them. Elenn was starting to worry about what ap Fathag would do. She knew King Conary wouldn't do anything awful to him whatever mad thing he did, because ap Fathag was an oracle-priest—and Conary's father, even if he had never been married to his mother. But she wasn't so sure Conary wouldn't be really cross with the rest of them for following him.

The king was sitting in one of the end alcoves playing fidchell with Amagien the Poet. There was a place above where the roof could be lifted off to give light on warm clear days, so they and the board were clearly illuminated. Both men sighed when they saw ap Fathag and his pupils approaching. King Conary didn't look as handsome as usual when his face had such an irritated expression. Elenn found herself remembering stories about his terrible rages. It was said he'd killed his sister Dechtir in a fit of temper.

"I can guess what you want," he said, crossly. Elenn kept her face still, the way her mother had taught her.

Ap Fathag laughed loudly, the way he did sometimes. It sounded more like a raven than a man; there was no mirth in that sound. Elenn saw Nid shiver, and she would have shivered herself if she were younger.

"What did Darag tell you?" Inis asked.

"He told me you told him it was the day fated for him and Ferdia and Laig to take up arms," Conary said.

"I told you your foolish nephew was lying," Amagien put in. Conary glared at him.

"I told all my pupils that it would be a good day for a mighty warrior to take up arms," ap Fathag said. "I did not tell Darag to come to you."

"Not lying," snapped Conary at Amagien. "Enterprising lad."

Conal hissed air between his teeth, but ap Fathag clapped him hard on the shoulder and he said nothing. They all just stood there. Conary stared at ap Fathag as if daring him to speak.

"Have you given Darag and Laig and Ferdia arms?" ap Fathag asked after a long pause.

"Surely nobody would doubt the right of the king to arm his nephew and fosterlings in his own hall," Amagien said.

"Quite right, too, I have every right to do it if I want to," Conary blustered.

"You have every right," ap Fathag said, very mildly. "But you must arm also these other nephews and fosterlings who stand beside me now."

"Sir, I am three months *older* than Darag," Conal put in.

"Do you think we could have forgotten your age?" Amagien asked. Elenn had never seen him snapping like this before.

"Of course I know his age," Conary said. "It is well past noon, Inis. It is too late to arm them today. They will never find a beast to kill before sundown."

"We will take that risk, sir," Conal said.

"Very willingly," Leary agreed.

Conary looked at them all as if they were something that had fallen from the thatch into his stew. "All of you?" he asked.

"I will," Nid said.

It was only then that Elenn realized exactly what was likely to happen. She wanted to be armed, yes, but not like this, not in a scramble and with no time to hunt properly. She wanted it to be an occasion, the whole court there out on a hunt and leaving the kill to her. She had heard all the stories of how her brother had taken up arms two years before. She didn't want it to happen this way.

"Not us," she said, thinking quickly. "Sir, my mother would not like it if we were armed in Oriel." That was nothing but the truth; Maga definitely wanted to arm all her children herself, as she had done with Mingor. "Besides, I am not ready."

"But I would be armed," Emer said. Elenn couldn't stop herself from gasping. It was as if her left arm had suddenly developed a will of its own and started reaching for things she had no desire to grasp.

"Nonsense, girl," Amagien said. "Your pretty sister is right, it would cause trouble with Connat. Besides, how can the younger girl be armed and the elder not?"

"If Elenn feels unready for arms, that is her choice," Emer said. "She has no wish to be a great warrior." Elenn winced, for all that it was true.

"Stout heart," ap Fathag said in something that sounded horrifyingly like an approving tone.

"My mother would wish to arm us herself. Elenn is right. But she would yield before the news of a fortunate day," Emer said boldly.

Elenn leaned forward. "Emer, think, you can't," she whispered.

"Oh yes I can," Emer said, keeping her eyes straight forward.

"Maga will not like it, but will she go to war for it?" Amagien asked.

"She will go to war with us for one cause or another within three years," ap Fathag said, rocking to and fro slightly in the stupid way he did when someone asked him a question. It was so unfair, as his main means of talking was by asking other people questions, but if you asked him one back, his response was to say something often unintelligible and always uncheckable and then go off into a daze. He was much madder than the oracle-priests at Cruachan. And his predictions were always so obvious, just like this one.

Conary leaned forward, looking at Emer. "Do you want to be a great warrior, then?" he asked.

"If possible," she replied.

"Has anyone seen if she can even fight?" Amagien asked. "Ah, I thought not. And she is two years away from age."

"She can fight," Conal said. Elenn frowned at him, but he took no notice; he wasn't even glancing at her. "She's young to be armed, but so are we all, sir. And time and daylight of a fortunate day are wasting as we stand here."

King Conary had shut his eyes. "She has not strength to fight hand to hand," he said faintly. "Anyone can see that."

"Strength as much as my daughter Dechtir had," ap Fathag said.

Conary's eyes snapped open and he sat bolt upright, but when he spoke, his voice still sounded weary. "Do either of you youths need a charioteer?"

Leary and Conal both stared at Nid, who shrugged. "I have driven you both and would willingly drive either of you," she said.

"You have far more often driven me," Leary began.

"Then let her drive you now," Conal said, "If Emer will consent to drive me?"

"It would be an honor," Emer murmured, looking down and sounding her usual self again.

"Let her be armed as a charioteer then," Conary said, as if he were tired to death of the whole business. Elenn felt a great deal of sympathy for him. "Come, Amagien. Where is Finca?"

Finca came up immediately. Elenn suspected she had been listening in the next alcove. It was a large hall, and the alcoves were hidden from each other in the same way they were at Cruachan. It meant proper privacy for eating, but it also meant it was very easy to hide in them and spy on people when the hall wasn't full. If she built her own hall, Elenn thought she would prefer to have a great table to eat on the way the poets said the Vincans did. Except that it would make it difficult for people who were at bloodfeud with each other and so could not eat together. She wondered how the Vincans managed about that.

"You called for me, my brother?" Finca asked.

"Rejoice, for today your child becomes one of the people," Conary said with an ironic nod of the head to Conal. "If you can find Elba and Ringabur, and Ugain and his wife, they may wish to hear the same news. Regrettably, Maga and Allel cannot be here. Also, the feast I bade you prepare for Darag's return should perhaps be expanded a little."

"Yes, my brother," Finca said, as if his words had been quite ordinary. She gave hardly a glance to Conal and no glance at all at the rest of them.

"Oh, and sister, take the elder princess of Connat to help you," Conary said. "She does not need to be armed today."

"No," Finca said, looking at Elenn a little curiously. Elenn kept her head up and looked back. "Very well, you can help me prepare the feast. Come along, child."

It was only then, hearing that familiar form of address, that Elenn realized what she had done. She would still be a child, when the others, even Emer, would be adults in everyone's eyes. It was not quite too late to change her mind, but entirely too late to do it and maintain dignity. She lifted her chin high and walked off after Finca without a backward glance.

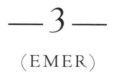

# — 3 —

## (EMER)

King Conary gathered up champions and parents and guards so that there seemed to be a crowd of them before they even left the Red Hall.

Emer was starting to feel almost sorry that she had spoken up. Elenn's face had been like thunder as she went off with Conal's mother. No doubt she would never let Emer forget it. Worse, she would tell Maga. Maga hadn't wanted to send them to Oriel in the first place. Having fosterlings at Cruachan was one thing. Sending her own children off into danger was another.

Not that there was any danger. Emer couldn't see how such a thing could even cross her mother's mind. Maga and Allel had fought over it until Emer's head hurt. Eventually, Allel suggested that Maga's reluctance wasn't fear for her children but an intimation that she herself would break the sacred bonds of guesting and harm a fosterling. Emer thought he was entitled to say so. After all, the idea would never have crossed anyone else's mind. All guests were sacred, even in the middle of a war, and fosterlings were the most sacred guests of all. Maga had clawed Allel's face so hard that he had marks for days. After that, there had been no more words Emer could hear through the wall, only moans and cries. That fight had ended up in bed, as her parents' fights so often did. Emer had wondered at them the next morning, seeing her father with a scratched face and her mother purring. She had been overjoyed when Allel had told them that they would at last be allowed to spend a year at Ardmachan. She had been waiting through all of Maga's excuses since she was nine years old and the royal children of Oriel had gone home without them.

King Conary marched out of the Red Hall with everyone close behind him. Emer blinked at the sudden sunlight. There were some champions playing hurley on the field laid out for it over against the east wall. Their excited cries rose up in the warm air as someone scored.

"Don't you just wish you were with them?" Conal whispered. Emer turned and grinned at him and he rolled his eyes towards the adults. King Conary was walking very fast, with an expression as if he had bitten a sour apple. Everyone else except Inis was scurrying to keep up. The king's counselor ap Carbad was almost smiling. Nid's parents looked apprehensive, and Leary's looked confused. Conal's father, Amagien the Poet, was frowning as usual. Emer thought it was awful that Conal's mother hadn't even bothered to stay to see her son armed.

"Not really?" she said tentatively, making it a question.

"Oh no, not really," Conal agreed.

"Besides, hurley is a stupid game," she said.

Conal laughed. "I don't know how you dare say so," he said, sounding surprised. "Though in many ways it is a very stupid game. I enjoy it sometimes. But such a lot depends on things you can't do anything about."

"Like how many people there are on each team, and when they switch sides," Emer said. "Is it true that Darag once played alone against all the rest of you?"

"There was a game once that started off like that," Conal said carefully.

"He didn't want to wait to pick sides," Leary said. "He won, though."

"Who was left on the other side at the end?" Emer asked.

"Just me," Conal admitted, and lowered his voice. "But that isn't the sort of thing that's worth making songs about."

"Hurley is good training for war," Nid said. "It teaches you how to move in battle."

"May the wise gods send that I never have to fight a battle where everyone changes sides as they see their advantage," Conal said.

Nid and Leary laughed, but Emer just looked at Conal, knowing he wasn't joking. His eyes met hers for a moment, dark and serious. An instant later he was laughing lightly again as they all hurried to catch up.

Then King Conary flung open the door of the Speckled Hall and stopped abruptly, forcing everyone behind him to stop just as fast. Leary's father fell over his feet and caught himself. Nid giggled nervously.

The two guards inside the Speckled Hall looked incredibly guilty, as if they had been caught stealing from the storehouses rather than guarding them. They leaped to their feet with their spears ready. As far as Emer could tell, they had been doing nothing worse than sitting talking. King Conary looked them up and down for a long moment. "Better," he said at last, and both guards relaxed a trifle.

"I wonder what they were doing *last* time?" Conal asked, almost in her ear. Emer bit back a giggle.

"Ap Carbad, take all these people whose children are not here today down to the stables to wait," Conary said without even turning his head to look.

Ap Carbad gathered up the extra people, pausing when he came to Inis but passing on as Inis beamed like an imbecile and indicated Conary. Inis was very clever about using his madness to his advantage when it suited him. He could be absolutely outrageous and nobody would challenge it. Emer had been afraid of him at first, but now that she knew him better, she liked him.

King Conary led the ten of them remaining into the Weapons Room. Emer had never been right inside the Weapons Room of the Speckled Hall before. As a child, she had had no weapons of her own to leave, and for practice, they used weapons kept down at the stables. The light came in under the eaves where the roof met the walls. The walls were plastered and painted with pictures of champions fighting in chariots. Maga would have sneered at the paintings, which were crudely drawn and used too much blood-colored paint. Emer quite liked them. The way the people were standing looked right, almost as if they could move. It took a moment or two for her to lower her eyes to the arms they had come to find.

The room was almost full of weapons of all descriptions, clearly care-fully arranged, but equally clearly using some system she could not imag-ine. There were spears and knives and slings in great profusion, and piles of round slingshots, lime mixed with blood and set harder than stone. Among them were swords, more swords than she had ever seen. At home her father had a sword of course, and her brother, and maybe half a dozen of the other champions. Here, there seemed to be uncountable numbers of them. Emer stopped. She knew better than that. Ap Fial had taught her the Thorn Knowledge, how to count large numbers. She ran her eyes over the swords, counting by threes and twelves. "Forty-five and two," she murmured, impressed.

"What?" Conal asked, setting down a sling and turning to her.

"Forty-seven swords," she said. "That must be one for each champion of Oriel."

"More," King Conary said, stopping abruptly again and turning to Emer. "Many of these swords are mine, battle spoil that I have not yet gifted to any champion." He bent and picked one up to show her. "This is a Vincan cavalry sword. I won it fighting them on the coast of Demedia five, no, six years ago." He half drew it out of the scabbard. "Look at the edge on that!" He set it down again carefully in its place and picked up another nearby. "This one belonged to the champion Ardan of Muin; before I killed him. It is called Oakheart. See how the hilt is carved and the blade is veined a little like an oak leaf? It was made by a smith of Muin, you do not see those patterns on swords made in the north."

Quite suddenly King Conary seemed to notice that everyone was watching and listening. His face twitched and he set the sword Oakheart down carefully. "Well, why are you waiting?" he asked. "Arm these chil-dren; it is why we have come here." Then, as they began to bustle about, he put his hand on Emer's arm. "Do you just admire good weapons, or can you use a sword, ap Allel?" he asked.

"I can use one a little," Emer admitted. "My father taught me. But he said I should wait until I was tall enough to use a real one. Mostly I have used a wooden one made the right size for practice."

"Very wise. The sword must work with the arm, and if you started using an ordinary sword before you were tall enough, you would have too much to unlearn, or you would need a sword as tall as that one—" he indicated the Vincan sword "—when you had all your growth."

"Is that the sword of a Vincan who made that mistake then?" she asked. "Or an ogre?"

He laughed. "Neither. It is a cavalry sword, meant to be used from horseback."

"Riding on a horse? For battle?" Emer was astonished. "I have ridden, but I would never have thought of such a thing."

"Their horses are larger," Conary said. "Much larger. Even their ordinary horses are almost three hands larger than ours, and their war horses maybe six hands higher. They can bear a heavy man in armor. They use them in preference to chariots. I might do so myself if I had horses of that size."

"And they use those swords?"

"They use thrusting spears first, and then the swords."

"Sir, I did not realize before what a feat you were recounting when you told me you won that sword in battle," Emer said, bowing with both hands on her heart, the bow given to a mighty warrior, not the bow given to a king.

Conary laughed and looked distinctly pleased. "If you have to fight against them, use spears," he advised. "Spears have the reach. Get the horse fast, and then they will be down on your level. Best of all, use a belly-spear." He reached out without looking and drew forward a spear with a wicked barbed head. "It twists on the way in and can't be drawn out straight, so it's almost sure to kill. I keep those for fighting against cavalry. Horse-warriors are a nuisance, but the good thing is that there are not very many of them. They cannot be everywhere at once, else raiding Demedia would be a foolish pastime indeed."

Emer laughed, knowing that Oriel raided Demedia every summer they were not at war elsewhere.

"You must be armed today," King Conary said, sounding much happier about it than he had earlier. He touched her elbow and then her wrist, then held his hands apart at that distance. "I know," he said and looked about him. Then he frowned. "Conal!"

Conal was on the other side of the room with his father, looking desperately unhappy. He was wearing an armor coat, leather set with iron rings, and holding a spear. He and Amagien both looked up at Conary's call. As Conal looked up he smiled easily. Emer was surprised how at quickly he could do that. Inis, who was standing by the door turning a knife in his hands, also glanced over, then away.

"Conal, where are those Jarnish swords I said you could use for practice?"

"If you have lost the king's swords—" Amagien began.

"Oh no, they are not lost," Conal said, with a smile like ice over deep water. "They are here with the sling I use." He took a few paces among the weapons, dodging Leary who was pulling on his armor coat, clearly entirely at home in the room, and took up a pair of long knives and handed them to Conary.

"They are mine, and should not be kept with your father's weapons," Conary said, frowning.

"Useless boy!" Amagien said. "Can't you do anything right?"

"I am very sorry, sir," Conal said, looking at Conary.

"Humph. They're not harmed by it. Have you outgrown them yet?"

"The smaller, yes, but I am still using the longer." He turned to Emer. "I use them for practice. Using a weapon with an edge is different from using a wooden one, even when the weight is the same."

King Conary measured Conal's arm the same way he had measured Emer's, and frowned.

"This will be the summer he will grow," Amagien said grimly, as if he would personally make sure of it.

"He is smaller than Darag but taller than Leary. He is not small for his age," Emer said, surprising herself. Conal gave her a swift frown and shook his head a little. Amagien looked furious.

Conary laughed. "Does your charioteer defend you already?" he asked. "Well, so it should be. Emer ap Allel, take this sword. It is a Jarnish weapon. These were won in a sea-fight, years ago. When you grow taller and wish to change it, bring it back to me. Conal, you keep the other until you too, need a longer sword."

Emer took the smaller of the pair and turned it over curiously. It was not quite like a sword sized for a sixteen-year-old. The shape was unusual, but the balance was good. Conary handed the other to Conal just as Nid's mother came up with an armor coat for Emer. She shrugged it on over her clothes. There would be time at the stables to take off her overdress. She belted up her shift and fixed the sword to her belt. Beside her, Conal was doing the same.

"And a spear," Conary said. He touched Emer's head briefly and made for the wall where many spears were standing propped. He took up one without hesitation and strode back to her with it. She hefted it for a moment. It was just the right length. She was glad to see he had chosen an ordinary throwing spear, not a barbed belly-spear.

Conary went over to Leary then and after exchanging a few words found him a blade.

"If we are done here, then to the stables," Conary said. "Time is wasting."

As soon as they were back out in the sunshine, Inis came up to Emer quietly. "I thought you would need a knife today," he said.

Emer bit back the first six things she wanted to say, all of which were questions. "The king has given me a sword," she said, showing him.

"I saw," he said. "That was well done." Without another word, he turned and walked off, towards the gate of the dun, back towards the grove.

Emer stared after him.

"Sometimes he is just impossible," Conal said.

"I don't understand him," Emer said.

"To understand him, you'd have to be him, study all the branches of knowledge for twenty-one years, and at last come to the depths of the Oak Knowledge that drives people mad. And after that, he has spent half the rest of his life spread out across lots of worlds. He's my grandfather, and I've known him all my life and he has been nothing but good to me, but I wouldn't want to understand him."

Emer felt almost afraid of the intensity Conal was letting her see. "Come on," she said. "We ought to catch up or we'll be left with the chariot with the wobble."

"Oh, no," Conal said. "This isn't practice. We don't use the practice chariots. We'll take my father's chariot. And his chariot horses. He will do that for me, and I'll make him proud of me."

Emer looked. Amagien was up ahead talking to the king, taking no notice of them at all.

"Thank you for asking me to be your charioteer," she said.

"I meant it," Conal said. "Not just for today. I mean to be a great warrior. I will need a charioteer. I want you."

"Why?" Emer asked. Then, as she saw his face fall, she added hastily, "I mean, yes, yes of course, but why me?"

"Because you are brave," Conal said. He looked as if he might say more but he just shrugged, as if that was enough.

Emer grinned, too full of words to speak any of them, then ran off after the others, with Conal running beside her.

Finca had sent word to the stables, and both chariots had been harnessed ready. She was even here herself, fussing with the horses. Elenn was with her, still looking downcast. Ap Carbad and a great crowd of champions of Oriel were gathered around talking busily.

Emer stole a moment to dress herself properly in one of the stalls before they set off. Nid came with her and they helped each other bind up their shifts tightly and tie back their hair. "My mother's upset," Nid said, frowning. "She wanted to have time to make me new clothes for when I come back, and she's only just started to warp the cloth for them never mind got them done. She doesn't care about lucky days. She says this is a scramble."

"She'll be glad when you come back," Emer comforted her. Nid looked unsure for a moment. Then they went out and rejoined the others.

The grooms handed them the reins and they mounted up. Emer put her spear into the slot for it at her side. Nid looked much steadier once she had horses to control. Emer's pair seemed well matched, both in color and temperament. They were dun mares, each properly mealy nosed and raring to go.

Then King Conary raised his hand for quiet, and everyone stood together without saying anything. Amagien kept shifting his weight and scowling at Conal.

"You stand before me children," King Conary said. "Children of my blood, children of my dun, or fosterlings of my hearth, but children all. Today you take up the arms you bear, not now in practice but for the first time in truth. Bear them well and worthily, and as long as you may bear them in honor. Go now and hunt, and carry back whatever you may kill in token that you return to me children no more, but men and women grown and champions of my household."

Nid's mother and Leary's father were weeping openly, and Leary's mother was wiping her eyes. Nid's father was grinning like a man who was ridiculously proud. Amagien continued to scowl. Finca looked emotionless. Elenn was smiling distantly, like a queen painted on a wall. Emer was deeply relieved that her parents weren't here and that she had got out of doing this before the whole court in Cruachan. There would be a fight over it, she knew, but just one fight, not a whole drawn out campaign.

At a signal from Finca, she and Nid let the horses go and a moment later they were driving down the track that circled Ardmachan.

"Where to?" she asked, wishing she could turn and see Conal's face. Then he came and stood beside her, so close she could feel the warmth of his body.

"Anywhere we want," Conal said. "Anywhere, anywhere at all, anywhere in the whole island of Tir Isarnagiri. Nobody can stop us." He laughed, and they all laughed with him. Emer felt as if she had managed to escape a cage that had been around her all her life.

The farmers in the fields looked up as they heard them. "They probably think we're mad," Nid called, and that made them laugh all the more. They came towards the first track leading away into the countryside.

"There are four hours to sunset," Conal said, sobering a little. "There's likely to be game in the woods. Let's go that way."

Emer obediently turned the chariot southwest, full of delight.

# —4—

## (FERDIA)

"I f it's such a fortunate day, why haven't we found anything yet?" Laig
called.

Ferdia would have shrugged, but he knew what shrugging did when
you were holding chariot reins. "I don't know," he said, too quietly for
Laig and Darag to hear. He didn't want to talk. He wanted to think about
what he was going to do when they did find something. He'd been thinking about that all afternoon. He almost had it clear, but it made such a
difference what they found that it wasn't easy to make a plan. Darag would
be all right. Darag was always all right.

Anyway, it was easy to make a kill from a chariot if you had a charioteer. It was a different matter if you didn't. He'd either have to stop and
get down or be extraordinarily lucky. He'd have to be lucky to kill something on foot, too. Or maybe he would see something, stop, draw the
spear, aim and throw. If only the horses didn't move just as he was throwing and draw off his aim. If he didn't kill something he wouldn't be a
man. He wouldn't be a boy either, since he had taken up arms. He didn't
know what he would be.

"We should have gone after the hares," Laig said.

"Don't be a fool," Darag said roughly. Ferdia glanced over. Above the
dust of the chariot wheels, Darag was standing without holding on, the
way they'd been practicing. His hair was clubbed together on his neck,
the rings set in his leather armor were shining in the sun. He had his spear
drawn back ready, as if he was expecting to sight a quarry at any moment.
He looked like a hero in a song, like Young Lew going to fight at the
Plain of the Towers. But there was still nothing to fight. The countryside
rolled here, with green fields spread out on either side of the track and
the young corn green and growing. Ferdia hadn't seen so much as the tail
of any animal but those hares since they had left Ardmachan, and they
must be almost to the borders of Connat.

Ferdia sighed and turned his eyes back to the space between his horses
where they ought to be. You had to pay attention all the time to drive a
chariot, it wasn't anything like a cart. Even going slowly was fast enough
to tangle the traces and bring the horses to their knees, and maybe lame
them or worse. Ferdia had gone off over his head a few times before
getting the hang of it, and once Finca ap Inis had called him a clumsy oaf
and said he'd have killed his left horse for sure if she hadn't been there to

catch them. He had a good pair today; he doubted that King Conary had
a better pair in his stables, except for his own, which Laig was driving.
He had given Darag his own pair and his own chariot. It was an incredible
sign of favor. He had been very kind to Ferdia, too. These were very
good. They were better than any he had ever driven in practice. They
were both six-year-olds, used to working together, one bay and one dun,
each with the sprinkling of white hairs on their muzzles that mark a hardy
horse. They had been going steadily all afternoon without complaint. If
he did not kill today he could not blame them. Nor could his father blame
King Conary for sending him out badly equipped. He had even refused
the king's offer of an experienced charioteer.

"A hare would make a useless trophy to show in the hall," Darag said.
"Don't be afraid, Laig, we'll find something better. A stag. Or a wolf. Or
a boar. Or even a bear. A bear would be best of all."

Darag was always so sure about everything. Ferdia, who was never
sure, who always stopped and thought things through two or three times,
found Darag's certainty compelling. "I'm not afraid," Laig said. "A bear
each would suit me." Ferdia had been on a bear hunt once with his father,
and all the champions of Lagin. He would have been worried by Laig's
overconfidence if this was anything like bear country.

"My kill would count for yours as well, you're my charioteer," Darag
said. "If we found a big bear and all three of us killed it together that
would count for all three."

"But there aren't any bears in the southern part of Oriel," Laig said.
"And we're coming around in a loop and this road leads back to Ardmachan."

"It does?" Ferdia asked, startled. Sometimes Ferdia wished he'd never
left Lagin where he knew every stone and tree and, even better, felt that
they knew him. All the same, he should have been able to tell by the
shadows if he was paying attention. The next moon would mark the Feast
of Bel. That meant by the shadows that there were three more hours of
daylight and they were indeed heading back northeast.

"I forgot you wouldn't know," Darag said. "Sometimes it seems as if
you've always been here, not just since midwinter." That offhand comment made Ferdia feel welcome all through. "The road does lead back to
the dun. I didn't want to exhaust the horses. But don't worry, it goes
back through the woods. There are always animals there, it's where people
go to hunt."

"So why didn't we go there first?" Laig asked.

"Do you need a charioteer?" Darag asked.

Ferdia glanced at Darag again. He was actually leaning towards him.
"Do you want to kill yourself?" he asked, getting his eyes back where

they belonged. He could see the trees up ahead. He looked forward to the shade. He hoped the woods would be teeming with wildlife. Even a hare, even a squirrel, would be better than going back with nothing.

Darag laughed a little uneasily. "Not even when I am ready to throttle Laig," he said. "I am no charioteer. We should have brought Nid."

"I would have, though nobody drives you but me," Laig said. "She'd have been glad enough to drive Ferdia. But she was playing fidchell, and there was no getting her away from Leary. He would have wanted to know and wanted to come. He's going to be spitting furious when he finds out."

"Not half as furious as Conal's going to be," Ferdia said, laughing.

Going to the king and asking to take up arms on the fortunate day had been Darag's idea. It had taken Ferdia to see the advantage of not telling the others. It wasn't just that they would be men and great warriors and the others would not. That would be churlish, for a great warrior wants other great warriors around him. The real advantage was to Darag, for it would put him clearly ahead of his cousins in the rivalry for Oriel. King Conary's children were dead, it was very likely that one of his nephews would be chosen to be king after him. Darag just seemed to assume it would be him, but Ferdia knew that sometimes things didn't work out like that. Darag was the best champion, but Leary was tough and Conal was clever, and anything that would give Darag an advantage when it came to choosing was a good thing.

Ferdia meant to do everything he could to see that when he was king of Lagin, Darag would be king of Oriel, so they would still be equals. It would be ridiculous for Darag to be set below him or have to be polite to him. They would both be kings and both be friends and Lagin and Oriel would never go to war. They would always fight together against Muin and Connat and Anlar and the Isles—especially Anlar, whose king Lew ap Ross was a boring old windbag.

"What's that?" Laig asked, drawing his pair to a halt. Ferdia had been so far off in his thoughts that he was surprised to find they were deep under the shade of the trees. He hadn't heard anything, but he was glad of a moment's rest. He halted beside his friends and spat, clearing his mouth of the dust of the road. He took a mouthful of water from the skin at his belt and put it back to stop himself from taking as much as he wanted and draining the skin.

"Could it be deer?" Darag asked.

Ferdia listened for a moment. "Sounds a lot more like horses to me," he said.

"Better let whoever it is pass, then," Laig said, drawing his chariot over to the side.

Darag put his head on one side as if he were listening, too. "No, let's go and find them," he said.

Ferdia twitched the traces and the horses responded at once with a surge forward. A moment later, the other chariot came up beside him. They went forward along the track through the woods. The trees along the right side of the path were a line of planted alders, so although he had never been here before, Ferdia wasn't at all surprised when the woods widened out ahead and there was a mere on his right, full of reeds and rushes. What did surprise him was the sight of two other chariots, drawn up facing the water. The nearest held Nid, driving Leary, and the other was little Emer of Connat, driving Conal. Ferdia could hardly take it in that they were there at all.

"Ah, greetings cousin," Conal said, bowing in his typical sardonic way. "Have you made a kill yet?" His eyes ran over their empty chariots. "No? What a pity." Emer laughed. Ferdia scowled.

"I wondered if you might make it after all," Darag said in perfect good humor. "No, we have seen nothing all day. How about you?"

"We have only been out an hour, and naturally we used our wits and made straight for the woods as the most likely source of game," Conal said. "But we have seen nothing yet worthy of our spears."

He was also holding his spear. He didn't look as good as Darag, but only because his chariot wasn't moving. Conal had the sort of smooth good looks that made Ferdia want to break his nose.

"Why are you stopped here?" Ferdia asked.

"We were looking what birds are on the water," Nid said.

Ferdia looked at the water. Moorhens and a handful of ducks. He enjoyed eating duck as much as anyone, but it wasn't game for a warrior; ducks were caught with nets. Anyway, they couldn't be killed now, unless someone was likely to starve to death otherwise. It was late spring; they might be nesting.

"There's nothing," Laig said after a moment.

"We were just looking," Leary said gruffly.

"Well, since we have met, cousin, should we hunt together or separately?" Conal asked.

Ferdia longed to answer that they should separate, but he looked to Darag for a response. As he turned, he saw them, gasped and pointed. Darag immediately turned to see, spear ready. A flight of six swans was coming down towards the mere, dark against the sky. Swans were warriors' game if speared from the sky. They might not be as good as a bear, but they were a lot better than a squirrel.

His spear was in the charioteer's slot beside him. With the chariot stopped and facing towards them it was much easier than it would have

been. He drew the spear, chose a swan, aimed and threw. He knew almost
at once that he had missed. But even as he realized, he saw that Darag
had hit. He saw another spear miss and plunge into the water. He was
surprised Conal or Leary had even tried, from that angle it would be quite
impossible. Darag's spear struck the swan cleanly, as cleanly as any such
hit Ferdia had ever seen, and it fell straight down, into the water. The
other swans landed, swishing in one by one and settling to sit serenely on
the surface. They turned and honked angrily. Ferdia wondered if they
knew they were safe on the water.

"I hit it!" Darag said. "Bad luck, Ferdia. You were very close."

"You didn't have anyone to hold your chariot still," Laig said.

"There'll be another chance," Ferdia said, furious with himself. "Will
you hold my traces while I get my spear?" He handed the traces to Laig
and stumped off toward his spear. He could see it clearly against some
fallen leaves already half returned to loam. It was a good cast, though that
was no consolation as he hadn't hit; all it meant was farther to go to get
it back. The ground was very muddy. He wiped the spear on some moss
as he retrieved it.

When he got back, Darag and Leary and Conal had all got down and
were looking at the floating body of Darag's swan, a tall man's length from
the edge of the water.

"My spear is sunk forever," Conal said with a wry smile. "If we didn't
need the swan for you to show, I'd suggest leaving it."

"My mother keeps dogs to bring back game," Emer said, staring out
over the water.

"So do we. We just didn't think to bring any," Leary said.

"I'll fetch it back," Laig offered. "It's part of my job. I was only
waiting for Ferdia. Here, have your reins back."

Ferdia was in no hurry to take up the reins again. He ignored Laig.
"I might be able to reach it with my spear," he said. He took a couple
of careful steps into the water and reached with his spear, hoping to hook
the swan and have it drift towards them. The live swans were moving
away elegantly. The dead one was a revolting object, all its grace gone.
He could almost reach it. The surface beneath his boots was made up of
slippery mud and the roots of reeds and trees.

"You'll get very dirty if you fall in," Conal said in his mocking way.
Ferdia took another step, less carefully, and slipped. He went down on
one knee and instinctively put his left hand down to save himself. The
bottom squirmed away under his hand. His right hand, holding the spear,
reached the swan and poked it farther away. His breeches were soaked.
Beyond caring now, he pulled himself to his feet and waded out towards
the swan. The water was thigh deep. One of the live swans glided towards

him, hissing ominously. He wondered if it was the mate of the one Darag had killed. He knew it was wrong to spear a bird on the water, but did that apply to self-defense? The swan's beak looked quite threatening. Ferdia made a warding gesture with his spear, hoping to scare it off. At the same moment he grabbed the dead swan with his left hand and took a step back towards shore. Then another swan got inside his guard and made a determined strike at Ferdia's right knee, hard, and he went down again, going right under the water this time, dropping the dead swan and almost losing his spear. He pulled himself half up and used the spear like a quarterstaff to push the swans away.

He could hear Conal laughing, and some of the others as well.

"Hold on Ferdia, I'm coming," Darag called from the shore.

"I'm all right," he said, though he wasn't. He heard Darag splashing into the water. He attempted to stand up straight. His armor was heavy and his knee hurt where the swan had hit him. The water was all churned up with mud and he couldn't see the bottom at all now. There were big bubbles breaking all around him. At least he'd made the swans back off a little, though they weren't far away. He made another grab for the dead swan just as everything exploded.

He had been in the water, and now he was looking down on the water. He had been standing, or crouching at least. Now he was upside down. The swans had been going for him, but now he was being squeezed around his waist. He tried to see what was squeezing him, but he couldn't make it out. It seemed to be a huge silver coil. That made sense, because there were other huge silver coils coming out of the water. Darag was in the water, fighting the coils with a spear. Leary wasn't far from him, also with a spear. This made Ferdia remember that he ought to have a spear himself. He looked around for one. There was a spear stuck hard in the smooth coil, though it was not bleeding. The spear was quivering slightly and stuck quite far in. Ferdia wondered if he had put it there, though it looked as if it had been thrown there. He stretched his arm to see if he could reach it, and found his arm encircled with another loop, a thinner one. People were shouting, but the sound of thrashing water drowned out their words.

What was this thing anyway? It was like a snake, but everyone knew there were no snakes in Tir Isarnagiri. And where was its head? He looked up and saw nothing but sky. He was starting to feel faint from lack of breath. The coil seemed to be moving him downwards towards the water. There was a huge splash and he was immersed in the mud and water again. He struggled, but the harder he struggled the more the loop squeezed him. Just as he was about to give up and try to breathe water, someone rolled him over. He just lay there for a moment, breathing.

Breathing was wonderful. He was on his back in quite shallow water. Close above him were Conal and Emer, laughing. They both held big knives, or maybe funny little swords, and were soaked and muddy.

Ferdia sat up gasping and saw Darag, still holding a spear, looking concerned. "Are you all right?" Darag asked. There was nothing behind him but Leary and Nid, muddy and dripping, both their spears running with water.

"Where did it go?" Ferdia asked and coughed painfully.

"We killed it," Emer said, then amended herself. "Conal killed it."

"Emer killed it," Conal said, bowing. "You're a true warrior, not a charioteer."

"I'd much rather be your charioteer," she muttered.

"If you killed it, where's the body?" Laig interrupted. Ferdia looked to the bank. Laig was standing there dry and clean, holding the traces of both chariots.

"It melted away when we killed it," Emer said.

"What was it?" Ferdia asked. "Was it a snake?"

"It may have been," Conal said. "I've never seen one, but it was like the way they are in songs." He leaned down and offered his empty hand to Ferdia and pulled him to his feet. The water wasn't even up to his knees here. Now that he could breathe again, he felt chilled all through. He took a step toward the bank and stubbed his toe on something hard. He saw a gleam through the murky water and bent for it. It was his spear. He pulled it out and leaned on it.

"I didn't know they were so big," Nid said. She looked cold as well, her teeth were chattering. "And I didn't know about the wings. I thought it was like a huge swan."

"What wings?" Ferdia asked, puzzled.

"I didn't see any wings. It had scales like snakes are supposed to, but I think it was a great big fish," Leary said.

Ferdia looked about for the dead swan he had come into the water for. There was no sign of it. There was no sign of any life at all, except for one solitary moorhen cowering in the reeds.

"It wasn't a swan or a fish or a snake, and we didn't kill it," Darag said. If it hadn't been impossible, Ferdia would have thought there were tears in his voice. He must have swallowed some of the water. "She was the Guardian of the Creatures of the Island of Tir Isarnagiri, and it's all my fault and I nearly got you killed, Ferdia. I shouldn't have killed the swan, I knew it was out of season."

"The swan was flying," objected Leary. "You're allowed to spear swans in the sky all year 'round."

"But he was coming down, and he fell in the water," Darag said.

"*If* it was the Beastmother, and I do not for one moment concede that it was," Conal said, his voice like sharpened ice, "then how is it that you know this and we do not?"

"It's just how things are," Darag said. He ran his wet hand through his wet hair. "I know you won't believe I don't do this sort of thing on purpose, Con, but if I could be free of it, I would. I'd happily give it to you and have it be you who hit the swan and you that Rhianna spoke to. It's as if everything I do has significance beyond anything I would want for it. I can't just come out and kill an animal and go back a man, something has to happen to make it special. It's as if nothing of my life belongs to me and all of it is tied to something else. It's as if I don't have any choices. Everything I do is ringed about with strangeness. I saw a target and went for it and I could have got Ferdia killed." He sounded completely despairing.

"Ap Fathag said—" Emer began, but Conal raised a hand and she fell silent.

"Any of us could have done the same," Conal said. "But speaking to the gods is—"

"It was because he killed the swan," Leary said. "He's the king's nephew, we all are, she would have spoken to any of us if we'd killed it. I didn't even throw, impossible shot from where I was. You missed, lost your spear. Darag hit it, we all fought the Guardian, whatever it was. When we did well enough against her she relented, spoke to Darag to tell him what he did so he wouldn't do it again. That's all."

"And I'm all right," Ferdia said to Darag, as reassuringly as he could. "Really I am." Darag came nearer and embraced him wordlessly. Ferdia hugged him back, as if they were family.

"Did we kill it?" Nid asked. "Or do we have to go and look for something else?"

"Emer killed it, but it counts for all of us," Conal said doggedly. "The same as it would in a boar hunt."

"No head," Leary said briefly, looking around as if hoping to find one. "Supposed to show the head in the hall."

"They will have to take our word," Emer said.

Conal laughed suddenly. "Yes, they will. After all, would they accuse all of us of jumping in a duck pond to muddy our clothes and making up a story about it?" He bowed to Emer and took her arm to escort her out of the water, for all the world as if they were going in to dinner.

Ferdia shook his head at Darag. "Will they believe us?" he asked.

"They'll have to," Darag said fiercely.

In the end, it didn't matter, because a herd of deer crossed their path on the way out of the wood so they had venison enough to feast all King's Hall.

# 2

# THE FEAST OF BEL

# — 5 —

## (CONAL)

Conal feinted high and thrust low. Emer blocked smoothly, then signalled a stop. They both stepped back.

The grass behind the smithy was flattened in a rough circle. They had been coming here to practice alone for half a month now. It was as private a place as there was in reach of Ardmachan. Conal had found it three years ago. The willow-bordered stream ran out of the trees and alongside the low stone smithy. This patch was one of the very few pieces of land outside the dun bare of trees and not planted with crops. The smith kept a cow, but she did not mind her pasture being trampled. And the smith didn't mind the noise, he always made enough himself. Conal had come to an arrangement with the smith. When the cow was ready, he would bring his father's great bull down to her, and this kept the smith in milk and cheese and meat, or even profit if it should be a heifer that he could trade. The smith was well pleased with this bargain, always greeted Conal kindly and sometimes even brought him out a cup of milk on hot days. Amagien knew nothing about it, but it suited Conal very well. Inside the dun, there was plenty of room for practicing. But inside the dun, there were also the others.

"What's wrong?" Conal asked. She couldn't be tired already. She wasn't even breathing hard.

"Nothing," she said. "Just getting my balance a moment. You're right about how different it is using the blades."

"I'm not going to hurt you," he said. He wouldn't have agreed to it if he wasn't sufficiently confident of his control of the sword. He had always been told never to practice steel against steel, but Emer had wanted to so much, and he knew he could stop in time.

She laughed. "Of course not." Conal felt a sudden wave of protectiveness, a desire not just to avoid hurting her but to keep her from being hurt by anything, ever. "But I suddenly realized I could hurt you. The next move after the block would be—" She mimed the upward strike, slowly.

"Yes, and I would block," Conal said, bringing his shield around equally slowly. "We've done this with the wooden swords. You're fast, and you're getting much smoother."

"But if you didn't block in time, I could hurt you. With a wooden sword, that doesn't matter." Conal grinned wryly. They had both felt the force of the wooden swords in the time they had been training hard together. "Well, if you don't count bruises, it doesn't matter," she amended. "But with this if I don't stop, I could gut you. And I know I shouldn't be thinking about stopping."

"You're right, it's the last thing," Conal said seriously. He sat down and patted the ground beside him. For a wonder, the grass was quite dry. Emer sat obediently, quite close. "That's what Meithin always says, and I see now how right she is. That's why we always practice with wooden blades. If you learn to pull your blows, then you'll pull one in battle, when you need to be gutting someone. And they won't do the same and then you'll be the one who's dead."

As he was speaking the smith's hammer stopped for a moment and the last word came out unnecessarily loud in the sudden silence. The sound of the stream came to him clearly, and a thrush singing in the woods.

"Have you ever fought anyone for real?" Emer asked quietly.

"Not with swords." Conal didn't want to think about the times he'd fought Darag. He wasn't sure it counted anyway; real as those fights were, they weren't trying to kill each other, only to win. "Only that thing in the water."

"That wasn't at all the same," Emer said, turning her sword in her hand. "It didn't have hands or a head. It was a monster. I just wanted to stop it. It wasn't like fighting a person. I didn't use any technique until you told me to cut through it with you."

"We were very lucky, I think," Conal said.

The hammering started up again, louder than ever.

"It felt different from practicing," Emer said, raising her voice. "I think fighting people for real would feel different again."

"I think so, too," Conal said. He hesitated, looking at her, still feeling strangely protective. "You don't have to fight if you don't want to," he said.

Emer looked startled. "Of course I want to! Do you mean you don't think I'm good enough to be your charioteer after all?"

"You're better with the chariot than a lot of charioteers already," Conal said. "Even my mother says so, and my mother never gives more praise than she need. I didn't mean that at all. It's what I want. But if you would rather not fight and kill, rather stay home safe, nobody would think any the worse of you, and I would defend—"

Even as he found the words, he knew he was saying the wrong thing.

"I think you are mistaking me for my sister," Emer said, her voice very hard. She turned her face away, wiping it on her sleeve.

"I'm sorry," Conal said after a moment. "I wasn't mistaking you for anyone else. I just—" Her hair was tightly braided, as if to go under a leather battle-cap; she seemed all eyes, as always. She wasn't beautiful, not like Elenn. But she was unmistakably herself. He wanted to take her in his arms and kiss her. He wished she weren't so young. "You are special, and I want to keep you safe."

She turned her head back, her eyes still bright with tears, but there was anger in her voice. "And how would you feel if I said that to you?"

He thought about it for a moment, giving it consideration. "Treated like a child," he admitted.

"Well then!" she retorted, and threw a piece of grass at him. It landed on the leather practice coat around his chest. He looked at it for a long moment as it moved with his breathing. "I want to defend you, and be defended by you," she said. "I want to be your charioteer and fight beside you."

Conal reminded himself again how young she was, almost a year younger than he was, not even seventeen yet. "Yes," he said. "And later, not yet, later, in a few years' time, we could get married, and keep on fighting together."

Emer didn't say anything for a moment, and he thought he had spoiled everything. Then she put her hand on top of his where it lay on the grass. "It would be like a song," she said quietly. "If my mother would let us."

"You said she wanted to marry you to Darag," Conal said. He felt far more aware of his hand where hers touched him than of anything else. "There are no bloodfeuds between our houses. I am of the royal kin of Oriel. If she would consider Darag, I ought to do as well, if not better. Through my father, I am also of the royal kin of Anlar."

"Maybe we could persuade her," Emer said. She ran her long fingers over the back of his hand. He shivered. "It isn't blood she is concerned about, but alliances. Kings." Emer frowned.

"Darag is not bound to be king of Oriel," Conal said. He felt as if his hand was his whole body, his whole existence. He wanted to move, to put his other hand on her hand, but he dared not. "And surely if you tell your mother your preference, she will take account of it."

"My father might," Emer said, biting her lip. "My mother thinks that if Elenn is married to Ferdia and he is king of Lagin, and I am married to Darag and he is king of Oriel, then they will do what we say."

"That's nonsense," Conal said. "I mean, when my father married my mother, I am sure my Grandfather Ross of Anlar and everyone here meant it to be an alliance to bind Anlar and Oriel. But we go to war with Anlar whenever we want, and my father goes along and takes care not to kill his friends and then makes up songs about it afterwards."

"Maga's plan is that we should make the marriages as alliances for Connat before anything else, and use our wiles to keep our husbands firm to our alliance," Emer said, screwing up her face. "She is full of good advice about how to do this, and how to be a queen, all of which sounds the most vile nonsense. Not to mention that it demonstrably doesn't work, or she and Allel wouldn't fight so much. But she says that if we do it right there will be nobody to attack Connat except Muin."

"Or Anlar, or the Isles," Conal objected. "But no, I suppose Anlar couldn't attack except through Oriel, and the Isles would have to attack by sea, and I suppose that's why she wants your brother to marry Atha."

"She doesn't want him to!" Emer said, surprised. Her hand stopped moving, and Conal's breath caught. "My father wanted him to, but Maga says that Atha is a famous warrior and will always want to be fighting someone."

"She would, you know," Conal said, grinning at the thought. "I met her when she was here last year. She's not happy sitting still. She had the champions racing and playing hurley all day and dancing all night. My aunt Elba kept threatening to take to her bed with exhaustion, and my mother kept forcing her to join in with dire threats."

Emer laughed and stroked his hand again. "I wish I'd seen that. Is Atha really as ugly as people say?"

"No, nothing like. She's not pretty, but she wouldn't crack a plate either. Just like anyone. But I hear she always spikes her hair and paints herself ugly all over for battle."

"Does she fight naked, then?" Emer asked.

"Apparently. Almost all the champions of the Isles do. I haven't seen her in war paint. But that's what my mother said."

"It shows great trust in the gods," Emer said dubiously. "Our people paint their faces and arms and legs, but they wear armor where it will cover."

"Very sensible of them," Conal said. "But you're right that Atha fights in a frenzy, and your mother is right that she'd not be happy without fighting. Besides, I have heard that she might be going to marry Urdo ap Avren."

"Really? And go off to Tir Tanagiri and fight the Jarnsmen?"

"Ah, that's the snag. Urdo would like that, no doubt, but she'd like him to send her some Vincan horse-warriors to fight against us."

Emer rolled her eyes and took back her hand. "Marriage alliances!" she said. "This is getting like dinner conversation at home."

"I wasn't talking about an alliance, except incidentally," Conal said. Now that he was free to move he reached out his hand, meaning to take hers back, but she turned, and she was in his arms and he was kissing the top of her smoothly braided head. Her scent was stronger than the scent of the grass. He felt overwhelmed. "Emer!" he said. "Emer!" The hammering stopped again. "Emer," he whispered into her hair.

He knew exactly what he wanted to do, though he knew he wasn't going to do it. She might be a grown woman before the law, but she was not seventeen yet, and she was his uncle's fosterling. No matter what his father said, he wasn't an irresponsible boy. He could master his desires. But she turned her face up and looked at him, and in her eyes was such trust that he almost wanted to close his own eyes. "Conal," she said, very quietly.

Then there was a hesitant cough, and they leaped apart as if they had suddenly grown red hot. It was the smith, bringing a cup of milk as he often did on warm days.

He held the wooden cup out to Conal, who stood and took it awkwardly.

"Shall I bring some more for the lady?" the smith asked slyly, looking at Emer.

Conal's first thought was to say no and get the man away as fast as he could, begging him not to tell anyone what he had seen. Then the things he had learned took over. If he acted guiltily everyone would assume that there was something to be guilty about. Nothing would make the man gossip more than him trying to stop him. Much better to act as if there was nothing unusual. "Yes, thank you very much," he said casually, sipping at his cup. "How do you keep the milk so cool on such a warm day?" he asked. Emer was sitting down with her back to them.

"Well now, I keep the bucket in the stream," the smith said.

"What a good idea. I shall have to tell my mother about that," Conal said. "I suppose you have an iron bucket?"

The smith laughed. "Iron fittings on it," he said. "A bucket all of iron would be too heavy."

"Of course," Conal said. "I was thinking you could have made one without the carpenter."

"Iron fittings, and the wood swelled to be watertight, for a bucket," he said. "I'll fetch some more milk for the lady now."

Emer looked around when he had gone. "How could you talk so calmly?" she demanded.

Conal laughed. "I'm good at that," he said.

"I know, I've seen, but even so. My face was burning. It still is. I've never been so embarrassed in my life."

"We weren't doing anything wrong," Conal said, draining his cup.

"My mother would scream for days," Emer said. "Worse, she'd make me come home. She may anyway. She may not like my taking up arms." She bit her lip again.

"Surely she'll take it all right?" Conal was alarmed. "Uncle Conary sent ap Usli to explain, and he's good at explaining. She won't really make you go home, will she?"

"I've begged Elenn not to ask her to," Emer said. "And she wrote as well. Maga takes more notice of her. But Maga didn't want us to come away. Ap Usli could be back by now, if she had been happy. It's only five days to Cruachan."

"They'll have asked him to stay for the Feast of Bel," Conal said. "I can't see what Maga can object to, really, when it was a fortunate day."

The smith came back out with another cup of milk. Emer took it and thanked him seriously. They all bowed, then he went back inside and began clattering again.

"It will be the Feast of Bel in three days," Emer said, drinking her milk.

"Yes?" Conal said. Then he remembered what that meant. "No," he said in a different tone. The Feast of Bel had three meanings. The first was that the season of planting was over and the season of war could begin, between planting and harvest. The second was the renewal of the ancient ward that protected evil from coming to the island of Tir Isarnagiri. The third was the dance of fruitfulness. Everyone danced it once, around the relit fires, that the crops and the beasts should be fruitful in the next year. Then, after the children were sent to bed, it was danced again by men and women. Conal had heard that nobody ever asked where anyone had slept on the Feast of Bel. It was a time when the gods came into the world in disguise looking for willing partners, a time when women whose husbands had not given them enough children could seek a more fruitful coupling, and a time when many married couples would try to kindle children in the fields who had not come to the marriage bed. So many children were conceived at the Feast of Bel that the Feast of Mother Breda came exactly nine months later.

"Nobody asks where anyone sleeps on the Feast of Bel, and we are adults now," Emer said, smiling in a way that made Conal want to hold her again.

"You are not done growing, you are too young to bear children yet," Conal said. His voice came out almost as a growl. "Besides, if we go to war with the Isles this summer, you won't want to be feeling sick as the chariot lurches."

Emer frowned. "But I'm not married, and unmarried women don't have babies."

"They do after the Feast of Bel," Conal assured her. "If the gods want them to. That's what it's all about."

"My mother never explains things properly," Emer said crossly.

Conal had heard tales of what Maga did on the Feast of Bel. He didn't like to think what she might have told Emer. "There will be plenty of other chances," he said, stooping to pick up the wooden swords. "But not yet." He tossed a sword to Emer. She caught it left-handed; she still had the cup in her right hand.

"Not here," she said, looking at the smithy and setting the cup down. "Not in the dun, not anywhere in the dun."

"No, there's no privacy there unless you have your own house," Conal agreed. "If we get married, we could have our own house. Next year, maybe."

"You could sleep in the king's hall now if you wanted," Emer said, picking up her shield and getting into position.

"I'm not ready to fight that battle with my father," Conal said. "I need to do it from a position of strength. He isn't ready to see me as a man yet."

"Anyway, apart from the poetic side of it, it wouldn't do any good. I sleep with Elenn and Nid."

"What poem do you mean?" Conal asked, taking his stance.

"Really, for someone whose father is a poet anyone would think you never heard any," Emer said. "Cian's poem *Spring*. He's in love with a woman and they both sleep in the king's hall. '*How can I sleep when your soft breathing fills the air of the hall, echoes through the whole island*'."

Conal laughed. "Sounds to me as if she snores."

Emer looked horrified for an instant, then began to laugh so hard she dropped sword and shield and sat down abruptly.

"I'm not very poetic," Conal said apologetically.

"Oh, that's all right," Emer said when she could speak again. "It's Elenn who wants poetic. I just want you."

Conal put out his hand and pulled her to her feet. "And I, you know I—" Words had always come easily to Conal, but now there didn't seem to be enough of them to say what he meant. "I want you, too," he said clumsily, and angry with himself for being clumsy. "Now pick your sword up and let's get back to it."

"With the wooden blades?"

"Yes. Now I really understand why it's not good to learn to stop, or to gut your friends in training. We can use the real swords for practicing alone. Or maybe we could use them with ap Carbad, if he keeps coming down to morning practices the way he has been these last few days. You wouldn't mind if you gutted him."

"Not in the slightest," Emer said, sounding entirely as if she meant it. "No more than I would an enemy. But he's going to be very surprised tomorrow when he sees how much better I am."

They practiced until hunger drove them back to the dun.

# — 6 —

## (ELENN)

When Finca shouted outside the door, they all got up and dressed by candlelight, getting in each other's way. Nid kept yawning and complaining about having to be up so early, as if she didn't care what day it was.

At home, they would all have had new clothes. Maga had sent new overdresses for both girls, pale green with red and blue hatchings. Elenn smoothed hers down carefully. It was the first dress she had had for years that she hadn't worked on herself. She had neither helped weave the length nor sewn the finished cloth. She might have carded or spun the wool before she left home, and she found herself hoping she had, that when Maga had come to choose the wool to weave, she had run her hands carefully along the store until she came to some Elenn had spun. It was strange to wear a dress that had none of herself in it. She had only her old shift to wear underneath. Maga had not sent a new one, and Elenn had not thought in time to beg Elba for wool and the use of her loom.

They did not seem to make new clothes for the Feast of Bel in Oriel. If they had all been preparing, she would have remembered. But nobody had said anything about it or been extra busy at the looms. Nid was wearing the overdress she always did. Elenn had seen her wear it every time she'd seen her more dressed up than the shift and jerkin she wore every day, like a boy. Nid's hair, left bare and unbound for the festival, looked like a rat's nest. Elenn took up her comb, a very good hawthorn comb her father had made. She combed her own hair smooth and left it loose on her shoulders. She turned to Emer and was about to offer her the comb when she saw that her sister was wearing her usual mottled heather-colored overdress.

"You forgot your new overdress," Elenn said.

"It doesn't fit," Emer replied, untwisting her hair from her sleeping braid.

"How can it not fit? Mine fits."

Emer shrugged and looked down. "I've grown a lot since I left home."

Elenn frowned. She had grown, too, and her dress fit. But it was true that Emer had grown a lot.

"You should have said before," she said. "I'd have helped you let the seams out. It's fortunate to have new clothes for the Feast of Bel."

"Is that a custom of Connat?" Nid asked.

"It's what we say at home, yes," Elenn said, trying not to sound as if she thought less of Oriel for doing differently. Maga had warned her about that. She had warned her about a lot of things, but not of the important one. She didn't think Maga had ever imagined the possibility of Emer's mutiny.

Emer still wasn't meeting her sister's eyes. "The dress isn't long enough," she said.

"An overdress doesn't need to be long," Elenn countered. "Let me see if I can do anything with it." She couldn't force Emer to do anything anymore. The last half month had shown that only too clearly. But she could persuade her.

"There isn't time," Emer said sulkily.

"She's right," Nid said. "It'll be light soon. I need to find my parents and you need to join the king."

Without waiting for Elenn, or even combing her hair, Emer took up the candle, parted the curtain on the door and started out into the hall. Elenn and Nid had no choice but to follow.

At home, Maga and Allel would have had every fire in the hall lit, ready to be doused. Then they would lead the way around all the houses of the dun and down into the village, making sure there was no fire anywhere before Maga made the sunrise vow. Here, there were hardly any fires lit. Well, nobody could say it had been cold. It was one of the warmest springs Elenn could remember.

The hall was dark and shadowed. King Conary was standing with Ferdia, Darag, Leary, and Leary's parents. As Elenn came out of their room, Conal and his parents came into the hall through the outside door, letting in a little dawn light with them. Inis came in a little behind them. Emer went straight to Conal and stood beside him, abandoning her sister. Nid joined a group of people going outside, and slipped off to join her family.

"The fires in the dun are cold," Finca reported.

Elenn walked over to stand by Ferdia and Darag. At least they looked pleased to see her. Ferdia was even wearing new clothes. That made Elenn feel more comfortable somehow. It was so strange when everything was the same and different. She wished she was at home with her brother teasing her and her father making special porridge for them to eat before the fires were put out. Nobody had offered her any early breakfast, so it would be nothing but cold food all day. Ferdia smiled at her, and Darag complimented her on her dress. It was nice that somebody noticed.

King Conary led the way around the whole hall, starting in the kitchen. The fires were almost out already. He quenched all those that were still burning, using water. At home, Maga would have used her charm. Everyone knew the charm for lighting fires, but the charm for putting them out again was something special. Maga had promised to teach it to her daughters when they were grown. Elenn bit her lip and hoped she would not teach it to Emer first now. There had been a message for Emer with the clothes, but nothing for her. Was Maga angry with her? And if so, for what? For letting Emer take up arms, or for not doing the same herself?

Conary led the way back through into the main hall and they all trooped after him. Even the hearth-fire, which never went out except for the Feast of Bel and the Day of the Dead, was little more than embers. Before bending to it, Conary touched the heads that hung on each end of the stone mantle above the fire. Elenn knew they were only vanquished brave enemies, protecting the hearth, the same as the ones at home. But the ones at home were familiar; she had heard their stories told many times. There were no more here than at Cruachan, but they somehow seemed more sinister. She wondered if any of them were people she had known. It was not polite to ask.

Conary took up a poker and stirred the embers apart. When they sparked to life he poured water on them, sending up a choking cloud of smoke. Emer coughed, and for a moment Elenn almost went to help her. Then she remembered that her sister wouldn't want her help anymore and stayed where she was. When he was quite sure the fire was out, Conary blew out his candle. The others who had candles hastily blew theirs out, too.

Ap Fathag opened the door outside, and they all followed Conary through it. The sky was quite light now. Everyone was gathered in the space between the hall and the hilltop. It looked as if not only everyone in Ardmachan but all the farmers for miles around had come. On the hilltop was a cold bonfire, ready for sunset. Conary strode toward it through the crowd.

"Do we follow?" Elenn asked Ferdia. The grass was wet and cold with dew, chilling her feet. But it wasn't really cold, not like sometimes. There had been Feast of Bel mornings at home when she had shivered in her bare feet almost as much as on the Day of the Dead six months later.

"We can stay here," Darag said. "We have seen the fires put out, the king doesn't need his household with him now."

Conal's family, with Emer, her eyes red and streaming, stopped a little way ahead. Leary's family followed Conary almost all the way up to the crest.

"Shhhh!" Ferdia said.

Conary had reached the top and was looking out eastward, waiting for the first sliver of sun to clear the horizon over the distant sea. A hush grew through the crowd, a quiet expectancy. This, at least, was just as it was in Cruachan. At this moment, Elenn knew, her mother would be waiting as Conary was waiting, as the kings of Muin and Lagin and Anlar and the Isles would be waiting.

As the sun revealed itself, Conary raised his arms, first palm up and then palm down. "Hear this," he said loudly. "Lord Bel, Mother Breda, and all gods of earth and sky and of home and hearth and clan. And hear this, my people assembled here before me. The fires are cold. The folk of Oriel have kept the Ward."

Nobody moved or spoke. Behind them, Elenn knew, the sun was rising slowly. Usually she stood beside her family and watched it rise. It seemed a great deal of trust to put in Conary to let him watch alone, though he was the king, and he had no wife or children to stand beside him.

After a time that seemed endless, Conary spoke again. "The sun is risen, Lord Bel, master of life and death. No fire will be kindled again in Oriel until we see the fire that has been kindled on the Hill of Ward." It was much too far to see the Hill of Ward from here, of course. But there was a bonfire prepared on each hilltop, and as each hilltop sighted the fire on the next, they would light their fire until every fire in the land was lit. Then the feasting and dancing would begin.

"Let the Ward hold across Tir Isarnagiri," Conary said. "Let there be death in bright sunlight, life out of darkness, war without hatred, strife without bitterness. And let the evil time come not."

Everyone murmured their assent. Then they sang the Hymn to Dawn, voices rising together. When it was done, people started moving and talking. Elenn stayed still. Weren't they going to sing again? But it seemed they were not.

"Come and have breakfast," Darag said, taking Elenn's arm.

"It seems strange to do this and be hungry," Ferdia said, taking her other arm.

Elenn smiled up at him. "Do you eat first in Lagin, too?"

"Ah, but breakfast is the best part," Darag said.

People were going into the Speckled Hall and coming out with baskets. Finca was setting up an ale barrel. "Are people going to start drinking already?" Elenn asked.

"Some people will, others will wait until this evening," Darag said.

"We could drink some ourselves," Ferdia said.

Darag grinned. "I hadn't thought of that. Have you ever had any?"

"A little cup at dinner with my father sometimes," Ferdia said.

Elenn smiled to cover her uneasiness. She wouldn't have wanted ale even if she had been allowed it. Maga had told her all about it, how it muddled people's minds. She did want something to eat, though. She wondered what was in the baskets. She saw Emer going with Finca into the Speckled Hall. "Should I go to help?" she asked.

"They look as if they know what they're doing, but I expect they wouldn't turn help away," Ferdia said.

"You should stay with us," Darag said. He smiled at Elenn, and she smiled back. She liked Darag. There was just something strange about him, even now, when he was being nice.

Leary came running up to them, whooping. "Ale. Did you see?" he asked.

"We saw," Darag said, smiling amiably at him.

"Get some for you, Elenn?" Leary asked.

"I'd prefer to have some well water," Elenn said, meaning it.

"Get you that, then?" Leary begged. Elenn smiled graciously at him and gave him permission. Then they went to collect some food.

There were apple pies and meat pies, cold but delicious. They filled their sleeves with them. The boys got wooden cups of ale, and Leary came back with Elenn's water. They sat down to eat on the far field, right over by the wall. Nobody was playing hurley or practicing slingshots today. There were other people around, but nobody was really close. Elenn sat down, spreading her skirts out and putting her pies on them. The boys sat sprawling, Ferdia and Conal on each side of her and Leary opposite.

"Aunt Finca's been baking for days," Darag said, munching on an apple pie. "She says they've used up every last one of last year's apples and she's asked Uncle Conary if we can have a big hunt soon to replenish the meat stores."

"Hunt?" Leary sat up a little. "For what?"

"Boar, deer, whatever we find to fill the smokehouse," Darag said, spraying crumbs.

"But we could go with the champions?" Ferdia asked, looking eager.

"Of course we could." Darag grinned. "We're champions now, just the same as the others."

Elenn didn't say anything. She took neat bites out of her pie. She didn't want to go hunting anyway.

"Do you think it'll be tomorrow?" Ferdia asked.

"Probably Conary will leave it a day or two, to let people get over tonight." The three boys laughed.

"Oh, that happens here, too?" Elenn asked. She had heard about that from Maga. Nobody cared who slept where on the night of the Feast of Bel, once the children were put to bed. It was a wild festival. "People getting drunk and dancing and plowing the furrow in the fields?"

The boys looked at each other, and then awkwardly at her. "People will get drunk," Ferdia said. "Then they'll be hung over tomorrow and not ready to hunt."

"You going to do that?" Leary asked.

"Definitely not," Ferdia said. Elenn looked at him approvingly.

"I don't know," Darag said. "I've never had the chance before."

Ferdia looked disappointed in his friend. "I'm not going to," he said again.

Leary giggled. "Drunk, plowing the furrow . . . know what they say about the Feast of Bel? Feast of the Mother comes nine months later."

Ferdia laughed.

Elenn was horrified. It just wasn't the sort of thing people talked about, and especially not men and women together. It seemed almost an impious thing to say. She looked at Darag, who had neither said it nor laughed, and saw that he was also looking shocked.

"You know what they say," Ferdia said, grinning, oblivious of the fact that nobody wanted to hear this. "They say children born at the Feast of the Mother always know for sure who their *mother* is!"

"They don't say that to me," Darag said, forcing the words out. He looked as if he'd been hit quite unexpectedly and very hard. Elenn put her hand out unthinkingly and pressed his shoulder for a moment, offering comfort.

Ferdia looked surprised and a little taken aback. "Were you born at the Feast of the Mother, then?" he asked.

Leary also looked chastened. "Didn't mean you," he said.

Darag looked as if he was never going to get a word out again.

"I was born at the Feast of the Mother," Elenn said. It was true. She had always thought it a good time of year for a name day. Mother Breda gifts all children to their mothers, but Elenn had always felt especially close to her because she had been born at her festival. Besides being true, she said it because she wanted to distract Ferdia and Leary from going after Darag when he felt so bad. Maybe he really didn't know who his father was. Both his parents were dead, after all, and both had died when he was very young. She'd never heard him addressed by his father's name since she'd come here, he was always Darag, as if he were king already. "Maybe my parents went out to the fields," she said, smiling.

"Yes, definitely," Ferdia said, much too quickly. "I'm sure they did. Lots and lots of married couples do."

"Lots of married couples go together," Leary confirmed unhesitatingly, clearly not believing a word of it.

Elenn now understood something of what Darag might be feeling.

She felt stupid. She knew that Maga didn't go into the fields with Allel, but alone, to find a new and willing partner. She had never thought before, how Mingor and Emer looked like Allel but she didn't. Where babies came from was a Mystery, a Mystery of the Mother. People shouldn't talk about it like this. Not that it mattered. She'd ask Allel if it was true when she got home. Allel, not Maga. Maga knew a lot and understood things really well, but sometimes she said what she wanted to be true. Allel didn't always know, but he always told things straight out.

Darag looked as if he was a painted statue of a young man someone had set up in the field. Ferdia looked anguished, clearly realizing he had hurt her, though he was staring at Darag, obviously too distressed even to look at Elenn. Leary looked uncomfortable.

"Think we should get more pies," he said and took Ferdia's arm.

"I think not," Ferdia said, shaking him off. "Darag—"

"Darag's thinking. Be fine in a little while. Elenn wants more pies, don't you, Elenn?"

It would give her a few minutes to gather herself, at least. Darag looked as if he was going to be quiet for a long time. She raised her chin affirmatively. But as soon as they were gone, Darag stirred.

"You are festival born?" he said.

"Yes," Elenn said. There was hardly any point in denying it. "But it's a Mystery. Leary shouldn't talk about it like that."

"He shouldn't," Darag said, very quietly. "Or Ferdia either."

"Ferdia didn't know," Elenn said. "I didn't know."

"My mother didn't know who my father was," Darag said. "She told my uncle he was a god."

"I have heard stories of that happening at the Feast of Bel," Elenn said. She was starting to wish she had gone with the others. "Nive, or Lew, or Govannon coming to join the feast."

"But my mother wasn't married," Darag said. "So it must have been a god. Or maybe not. I've never known. Sometimes it seems that it was just some lucky man, and other times I think it must have been—" He stopped and put his head in his hands.

"It is a Mystery, truly," Elenn said. "But it would explain a lot if it was," she added.

"Explain, yes, but what's left for me then?" he asked. "Who would want me, or even see me, when everything I touch turns to wonders?" He shook his head. Elenn saw Leary and Ferdia coming back slowly, talking to a pretty girl she didn't know, laughing with her. "I know I'm not a normal man. Strange things happen to me. Omens. Portents. And I keep dreaming such strange dreams."

"About your mother and a god?" Elenn asked gently.

"No. Not that. I keep dreaming about how they built this dun," Darag said. Elenn blinked, surprised. "There wasn't even a hill to start with. They brought all the earth here, piling it up and up, little horses pulling it up. It's this place, this dun, before it was a dun." He gestured around him, as if he could see it. "One of the horses is a mare, and she's pregnant, worse, she's actually giving birth, shuddering with it, and the man, the king, keeps on driving her up with load after load, whipping her, whipping all the horses, forcing them. And then she stops and gives birth to a filly, just over there, where the Red Hall is now. And the king takes the filly and draws his knife to cut her throat. And then, talk about mysteries, then the filly changes and grows and it's Beastmother he has hold of, Rhianna herself, and she's huge and powerful, like a horse but not, like a woman too, and black, black as night, flecked all over with blood and sweat. And she shakes the man in her great teeth, and then the hill is built, all finished, but the people are clutching themselves and crying out in pain, and the horses are gone."

"That's horrible," Elenn said and shivered.

"I don't know why I keep dreaming it," Darag said miserably. "I don't know what it means."

"Have you asked ap Fathag?"

"It's impossible to ask Inis anything," Darag said. "I haven't told him. Maybe I should try. But he always looks at me as if he isn't really seeing me, or he's seeing too many of me."

"I think you should try," Elenn said. The others were nearly up to them. She wondered who the girl was. Ferdia seemed to be paying a lot of attention to her. "And tell me what he says. Now, quick, stop being upset about it. Whatever it is, it doesn't matter. You and I, we know who our mothers are, and for both of us that's the important thing. Don't let anyone see you're upset."

"I have to fight anyone who says anything against my mother's honor," Darag said.

"When you'd kill them? Where's the honor in that?" Elenn asked. "Besides, what's against her honor to say she lay with a god in the fields on the Feast of Bel? She was the king's own sister, after all."

"Thank you for understanding," Darag said. Elenn gave him one of her best smiles. She wasn't at all sure she understood, but she wasn't about to let him know that.

# — 7 —

## (EMER)

She thought the best thing would be if she could provoke him into saying something disparaging about Connat. Anything would do. Then she could fight him in honor, without making Conal a cause. She thought she could do that without causing Conary to throw her out or Maga to summon her home. Maga's words had seemed almost scorched into the paper as it was, demanding to know what she thought she was doing. She wouldn't tolerate any more independence right now. Defending Connat's honor, or better, Maga's own honor, would be ideal. Amagien didn't guard what he said at all. She thought she could kill him quite easily. He was slow, and he rarely came to practice. The only problem then would be the impiety of marrying Conal after she'd killed his father. No, she couldn't do it no matter how much he annoyed her. It would be a bloodfeud, and people with a bloodfeud between them couldn't marry. That would be a disaster. She'd heard of a bloodfeud being reconciled so that people could marry, but only after six generations. Though maybe she could provoke a quarrel between Amagien and another warrior. Only she wouldn't do anything so dishonorable.

Emer had never thought Maga's lessons in how to smile sweetly whatever you were thinking would come in useful. She'd never been as apt a pupil as Elenn. Yet now she found herself doing it every time Amagien opened his mouth. He didn't seem to be able to say anything at all without making Conal squirm. It didn't matter than Conal didn't show it. It was just the same as standing by while someone stuck little knives into him.

The clouds in the western sky blazed purple and red. The sun was down and Conary had made the sunset vow. They were waiting to catch sight of the first fire. Conary was standing alone by the piled wood that would be the fire. Near him were Elenn and Ferdia, arm in arm. Elenn had been ignoring Emer all day. Emer had almost repented of not wearing her new overdress when she saw how unhappy her sister was. It wouldn't really have made any difference. The one she was wearing was just as much Maga's gift if she stopped to think about it. She just didn't want to take a gift from her mother right now. Also, she didn't want to wear the same colors at the same time as Elenn ever again. She was tired of being dismissed as the ugly sister. She wanted to be seen as herself. No, she had made the right choice and been right to stick to it. It was strange to feel pity for Elenn. But now her sister couldn't do anything to stop her. Even what she said didn't hurt. It just sounded like a weak echo of Maga.

Her eye moved on through the crowd. Elba and Ringabur stood with Leary, who caught Emer's eye and grinned. Next to him was a woman Emer didn't know. She was stocky and well balanced, and her face marked her as obviously kin to Leary. Darag was next to her.

"I didn't know Leary had a sister," she said to Conal.

"Where?" He turned to look.

"The elder ap Ringabur came back from Rathadun of the Kings today," Amagien said. "She has been there nine years learning the law."

"She's back to stay?" Conal grinned. "You'll like Orlam, Emer. Let's go over and I'll introduce you."

Anything that got them away from Amagien was all right with Emer. She raised her chin affirmatively.

"You're not to waste her time," Amagien said. "She won't want to be bothered now she's a lawspeaker. Let her see that you're a man now, don't behave like a puppy dog."

Conal froze. Emer decided to change the subject before one of them said anything they regretted.

"Have you ever been to Rathadun?" she asked.

"Never," Conal said.

"You'll go there one day," Amagien said. "I went there for my initiation, and you'll go there when you're chosen to be king—if you ever shape up enough that you are chosen. Rathadun of the Kings is a wonderful place, very holy. The nine hills have a peace like nowhere else. The Hill of Ward, where even now the fire will be alight, is the very heart of it. And nobody stays there but priests and initiates, and they make no difference between initiates for law or poetry or priesthood or kingship. It is a wonderful way to live."

Emer smiled another excruciating Maga smile and wanted to scream. She hadn't exactly forgotten that Amagien was a poet. How could anyone, when he went on about it all the time? Nor had she forgotten that poets were, like kings and priests and lawspeakers, immune to challenge. But she somehow hadn't connected it up. He didn't act like a poet. Even when he sang his stupid song about how pretty Elenn was, he just seemed too full of his own importance. Still, she should have remembered, and it ruined everything. He could say anything in perfect impunity and nobody would be allowed to challenge him over it. At least this solved the riddle of how he had lived to grow as old as he was. He could say whatever he liked and nobody could even kill him. It really wasn't fair. What was so sacred about poets anyway? A king, yes, or a lawspeaker—of course they shouldn't be challenged, because then they might be afraid to judge fairly. As for priests, challenging them insulted the gods. But poets? Nobody would challenge someone because they didn't like their poetry.

"There!" Conal pointed, and a rustle went through the crowd as everyone craned to look. The first faint spark of fire blazed out to the south, looking distant as a star. "That's Mornay," he said. "And now watch to the west, we'll see Lusca next."

"Nemglan next," Amagien said. "Then Lusca."

It didn't matter. But if she said it didn't matter, it would make Conal feel worse. The points of light spread, like red flowers bursting into blossom. Conal named them all for her until at last it was time. Conary raised his hand and the bonfire beside him burst into flame. People stepped back from the sudden heat. The drummers began to play, and the harpists joined them. From somewhere came the sound of a pipe, the music twining around the harps.

"I must join Finca," Amagien said. "Take good care of ap Allel, Conal. And make sure you take her safely to the Red Hall after the dance."

Emer smiled a farewell. Conal raised his cup and took a relieved sip. "Why are poets sacred anyway?" she asked him.

He choked on his ale. "To keep words free," he said when he had recovered. "But why were you thinking about that?"

"Your father made me wonder," she said. "Look, the fires are spreading north."

Thankfully, Conal accepted this distraction and turned to look. The fire was indeed still leaping from hilltop to hilltop across the darkened countryside. "That's Edar," Conal said, pointing at a nearby blaze to the northeast. "My father's farm."

"I didn't know Amagien had a farm so close," Emer said.

"We used to live out there," Conal said. "But since my mother is Uncle Conary's keykeeper, we have all moved into the dun."

"Do you ever go out there now?"

"All the time," Conal said. "Not so much recently, but whenever my father can find an excuse to send me with a message or something to do out there, he does." He laughed. "Don't tell Amagien, because he thinks it a punishment to send me. But I like going. I like the farmers there—and see what a great blaze they have made."

"Why does your father think it's punishment?" Emer asked. "Like 'Pleeeease don't turn me into a bird, Uncle Math'?"

"Partly that," Conal said, grinning at her Little Wydion voice. "But I used to be afraid of the bull, a few years ago. He's a huge creature, and fierce. My father made me lead him about and take charge of him."

"Your father is a monster," Emer said before she could help herself.

"Well, but it worked. I'm not scared of the bull anymore. And he isn't a monster. He means well. He wants to help me grow up to be the best."

Emer knew she couldn't say what she wanted to say. She knew too much about parents who wanted things for their children. Instead, she looked away at the distant lights. "I wish we were out there," she said. "Away from them all." The music was getting louder; people were forming up for the dance around the fire.

"It's a pity we didn't think of that earlier," Conal said. "We could have gone out to Edar. The farmers there are good people. They'd have been glad to share their feast with us."

"We still could go," Emer said, all at once eager for it.

"It's two hours' walk," Conal said. "And it's nearly dark already."

"We could take the chariot," Emer said. "We'd be there much sooner. And people won't stop celebrating tonight until late."

"Do you mean stay the night out there?" Conal asked.

Emer felt her cheeks heat. Elba came by before she could say anything and gave Conal a little push. "Take your places, we're starting," she said. Emer realized that almost everyone was lined up ready to begin the dance. Conary was at the head, with Orlam ap Ringabur. Elenn was with Ferdia, and Darag with Nid. Conal and Emer hastily took up a place as the music grew insistent. Some of the champions grinned at them and made teasing remarks.

"Yes, I did mean stay the night, but not what I said before," Emer whispered under the music as they started to move. "I believe what you said. But if nobody minds where we sleep, then we could just sleep out there, in a storehouse or something, and come back in the morning. No parents, no Darag, no Elenn. Strangers are lucky on the Feast of Bel, they'll be glad to see us."

Conal danced in silence for a moment, looking torn. They circled the bonfire, then Conary led the chain of dancers around the wall of the dun. "Can you drive in the dark?" Conal asked at last.

Emer raised her eyebrows and smiled. "Of course."

"Have you done it?" Conal persisted.

"It won't be very dark," she said. "There's light in the sky still, and the moon is rising. And you know the way."

Conal shook his head and grinned. "All right," he said. "Let's do it. Straight after the dance."

Emer felt as if they were escaping as they made their way down the hill. Nobody noticed them in the general confusion. People were preparing food and hurrying children to bed and bringing animals to be led around the fire. They could still hear the merriment as they came to the stables.

There was nobody there, and no horses either except for one strange horse. "That will be Orlam's horse," Conal said. He dragged out the chariot while Emer went out to the paddock and caught the horses. She had been afraid they might be hard to catch, but they all came running as soon as she whistled, and the problem was separating out the pair she wanted. She had to light a lantern to see what she was doing with the harness, but before long, she had them safely yoked to the chariot. She looked up. Conal was watching, smiling at her in a way that made her feel warm all through, despite the chill of the night.

"We should have brought cloaks," she said. "The wind's cold, even if it is the Feast of Bel."

"Our armor coats are down here," Conal said. "They'll be warm."

As they were coming back with the coats, they heard the sound of someone whistling a plaintive tune. They glanced at each other guiltily. The chariot was waiting outside; there was no sense in trying to hide. The whistling stopped as they came out. Meithin ap Gamal was looking at the chariot. She laughed when she saw them. "Oh, so it's you two new champions? I might have guessed."

"We were just—" Conal began.

"Sneaking out?" Meithin laughed again. "Well, you're not children, I'm not going to stop you. I'm not even asking you for an explanation. I'm just here to fetch my Swiftfoot and Windeyes up to take around the fire, and if anyone asks, I haven't seen you. But what horses have you got?"

Emer breathed a sigh of relief and set down the lantern beside the chariot so Meithin could see them properly. "Whitenose and Crabfoot," she said.

"Very sensible of you," Meithin said approvingly. "Nobody's going to want the geldings tonight. You have been careful to put Crabfoot on the right?"

"Yes, I'm quite used to him," Emer said.

"We make sure you have difficult horses for training so that you get used to challenges," Meithin said. "You're not going to do anything crazy, are you, not going to blindfold yourself and drive three times around the dun backwards? Or go down the waterfall road in the dark?"

"Of course not!" Emer hoped she sounded as horrified as she felt.

"Orlam and I went backwards around the dun blindfold one Feast of Bel," Meithin said, sounding wistful. "We were only a year or so older than you two."

"We're just going out to Edar," Conal said. "I know the way, and we won't be blindfold."

"Edar?" ap Meithin sounded taken aback. "What's there?"

"It's my father's farm," Conal said. "It's a fire hill, so they have their own festival there, with good ale and dancing. They roast a sheep, which might even be done not long after we get there, if they had it ready, unlike the cows here, which won't be cooked until breakfast. There'll be room for us to sleep out there, and we'll come back in the morning."

"And it's a long way from parents and everyone you don't want to see," Meithin said. She sighed. "Well, have fun. I almost wish I was ten years younger and coming with you."

Conal looked at Emer inquiringly. She squeezed his hand, loving his generosity and his consideration.

"Why don't you come, then?" Emer asked. "There'll be a fire there for you to drive your horses around."

"I'm not so young and wild," Meithin said. "Besides, the last thing you two want is me coming along like a third horse to your yoke."

"It isn't you we want to get away from," Conal said, saying exactly the right thing, as always when he wasn't with his father. "You'd be very welcome to come with us. But you do know Orlam's back?"

"I could hardly have missed her," Meithin said. "But she . . . but I . . . well. Sometimes what you wait for isn't what you were hoping for. Orlam's back, but . . ." She hesitated. "Well, maybe it wasn't a good day for it. But she said she isn't going to need a charioteer."

The misery in Meithin's voice was so painful that Emer wished she knew her well enough to hug her.

"That's too bad," Conal said sympathetically. "Come on, yoke up, or the sheep will be eaten before we get to Edar."

"I haven't said I'm coming," Meithin said, but she so clearly wanted to that Emer couldn't bear it any longer.

"We'll get your chariot, you get the horses," Emer said decisively. Meithin raised her chin and went off to the paddock.

Fortunately, Conal knew which chariot to take, even in the darkness of the stable. "You don't mind, do you?" he asked as they dragged it towards the doorway, gray against black.

"Mind? I asked her. How could I mind?" Emer let go of the chariot and put her arms around Conal, resting against him for a moment. "I want to be with you. You wouldn't be you if you didn't want to ask her to come. Besides, I like Meithin."

Conal squeezed her tightly, and her body felt as if it were melting. Not tonight, she thought, not tonight, but soon. Then, wordlessly, they each let go and took up the chariot again.

"I like Meithin, too," Conal said. His voice sounded strange, as if he barely had it under control. "She's helped me more than anyone with my swordwork these last few years."

"Me, too," Emer said, and she was surprised to find that her own voice shook a little. "I didn't know she was a charioteer."

"She used to be," Conal said. "She's mostly a champion these days. But she was Orlam's charioteer, before Orlam went off to Rathadun. They were very wild, and very close, too."

"I'd gathered that," Emer said. Then they were outside, and they could see Meithin coming back from the paddock with her mares.

The lower gate stood open, with no guards. Emer had expected they'd need to talk their way out. "Where's the guard?" she asked.

"Nobody would attack on the Feast of Bel," Conal said. "We leave it open for the gods to come in, if they choose to visit, and the farmers. It doesn't seem worth making someone miss the festival to guard it. It worries me less than leaving it unguarded in the daytime when it's quiet, really. If an enemy isn't stopped until the top gate, we'd have given away a lot of ground for free."

"Have you said this to Conary?" Meithin asked.

They turned westward around the hill, to meet the northern road. It was lighter than Emer had feared. The moon and the stars were bright. She could easily tell the road from the fields. The horses were eager, but she kept them at the pace Meithin set beside them.

"He won't listen to me," Conal said. "He said I'd soon learn how much champions enjoy guarding gates when there's no war."

"I suppose he does have to manage his champions as well as his enemies," Emer said.

"He'd have heard it if Darag had said it," Conal said.

Then they came to the northeast road and turned, and Emer let the horses have their heads for a little, and Meithin did the same with hers, and for a while, they raced down the road. Meithin would have won, having less weight, but they pulled up after a little and went on more sedately, talking sometimes but mostly in a companionable silence. There were no other chariots, no sign of anyone else at all. Only the fires on the hilltops told them that they weren't the only people left in the world. It felt peaceful and exhilarating to go along through the dark like this. Emer would have been happy to have traveled on like that forever, Conal close beside her and the horses eager under her hand.

Edar turned out to be bigger than Emer had expected from Conal's calling it a farm. There was a ditch around the bottom of the hill, almost dry after this very dry month, and a palisade around the top of it. The night was completely dark by now, but the moonlight was sufficient to show them that the way up was too steep to drive.

"Should we unyoke the horses?" Meithin asked.

"But then there's nowhere to put the chariots except just leaving them out here," Conal said, biting his lip. "I think we'd better leave them yoked and lead them up. It's not too steep if we're careful. If I drove out here more often, I'd suggest we ought to build a stable at the foot of the hill like at Ardmachan. But I always walked before."

As they neared the top of the hill, the wind changed, taking away the scents of hot ale and cooking meat and bringing Emer the scent of salt-water and tide-wrack. "Are we so near the sea, then?" she asked.

"It's just two miles east of us here," Conal said.

They led the chariots up and were met at the top by a cluster of delighted farmers. Emer gathered that they loved and honored Conal and had not seen him for some time. She soon found herself plied with marvelous hot ale and, not long after, with roast lamb and palm-sized griddies hot from the pan.

"I haven't had griddies since I left home," Emer said, thanking the smiling farmer who had brought them. "I thought you didn't make them in Oriel. I like them so much better than bread."

"We always make them on special occasions," the farmer said.

"You couldn't have said anything better," Conal murmured when the farmer had moved on to share the griddies with everyone. "Ap Anla prides herself on her griddies."

Emer ate seven griddies and felt ready to burst. After they had eaten, everyone was needed for driving the animals around the fire. Emer had never seen this done; she had always been sent to bed long before. The animals were garlanded and driven around while everyone sang to Rhianna, the Mother of Beasts, and danced with them. There were no instruments, and Emer found herself thinking that next year she would bring a harp, if she could. Meithin threw herself into the celebration, drinking and dancing and laughing. At last, she went off with two of the young farmers, one on each arm.

"Do you think she'll feel better about Orlam?" Emer asked, watching from where she sat with Conal near the fire.

Conal put his arm around her, and she leaned back against him. "Not really," he said. "But at least she hasn't had to stay in Ardmachan with Orlam there and not with her. I'm glad we brought her."

"I'm glad we came," Emer said. "Maybe we could come every year. I really like the people here."

"You really like the food," Conal said.

"Maybe we could live out here," Emer said. "Your father isn't using it, and he isn't here, and we could be in Ardmachan if Conary needed us."

Conal hesitated, and Emer wondered what she'd said wrong. "I need to be under Conary's eye, and where all the champions know me well," he said. "If they're to choose me king over Darag, I have to be in Ardmachan."

"You don't have to be king," she said. "It isn't the only good thing to be."

"Anything else is a failure," Conal said decisively.

Emer bit her lip and didn't say anything. There were so many things to be, why did he have to set his heart on that one? It was his father insisting on it, she knew it was. She couldn't say so, she could never make him see it. She just sat there and watched the dancing and the people going off together in pairs.

At last her eyes started closing, and she and Conal staggered off to lie down in the hall. They kept all their clothes on, except for their armor coats, but lay all night curled up very close together, sharing the warmth of their bodies and feeling each other breathe. Soon, Emer thought sleepily, but for now, this was enough, this was marvelous, she didn't want anything more than just to lie together like this for as long as they possibly could. She drifted between sleeping and waking, feeling happier than she ever had.

She must have slept at last, because she was woken at dawn by one of the farmers coming to tell them that ships from the Isles were landing troops down on the shore, and they wanted Conal to tell them what they should do.

— 8 —

(FERDIA)

Ferdia's father Cethern, the king of Lagin, had told his son there was no point in drinking to drown your troubles, because troubles can swim. It was just as well Ferdia knew this, or he would have been very tempted to try it. He kept out of the way, leaning on the wall of the Speckled Hall, and looked at the reflection of the lights in his ale. Everything had gone wrong. First he had unwittingly said something to offend Darag. Then he'd been unable to get Darag alone to talk about it properly. Leary had stuck to them like a leech, and Darag had seemed, as so often lately, to want Elenn ap Allel to be with them.

Ferdia understood why, of course. Elenn was beautiful. He knew how beautiful women liked to be talked to, and he was always polite. He had two older sisters, and there were other girls his age at home in Ernachan. He knew what they liked, and Elenn wasn't any sillier than the rest of them. Besides, Darag was right—she was nice to look at, and it did make a difference. Conal's father had made up a poem about how beautiful she was, which he hadn't liked much. Leary had made up his own afterwards, and then Darag had wanted to, so they sat down to it together.

The best Ferdia could come up with was to say that the way she looked reminded him of the smell of snowdrops. Darag didn't understand, and asked how a look could remind him of a smell. Ferdia wished he were better with words so he could explain properly. It was something about the fragrance in the cold air, with the loam smell and the green growing smell. He was thinking especially of a wood near home where he always found the first snowdrops in the early spring. That's what she looked like to him, not how they looked, the smell. She looked nothing like them, the green shoots in the dark earth and the nodding white blossom, but there was something about the smell. Or maybe the taste of the very first blackberries of autumn. Something like that. Darag laughed and said he'd never be a poet. Ferdia knew that already.

All the same, he quite liked Elenn. Sooner or later, he knew, he'd have to marry somebody, and if not for who her parents were, he wouldn't at all have minded if it turned out to be Elenn. It would be nice to have her around to look at, her manners were very good, and a queen everyone thought was beautiful was an asset to any kingdom. As it was, with her being Maga of Connat's daughter, she wasn't even on his father's list. Leary's sister Orlam was, and from what he'd seen of her today, she would probably do well enough, though she was a lot older than him. That wasn't so good. But a queen who was a lawgiver would be a good thing for Lagin. Orlam seemed to be quick and clever, which would also be useful.

It was such a pity Darag didn't have a sister. Then he could marry her and Darag could marry his sister Locha. Or his sister Moriath, if Darag preferred her. It didn't matter which one. If they could have done that it would make them brothers twice over. But Darag could marry one of his sisters and be his brother anyway. Unless Darag insisted on marrying Elenn. That would spoil that plan. He sighed and drank another mouthful of ale. She had been with them all spring. She would be here until next spring, and he would have to go home at midwinter. He had been hoping Darag might come with him and spend a year in Lagin. But not if he wanted to stay with Elenn. She wasn't so bad. She was always polite, and she seemed to like him. He didn't usually mind having her around at all. He didn't even mind Darag liking her. Usually.

Today it was different. He just wanted to talk to Darag about what he'd said, and apologize. He doubted very much if Darag's mother had done anything she shouldn't. In any case, she was dead, and it was no reflection on Darag. He just wanted to say sorry, but he couldn't get Darag on his own, even for a moment. It wasn't as if Darag wanted to be with Elenn as well as Ferdia; it was as if he wanted to be with her instead. The only way Ferdia could think of to deal with this was to act as if he really wanted to stay with Elenn, too. Leary was doing the same, as usual. So they had ended up in a nonsensical wrangle about who Elenn was going to dance with, which Ferdia realized halfway through he could only lose, whatever happened. What he wanted was to dance with Darag, and they couldn't do that. This wasn't a dance men could do together, the dances of Bel were men and women dances. Conary had taught them that when they realized the thing they wanted wasn't on the table, it was time to stop negotiating. Unfortunately, as so often, life turned out more complicated.

He danced with Elenn. She danced very well, in the southern fashion of Connat and Lagin and Muin, quite unlike the way it was done in Oriel and the Isles. He could feel Leary shooting him jealous glances as they danced. He hoped Darag wasn't doing the same. He tried not to look. After the dance, he took her safely back to the Red Hall, with the children. Elenn hadn't taken up arms with the rest of them, so she had to go inside. She said she wanted to. Ferdia smiled and said she was taking the light inside with her. He had heard his father saying that. There was a guard on the door of the Red Hall, to stop the children coming out again. It was gray-haired Senna, leaning sleepily on her spear. He supposed she had grown too old to mind missing the rest of the feast.

He had come straight back, and he couldn't find Darag. He had found Nid, who had danced the first dance with Darag. She had drunk more ale than was good for her and insisted on kissing Ferdia for luck. And after that, she didn't even know where Darag was, only that he had been dancing with Orlam when she had last seen him.

The dun was crowded. There were people and animals everywhere, all moving. It was impossible to find anyone. The music never stopped; when one player got tired they handed their harp on to another. Ferdia realized after a while that as everyone was moving, he had more chance of finding Darag if he stayed in one place. So he had been leaning against the Speckled Hall, watching the crowd. He had seen lots of people, but not Darag. He hadn't seen Conal either.

Then he spotted Laig. Laig was drunk. His clothes were disordered and his hair was rumpled. Ferdia thought almost everyone looked better with their hair tied back. He didn't know why keeping it loose at festivals was a sign of respect for the gods. If he was a god, he'd prefer people to stay tidy. If there was ever a chance to mention it to Inis ap Fathag, he thought he might, because it would be interesting to know. Just looking at Laig made Ferdia want to straighten and smooth down his own hair. Elenn's hair always looked smooth; he wondered how she did that.

"Have you seen Darag?" he asked.

Laig stopped and ran a hand backwards through his hair, which might have accounted for the state it was in, except that it also seemed to have grass in it. "Yes, he's down by the hurley field," he said, his voice slurring a little. "But don't go and disturb him. Tonight all the young married women are looking for dancing partners. Darag's got his hands full. Even I have had offers. More than offers." Laig leaned towards Ferdia confidingly. Ferdia shrank back a little from the ale on his breath. "That's where I was," Laig said. "Pressing the grass flat. Plowing the fields. And with a champion, too. I won't tell you her name, that isn't the thing to do, but definitely not one of the ugly ones."

As Ferdia remembered Conary's champions, that left two possibilities, and one of them had three children already. Though Laig might be counting charioteers as champions, being a charioteer himself, which left much more scope. Not that Ferdia wanted to guess, but how could anyone avoid it when he said things like that? "Well done," he said, because Laig was definitely expecting some such response.

"You should try it yourself," Laig said. "Plenty of them would want you, being a king's son. You'd be even more popular than Darag, and Darag is very popular." He laughed.

Ferdia shook his head, absolutely certain. "I don't want to," he said.

Laig giggled. "You might find you liked it if you tried it. But it's up to you. The unwilling gift isn't a gift at all, better a gift unoffered than a gift spurned, and all that. Well, I'm going to find more ale and then see what other dances I can learn tonight."

He wandered away unsteadily. Ferdia set down his own cup in sudden disgust. There wasn't anything here for him. He wished he was back home in Lagin. He wished he were still a child to go to bed after the first dance. He thought he might as well go to bed anyway as stand here watching the people dancing in the firelight. The only thing that stopped him was the thought that it wouldn't be quiet enough to sleep for hours yet. Standing here wasn't good, but being inside awake listening might be worse. Ferdia hesitated, then decided he could always stuff his blanket into his ears. He set off through the press towards the Red Hall.

Everyone seemed to be laughing and touching. Several women, some he barely knew, insisted on kissing him for luck. He realized that Laig was right, he would have no trouble finding partners if he wanted them. He was quite sure he didn't, not at all. He was glad to win safely to the shelter of the Red Hall. He made his way to the other side of the building, where the door was, away from the crowd.

Old Senna had left the door, there was nobody there now but Inis, who was sitting on a stool by the door, rocking to and fro a little. He did not look up until Ferdia was almost up to him. His eyes seemed very bright in the lantern-light.

"Well met on the Feast of Bel, son of Cethern," Inis said.

"Well met, ap Fathag," Ferdia said uncomfortably. He wanted to get past Inis and go in to bed. He hated the necessity of being polite while making sure to ask no questions, even the most innocent.

"Not dancing?" Inis asked.

"I've had enough of it for tonight," Ferdia said. "I'm tired and ready for my bed."

"Seeking your lonely bed," Inis said.

Ferdia didn't know if he was making a comment or quoting something. It sounded like a quote, but it wasn't from any song he knew. He didn't know if it was something he might reasonably be expected to know but had never heard. With Inis, it could be something really unusual, or something from another country or even another world. The worst, the absolute worst, would be if it was something from another world written about him, now, and Inis knew that. The problem with Inis was that he was both very mad and very wise, which made him just impossible. Most people were limited in what they would say by politeness, but never Inis. Sometimes Ferdia thought the Vincans were right to kill all the oracle-priests or drive them out of their empire. But then, Inis was especially rude even for an oracle-priest. It might have been because he was the king's father. Nobody even dared reproach him.

Whatever Inis meant about the lonely bed, Ferdia didn't want to talk to him about it. He realized he'd just been staring at him for a long time without saying anything.

"I don't mind if it's lonely as long as I can lie down," he said, and faked a yawn.

"Darag won't be there," Inis said plainly.

Ferdia wanted a god to swoop down from the sky and catch him up to the clouds. He wanted the hill to open so he could dive inside. He felt his cheeks heating so much he feared that Inis would see. He swallowed and tried hard for a casual tone. "No, he's still dancing. He'll probably get to bed late. Or maybe not until tomorrow." He tried to sound amused rather than distressed, and thought he did quite well.

"I wish you could stay boys forever," Inis said, and he sounded really sad. What did *that* mean?

"Too late," Ferdia said. "We are men already and have taken up arms."

"He has killed the deer and the swan. Soon he will add a man. All of my grandsons will, and you will fight, too, son of Cethern." Inis rocked again and closed his eyes. Ferdia bit back questions. "Soon" must mean this summer, it had to. He didn't want to know more than that. He didn't want to know anything. He knew he would have to deal with oracle-priests all his life, but he just wanted to do things without it all being doomed and prophesied. Often enough if you listened to them, you ended up worrying about things that didn't happen anyway. His father told him that. He took a step toward the door. Inis's eyes shot open again. Ferdia froze.

"So, though you are a man, you go to bed early on the Feast of Bel, like a boy?" Inis asked.

"I'm tired," Ferdia said, and was horrified to realize it came out like a whine, like the child Inis said he was.

"This could be a night you would get strong sons," Inis said.

Inis knew that sort of thing. Everyone knew that he did. He was one of the three best reckoners of lucky days in the island of Tir Isarnagiri. The story was that years ago King Nessa had asked him what the day was fortunate for, and he had replied that it was a lucky day for begetting a king on a king. As he was the only man around, she had taken him to her bed, for all that she had a husband and he had a wife, and the result was Conary. Nobody could deny that Conary was a king, and one of the best kings Oriel had ever had. But even if Inis did know it, what good would it do anyone? "I could beget sons maybe, but not sons of my house," Ferdia said. "They would be neither heirs for Lagin nor grandsons for my father."

"No," Inis agreed. "But children of your body. Heirs for Mother Breda. A son might come of this night who may not bear your name but who will take your face down the years."

"That would be a child denied to the wife I will one day marry," Ferdia said.

"Now there is the thought of a man who would live long," Inis said. Ferdia stared at him again, the whole world narrowed to Inis on his stool. What did he mean? That he was going to die soon? Or that he wasn't?

"I have two sisters and a brother," Ferdia said at last, as the thought came to him.

Inis smiled sadly and gestured to the darkness. "Then you may deny a wife nothing, if you can find her here tonight."

Ferdia didn't want a wife, or a child, not yet, not now, not like this. He just wanted to go inside and go to bed, and maybe later Darag would come back and it would be like every night. Or not. He didn't want to

do things Inis suggested, wide things without edges. He didn't want to
go to the hurley field and lie down with any of those laughing, kissing,
teasing women. Yet, to go inside past Inis now would be like running
away. Though to do something he did not want to do for fear of Inis was
also cowardice. What Laig had said to him earlier came back. "The unwilling gift is no gift," he said.

"No, it could not be unwilling," Inis agreed calmly.

Then he stood up and walked away into the night, around the hall
toward the lights and the dancing, leaving Ferdia gaping. He hesitated.
Nothing constrained him now. He could go inside to bed. But he did not
move. He stayed on the threshold, thinking it through. He shrank from
the thought of doing it. Yet somehow it felt impious to turn aside from
so clear an oracle. He wondered if this was how Darag had felt when Inis
spoke of a fortunate day for taking up weapons. He took a step toward
the door, then stopped again. No man was bound to have children. If he
let this lucky time go, then the gods might never smile on him and bless
his eventual marriage bed. Inis's words came back to him, the thought of
a man who will live long. That might have meant that he would die this
summer. It was a chance any champion took. Leaving a child of his getting
in someone else's marriage bed would not make much difference. Did he
want to leave a child who would grow up like Darag, fumbling at questions about the Feast of Bel? That was no legacy to leave. And yet, what
if turning away now meant no child ever?

He turned and looked up at the moon, who looked back at him,
offering no counsel. "Help me, Nive," he murmured. No answer came.
Then around the corner of the hall came a woman. Ferdia knew her a
little, though he didn't remember her name or how to address her. She
was one of the people who looked after the king's dogs. She smiled when
she saw him. He didn't know whether Nive the Beautiful had sent her
to him to make up his mind. But he decided he should make a willing
offering, if she had. The woman came straight up to him as if they'd
arranged to meet. She kissed him, and he embraced her. It felt strange.
He could feel the softness of her breasts pressed up against him, and for a
moment, he wanted to push her away in revulsion. Then she took his
hand and led him down to the hurley field.

# 3

# ATHA AP GREN

# — 9 —

## (CONAL)

On the waking edge of sleep, Conal drifted a little, half-dreaming across the worlds. He held as tight as he could to place and time. Even deep down in sleep, he had known he was in Edar. There was a smell to the place, that particular mixture of burning peat and heather bedding and hams hanging from the roof that told him he was home. He always slept better here than in his father's house at Ardmachan. Edar he knew as well as he knew anywhere. But this was not childhood. He could feel Emer curled up beside him, familiar and homely as his own heartbeat. Emer, in Edar, this place, this time, and no others. Drifting, he held to time and denied the gift. Asleep, he turned away and strove to close eyes closed already.

He heard the door to the hall open, and came nearer waking. It could still have been any time, anybody coming in. He was warm and Emer was safe beside him. But two pairs of footsteps came hurrying toward the alcove where his bed was made up. Conal's eyes opened, the struggle over, he was entirely and effortlessly there. When Old Anla and Garth came to the foot of the bed, he was awake, alert, and sitting up. Anla was the steward, responsible for Edar in Amagien's absence, but he was getting old and frail. For a year or two now, more and more of the responsibility fell on his daughter's husband Garth. If they were both here now, it must be something urgent.

"Raiders," Anla said, his voice quavering. "Folk of the Isles. Six ships, coming in down on the shore."

"I was going to wake the folk and go out to fight them, stop them stealing the cattle," Garth said, sounding angry. "But your ap Gamal insisted we stay inside. She shut the gates. She demanded we get you."

"Thank the Mother of Battles that she did," Conal said, pushing back his hair. "If a straggle of you had gone running down the hill, Atha's folk would have picked you off at their leisure."

"Then are we to cower inside without facing them?" Garth asked. "The cattle are together in the near pastures; they were all brought in for the blessing last night. They will take them like reaping corn."

Conary had told him that no matter what good plans you thought you had, you almost always became alarmed when a crisis hit, which was why it was necessary to have everyone know the plans well in advance so they could stick to them instead of each going their own way. Conal didn't have a plan made in advance; it was all coming to him now and cohering as he thought of it. He didn't feel alarmed, though, he felt unusually calm. Emer, too, seemed calm. She rolled over and began binding back her hair. But he could see already how it would have been helpful for everyone else to have known the plan before.

"Oh, no, we must fight," Conal said, getting the order of things clear in his mind. "Anla, wake Nerva and tell her to get the paint ready. Garth, wake everyone who can fight and get them painted as quickly as you can."

Old Anla jerked up his chin and went off to find his daughter, who was in one of the other alcoves of the hall. Emer stood up, stretched carefully, and reached for her armor coat.

Garth hesitated, looking at Conal. "I hadn't thought we'd have time for paint," he said sullenly. "Nor need to bother with it. We could keep them from the herd if we were quick. If they thought there would be easier pickings elsewhere, they might leave our cows alone and make for another farm. It isn't as if we can hope to stand and fight them all."

"We can hold them off long enough for King Conary and the champions of Ardmachan to get here," Conal said. "We can do it better if they think we're a lord's household and not just a bunch of farmers."

Garth frowned. "It won't work," he said. "They won't come. They won't know they're needed. What do you know about it? You're the lord's son, not the lord, and even your father is only the lord because the king gifted him this land. He wasn't born to Edar. You're only a boy. Why should I take your orders?"

Conal didn't know what to do. He could kill Garth for saying that, but that would not make him obey him nor keep Atha from the herd. Garth was a foot taller than he was, and twice as broad across the shoulders, so knocking him down was out of the question. It was essential that the people of the dun obey, or he could do nothing.

"Conal ap Amagien is one of the king's champions of Oriel," Emer said, her voice as cold as steel. "He was armed by Conary himself this season. What you have said would be accounted treason in Connat, and my mother would have your head for it."

Conal blinked at her. He had never heard her sound the outraged princess of Connat before, though Elenn did it often enough. Garth looked at her in amazement. "In these parts, we speak the truth to our lords," he said.

"And here I am speaking the truth back to you," Emer said. "Conal is young, true, but a king's champion."

"What is a champion but someone who has a chariot to fight from and need not be down in the crush with the rest of us?" Garth demanded, thrusting his chin forward.

"Someone who knows how to lead," Conal said, the words coming from his dream, or from nowhere.

Emer looked cross enough to spit. "Conal is your lord's son, he is here, he has a plan to save you, and while you stand here arguing with him, time is wasting that might mean all our lives, or the loss of all your herds."

To Conal's amazement, Garth hesitated only half a moment longer, gave a clumsy half bow and went off towards the door.

"I don't know how he dares speak to you like that," Emer said, twisting her hair into place behind her head with both hands. "I suppose it is from having seen you grow up and not really realizing that you are a man now."

"No doubt," Conal said, still a little dazed.

"What is most needful for me to do first?" she asked. She was standing ready, looking at him expectantly.

"I love you," Conal said, surprising himself even as he spoke.

Emer gave a little surprised laugh. "I love you, too, but—"

"I know," Conal interrupted. He stood up and buckled on his own armor coat. "Get the chariots harnessed. Find out where Meithin is and make sure she's ready. I need to see exactly where they are and how many of them there are. Six ships could mean two hundred warriors, but not if they are raiding and planning to take cattle back with them."

She bowed in acknowledgment and headed off without a backward glance. Nerva came in as she went out, carrying a great cauldron of paint and followed by most of the people of fighting age of the dun, naked and clamoring. None of them were blue so far.

Conal finished fastening his coat and went towards them.

Nerva made an awkward gesture with her head when she saw him. "We wanted to know what to paint," she said, swinging the big cauldron onto the hook over the fire. Nerva's daughter Hivlian, who was surely too young to fight, blew on the embers and started to add some wood.

Conal stopped. He had not the least idea. "What to paint?" he repeated stupidly, wishing Emer was still there. He was a champion of the king's house of Ardmachan, but paint was not something he knew anything about.

"Defense or attack, or which gods to call on . . ." Nerva said, stirring the paint. Then everyone started talking at once, each with their own suggestions and demands. Cevan slopped white paint onto the floor from the little pot he carried as he gestured too emphatically. Conal could not hear it all, and time was wasting in which he could be planning how to stop Atha.

"Protection, of course," he said. "And beyond that, victory. Paint yourselves to win, and do it as fast as you can, time is short."

That sufficed to create enough silence for him to leave, though he could hear their voices being raised again before he was quite clear of the hall.

The dun outside was in an uproar. Meithin was standing at the gate holding a spear. Garth was beside her holding another and wearing an old armor coat. Another part of his plan came to Conal, and he smiled. Emer was harnessing the horses. Women and children were running everywhere, dogs were barking furiously, pigs and hens were loose and complaining. Conal ignored them all as best he could and went to the point of the wooden wall where, by long practice, he knew he could swing himself up to see down toward the sea.

Six boats, Anla had said. How many people could Atha have persuaded to miss the Feast of Bel for this raiding?

He was looking almost straight into the sun, he had to squint. He saw at once that they had brought no chariots. But there were more of them than he had hoped. He did not let himself be daunted, but counted them as Inis had taught them. He made it eight twelves, two threes, and two, a hundred and four, armed and on foot, but there might have been more. They were among the herd already, which made counting difficult. Still, that could work to his advantage. Few of them were painted; they were not expecting much opposition here. They would be about even for numbers, so he would need what advantage he could take. They would not all be champions; some would be farmers come for the raid, and many of them would have come to sail the ships. But none of his people were champions except himself and Meithin and Emer. He squinted harder, looking among the cows, wondering.

He walked calmly over to Garth and Meithin. "Can you stand in a moving chariot?" he asked Garth.

Garth frowned as if he thought it some sort of test. "I never have," he said after a moment.

"Practice a little, once they are harnessed," Conal said. "I am not asking you to fight from one. That is a matter of years of practice. I just want you to stand in one until we are down there. Then you can get down and fight on foot. But you are the only one who has an armor coat and might convince them."

"Your lady was right to say I am no champion," Garth said, scowling.

"You are steward of this dun," Conal said, holding his ground.

"My wife's father is steward," Garth replied.

"And shall we set old Anla bouncing down the hill to frighten Atha ap Gren and her chosen champions?" Conal lowered his voice. "I am not trying to punish you for insolence. I am trying to save the herds. We all want the same thing, Garth, and I know how to get it."

"I will stand in your chariot," Garth said.

"Very well," Conal said and turned to Meithin. "Ap Gamal, when we are ready, take ap Madog here up behind you, go down the hill before the footmen, just a little behind me. At the foot of hill, let ap Madog jump out, then wheel as fast as you can and make for Ardmachan. Tell them what is happening and bring them here to our aid as fast as you can."

"As fast as I can is going to take an hour there and back, which will mean closer to two hours than one, even if Conary listens at once," Meithin protested. "It's better for me to stay here and fight. We can't really use both chariots properly, but a chariot with a charioteer and without a champion is better than nothing. And I am a champion."

"They will come in time if you are quick," he said. Meithin looked as if she would have liked to argue more. If they had been anywhere other than Conal's father's dun, he was quite sure she would have tried to take over. In some ways, he would very much have liked to take her advice, but everything screamed to him that doing so would be fatal to his already shaky authority. "Practice with ap Madog now," he said and walked away.

Naked people stained blue and painted on top in black and white were starting to emerge from the hall.

A small child started to scream. Anla picked him up and tried to soothe him. Conal could not wait. "Where is Old Blackie?" he asked. "Have they taken him already, or wasn't he with the herd?"

Anla blinked and continued to rub the child's back as his cries subsided into gurgles. "He is here," Anla said. "He is in the calving house. He came up last night for the blessing and he couldn't be left with the cows after, or they would all get in calf, and it isn't time."

Conal could feel himself smiling. "We really can do this," he said, and looked around.

Emer had harnessed up both chariots. Garth was practicing standing still as Meithin drove hers around in a small circle. Emer stood by theirs, holding the horses' heads. More painted people were coming out of the hall.

Anla had been talking, but he hadn't heard a word of it. "Where are the spears?" he interrupted. This wasn't Ardmachan. There wasn't a separate hall for weapons. But it wasn't the barbarian countries either, where people would take weapons in where they ate. How strange it was that he'd never needed a weapon at Edar.

"In the smokehouse," Anla said. "Shall I fetch them? Or shall I send Garth to fetch them? He has his own already."

"You fetch them, and take some people who do not fight to help you," Conal said. "Are there any weapons there besides spears? I know my father keeps most of his weapons beside him at Ardmachan, but did he leave anything here?"

"There is one sword of Amagien's, and there is another that belonged to Howel when he was lord here, and which his daughter did not want when she went to Rathadun. There are many slings besides, which we use for hunting, and a few shots for them, and plenty of stones."

"Does anyone here know how to use a sword?" Conal asked, knowing the answer would be no.

"Lord, it is a champion's weapon," Anla said.

"Bring the swords to me," Conal said. "And share the spears out to those who are ready to fight. Give the slings to those who can best use them."

Anla hurried away and Conal walked over to where Emer was waiting.

"He has two swords, but I have no idea what size they are," he said.

"Give one to Meithin. I have a knife if I need one for the traces," Emer said, showing the little belt knife no charioteer would go without even on a peaceful summer's night.

"Meithin is going to ride for Ardmachan as fast as she can," Conal explained.

"Then I will take one," Emer said, unruffled.

Anla came back with an armload of spears and started to give them to those who were painted already. It seemed to be taking hours for them to get ready, though the shadows had hardly moved since Conal had come out.

"You should get them ready, or they will fight each other," Emer said very quietly. "Shall I drive you to the gate?"

Conal could see that she was right. The young farmers were over-excited already and did not want to wait.

They looked up as he came over. He ran through what he would say to them in his head, but what came out of his mouth was his first thought. "Where are your shields?" he asked.

They were naked and painted blue. Across their chests, men and women alike—though it looked more horrific on the women—was a great black battle-crow. Down their arms and down their faces were white spirals. They had been boasting and teasing each other. Now they looked at each other in confusion at Conal's question, like children, and began to slink away to their houses to fetch their shields. By the time they came back, their fellows had joined them, and at last Nerva came out of the hall, painted and carrying the black paint.

Anla came back with the swords, which Conal took. "There were some throwing spears as well," he said. "Only five."

"My great thanks to you for keeping the dun so well," Conal said.

"It is Garth you should thank," Anla said grudgingly. "I have kept it for many years, but he thinks it is his time."

"His time will come," Conal said. "Now, as soon as we are out, get Blackie from his house. Watch from the gate. When I signal by throwing both hands up in the air and calling his name, let him go."

Anla hesitated. "You know how Blackie can be," he said. "There's no promise he'd know his friends in a battle."

"Do it all the same," Conal said, as firmly as he could.

Anla drew breath as if he would speak again, but Conal stared at him. He didn't want a conversation about what Amagien would say if Blackie were hurt. At last Anla raised his chin in agreement and went off to help with distributing spears. Conal arranged the throwing spears in the slots in the chariot so they would be ready to his hand. He set a long-weighted fighting spear beside them in case he needed it, then looked at the swords. They were both much bigger than the swords they had been practicing with.

"Which do you want?" he asked Emer.

She looked at them. "They're very old," she said.

"Anla said one of them was my father's and the other was left by the lord who was here before him."

"Which was your father's?" Emer asked suspiciously.

"I really don't know," Conal said.

"Then I'll take the one that's a little shorter," Emer said. "I wish I had my own that King Conary had given me for my use."

"So do I," said Conal, buckling on his sword.

Nerva had been painting Garth's face. As soon as she was done, Garth climbed into Meithin's chariot and Nerva came over to Conal. "We are painted," she said. "Will you wear the victory sign yourself?"

He bent his head, closed his eyes, and felt the pig-bristle brush sweeping across his face. Nerva murmured the charm as she painted, calling on the Mother of Battles for Victory, and he felt it taking effect, filling him with confidence, making him more ready to fight and kill. The calm that had filled him since he woke receded a little and although the paint was supposed to take away fear, he felt a little fear for the first time.

"And you, lady?" Nerva asked Emer.

Emer looked at Conal, then shook her head.

Conal waited until Nerva had set down the paint and picked up her spear. Then he raised his hands palms up and then palms down.

"Branadain, Mother of Battles, and Edar of the Spring, be with us now when we call on you. Right is on our side. These folk have come from the Isles meaning to take us by surprise, steal our herds, and harm our people," Conal said. Then he looked at the waiting farmers. "Our plan is to hold them off long enough for King Conary to come here with his champions and help us. Ap Gamal will be going to fetch him, so they will be back here almost before we know it, and well before the folk of the Isles can expect them. If I give a great howl like a wolf, break off and come back up to the dun, we will hold them off inside. We are fighting for time, and they have no help coming. And most of all, remember, the cows are ours!"

Anla swung the gate open and Emer drove out, Meithin close behind with Garth clinging to the side of her chariot. The painted farmers, giving a great roar, came boiling out behind. Conal saw heads turning among the raiders. He gave his own battle cry as Emer headed the chariot straight down the hill toward them, and suddenly his feelings, which had been far away from him all morning, came back and were close. He felt his love for Emer not as a distant knowledge, but as a burning presence. His fear that he might disappoint his father, or die with nothing done, his joy at being alive and going downhill fast enough to rattle his teeth, and the love and comradeship he felt for Emer, so close beside him—all welled up in him at once and he thrust them into the battle cry which rose up on the air above the howls and cries of the others.

Then they came up to them, and after that, there was only the fighting.

# — 10 —

## (ELENN)

Emer still wasn't there when she woke up. Nid was fast asleep and snoring in a beam of sunlight that had come in through a hole where the roof sat on the wall. Emer's bed was still as she had left it the day before. Elenn sat up and combed her hair and felt strange inside, as if she wanted to cry, but she didn't know what she wanted to cry about. She swallowed hard and kept back the urge. She had cried when she'd come in last night, and it hadn't helped at all. Anyway, if she cried now, it might wake Nid.

She didn't know if she was dreading or hoping for what would happen when Emer got found out. She didn't even know if anything would happen. She knew for sure that she wanted something to happen. There was a tightness in her chest that she thought an explosion of anger with Emer would clear. For a moment, she stopped still, considering being angry with Emer herself. She almost wished she could. But Maga said losing your temper was letting people know what you were thinking and something you should only do with a very good reason. Even Allel said it was better to control your temper, so Elenn never lost hers anymore. She had not lost control of it since she was a very small child having tantrums, and she felt embarrassed to remember that now. So she didn't want to be angry with Emer; she wanted someone else to be angry with her and make her feel better.

Elenn went out to find some breakfast and see if she could find Emer. Finca was stalking around the hall as if she were looking for someone to shout at. The cooks were keeping their heads down. They didn't even look at Elenn as she went up for some porridge from the pot over the fire, just ladled out a bowlful.

Elenn walked around the alcoves looking for someone to eat with. There was nobody there she wanted to see or who called out to her. It wasn't early, but maybe it was early for the morning after a festival. King Conary was there, but he looked so grumpy that she didn't want to try talking to him. In the end, she sat down next to ap Dair the poet and Leary's sister Orlam, who were talking about music. Music didn't interest Elenn much. But Orlam had only come back here yesterday and didn't know anything about Elenn, and ap Dair seemed like an old friend from home, because she had seen him sometimes in Connat.

As soon as they had greeted Elenn, they took up their conversation again. Elenn took a spoonful of her porridge. It was thin, and could have done with some fruit or honey. Maybe there would be wild strawberries soon. There would at home.

"You get the best music in the world in Rathadun, it spoils you for coming home," Orlam said.

"It has wonderful music," ap Dair agreed. "But I enjoy going around to different kings' halls and playing with different people, and learning the songs of the different places."

"Where have you heard the best music, then?" Orlam asked.

"I have heard very good music in this hall," ap Dair said courteously. "And I have heard very good music in Cruachan," he continued, turning to Elenn and half bowing as best he could sitting down, which meant that she had to say something back. She racked her brains for a proper response to that.

"Do you like traveling so much that you mean to travel all your life?" she asked. "Or would you like to settle down and sing in one place eventually?"

"When I grow old," said ap Dair, stretching. "There are certainly songs you can only learn by staying in one place, though they may be less obvious than the ones you can learn by traveling."

Orlam made a noise of agreement, though Elenn had no idea what he meant. Surely it didn't take more than four hearings to learn any song? And poets were supposed to be able to learn a song in two, ap Fathag said.

"But I'm not ready to be just ap Dair," ap Dair went on. "You know what I mean?" He looked at them and grinned. He put his spoon down and gestured with both hands. "The king's hall, full of people. They want music. The visiting poet is introduced, comes up to the great harp and sings a new song to much applause, rich gifts. Then the king's own poet comes out and people say 'Oh, it's just ap Dair our poet, whom we have heard many times before.' And even if it is a new song, they only listen with half their ears because they know they will hear it again. When I am old, I may be ready for that, but for now, I have too much vanity. I like to travel to different places and be acclaimed and eat my breakfast surrounded by beautiful women." He grinned at them again, and Elenn smiled back.

Orlam looked thoughtful. "I am not a poet or a warrior, but a lawspeaker," she said. "So fame plays little part in my desires. But there are many mornings when I would be glad to see not new and beautiful people but the same faces that delight me. It is the same with places. I have been nine years at Rathadun and at first I missed Oriel badly. Now I am home for the first time for longer than a few days and I am already missing Rathadun. A lawspeaker can go anywhere. Some of my friends are planning to travel throughout the island and see all the wonders. But I know if I did that, I would only find more places and friends to miss."

"And what of you, ap Allel?" ap Dair asked.

"I have never thought about it," Elenn said. "I have never been anywhere except Cruachan until this year. I have always thought I would live in one place. I've never thought about the alternatives."

She sounded impossibly naive in her own ears, but Orlam made a sympathetic noise. "I heard at Rathadun that your parents didn't follow the custom of fostering with you," she said. "I have met your brother, Mingor."

"We are fostered here this year," Elenn said.

"But this year you are what, seventeen?" Orlam asked. Elenn raised her chin in agreement. "That's old enough that you have largely formed your expectations of conduct already, and traveling never crossed your mind because you never did any."

"It's a good thing you don't want to be a poet," ap Dair said.

"My sister plays the harp," Elenn said, though she herself could play and sing well enough not to disgrace herself if called upon.

"What do you want to be?" Orlam asked.

Elenn looked at her blankly. "What choice have I? I have always been a king's daughter, although my brother is the heir, and I have always known I would grow up to marry to further Connat's alliances."

Orlam winced, and ap Dair frowned. "Like a princess in a song," ap Dair said after a moment. His voice sounded strange, as if he thought that sad rather than enviable.

"I am of the royal kin of Oriel myself," Orlam said, which Elenn naturally knew. She was Leary's sister, which meant that her grandfather was King Fiathach. "I could have made such a marriage myself."

"You still could," ap Dair murmured. "I saw ap Cethern looking at you yesterday when we were dancing. He isn't betrothed to anyone yet, and he will be king of Lagin unless things go very badly for him."

Elenn went cold all over, as if someone had poured well water straight down her back. She bit her lip to avoid saying anything. Even with her short hair, Orlam was very pretty, and of course she was quite grown up already.

"He's a child!" Orlam said, and laughed as if the suggestion was absurd.

Elenn breathed freely again. She would have liked to have put her face in her hands and shut her eyes for a moment of relief. She made herself smile. "He is seventeen, the same as I am. And he has taken up arms."

"And I am twenty-six, and a lawspeaker, because I have made other choices about what my life is about," Orlam said, rolling her eyes. "Marriage and children are things I want, and I am even feeling ready for them now that I am home. But marriage for policy and being a queen, well . . ." She screwed her face up. "I mean," she looked at Elenn in belated but well-intentioned courtesy. "That it is not for me."

Elenn finished her porridge and set the wooden bowl down carefully. "It is what I have been brought up to," she said.

"And you never wanted to be a king or lawspeaker or harper—" ap Dair began.

"—or smith, or champion, priest, or farmer?" Orlam finished, miming counting out the cherry stones.

Elenn laughed. "I never thought about it, but now that I do, no, I don't want to do any of those things."

"You are beautiful enough that you will doubtless have all the kings of all the world fighting to make you their queen," ap Dair said, getting up and bowing extravagantly.

"Thank you," Elenn said, as she had been taught.

Ap Dair bowed now to Orlam. "And as for you, ap Ringabur, they say your mother and her sisters were the most beautiful girls of their generation, but you outdo them all. I am sure all the men in the hall are jealous of me sitting here with the pair of you."

Orlam laughed, but a little impatiently, and got up herself, offering her hand to Elenn. "Let's go outside where the air is not quite so thick with prettily turned compliments," she said.

Elenn took the proffered hand and pulled herself to her feet. She liked compliments usually, but she had also noticed something odd about those, after the conversation. It was as if ap Dair had stopped addressing them as people and was saying something that could be addressed to any pretty girl. In some ways, it was more comfortable not to be seen as herself, but in others, it was refreshing and she liked it. She definitely liked the way Orlam talked to her.

She walked towards the door with Orlam, though she wasn't sure where they were going. "I hate how even the nicest men can just turn words to emptiness like that," Orlam said.

"Oh, yes," Elenn agreed enthusiastically.

Just then Finca intercepted them. If she had once been one of the most beautiful girls of her generation she didn't show much sign of it now. She was bony and hard faced and had scars on her arms from fighting. "Have you seen Conal?" she asked.

Elenn shook her head. "Not since I came home," Orlam said. "That's strange, now I think of it. He was still hanging around me like a puppy dog when I last visited. But like Darag and my little brother he must be seventeen and an adult, by what I hear."

"You hear right," Finca said, and walked away without another word.

Orlam laughed quietly. "That sounds like more than too much merriment. Do you think he's been out all night with some girl my aunt disapproves of?"

"My sister," Elenn said and sighed. It would be very unfair of Finca to blame Elenn for not keeping Emer in order, but from the set of her jaw this morning, it didn't seem beyond her.

"Your sister?" Orlam said. "I thought—"

Just then Darag came into the hall. He looked as if he had not slept enough. "Elenn!" he said. "Orlam!" Then he stood looking lost in the middle of the floor as if he had no idea what to say next. Orlam giggled, and Elenn had to fight not to giggle herself.

"Drink water," Orlam advised kindly. "Lots of water. You'll need it."

"Have you seen Ferdia?" Darag asked. Then he looked appalled, as if he said something terribly rude, though Elenn didn't know how he could have.

Orlam giggled again. "Not since the time I saw him with you after my brother introduced us yesterday. Everybody seems to have lost someone this morning."

"Who have you lost?" Darag asked, looking alarmed.

"Why, nobody," Orlam said, making her eyes wide. "But Finca is having trouble finding her little boy." Then Orlam took Elenn's arm and took her off, leaving Darag staring after them. "People who can't hold their drink can be disgusting. Do you think he will remember the water?" Orlam said into Elenn's ear, and this time Elenn could not keep her giggles to herself.

In other company, Elenn might have been distressed to see Ferdia looking ill and tired and making his way to the hall. Somehow, with Orlam, it just seemed like a continuation of the joke. "Drink water," she said as a greeting.

Ferdia started and rubbed his eyes. "Thank you, I shall," he said.

"Darag is looking for you," Orlam said. "And have you seen Conal?"

"Conal? No." Ferdia said, distracted. "Where was Darag?"

Elenn had just opened her mouth to tell him, when Meithin ap Gamal came running in through the gates and pelting across the grass towards the Red Hall as fast as her legs would go. Elenn stopped and stared at her.

"What's wrong, Meithin?" Orlam called.

"Invasion from the Isles, at Edar," Meithin said without stopping. "I have to get to the king, fast."

Ferdia's eyes widened and his shoulders went back. All the laughter went out of Orlam's face. "He's eating in the hall," she called after Meithin.

Meithin charged on into the hall. The three of them followed her. When she skidded to a halt in front of Conary, they were only a little behind. The other folk of the dun who saw Meithin running came pressing up behind them to hear what was happening. Conary had finished eating and was talking to Finca in front of the fire.

"Invasion, from the Isles, at Edar," Meithin panted. She sounded as if she had been saying it in her head all the way. "Six ships, a hundred and four people. The folk of the dun are holding them off, under Conal ap Amagien."

Finca's lips pressed into a hard line. Conary's eyes bulged. "Conal?" he asked, incredulously.

"We went there for the feast," Meithin said.

"He was here at sunset," Finca objected.

"We went out there after sunset," Meithin said, putting a hand to her head. "But this is all wasting time. He's there right now, fighting Atha for all I know. We need to arm and hurry to help him."

"Did you bring the chariot back and leave him there?" Finca asked. She looked so angry that Elenn took an involuntary step backward and trod on someone's foot.

"There wasn't any point in me staying, without a champion to fight or someone else to drive so I could fight," Meithin said.

This made sense to Elenn, but apparently not to Finca, who rushed at Meithin, her voice rising to a screech. "Was Conal not champion enough for you that you left him there on his feet?"

"We had two chariots!" Meithin said, sidestepping just in time. Ap Carbad caught Finca before she ran into someone and straightened her as if she was a child just learning to walk.

"So Emer ap Allel drives him? Babes to the slaughter," Finca said.

Elenn suddenly felt worried herself. She had thought Conal and Emer were pretty good. But Finca had taught them to fight from a chariot, she ought to know. She bit her lip. There was nothing she could do now. She'd worry about how to tell Maga that Emer had managed to get herself killed if it happened.

King Conary shook himself. "To arms!" he said. "To arms, my champions! Let us ride out and defend Edar and come to the aid of my valiant nephew. Finca, have the chariots harnessed. Ap Carbad, open the Speckled Hall. Time is short. We ride as soon as we are armed."

Everyone began to bustle about. Ferdia and Darag embraced, then rushed off towards the Speckled Hall together, looking much less as if they were suffering the aftereffects of drinking strong ale. Meithin went off after them. Nid almost knocked Elenn over as she ran past, dressing as she went. She did not even look back to see if Elenn was all right.

Orlam stayed where she was, with Elenn, an island of stillness in the midst of the bustle. She looked torn. "I was a champion before I went away," she said to Elenn. "Now I am bound to watch with the old and the weak and the children and be defended while others put themselves in harm's way. My little brother and my mother and father are all going, and I am staying."

"Have you sworn an oath not to fight?" Elenn asked.

"No, one not to be killed needlessly," Orlam said, putting her hand to her hair, cut in a lawspeaker's crop. "And one not to fight when there are other good choices. If it were a case of defending the hall and everyone needed, I should take up my arms again, it not being so long since I laid them down that I would have forgotten the use of them. But for a raid on a May morning? A hundred and four of Atha's people against all the champions of Oriel and the spearmen of Edar? They don't need me, and there is no honor to me to fight those who would find themselves cursed for killing me."

"Amagien fights," Elenn said.

"That rests on his soul," Orlam said. "But if someone's parents were to ask me to judge recompense when a poet had killed their child who was piously avoiding hurting them in such a battle, the laws would not find the poet guiltless. I do not wish to go to this fight." All the same, her eyes followed Meithin until she was right out of the hall. Then she sighed. "I'm sorry. It's just as bad for you, because your sister is in the battle. But next year you will be able to go out and fight, and I never will again."

"I don't know why I'm not more worried about my sister than I am," Elenn said. "I wasn't worried at all until I saw how worried Finca was."

"Finca fusses over Conal, though never where it would do him any good," Orlam said. "He was shaping up well when I last saw him, better than Leary. Unless he's stopped practicing since then, I doubt he'd get your sister killed. Not and survive himself, in any case, which may not be much comfort if he's fighting one to one against Atha ap Gren, but it's something."

"We should go and cheer them off," Elenn said, hoping it might brighten Orlam's thoughts.

Orlam hissed like a cat. Elenn looked at her in surprise. Orlam laughed. "It isn't so much even that I want to fight," she said. "It's how much I hate not being able to do anything."

"Oh!" Elenn said. "I understand that. I hate that too. Sometimes, even if I don't want to go, I still hate being left behind."

"Cheering them off seems like the very essence of being left behind," Orlam said. "But I do see how it is our duty to do it."

They walked together down the hill, avoiding running champions and charioteers as best they could. Outside the stables, Conary was trying to organize the people, the horses, and the chariots. There was a tremendous din as everyone shouted at once. Darag came up to Elenn and kissed her hand for luck before getting into his chariot. "Go with glory," Elenn said, as she had heard her mother say.

"Remember your healing charms," Orlam advised him.

He shook his head at her and laughed. "You've come back very wise, cousin, but I think it is my fighting I shall need to remember."

"Sometimes it's the charms, if you want to fight another day," Orlam said and embraced him.

Then Amagien came up and kissed Elenn's hand, and after him Leary and his parents, and a host of other champions. Ferdia was almost the last of them. She wished she could embrace him at parting, to show her friendship, but he made no move towards it.

There was some squabbling as Conary insisted that some of the older champions stay behind as gate guards. He had to raise his voice, which would have surprised Elenn when she first came but seemed almost normal now. Then everyone mounted up. When Conary gave the signal, they all surged forward and followed him up the road around Ardmachan. Only one chariot tangled the traces and had to stop; the rest swept off as creditably as the champions of Connat could have managed.

Elenn held up her hand until they were out of sight. Then she walked back up the hill to the dun, deep in conversation with her new friend.

# — 11 —

## (EMER)

After she stopped being afraid and before her sword broke, it was even better than Emer had imagined it would be.

It wasn't at all like the songs. The songs never said how noisy battle was. They sometimes mentioned the clash of arms, but the clash of arms was the least part of it, after the howling of battle cries, the dissonant music of the war trumpets, and the bellowing of the cattle. Even Conal yelled out the battle cry at the top of his voice. It was deafening, like a very loud game of hurley played for some mad reason in a byre. It tested her skill to the limit, but with Conal beside her, she found herself enjoying it all enormously.

To begin with, she had been nervous. It was clear that their reputations as champions would stand or fall on what they did today. She harnessed the chariot ponies with the same hollow feeling in the pit of her stomach with which she always anticipated a quarrel with her mother. She wiped her palms nervously on her shirt before fastening her gloves. Then Conal came to wait with her, looking calm and beautiful, like a young god in the morning of the world. She ran through all the advice she had ever been given about chariot fighting. She knew that in a fight like this, where nobody else was mounted, the most important thing was to keep moving; if they were brought to a standstill, they could be pulled down. Yet she had no other horses so she could not risk exhausting the pair she had. She worried that the horses would not fight properly, would not obey her. She had heard of chariot teams running away from battles when the charioteer wasn't firm with them. She thought of the things Finca always said at practice. Mistakes now would not mean embarrassment and bruises, but wounding and death.

Then ap Anla painted the battle-crow across Conal's face, changing him at a stroke into a wild and fierce stranger. Hardly knowing why, Emer refused the transformation. So it was as herself that she took up the traces and drove out of the gates and down the steep slope. She felt very young and inexperienced. When the horses pulled hard and tried to turn away from the raiders, she remembered that they at least had seen battle before. It was much harder than practice getting them back under control, but after a moment, they responded to her hand on the traces. She brought the chariot up beside Meithin's. The steward who had questioned Conal's right to lead earlier was riding in it, clutching the rails and keeping his balance uneasily. Meithin grinned at her and rolled her eyes. Emer found herself laughing, all the fear burnt off like mist in the sun now that there was something to do.

They caught the raiders entirely unaware, scattered among the herds, trying to bring them toward the ships. Meithin wheeled and set down the steward, then brought her mares around and set their heads for Ardmachan. Emer turned her horses only to give Conal clear room to strike to the right. Out of the corner of her eye she saw the farmers of Edar charging down the hill. They were painted to make a fearsome sight, and they held their shields above their heads. Those who had them waved their spears, the rest waved axes or mattocks or billhooks. All of them screamed out battle cries as they ran.

Conal took down three of the invaders with his throwing spears while they were still standing openmouthed. Anyone would have imagined he had been doing it for years. Emer gave a shout of encouragement and brought the horses around again, closer this time, forcing Crabfoot to turn in just the way he hated most. The invaders were starting to get organized, and some of them were forming a line, but most were still among the cows. Emer looked for Atha ap Gren but couldn't tell her from any of the rest of them. Several of them had limed hair. None of them had chariots, so they couldn't challenge Atha to a single combat, and there would be no fighting chariot to chariot.

The fight seemed to last forever. The farmers and the raiders fought each other. Conal and Emer and the chariot moved among them like one creature, scattering the raiders where they could, avoiding places where the raiders tried to trap and slow them, trying to stop them finding time to close up. A spear from behind narrowly missed Whitenose, and another stuck in the chariot beside Emer. Conal pulled it out and returned it to its owner or one of his friends.

Emer's arms began to ache badly as they turned again. A moment later, Conal put back his head, threw up his arms, gave a great shout, and the black bull came running down the hill, head lowered. The bellowing of the cows redoubled as the whole herd began to move, trampling enemies and the occasional badly placed friend alike. Then Conal had her drive along the edge of the stampeding herd as he leaned over, calling all the time to the bull, forcing the cattle to go where he wanted them, out along the shore, away from the ships and the raiders.

By the time they came back the raiders were scattered, some of them making for the ships with blue-painted farmers running after them. There seemed to be only one knot of organization. "Atha," Conal said, then gave a rallying battle cry again. Emer drove her tiring horses straight toward the knot of raiders.

She went right at them. They had been leaping out of her way all morning, though she could not tell whether they had been fighting for minutes or hours. Behind them, in the distance, on the road to Ardmachan, she could see a cloud of dust that might have been Meithin going for help, or help coming back already. Then Whitenose stumbled and before she could right him Crabfoot fell, leg broken, tangling the traces. Conal drew his sword as he vaulted neatly over the wheel on his side. Slingshots, Emer thought, ducking as she hacked at the traces; she had given them time for slings and the horses at least would die for it. Whitenose was still dragging the chariot and his fallen companion forward in lurches. If she survived she swore she would practice cutting traces. The leather was tough and the knife was not sharp enough. Her fingers were clumsy in her gloves. Everyone said how important it was, and made sure charioteers had a knife for it, but nobody practiced doing it. She was half sobbing for breath as she hacked at the leather.

"Jump!" Conal shouted from somewhere off behind her. She jumped and rolled without thought. Almost as soon as she was free of it the chariot and horses went down together with a crunch and squeals. Whitenose must have been hit again.

As she started to straighten to her feet she saw a huge grinning raider right in front of her.

His spear was coming down toward her. There was no time to draw her sword. She leaped at him, inside the arc of his spear, and thrust the little knife upwards into his belly as hard as she could. He looked completely dumbfounded. Then she leaped away as fast as she could, leaving the knife buried to the hilt. The raider toppled slowly sideways. Stupid knife might be useless for its purpose, but it could kill, she thought, and giggled. She reached for her sword, and Conal was there protecting her back.

For a moment, it was even more like hurley, the two of them against everyone, except that the enemy wanted to kill them. They could only move together, and the enemy could move as much as they wanted. Then some more of their side came up, the steward and a handful of others, and it was more even. Emer wondered if they might make a song of it if she and Conal died together in their first battle.

There was a woman with limed hair, fighting with a long knife in each hand. Emer couldn't get near her, but she managed to keep her away for a little while, because her sword had more reach. Then she parried one of the knives hard and her sword shattered. One of the fragments bit into her leg and another struck the raider on the shoulder. Emer stared at the useless hilt for a moment, then looked around for another weapon. As she did, the woman slashed at her face and cut it open.

For the first moment, she did not feel pain, only the wetness of blood, and then she felt the cut and clapped her hand to it. Her cheek was hanging by a flap of skin. If the knife had been a breath farther to the left, it would have taken her in the throat and she would be dead already. She had been wounded and could have been killed, could still be killed, she, Emer ap Allel of Connat, now, today.

She lay on the ground, not quite sure how she had got there, struggling to get up. Conal stood over her, and as he fought he gave a great battle cry again.

"Who are you to come marked for victory?" the woman with the knives asked.

"Don't you know me, Atha?" Conal replied.

Emer pulled herself to her knees, one hand still holding her face together. She looked around for a weapon. Conary said that everything could be a weapon to someone who truly knew how to fight. Could that really be Atha? She looked just like anyone else.

"I thought I knew all the champions of Oriel," Atha said. "But I don't know you."

There was a thundering sound. "Run!" Emer heard the steward shout, sounding far away. Somehow she couldn't get any further up, however much she tried. Everyone seemed to be running, except Atha and Conal, who were still engaged.

"I am Conal ap Amagien of Edar," Conal said. "You have hurt what I love best in the world, but give me your knife and I will spare your life."

Atha laughed and attacked again. "You were a child when I was here.

I am famous among champions. You have done very well, but it is I who am going to kill you."

"Listen," Conal said, blocking her. "Drop your knife, or you will die."

"Never," Atha said, her eyes on his.

"Look, then," Conal said. "If you do not drop your knife, we will all die together, but I can stop them."

Atha laughed again, spun around, weapons ready, not dropping her guard for a moment, and then, amazingly, as she spun back, instead of attacking again, she dropped one of her knives onto Emer's lap.

"Get down," Conal said, and he called out and raised his arms.

In one smooth movement, Atha crouched beside Emer, and then the herd was there all around them, parting around Conal's spread hands.

There was a long, hot moment as the herd ran past. Even half-dazed, Emer was aware how large and fierce and close the cattle were and how strong their smell was. Then they were past, and Conal was on one knee beside her, holding the knife to her cheek and singing a healing charm, weaving her name into it.

"Don't forget the charm against weapon rot," Atha said.

Emer could not move her head but she moved her eyes. Atha was standing watching, holding her other knife. Conal sang on, the charms against weapon rot and blood loss. When it came to the charm for strength, Emer felt well enough to join in. She ran her fingers over her cheek. There was a ridged seam of scar that felt years old already. She pulled herself to her feet, feeling as if she had just woken from a dream. Conal put his arm around her and she leaned on him gratefully. It hardly seemed strange that Conary and Finca should be there in the king's chariot.

"So, Atha?"

"So, Conary?"

"So you are defeated by the cows you came to steal?"

"So the battle was won by the courage and leadership of Conal ap Amagien of Edar. Conal the Victor I call him now, for he painted for victory and victory on the field is his. Nobody has defeated me in personal combat."

Finca smiled a little at her son.

"Even the youngest of my champions can win a battle against the best the Isles can send," Conary said and glanced approvingly at Conal and Emer. "Is this an invasion from the Isles?"

"No," Atha said quickly. "This is a cattle raid only. My mother knows nothing of it. There is no feud between your people and mine."

"There is no feud, only a cattle raid," Conary agreed. "It seems we have much to discuss. Will you accept my hospitality at Ardmachan?"

Atha turned her head. Emer followed her gaze. The ships of the Isles were rowing away. There were a straggle of raiders left on the shore. Between them and Atha was the herd of cows, now placidly grazing, and the assembled might of the champions of Oriel. Darag and Laig were in the front row.

"It seems I will," Atha said and bowed.

It seemed that Conal wanted to speak to every surviving farmer of Edar, and every champion of Oriel wanted to speak to him. Emer was happy enough to sit quietly and drink water and eat some bread and honey ap Anla brought her. She still felt far away from ordinary concerns. It wasn't until Conary suggested she ride back to Ardmachan that she woke up properly.

"I will drive Conal," she said.

"I don't mind if you want to rest," Conal said. Now that the battle was over, he looked exhausted.

"I want to drive you," she repeated. "I know we wrecked the chariot, but there must be another we can use."

"The horses will be eaten at the victory feast," the steward assured her. His arm was bound up. She hoped they could find the weapon and heal him properly. "We will all honor them, and you. We also honor the generosity of King Conary for leaving the captives with us."

Emer smiled at him, and he bowed. She could see the straggle of leftover raiders being brought into the dun. They looked sullen and resigned. Serving at Edar for the season was not at all what they had expected when they had left home. It was so near the beginning of the season, too; it would be months before they got back to the Isles.

"I still want to drive," Emer said.

"The warriors can make space," Finca said, meaning that some of them could go back three to a chariot. "You can drive my son if you want to."

Conary looked as if he was about to protest, but bit it back.

Conal and Emer took their place in the array of champions. Not far from them they could see Atha getting in beside Meithin. Emer laughed quietly.

"What?" Conal asked.

"Yesterday I'd have been so proud to be here, but today we are the only ones who have fought. We won the battle ourselves."

"Along with the farmers and the cows," Conal said. "Twelve farmers were killed, though no cows were either taken or harmed."

"And how many raiders?" Emer asked.

"Around thirty, many of them trampled," Conal said. "Garth brought me eleven heads he says are mine. One of them is yours, the big man you killed with the knife. I told Garth, and he will send it to you when it is ready."

There had not been time in the battle for Emer even to think about taking his head. "How very kind," she said. "I should have thanked him." She looked around. The steward was over by the gates now.

"It was your kill," Conal said. "And Garth understands that you were recovering from your wound. I thanked him for you. And indeed, he would hardly take a word of thanks. Edar will do well from this raid, when it could have done very badly, and Garth and Anla both know it."

Then Conary came over to them. "You both did very well indeed," he said. "I am proud of you. You did everything you could have, except maybe you could have tried to set fire to the ships to stop them getting away."

"I didn't think of that," Conal said.

"Nobody can think of everything. You might have sent Meithin off and held Atha negotiating and boasting for long enough, but it might not have worked."

"I didn't think Atha would agree to fight me," he said. "She wouldn't fight someone she'd never heard of and when there weren't any other champions present."

"She didn't have a chariot," Emer put in.

Conary looked at her, startled. "I wasn't suggesting that you fight her, just exchanged challenges and boasts to buy time, establishing that it was a raid, not a feud, speaking of a champion who would fight, meaning when we came up."

Emer met his eyes. "Conal held her off for a long time," she said proudly. "They stopped fighting because the herd came back, but he might have won."

"I wouldn't have," Conal said, and shrugged. "She's too good for me yet. But if I keep practicing—"

Conary laughed. "You did very well. And what you did with the bull was inspired. It was a great risk, but anything was a risk. You saved the herd and the farm. What you did worked, that's the most important thing." Conary embraced Conal then, and went to his own chariot.

They set off back to Ardmachan. The fields seemed very brightly green and the hawthorn blossom on the hedgerows almost unnaturally white. Emer felt as if she had run a hundred miles. Conal stood still beside her. "Conary's really pleased," he said after a while, as if he was turning the thought over in his mind.

"He ought to be," Emer said indignantly. "It's about time people started to appreciate you instead of making a fuss over Darag all the time."

Conal laughed. "Darag came and congratulated me while you were dozing under the tree. So did Leary. Leary used to be my friend, you know."

"Good for them," Emer said. "And your mother smiled. Maybe even your father will realize you've done something good."

Conal's smile was crooked. "No, I'm fairly sure my father will be angry that I endangered the herd by getting them to stampede and furious that you broke his second-best spare sword."

# —12—

## (FERDIA)

I t doesn't matter," Darag said. He threw his last spear at the target and without even looking, flung himself facedown in the grass.

Ferdia had to bite his lip to stop himself from complaining about it again anyway. He wanted to murder Conal. Everything he had done had been foolhardy at best and outright demented at worst. He had not only got away with it, but had won a praise name and was getting everyone's attention. And the rest of them hadn't even had a chance to fight. By the time they got there, it was all over. But try to suggest that a stampeding herd of cattle wasn't a legitimate weapon of war and not even Atha would agree with you. Even now, a month later, Ferdia couldn't leave it alone. He straightened his own last spear and looked at the target, where Darag's spear quivered a hairsbreadth from his other two spears, right through the throat of the champion-shaped target. One of Ferdia's spears pierced it through the gut, and the other stuck ignominiously in the turf low and to the left of the marked figure. He hadn't done as badly as this for years; it was as if he had completely lost the knack.

Down on the other side of the practice field, Nid and Leary had their chariot out and were endlessly turning and passing in front of another target. At least he could still do that right, he'd been practicing that enough. Everyone else had gone off to play hurley, but Darag had stayed to help Ferdia with his spears. The excited cries of the hurley players could be heard faintly. Ferdia looked back at his target. "Conal," Ferdia said in his heart as he aimed. The spear went straight and landed just above Darag's trio.

"Ha!" he said.

Darag sat up and looked. "Oh, much better, yes, well done," he said warmly. "You're getting it again." Ferdia smiled at the praise. "Sit down for a moment."

He sat down beside Darag and looked at his friend as he sprawled on the grass, dappled by the leaf-shadow and sunlight. Darag smiled up at him lazily, then rolled onto his back and stared up through the aspen leaves at the sky. "The thing is," he said, "Conal has always felt he's competing with me."

"He *is* competing with you," Ferdia said. Darag never took it seriously enough.

"Well, in some ways he is," Darag conceded. "But if he is, I keep on winning. I don't mean I don't want to win when we fight. I do, of course I do. I want to be the best, and I'm glad I am. But it's the same to me if I beat Conal or you or Leary or anyone. I just want to win, it isn't personal. But it is for Conal. Conal thinks we're competing even when I *don't* want to. He thinks so even when *he* doesn't want to, like with Elenn at first. He thinks so much that it ought to really do him good to get a really good win in against somebody else where I wasn't involved. Now maybe he can stop feeling he's losing to me with every breath he takes and we can be friends."

"You've thought about this a lot," Ferdia said. It wasn't exactly that he didn't want Darag to be friends with Conal. It was just that he didn't think he could ever manage it himself.

Darag sat up again and looked at Ferdia seriously. "Before you came, Conal and Leary and I were the only ones our age. I had to think about why he doesn't like me."

"But it's not just competing at practice," Ferdia said, having worked it out properly now. "Conary's children are dead, and he had four, so there aren't going to be any more, even if he gets married again. So when he dies and the people choose between the Royal Kin in your generation, it's going to be you and Conal and Leary and Orlam they're choosing between. That's the prize Conal has his eye on." It was a prize Conal had come closer to in the last month, Ferdia knew, winning Conary's approval and a great deal of popularity among the champions. He knew that Darag could have done even better if he had been the one who had had the chance. But now it looked as if there would be no more fighting at all this summer. It wasn't fair.

"It wouldn't matter if Conary's sons were alive or not, in Oriel," Darag said, yawning. "They choose the best of all the Royal Kin. Anyone whose grandparent was a king."

"Well, in Lagin too," Ferdia said, delighted that Darag was prepared to talk about it for once. "But in reality my father says it's perfectly easy for the king to make it really easy for the people to choose by making sure the heir you want is the one who has the experience and the opportunities. He's doing that for me, so that when he dies I will be the obvious choice to succeed him, the way he was for his uncle. Well, Conary can do that, too. So Conal thinks—"

"I don't care," Darag interrupted.

Ferdia blinked. "How can you not care?"

"I decided last winter, before you came. It sometimes seems like everything in my life is doomed, everything happens with a significance I don't intend. Things happen no matter what I do, no matter what I want. From my birth. Before that, from my conception. Remember the day we took up arms? Like that. Lots of things like that, things that seem to mark me out as special. Dreams, too, strange dreams all the time. I talked to Inis about it, and he said lots of stuff, the way he does. What it amounted to was that I was special, that in lots of worlds I do special things. And I thought all right then, but I'm only going to do what I want to. If that happens, it happens, but I'm not going to help it. I don't care about that, I can't. If doom wants me to be king, or war leader, then it's going to do that whatever I want. So I've been doing what I want and being who I want to be, myself."

"And what do you want to be?" Ferdia asked.

"Ah, that's the question." Darag paused for a moment, then leaned closer, speaking quietly. Ferdia's heart beat faster. "I want to have friends. I was always so lonely before you came, and then the girls. Now you're my friend, and Elenn is, and I'm getting to be better friends with the older champions too, now that I've taken up arms and they see me as one of them. Then later, I'd like to marry and have children. I'd bring them up properly, be there to do the things fathers do for their children. Like Ringabur carrying Leary home from the stables on his back when he was small. I think about that sometimes. And I want to be a champion. That's something I want for myself. I am good. I have a good eye and a good hand, and I want to be better. I want to be good enough that whatever doom has waiting for me I'm good enough to get through it and survive— survive past that, survive to have a life afterwards on the other side of it if I can. Because I want to find out what I want, and what doom wants from me, and get as much as I can of what I want in despite of it."

Ferdia thought for a moment, and Darag leaned away again and let him. That was something he really liked about Darag, he didn't mind Ferdia taking time to get his thoughts in order. He heard a great cheer from the hurley field. Someone must have scored.

"Inis says that if someone is doomed to do something and they don't do it, then if it really is doomed, someone else will do it," he said at last.

"He says it doesn't matter who does it, usually, only there are some things that can't be stopped from happening. He said most things aren't doomed at all, even when he's seen things in other worlds, its usually a chance that can be taken or refused."

He thought uncomfortably of the Feast of Bel. He kept seeing the dog woman since, with her husband, or with the hunting dogs. She kept smiling at him. He didn't know how he could ask her name, now, and if he asked anyone else they would just tell him her father's name so he could address her politely, which wouldn't help. He pushed the thought of her away resolutely. At the other end of the field Leary made his three attacks perfectly for the first time. "But my father says what you said, to do what you want and not worry about what may be prophesied. Live without looking over your shoulder, he says. And I think that's the best way, generally. Leave all that to the oracle-priests. Though if you have dreams, I suppose that's hard." He stopped, uncertain.

"They're not oracle dreams," Darag said.

"It can be difficult to ignore even ordinary dreams sometimes," Ferdia said, from heartfelt experience.

"Oh yes," Darag agreed. "Shall we throw another set of spears and then go join the hurley before they finish?" He rose to his feet with his usual grace of movement. Ferdia pulled himself to his feet, feeling clumsy and as if he had said the wrong thing.

They started walking over to the target to retrieve their spears. "I know I can trust you," Darag said. "I can talk to you about real things."

"Of course," Ferdia said, his heart overflowing.

"Do you want to be king of Lagin?" Darag asked as Ferdia was bending down to pull out the one that had missed last time. It left a clear gash in the turf that covered the peat.

"Yes," he said, straightening. "Not now, but when my father dies, yes, of course I do. It's my duty."

"If I felt it was my duty to be king of Oriel then maybe I would want to. I'd certainly do it. As it is, I feel it's a prize Conary is dangling in front of all his nephews, setting us against each other. And it's actually a false prize, an empty one, disguising the real one. He talks about kingship to all of us, kingship and strategy and never about what the land wants, what the farmers need, the demands of the gods. It's not just him, it's his sisters and their husbands as well. Maybe if my mother was alive she'd be just like that, but I like to think she was different."

They turned and walked back up the field. "What happened to your mother?" Ferdia asked. He had heard stories about the death of Dechtir ap Inis, of course. The worst of them he had only heard whispered.

"She died in a chariot accident when I was five," Darag said, staring straight ahead. "She and Conary were going around the dun, I don't know if it was practice or if they were going off somewhere. They never got there anyway, never got off the road around. She pitched right over the rail and hit her head on a rock, a godstone beside the road. She cracked her head open and died before anyone could do anything."

He gestured southeast, and Ferdia realized he knew the very stone it must be, a looming single stone that stood between the fields and the road.

"How awful," Ferdia said, hearing the banality of his words but unable to catch them back.

"The worst of it is that it was such a freakish accident that some people whisper Conary must have thrown her out. Nobody with any sense has ever believed that. Not only was she his favorite sister and his charioteer, but he was absolutely heartbroken, really inconsolable. I can just remember. People have told me he was even harder hit by her death than when my aunt and cousins died in the plague. He blamed himself—I suppose they must have been going fast for it to have happened. He does have a temper, it's true, and I can almost imagine him getting angry and hitting her. But can you imagine anyone getting angry enough to throw their charioteer out of the chariot? Anyone at all, let alone Conary?"

"They'd have to be mad," Ferdia said, shuddering just thinking about it. "It would risk their own life."

"Not to mention the difficulty of doing it," Darag said. He gestured with his spear toward Nid and Leary. "Think of the angle you'd have to get."

Ferdia looked and on reflection, thought of a couple of ways it would be possible. Just as they straightened out of a turn, if the charioteer wasn't expecting it, bend and heave. It wouldn't be easy, and it would certainly be dangerous. He doubted it could be spontaneous, but it was by no means impracticable, assuming you wanted to do it in the first place. The hardest part would be taking the reins just right to avoid crashing after the charioteer was out. He wondered if Conary had crashed. He opened his mouth to ask, then realized suddenly that Darag must have thought about it a lot and wanted very much for it to be impossible.

"The idea is just the sort of nonsensical gossip people like to pass along," he said. "They must have been going fast and hit a stone or something in the road when she wasn't holding on at all."

Darag smiled. "That's what I've always thought." They were back at throwing distance. "Head, throat and gut this time?" he asked. Ferdia raised his chin in agreement. "Your turn to go first," Darag said.

Ferdia stuck two spears in the ground, held the third straight and turned his back on the target. Then he turned and threw, without aiming, hitting it too low for head, somewhere between neck and chest. It would have been enough to kill if it had got through the armor. He took the second spear and tried for a throat shot. It seemed to skim along the same path as before, landing almost beside his first spear. Gritting his teeth he took up the third spear, the one that had made the throat shot last time, and sent it toward the gut of the figure on the target, putting all his force behind it. It ended up a little to the left of where it should have been but within acceptable range.

"Not bad at all," Darag said. He stuck his own two spears into the ground then turned his back on the target, the third spear in his hand. Ferdia loved to watch Darag like this, his whole body completely engaged in what he was doing. He looked as if he was born to do what he was doing, every action the only possible movement. He took a breath, spun around and hurled the first spear in one motion. He bent and took up the second, threw that, then a moment later, sent the third thudding home after it. "You're not looking," he said, laughing.

Ferdia realized that he had been so engaged in watching Darag that he hadn't even glanced at the target. "You always hit where you aim," he said. "I was trying to see how you do the shoulder movement with that turning and bending and still keeping the spear straight."

Darag put his hand on Ferdia's shoulder blade. "Turn from here," he said. "And just let them go. You put your eye out thinking too hard."

A woman laughed close by. Ferdia looked up quickly, and Darag dropped his hand as if Ferdia's shoulder suddenly burned him. It was Atha, spears in her hand. As she was being treated as a guest while Conary negotiated with her mother for her return, she was allowed arms and acted as if she was on an ordinary visit. Any hostage might try that; Atha succeeded. Ferdia had never met anyone with more pride.

"One of you thinks too much and the other too little," she said, grinning. "You do it so easily you don't know how you're doing it, Darag. You'll never make a teacher unless you know in your head as well as your body. It isn't the shoulders, it's the legs. Have you been practicing a lot in the chariot, ap Cethern?"

"Yes, and I'm much better in it," he admitted.

"Well, you have to do it more often, so it's just as well. But it can give you bad habits for throwing from the ground. The chariot moves under you, and you're trying to compensate for that when you don't need to." As she said it, Ferdia realized she was right. He remembered how hard it had been to get used to the chariot at first. She sent her own three spears casually thrumming down, each landing a thumb's width to the right of Darag's three.

"You're right, ap Gren," Ferdia said, as soon as she had finished, so he would not be distracting her. "I think that is the problem. Thank you."

"I'll fetch them all back and see if you can do better now you know what it is," she said, and set off down toward the target without waiting.

"Well," Darag said quietly, watching her go. "She may not be as pretty as Elenn, but she has an amazing amount of nerve. And nobody can deny she knows about fighting."

Ferdia looked at him in consternation. Darag laughed. "She knows all about fighting and has nerve yes," Ferdia said as quietly as he could. "But Elenn is notably beautiful, while Atha definitely isn't. I don't see how it could come into your mind to compare them like that."

"Atha's much easier to talk to, though," Darag said. Atha pulled all nine spears out of the peat easily, then turned and started back toward them. "Conary's talking marriage alliances with her parents. It would be a good thing for Oriel. Elba really doesn't want Leary to marry Atha, though Leary said he would if he had to. Conal has turned the proposal down flat, unsurprisingly. I said I'd think about it, and I'm starting to think it might be a good idea."

Ferdia was completely lost for words. He hadn't been delighted at Darag's devotion to Elenn, but it was such a different kind of friendship that he hadn't really been jealous. It was something he could almost share. But Atha could do everything he could do, do everything he could do better than he could. If Darag married her she would always be there.

She came back and handed them their spears. Ferdia took his with hands that felt cold. She stood between them. "Now, remember that your feet are on solid ground and let's see you do it," she said.

"It could be you I'm putting one through next season," he said, forcing a smile.

"Oh, yes. Or the other way around, which is more likely if you don't get better at it," Atha agreed cheerfully. Darag laughed.

Ferdia stuck his spears in the ground. Solid ground, he reminded himself. Then he turned, paused, turned back and threw. *Atha*, he thought. *Lagin against the Isles, next summer.* He made his head shot. He drew the second spear out, aimed, looking at the figure, black against the green turf of the target. *Conal*, he thought. *Fighting for Connat because of Emer. Lagin against Connat, a huge cattle raid, the biggest ever.* The spear went straight through the figure's throat. He took the third spear, not holding his breath, that beginner's mistake, remembering solid ground, practice ground, Darag and Atha watching. *Darag*, he thought before he could stop himself, remembering the laughter.

Then he wanted to catch the spear back, but it was too late. It soared smoothly and made the gut shot just where it needed to. He turned to the congratulations of the others, feeling sick. He knew now why his father had told him never to pretend he was fighting against anything but what was really in front of him. It was too easy for anger to make you think something you never meant to. He spat to take away the omen and bent to touch a fragment of fallen wood from the tree. Darag looked at him curiously, but said nothing.

When the other two had made their shots, Atha called to Leary and suggested they all go and join the hurley. Ferdia was the first to agree. He didn't want Darag to know he was hurt, let alone that he'd felt that angry about it. He needed time to think about this, to get it all straight in his mind.

# 4

# AMAGIEN'S FEAST

# —13—
## (CONAL)

"N ow Conal, you know your father's very proud of you," Finca said. Fifteen impossible answers flashed up ready to Conal's tongue, topmost of them the desire to deny emphatically that he had knowledge of any such thing. Next in priority came the urgent wish to ask his mother why, if that was the case, Amagien had never done anything by word or deed to indicate it. He swallowed all the responses whole and stood mute and choking on unsayable words, his eyes on the worn rushes at his feet. Words were his shield and his defense against the world. He went through his days skimming along on them like a dragonfly over the water, words to bring laughter and keep trouble away. It was only with his parents that their shield crumbled away and left him helpless.

At least he had managed to catch his mother alone. It was not easy. Most of the time she was in the king's hall or down in the stables, surrounded by people. What little time she was in their house Amagien was almost always there too. He could not even begin to think of facing his father about this directly. He had only caught her now because she had come over from the hall to fetch something.

He took a breath and looked at Finca, disconcerted to find that he had to look down and not up at her. He had noticed that he had been growing all summer. It had made him clumsy. He hadn't quite taken it in that he had overtopped his mother. Finca regarded him with visibly fraying patience. "This isn't what I want," he managed to repeat, pushing away the real arguments, the ones he knew she could never hear.

"The feast isn't just to honor you, it's to honor all the folk of Edar who fought the attackers. You can't refuse it without insulting them," Finca said. Her tone was deliberately reasonable, as if to say that nobody could disagree. It was a tone she used on Conary and Amagien all the time.

Conal winced and looked away from her, his eyes sliding over the familiar curved walls and chests stacked against them. He could deal best with Finca when she saw him as ally, not obstacle. "I know. That's why I didn't refuse at once," he said, keeping his tone reasonable. "But the more my father talks about it the more he makes it seem that it is to honor me, and—"

"What's wrong with you? Most champions would be glad of an honor feast to their victory," Finca interrupted. He looked back at her. She seemed more impatient than ever.

"Most such feasts would be given by the king, and Conary has honored me for it already," Conal said, not letting himself react, pulling the words together quickly and lightly. She was listening, at least. "The problem is, mother, that it's really not very subtle. It's too much, making too much of it in a way the others don't like." He stopped, seeing the idea take root. He could never get anywhere with Amagien. Sometimes he could with Finca, and then Finca could get through to his father.

"You won a great victory," she said more slowly. "You won it almost single-handedly. That cannot be remembered too much."

Now he bit back the urge to remind her that he could not have done it without Emer, or without the folk of Edar. It would only distract her from the scent he wanted her to take. "If it were Conary giving the feast here, maybe," he said, stroking the dark fuzz that was beginning to grow on his chin, which only Emer called a beard. "But my own father doing it at Edar, and building onto the hall to do it? That could look like ambition rather than boasting."

Finca hesitated, and for a moment, he thought he had her. Then she shook her head swiftly. "At last I understand the direction you are wandering with all this reluctance and I don't have to think you've taken leave of your senses. But you're worrying too much. Nobody will think it is ambition. That is a line which is very clear to me, much clearer than it is to you. You think they will see that because there *is* some ambition in there. You do want to be king, after all, and this is a step toward that. But nobody else will notice. Conary will be there, he will honor you, and it is there that you won your name. Nobody will see it as ambition on your part when we feast the whole farm of Edar and all the king's champions."

Finca stopped and looked at him keenly. "You need to stop being so shy. That's half of why Conary doesn't notice you as he ought. You think you are putting yourself forward too much when in fact, you are too retiring. If Amagien had written a praise song about his own son, that might have been seen as ambitious, maybe. It was fortunate that ap Dair was here to do it, and he did a very workmanlike job. A little too much about Oriel and Connat working together, perhaps, but it is a song that will begin to make your fame known." Conal felt his cheeks heating at the thought of that song, and perhaps his mother noticed, because she laughed. "Let me worry about such things for now," she said.

"I am not a child," Conal said, and then immediately regretted it as his mother's face froze.

"Then don't act like one," she said, and turned on her heel and left the house without whatever it was she had come in for. Conal stood still for a moment staring after her, his hands clenched.

It took him some time to find Emer. Discovering that she was not among those on the field playing hurley made him muddy and sweaty, but cheered him up a little—he got to outrun Atha and to cause Darag and Ferdia to run hard into each other.

When he ran out of places to look in the dun, he went down to the stables. As he walked down the hill, he was struck by the beauty of the trees and hedgerows spread out below him, gold and red and brown in the afternoon sunlight that was so gold as to seem almost green. This was the light in which he pictured Manan's underwater halls. Although the afternoon was still warm, it was an autumnal light. It made him think of the short days to come. He could not decide whether he would be sorry to be done with this summer. Some of it had been so good, and the rest so painful.

The stable yard was full of people. Uthidir the chariot maker and his assistant were arguing with one of the leather workers who made harness. Meithin was trying to calm them down. Ap Felim, the kennel mistress, was trying to quiet a bunch of puppies who kept leaping up and barking. In the corner, Casmal was arguing with ap Carbad about training schedules. It was turmoil, and Conal could not see Emer anywhere. He edged around the buildings and saw Nid and Leary off at the far end of the rough paddock turning circles in a chariot. Then he saw Emer quite close, walking a pair of horses around her on a long rein, getting them used to the feeling of being yoked together before adding the weight of a chariot to the mix.

Conal stood for a moment in the shadow of the kennels watching her. She was completely absorbed in her work. As always, his eyes went to her scar, and then quickly away. It was an honorable wound, yet it made him feel as if he had been given something precious to guard and had broken it. She was not crippled, or even really hurt, but she could so easily have died if Atha's knife had found her throat instead. Whenever he saw it, it made him know what a mad risk he had taken with her, with them all. There had been no time to think about it until afterwards, when there had been time to think about almost nothing else. The scar made him apprehensive in a way he had not been in the battle. He had said nothing to her about that. He already knew how she felt about being taken care of. That she would go into battle beside him was just something else he would have to endure, quietly, every time, until she died, or he did. He would smile and fight beside her, and keep what he felt in his heart buried. In some ways it hurt most that there was already something he could not say to her. There had been such a little time when he felt he could tell her everything.

He walked out onto the muddy field toward her, noticing how she had grown into her legs over the summer. She looked like a charioteer now, not like a colt. She seemed absurdly pleased to see him, but did not stop. He waited, well out of the way, and watched her working. The outside horse was an older mare, pale brown, with the scattering of white face hairs that marked her stamina. She was slightly tubby with easy living. The other was a leggy two-year old gelding, mostly white but with patches so dusky as to be almost black. He was just getting the feel of being yoked to another horse and not sure he liked it. He kept throwing up his nose, and Emer kept holding him back to the pace of the steady mare on the outside. After a few even circuits she drew them to a halt so Conal could come closer and embrace her.

"I think Patches is finally getting it," she said, smiling up at him. "Did you see him stop then?"

"I managed to speak to my mother," he said quietly.

Emer turned her face up to him, all at once serious. "Did she hear you?"

"Not a word of it. I would rather have my hair torn out by sparrows, but we will have to go, and endure whatever humiliation my father heaps on me."

Emer sighed. "Oh, well. One evening, some speeches, a feast, how bad can it get? You're worrying about it too much. It'll soon be over. And afterwards Atha will be gone."

"I keep having dreams about it," he admitted.

Emer started the horses moving again. "What kind of dreams?" she asked after a moment, when they were moving evenly. "You know what Inis said about the three kinds of dreams."

"I think they're the silly mixed up worry kind of dreams," Conal said. "But they don't quite feel like that. They feel ominous."

"Did you tell your mother that?" Emer asked.

Conal shook his head, looking out over the horses' heads at the hill and the dun behind them. "She wouldn't have heard that at all."

"How about talking to Inis, then?"

"Inis's remedies are often worse than the problem." Conal sighed. He could, he supposed. But Inis had been very close to madness all this summer and he didn't want to make him worse. It seemed that talking about this would be likely to push him off balance. What could he do anyway against Amagien's determination? "I think you're right and we're going to have to go through with it."

"Did you ask your mother about the other thing?" Emer asked.

"I just didn't have the chance. There's no point asking when she's angry. There's time yet. We couldn't possibly get married for another year at the earliest."

"I'll have to go back to Connat at the Feast of the Mother next year," she said, not looking at him, her hands busy with the reins. "You think your parents are difficult but you don't know what my mother's like for making arrangements people don't want. We should get something sorted out before that."

"I don't want to be away from you either. Maybe you could speak to my parents and I could speak to—" Conal began.

"Look out!" Leary screamed, much too close. Conal could hear the horses and chariot tearing down toward them out of control. Emer dropped her reins and leaped to the side. He followed her, diving to the ground and rolling, coming up just in time to see what happened. The chariot careened past them, almost through where they had been standing. The iron wheels looked huge and much too near. He could picture one of them rolling over Emer's head, crushing it, almost as vividly as if it had really happened. His heart was pounding so hard it felt as if it would beat its way out of his chest. He took a deep breath and tried to calm himself.

Emer's horses, spooked, ran in different directions. Leary seemed to be driving—or attempting to drive—the chariot, though it was clearly out of control. There was no sign of Nid anywhere. He was pulling the horses to the left, to get as far from Conal and Emer as he could, or maybe in the hope of making a circle around the field and drawing the team to a halt when they were exhausted. But when the gelding bolted in one direction and the mare in the other, she went straight into the side of the hurtling chariot. Conal felt frozen in place. He could see what was about to happen. He held his breath. Emer clutched his arm. Neither of them could do anything to prevent it. Horse and chariot met with a great crash, and the chariot collapsed in a shattering of timber. The mare screamed. Leary's bolting horses were pulled to their knees.

"Oh no," Emer said under her breath. "Oh no, oh no, oh no."

"Come on," Conal said. Starting to move was hard, but once they had begun they ran and reached the fallen chariot in a few moments. People were coming running from the stable yard; they must have heard the crash even over all the tumult. Conal took in the scene with one rapid glance. Leary was half lying over the rail, his eyes closed. His left side was bloody and bruised. Nid was slumped on the floor of the chariot with blood on her temple, but she seemed otherwise unhurt. The mare was still alive, but breathing heavily with blood and foam around her mouth.

"Help me get them out, then look to the horses," he said to Emer. He went to the other side of the fallen chariot and began to pull Leary out. He was breathing, and Conal felt his own breath come easier for it. They had quarreled a lot in the past year, but before that, Leary had been his friend.

He laid him safely on the muddy grass and went back to help Emer pull Nid out. As he carried her over to lay beside Leary, Ap Felim and Uthidir came to help. Soon they were singing charms Conal did not know over Leary and Nid and there was nothing he could do.

He looked up. The chariot horses had been cut free and people were seeing to them. Meithin was with Emer by the wreck looking at the mare, who was plunging wildly and struggling to breathe. They both had tears on their faces. Conal stood up and took a step towards them. He was surprised to discover that his legs quaked like a bog.

"I knew her," Emer said. Meithin made a motion, but Emer drew her knife. "Forgive me, Barley, forgive me Rhianna," she said, made the Beastmother sign, and plunged the knife into the mare's neck.

Blood spurted out, covering them. The mare slumped for a moment, then swelled. The sun went behind a cloud. The mare's flesh fell away from her bones, like cooked meat falling away from a bone in stew. Conal could not move his eyes away. The mare's bones fell apart on the ground, and inside her there was something small and bloody and very ugly. It grew and darkened until it was unmistakably a horse, an enormous black horse, bigger than the chariot, bigger than any horse that ever was, with huge yellow teeth. Conal did not know how his legs had given way but he was sitting staring up at the great and terrible horse shape.

"Forgive me, Rhianna," Emer said again. She was still upright, the bloody knife in her hand, and her voice shaking only a little. Meithin, who had been beside her, was facedown on the ground.

"Thou I forgive, brave charioteer of Connat," Horse Mother said. Her voice was like the thunder of hooves towards battle. "Thou struck from mercy. But Oriel—no. This is the third time I died at Ardmachan."

"Accident," Leary gasped. Conal half turned and saw him sitting up, looking ghastly. Nid was still unconscious. Uthidir and ap Felim had flung themselves facedown like Meithin. "A stone struck my charioteer, and I couldn't hold the horses. The mare was—"

"Careless and cruel are not far apart," Rhianna said. Conal turned back to her. Her face seemed more like a woman's now, but still with those huge rending teeth. "Once it was cruel, once it's a tool, and now it's a fool. Beasts are not tools to bear your burdens, they are companions. Well that you learn this. I set a curse on the folk of this dun once, now I will call it to force. And all of my beasts who are here I will take."

Conal wished desperately that Conary or Inis were there to speak for Oriel. He cleared his throat to speak. "Mother of Beasts, we love our horses and mean them no harm. We risk them in war, but only as we risk ourselves."

Rhianna stared at him, and her eye was like a woman's and a horse's at the same time. Then she nickered, and the two chariot horses and the gelding, Patches, went running towards her. Patches was still tangled in his harness. One of the chariot horses was limping. They went right up to Beastmother and pressed close. They did not seem even slightly afraid. Conal dared not drop his gaze. He felt she was weighing every time he had ever had to do with animals, from his childish fear of Blackie the bull to his killing the two chariot horses in the battle at Edar.

She threw back her head and shook it, like a horse bothered by a fly. "True are your words, son of Oriel, you love them," she said. "And the beasts say they stay. Still, I will bring down the curse that I gave you long, long ago when the dun here was raised. When next the red tide of battle is flowing, when folk in arms cross the borders to fight, then will my curse come to make you remember, the fighting folk of Oriel will suffer that night."

"Suffer?" Conal asked.

She reared up, dark against the sky, as tall as the dun, taller, blotting out the hill, her eyes red and her mane tossing like stormclouds. "As the mare suffered, as the mare suffered, as the mare suffered," she said, each repetition more like thunder. Then she was gone from the paddock into the sky.

Conal sat staring up at the racing clouds, his mouth still open.

# — 14 —

## (ELENN)

Edar wasn't much of a place. It was just a farm on a hill with a palisade around it, like hundreds of other farms. And the hall wasn't big enough for everyone, even though it had clearly been extended recently and given a fresh coat of limewash. There wasn't even a proper kitchen. The far end of the hall, the old end, had a sturdy stone fireplace. It was there that the ox had been roasted, whole. It still hung there, a little away from the fire, smelling wonderful, waiting for Amagien to come and carve it himself. There weren't enough alcoves on the hall so trestles had been set up with boards placed over them, and everyone was lined up sitting along them, Vincan fashion. She liked being able to watch everyone. There were three tables, two of them running down the hall and the top one running across. One of them was packed tightly with the farm people, one was full of the champions and court of Oriel, including Elenn, and the top table was for the king, his family, and those who were being especially honored, including two of the farmers.

Conary sat at the centre of this table, with his family around him. Everyone was dressed in all their finery. Finca looked very dignified. Elba was wearing a new overdress embroidered with pearls. Ringabur was engaged in a long conversation with Darag about something that seemed to need lots of arm gestures. Leary put in the occasional remark. They really did look like champions now, not like boys. Conal, looking like a poet, was talking to Emer, who was looking respectable for once, with her hair combed and wearing a clean overdress. Beyond her were the two farmers, who looked clean but uncomfortable.

Elenn wished she felt more certain that Maga would approve of Emer behaving like this and being singled out. It was certainly an honor, but it might not be the right kind of honor. She hoped Emer wouldn't do something to bring disgrace on Connat. She didn't know what her sister could do to disgrace them, but she would never have been able to imagine half the things Emer had done already. Emer was wearing a gold arm-ring Conary had given her after the battle, and another one of thick twisted bronze snakes which Conal had given her. Elenn didn't know if it was right of her to accept them, but she was quite glad she had them now, because she was too young to have adornment of her own and without those she'd have been the only one at the king's table bare of it, except for the farmers, of course.

"In Lossia, they eat lying down," Ferdia said. The other good thing about the seating was that she could sit between Ferdia and Orlam, a little way down the right side of the champions' table. No ordinary seating arrangement would have put her with both of them for a formal feast. She would normally have been tucked away in an alcove with Emer and Atha and some of the lesser champions of Oriel.

"Lying down?" she asked, trying to picture people eating stretched out on the floor—or maybe they ate in their beds? "That's absurd."

"It's true," Orlam confirmed. "There are two songs that mention it."

Orlam was looking especially beautiful. She was wearing a pale blue overdress, a gold arm-ring on each arm, and a circlet of silver and pearls on her head. She made Elenn feel very young. It didn't matter if Amagien had written a song about how beautiful she was, her friend had so much more style. She herself was wearing the overdress Maga had sent for the Feast of Bel. Lacking adornment, she had made herself a headdress of dusk-purple daisies, which sat comfortably on her black braided hair.

"How do they do it?" Elenn asked.

"I don't know," Orlam said. "I'd imagine they'd suffer a great deal from indigestion." They laughed.

"Where is Lossia anyway?" Ferdia asked.

"Far off across the sea, beyond Tir Tanagiri, beyond Vinca, way off farther than anyone's been," Orlam said, looking dreamy. "I'd like to go one day and see what's really in the wide world."

"Raiding?" Ferdia asked, looking interested. "My father has raided Demedia."

"Farther than Demedia, and not raiding, just exploring," Orlam said. "Just to see what they do and what they eat . . ."

"And how they eat," Elenn put in, smiling. "I'd like to do that, too."

"I'd like to eat now, I'm starving," Ferdia said.

"Well, you're about to get lucky. Here comes Amagien at last," Orlam said "Be quiet."

People were shushing each other all around the tables as Amagien came in. He was dressed in his best for the occasion, glittering with what must be every torc and arm-ring and brooch he had ever won as a poet. Elenn's heart sank to see that he was carrying his little harp. She saw Leary whisper something to Darag and roll his eyes and wondered if they too would rather leave music until after they'd had a chance to eat.

"Be welcome to my hall of Edar, King Conary, champions of Oriel, Atha of the Isles, prince of Lagin, and princesses of Connat," Elenn inclined her head politely as she was mentioned. Emer visibly squirmed, at the top table, though it was no more than courtesy. "Never was such a splendid company gathered in this hall, nor were such splendid deeds done at Edar as those we gather here to honor today. Edar was threatened, and on the very first day of summer. With only the folk of the farm and two chariots with their charioteers, my son Conal beat off an attack by Atha ap Gren herself and by the champions of the Isles." Now it was Conal who squirmed. Some of the farmers didn't look very happy to hear their part played down so much.

"Nothing can be sufficient to honor those who fought and fell, those whose names will always be remembered. This feast is my small offering for those who fought and lived to see the victory. The herd was saved, until today when one of them will be served up to you." It was a feeble enough joke, but people were laughing at it, so Elenn made herself smile politely. Orlam's stomach growled.

"I have made no praise song for the victory at Edar. It is a little much for a poet to write praise songs for their own family. But Gabran ap Dair has made a song, which I shall sing now before we eat."

Everyone's face fell a little, even Conary and Finca lost a little of their air of pleased expectancy. People kept looking at the fine roasted meat as if to ask whether letting it get cold was a good idea. Only ap Fathag settled back comfortably as people usually did while harps were tuned.

Amagien began to sing. His voice and his playing were as good as ever. Elenn had heard the song before, when ap Dair first performed it in Ardmachan, so there were no surprises. When it came to the part about the cooperation between Connat and Oriel, she glanced at her sister. Conal and Emer were both listening with sober expressions and their heads down. If Elenn hadn't known that Emer had been brought up properly she would have wondered if they could be holding hands under the table.

At last, after much too long, Amagien brought the song to its dramatic conclusion with the charge of the bull and the capture of Atha. Atha, knowing everyone would be looking at her, was grinning back with a little malice in her expression. Elenn wondered what it would do to Atha's reputation to have that song widely sung. She supposed it spoke well of her that she had been so honorable in defeat as to give Conal a praise name.

Everyone drummed their feet politely at the end of the song, Elenn among them. The farmers of Edar around their table were extremely enthusiastic, drumming and cheering. They liked it so much that Elenn was afraid they might ask for a repeat. The old man sitting by Emer had tears in his eyes. But at last Amagien put down the harp and picked up a carving knife. Even so, Elenn was afraid it would be hours before she got any dinner. Carving could be a slow business. A quiet buzz of conversation rose as everyone began telling each other that they would faint with hunger in another moment. Then one of the farm women came around with a tray of hot fresh griddies. Elenn thanked her and bit into one gratefully. Before the woman had reached the far end of their table with the griddies, Amagien had carved the first piece, the top of the rump, sometimes called the "hero's portion."

Elenn ate her griddie delicately, catching the crumbs, and watched Amagien put the first serving onto a bronze plate. Everyone watched, admiring his hospitality or just waiting for him to give the plate to Conary and get on. The air of hungry impatience was almost tangible, especially at Elenn's table, where they could not hope to be served for some time. Instead of giving the portion to Conary, Amagien took the plate to Conal and bowed his head to his son. A silence spread out from them. Amagien spoke into that silence, his poet's voice filling the room. "Take the hero's portion, my son, for your victory, the first serving to honor the first among the young champions."

Conary closed his eyes. Conal looked sickly up at his father. He reached for the plate slowly but before he could take it Leary leaped to his feet. "Conal's victory I will honor," Leary said loudly, almost shouting. "But I won't sit still to hear him called first among the young champions. That is yet to be decided."

The woman with the griddies froze, and shrank back against the wall.

"That is yet to be decided," Conary echoed. "Divide the hero's portion into three, ap Ross, and share it between the sons of my three sisters."

Amagien hesitated. Finca put her hand on her brother's arm. "Conal has earned it," she said. "What have your other nephews done since they have taken up arms? Maybe it is time to decide."

Conary looked at her with dislike.

"What chances have they had this summer?" Elba asked, from Conary's other side, in reasonable tones.

Conary turned and gave her the same look. "It will be for the champions of Oriel to choose between my nephews when I am dead," he said. "They will have plenty of time to show their prowess before that, if the gods are kind."

A murmur ran through the hall as everyone invoked the gods to give Conary life and strength. Elenn joined in, sincerely enough.

Ferdia stood up as soon as the informal prayer was over. "We are not talking about inheriting Oriel now," he said. "But it seems to me that the question of which of the king's nephews is now the best among the young champions could easily be settled by some friendly contests—after dinner."

There was a general laugh at the last two words. To her surprise, Elenn saw that Darag was frowning urgently at Ferdia.

"Very well," Conary said, looking like a man seeing a clear way out of a maze. "We will have contests after dinner, and Orlam ap Ringabur shall arrange and judge them."

"But she's ap Ringabur's sister," Ferdia said. Darag shook his head at him fiercely.

"I am a lawspeaker of Rathadun, I am sworn to judge fairly," Orlam said quietly, yet all the room heard her. "Nor do you see me sitting with my brother and my parents as royal kin at this feast. Is that a challenge to my honor?"

"No," Ferdia said and sat down. Elenn breathed a sigh of relief.

Orlam looked down the table, and sighed herself. "Still, who will say that I can truly decide fairly between my brother and my cousins in such a case as this, when it will be remembered in the far time when it comes to time to choose kings again in Oriel? This is the blind spot I did not see which makes coming home a burden and not a benefit. We are all too close akin here, Conary, your lawspeaker is your niece, and your oracle-priest is your father. You had best set the contests and judge them yourself."

"Not I," Conary said. "That is advice, not a judgment, and I reject it. If you will not decide, I call on you to choose another to judge these contests."

Orlam stood up and sighed again. Elenn moved a little away from her. She looked different, more serious, older. Everyone kept very quiet, hardly moving. Orlam pulled off her pearl circlet and dropped it onto Elenn's lap. Elenn took careful hold of it; it was delicate work and could be crushed easily. Orlam let down her hair, shaking it until it was loose around her face. She extended her hands, palms up and then down.

"Before all the gods of home and hearth and of our people, and especially Damona, Lady of Justice," she said, "I am Orlam ap Ringabur, a lawspeaker of Rathadun, and this is my judgment." She looked all around the hall, making eye contact with everyone in turn. She did not take any less time with the farmers than with the champions. Nobody fidgeted while she was doing it. Elenn could hardly breathe as her eyes followed Orlam's gaze. Darag looked calm. Leary looked defiant. Conal looked desperately unhappy.

"These three young champions are the heirs of Oriel," she said at last. "Nobody here could choose between them without room for some to say that there was bias, one way or another. There must be four contests, each arranged and judged by the other four kings of Tir Isarnagiri." She paused, lowered her hands, and everyone drew in their breath all at once. "I do appreciate that this isn't going to happen immediately after dinner," she added. There was a feeble laugh. Orlam sank down beside Elenn, looking exhausted.

"And for now?" Amagien asked. Elenn offered Orlam her circlet back, but she shook her head vigorously.

"Put aside that portion," Conary said. "Serve the rest of us first, for we are all hungry. The young men can wait for their meat until all is decided, for honor is the best sauce, as they say."

For the first time, Darag looked as if he wanted to speak, but he just shook his head. When the woman with the griddies came to him, Elenn noticed that he took two.

Elenn offered Orlam the circlet again, under the table, questioning with her eyes. "Keep it," Orlam said. "It'll look good on you. And I never want to wear the thing again. But for that pressing on my head, reminding me that my mother gave it to me and it was my grandmother's, I'd have felt I could have judged fairly myself."

"But if it was your grandmother's, it's an heirloom, and I can't take it," Elenn insisted.

"It was given to me freely," Orlam said. "And now I want you to have it. It won't weigh so heavily on you. Wear it, and remember to make good choices."

"Thank you," Elenn said after a moment, turning it in her hand. It was very beautiful.

"How are they going to manage to get the four kings to judge?" Casmal asked from across the table.

"That's their problem now," Orlam said.

"It's only Muin that could be a problem as far as I can see," Ferdia said, looking self-conscious, glancing at Atha and then at Elenn.

"Damona alone knows how they will decide," Casmal said.

"It's her business to know," Orlam said, smiling a little.

"They should be able to choose fairly, as they have no stake in the outcome," Elenn said.

Casmal opened his mouth to comment, then looked at Orlam and thought better of whatever he was about to say. Elenn smiled at him encouragingly. "They're bringing us some meat at last," he said.

# —15—

## (EMER)

A re you feeling any better?" Conal asked, bending over her.
Emer lay still and wished that the deck below her would do the same. "Is the storm over?" she asked. It had stopped raining and the heaving of the deck was definitely better than it had been. She was chilled all through.

"We've rowed around the cape and we're inside the bay here, so it's more sheltered," Conal said.

"What cape?" Emer asked.

"The wind has changed again and it's all wrong for Oriel. We had a choice of going back to the Isles or making for Fialdun, and decided not to go back. So this is the Firth of Anlar we're going into."

Emer's stomach heaved. Going back to the Isles was unthinkable. It would have taken them another day and night at best, and leave them with the prospect of attempting the crossing again later in the season, when the winds would be worse. "How long before we reach shore?" she asked.

"I don't know," Conal said. "Not long, I hope. I wish we were there already. Shall I see if they'll spare some water for you? You look almost green."

"It would only come out again," Emer said. That was what had happened last time. A hot drink might be different, but she knew that was impossible on a boat. "How are the others?"

"Laig and Leary are pretty near as sick as you are, and lying down on the other side. Darag's feeling a bit unsettled but rowing, and Nid is running about as cheerfully as if the ship were a chariot. Darag says it's a pity we didn't bring Ferdia, who knows all about boats."

"Ferdia isn't in the contest. He'll be all right back at Ardmachan with Elenn," Emer said. "And how about you?" She clutched the wet blanket around her more tightly for the tiny bit of warmth and comfort it provided.

"I felt bad for a while, but I took a turn rowing and I found looking out at the horizon made me feel better."

"Do you think I should try it?"

"I can't see what harm it would do," Conal said.

He bent and put out his hand. Emer didn't want to move at all, but she took it and pulled herself up. Standing made her head swim, and almost at once she retched, heaving and gagging over the rail though there was nothing left to come out.

Conal kept his arm around her, supporting her. "I'm sorry," he said.

"Not your fault my stomach is heaving," she said and clutched the rail. She clamped her teeth and looked out at the horizon as Conal had recommended. To her surprise, there was a steep-sided rocky coast quite close.

"My fault you came at all," Conal said. "You could have lived your whole life on land and never known that the sea made you heave."

She laughed. One of the sailors came pushing past them and they moved to let her go by. "I'd have missed seeing the Isles then. And missed the contests. And missed being with you."

Conal smiled down and tightened his arm around her. Even feeling so terrible the touch was a great comfort to her.

"It's so good to be away from our families," she said. A gull soared out ahead of the ship and she followed it through the air with her eyes. The half month of contests in the Isles had been wonderful. The weather on the way over had been smooth and she'd barely felt ill at all. Gren and Skatha had treated them like adults and given them a room to themselves. Maybe it was because the Isles were so close to Demedia, but they seemed to have a positively Vincan attitude to blanket-sharing, smiling indulgently. They hadn't even blinked when Atha went off with Darag after supper every night, though Emer had. She felt there was something very strange about the pairing, as if she wasn't sure which of them was more of a danger to the other. She didn't think she would ever like Darag.

There had been contests all day, then feasting and sweet nights alone with Conal. She couldn't even feel a ghost of desire with her stomach wanting to turn itself inside out, but she could still remember. She smiled. The contests had gone well, too. Darag had won the spearthrowing, but

Conal had won the sword-fighting. She was still kicking herself about the chariot race, but it had been very close. Conal hadn't reproached her for it, and there were other chances. Next time, they'd do it. Lagin, Muin, and then Connat. Cruachan. Maga. But she didn't want to think about that yet. She looked at Conal and pushed the thought away. She was feeling a little better.

"If we're landing in Anlar we'll be away from them a little longer."

"Lew ap Ross of Anlar is my uncle," Conal said regretfully.

"Of course, your father's brother, how could I forget?" she said, her heart sinking and her stomach with it. She looked at the shore and saw a palisade around a hill and limewashed buildings curving up inside it. There was a scattering of small buildings around the shore. It was shadowed by the higher hills all around, making it seem a gloomy place. "Is that Fialdun?" she asked.

"Fialdun at the head of the bay," Conal replied, clearly quoting something. Then, in quite another tone, "I must get them to change the banner. Lew will think he's being invaded again."

"He's not at war with the Isles, is he?" Emer asked. Surely she would have heard.

"No, but his wife and daughter were killed raiding them last year, so feelings are running high. There isn't a war, but Lew personally has a bloodfeud with Atha. One ship couldn't really be an invasion, but it could be Atha coming to challenge his champion to single combat. It's the kind of thing she made her reputation doing."

"She can't challenge him. He's a king," Emer said.

"Challenge his champion, I said," Conal said. "Wake up. But anyway, I think that if we put an Oriel oak branch under the Eye of the Isles, he'd find it reassuring."

Conal patted her arm and went to speak to the master of the boat. Emer held on to the rail and watched the land approaching. She stayed there until the boat was drawn up, then climbed down to splash through the last few feet of water.

"If I never set foot on a boat again, I'll die thanking the gods for it," Leary said. He looked wretched and his clothes were filthy. She laughed ruefully. "At least your sister isn't here to see," Leary went on.

Emer looked at him blankly. "Elenn would probably have been puking over the side with you," she said.

"Oh, surely not," Leary said, his face full of serene confidence.

Emer gave up. Elenn had never looked at him for more than long enough to make sure he was still dangling after her, but that seemed to be enough. Poor Leary. Poor Elenn for that matter. How terrible not to love Conal and be loved by him. Emer followed Darag and Laig up the

beach. She wondered if Darag loved Atha and if she loved him. How
could she? How could anyone? They waited for Conal up on the shingle.

Some of the people of Fialdun came to find out what the sea had
brought them. Most of them seemed to be expecting a trading voyage.
They were taken aback to find three princes of Oriel and their charioteers.
There was a little flurry of confusion, during which Emer found herself
shivering, and she gratefully accepted a dry, warm blanket someone
brought out of one of the houses. Then they had to wait for the boat to
be secured before they could go up to the dun. It was too much to hope
that Lew would come down and welcome them so that they could
have a hot drink immediately. Once the horses and chariots were off-
loaded, she forgot herself in concern for them. The horses, all geldings,
were more miserable than she had ever seen animals. They took careful
awkward steps when she kept them moving for warmth. If Rhianna came
and reproached her for the state of them now, she would just lie down
and agree with her.

When everyone was ready, Emer reluctantly handed back the blanket
and made her way up the hill with the others.

As at Ardmachan, there was a lower gate and an upper one. They
gave their names at both. Emer was reluctant to leave the horses at the
bottom of the hill, but there really was no choice. There was a stream,
fortunately, and some pale, late sunlight was spearing its way through the
clouds. She kept glancing behind her, and noticed that Nid was also looking back at the horses. There were stables, but nobody came out to see
to the animals.

"When I heard about the welcome given to travelers I always pictured
it as a bit more . . . well, welcoming than this," Nid whispered.

"I suppose they're waiting to make sure we're peaceful," Emer said.
"But the horses go right into the stables at Ardmachan." She remembered
that from when she had arrived from Connat. But she had been with ap
Carbad then, who had escorted them all the way. Maybe that made a
difference. It had been raining. Conary had welcomed them and then
Finca had taken them off to get dry. She wasn't sure what happened at
Cruachan. When she got back, she would find out and make sure the
horses didn't have to wait about.

Lew met them at the door of his hall with the welcome cup in his
hand. He had long mustaches, longer than his beard. Apart from that, he
looked a lot like Amagien, until he saw Conal and smiled. Then suddenly
Emer could see a resemblance to Conal. If Amagien ever smiled like that,
she had never seen it. She had always thought Conal looked like Inis and
his mother, but there must have been something of Amagien in him after
all. Lew handed the welcome cup to a champion who stood beside him

and came forward to embrace Conal as kin. Then he took up the cup again and offered it around to all the others and exchanged the ritual peace and welcome greetings. The champion came behind with salted bread to complete the ritual. Emer was almost the last. She had given her name twice already, but when Lew heard it, he gave her a shrewd look, as if to take note of her.

Inside, the hall urgently needed new rushes. The floor was musty and almost slippery-smooth. The hall was very dark. There seemed to be a lot of people there but not very much organization. After a little while Emer was given a bowl of hot broth which she sipped gratefully. It was much too salty and had fish in it but it gave her strength. As her eyes adjusted to the dark hall, she saw that there was dust and cobwebs in all the corners. There were dogs lying in front of the fire; champions and servants stepped over them.

Lew came up to them and bowed politely. "I had heard of your contest, but I thought I'd been left out of the list of kings you were to visit," he said to Conal.

"Indeed, Uncle, this visit is not part of our contest," Conal said.

"What are they teaching at Rathadun these days if ap Ringabur could give a judgment that the five kingdoms of Tir Isarnagiri include the Isles and not Anlar?"

Emer wanted to laugh. It was well known that Tir Isarnagiri was divided into five parts, but what exactly those five parts were was a great matter of dispute. Maga considered Anlar almost a part of Oriel. Muin had once been two kingdoms. The kingdom of the Isles had long ago been a part of Demedia and not Tir Isarnagiri, but not for hundreds of years. It seemed strange to hear Lew saying it seriously. She'd always heard the five parts of Tir Isarnagiri talked about as one of those questions where asking two people got you three different answers.

"I'm sure she meant no insult, only that you are my uncle and could not be seen to judge fairly, as she herself could not," Conal said. Emer met his eye and saw the laughter bubbling up under his sober words.

"Maybe," Lew said, looking mollified. "One of my counselors suggested that was the reason, and it may well be so. Another suggested that this was an insult in itself." Lew frowned again.

"I don't see how it could be," Emer said firmly. "She wanted to avoid even the appearance of partiality casting a shadow on the outcome."

"I see," Lew said. He looked relieved.

Just then, Nid came over to them. "Excuse me for a moment," she said. "I'm going to go down and see to the horses. I've just said this to Laig as well—I'll do all of them because you two are recovering from the journey and I'm fine. You can owe me some other night."

Emer shook her head. "I'm quite recovered now. I'll come with you."
The stables, whatever they might be like, seemed a much more pleasant
place to spend the next little while than the hall.

"People will have seen to your horses already," Lew said, waving his
hand vaguely. "There's no need to go."

"I don't mean to doubt the hospitality of your stables, but charioteers
are always concerned about their horses, and these have had a bad voyage," Emer said.

Lew smiled kindly. "I understand. Yes, of course, a good charioteer
always wants to see to the beasts. I won't stop you. Come back soon, we
will eat in a little while and I would like you to eat with us, ap Allel."

Nid and Emer bowed to Lew and Conal and went out. The wind
that was a storm out to sea was strong even here, blowing away the
fustiness of the hall. It was chilly. The sun was already behind the shoulder
of a hill to the west and they walked down into deeper shadow.

Somewhat to Emer's surprise, their horses had been taken into the
stables, rubbed down, fed, and were in stalls with blankets over their
withers. They thanked the grooms, who made nothing of it, just admiring
the horses. They could easily return the compliment—the horses in the
stables were in very good condition.

"The stables are cleaner than the hall," Emer said as they walked back
up the hill.

"Lew has a good head groom," Nid replied. "He clearly needs an
equally good key-keeper."

"His wife was killed in battle last year," Emer said. "Conal mentioned
it."

"That would explain it," Nid said. "But there should be someone
else."

"His daughter was killed too, apparently. Maybe he's been too struck
with grief to get organized."

Nid rolled her eyes. "He needs to find a key-keeper quickly. I've heard
people say that Lew sways with every wind, and that he thinks too much
of himself. He won't like it if they start saying he keeps a dirty hall, and
they will if he keeps on."

"Although I've only just met him, I suspect it's true that he sways
with every wind," Emer said. "But he seems a good enough man. He
needs guidance."

"A good man, maybe not a good king," Nid said. "I don't know. I've
also heard that he makes shrewd alliances."

They went back into the hall. Lew was still talking to Conal, who
looked even more pleased than usual to see Emer.

"Think about it, Conal," Lew said as she came up. He patted Conal on the shoulder. He smiled at Emer in a friendly way, then went to speak to Darag.

"Think about what?" she asked quietly.

Conal looked stunned. "He asked me if my heart was given to Oriel or if I might like to come here," he said, gesturing at the hall. "There are only three people in our generation who are Royal Kin of Anlar, and none of them born here. He said that if I came, he'd treat me as his heir."

"Well?" Emer asked. Half of her mind was making rapid plans for cleaning up the hall and putting heart into the place, but the other half of her mind knew that Conal would only accept one kind of success.

"It isn't Oriel," he said, as she had known he would. His eyes were on Darag, who was talking to some champions on the other side of the hall. "Lew isn't so old, not forty yet. He could marry again. He said he would if I wasn't interested." He looked back at her, his eyes full of ambition. "Who would have Anlar if they could have Oriel? Who would guide good, weak Uncle Lew for the next thirty years and hope nobody said anything to change his mind between the desire and the action?"

"It's away from the curse," Emer said, lowering her voice to a whisper. "And it's away from your parents." As soon as she'd said it, she knew she shouldn't have. He wouldn't want anyone to think he was afraid of the curse. And he couldn't see what his parents did to him, not really. She also wasn't sure that she wanted to live here. It was a strange place, and it felt more distant than it was because of the way they'd come here. It was barely a two-day ride from Ardmachan, and hardly more than six from Cruachan.

Conal laughed shortly, as if he'd hardly heard her. "Lagin," he said. "Lagin, Muin, and then Connat. We'll see what we see. You know how I've been practicing. And I've grown. I'm taller than the others now. I won the sword-fighting fairly. I'll show them. I'll show Darag. I don't need any second-best kingdoms."

# —16—

## (FERDIA)

I t has been an honor and a pleasure," Conary said. "You came to me a boy and I am sending you home a man any father could be proud of. These gifts I send with you are a token of friendship between you and me, and between Oriel and Lagin." He took a wrapped bundle from Finca and gave it to Ferdia. Everyone tapped their feet in restrained applause and looked pleased, except Finca, who looked as prune-faced as always. The hall was quite full, but at least the dog woman wasn't there. If the weather had been warmer, they would have been doing this outside and he could really have just got in his chariot as soon as they were done.

"Thank you," Ferdia said, taking it and wondering what it was and where he could put it. "And please accept this small gift in thanks for the hospitality you have shown me." People tapped their feet again. They would have whatever he said. He hoped it was all right.

He handed his own bundle to Conary, who politely bowed over it without uncovering it. Of course nobody would ever refuse a gift, it would be a fighting matter, a rejection of friendship. The only time it was ever done was in ritual declarations of war, where the cover would be drawn off and the gift, whatever it was, scornfully returned, broken, or passed on to someone else. Ferdia was more worried that it would not be good enough when examined. It was an embroidered sword-sheath he had asked his mother to make and send. Conary was very fond of swords. It was well made, and his mother had sewn pearls onto it, and gold thread. He thought it was a rich enough gift that nobody could reproach him. It would not be right for him to give any greater gifts on leaving. His father would send something later to match whatever Conary had sent him, gifts of friendship from Lagin to Oriel. This gift was supposed to be personal from Ferdia to Conary.

Conary had set his gift down on a table. He looked at Ferdia expectantly. Ferdia looked about helplessly, and put the bundle down by his feet. Then Conary leaned forward and embraced him as a foster-father. Ferdia returned the embrace. He hadn't thought he would be glad to leave, but he was. He hadn't thought he would spend the last season almost alone either. He'd never imagined Ardmachan without Darag or realized how lonely it could be. When they left, he had thought they would be back in a month, but it had proved an unexpectedly slow contest. All the kings seemed to take forever to devise different testing feats. They had been half a month in the Isles, then his father had kept them a half a month, and then they had sent word that they would need to stay in Muin for a month. That time was almost up, but they hadn't even reached Connat yet. Anyway, it was too late. It was midwinter. Ferdia had been in Oriel for a year and his father wanted him home.

He picked up his bundle and stepped aside with it. It was bulky. Elenn came forward. She was wearing warm traveling clothes with a soft blue cloak over everything. She was carrying a little wrapped bundle. He wondered where she had found whatever it was. There hadn't been time for her to send home for something. She looked cool and beautiful and assured, not at all the way she had looked when she had begged him to escort her home. She should have stayed another few months; she hadn't been here a year. But she had said she was desperate to get home, and looked it. She said she couldn't bear to stay here entirely on her own after he left. He couldn't help feeling sorry for her. She said she would tell Conary her father was ill. It wasn't all that far out of his way to take her to Cruachan, really. She was still a child, so she couldn't go on her own, and it was a bit much to expect anyone to take her before it was time. He was glad he'd stuck out his year, even if the last part had been lonely.

Elenn and Conary exchanged the same kind of gifts and ritual farewells that Ferdia had. He tapped his feet when everyone else did. Fostering was an ancient custom. His father said that it was one of the things that helped to bind the peace between the kingdoms, just as much as the Ward, in its way. He had thought he agreed. But now he wasn't sure he knew what his father meant. He looked forward to asking him about it, about lots of things. There were things you couldn't say in a letter. And, of course, there were things you couldn't say at all. Maybe that was the real difference being grown up made—not taking up arms, but having things you couldn't ask anyone.

Conary embraced Elenn and she came over to Ferdia. They had officially left but they were still here, which was awkward. He shifted the bundle in his arms. He had packed the chariot already and he wasn't sure there was room. It was five days to Cruachan, and then four more days before he got home. He knew exactly where he was going to stay every night, but he had food and a leather tent in case he needed them. It wasn't the best time of year for a journey. It was cold. But the weather looked settled. One good thing he had done this year was to learn weather signs from Inis. He couldn't say he had mastered the Fir Knowledge. He certainly couldn't control the weather as some people said they could. Still, it was useful to be able to look at the sky and see if a storm was coming.

"Shall we go?" Elenn asked quietly. She also held a bundle. He wondered if they were the same. They pretty much had to be, unless Conary was meaning to indicate more friendship to one country than the other, which might be dangerous.

Nobody was looking at them, though people were still gathered around expectantly, as if something was going to happen. But there was nothing else. They were gone already. "Come on," he said, and led the way out of the hall.

He blinked at the sunlight as they came out. Frost limned each blade of grass, making the world glitter.

"I'm so glad to be leaving," Elenn said, leaning toward him in her confiding way. "Thank you for taking me."

"It's not far out of my way," he said, knowing he sounded awkward. "Did anyone make any difficulties?"

"No, they didn't mind at all," she said. She sounded a little hurt, but when he looked, she was still smiling.

They walked down the hill. Elenn said good-bye to the guards on the gate as they passed, so he did the same. The trees and fields were glistening. He felt filled with relief at leaving. No more Ardmachan. No more trying to make decisions on his own without enough time to think.

One of the grooms had yoked up the chariot ponies ready. There was probably just about room for the bundles. Ferdia was about to tell Elenn to get in when, to his dismay, the dog woman came out of the kennels and smiled at him. Her breasts and stomach were hugely swollen with pregnancy. She had two hounds with her. She looked as if she was going to walk right over to Ferdia.

"Wait here a moment," he said to Elenn. She looked puzzled. He crossed the yard to the dog woman.

"Ferdia," she said.

He hadn't heard her voice before, not talking, only whispering and then crying out. He still didn't know her name, and he writhed with embarrassment. He had hardly exchanged a word with her before or after. He had thought he ought to talk to her, but not known what to say. There had been too much and not enough between them. Her belly stood between them now. A child to be, a child that was and was not his. He couldn't ask her name. He should have asked it on the feast of Bel, or he should never learn it. "I'm going home," he said.

"I know," she said, looking down at her dogs. "I wanted to give you something."

"I don't have anything for you," he said. He was conscious of Elenn and the grooms across the yard. They couldn't hear, but he knew without looking that they were watching them.

"You've given me a gift already," she said. "Come inside for a moment."

She turned, and he followed her into the kennels, the hounds padding silently beside them. At least there was nobody else there to see. The light came in under the eaves, so he could see quite well, but it was shadowed after the brightness of the yard. She walked over to one of the pens. Inside was a bitch, her teats swollen in a way uncomfortably reminiscent of the woman's, and a litter of pups. He hadn't known what he'd expected her to give him, but it wasn't a dog. Though what else would she have to give? He didn't know what he could do with a dog.

"This is Swift," she said, bending down and patting the bitch. He wished she'd think to introduce herself like that.

"She's lovely," he said inadequately. "Does she live up to her name?"

"She's one of the three best hunting dogs in Oriel," the woman told him, pride in her voice. "And she's mine, not Conary's. She came into heat very late this year, and the father of this litter is Conary's famous Blackear. These pups should be great hunters, and half of them are mine. Choose whichever one you want."

He looked at them. They all looked alike—puppies, grayish-brown, with darker gray brindling just beginning on their coats. His father had a kennel full of hunting hounds at home. How could he explain bringing one from Oriel? "Are they old enough to leave their mother?" he asked.

"They're just ready," she said approvingly.

He looked at her. She was standing with one hand on her belly, and he thought he saw it move. He looked hastily back to the dogs. He didn't know her name, and the baby would have her husband's name, which he didn't know either. It was so strange to think that what they had done on the hurley field had swollen so and would soon be a child, a person. He looked away, back at the puppies. "I don't know enough to choose," he said honestly.

"Then I'll give you the pick of the litter," she said and put her hand in and drew one of the puppies out. It tried to squirm away but she held it tightly. "She doesn't have a name yet. You can give her one."

Ferdia took the puppy awkwardly. She tried to get away. He couldn't think how he would manage in the chariot, but he wanted to get away as much as she did. "Thank you," he said.

"No, thank *you*," she said, and turned away to fuss with one of the other hounds.

Ferdia was left standing there feeling that he didn't know whether the encounter was over or not. The puppy licked his ear. He backed away, and the woman didn't look back at him. Maybe he would never have to see her again. But in a way, he would like to see the child, even if he had no claim on it.

He blinked a little again as he came out. The puppy whimpered. Elenn was staring at him. She was going to ask questions, he just knew she was. What was more, she was going to have to hold the puppy while he drove.

She amazed him by taking the puppy from him without protest. "Isn't he sweet," she said. "Aren't you the sweetest thing? Look at his brindling just starting. Oh, look, the hair underneath is so much lighter."

"She's only just old enough to leave her mother,'' he said. "She doesn't have a name yet. Her mother is a hound called Swift, and her father is King Conary's Blackear."

"She's a little beauty," Elenn cooed. The puppy clearly returned

Elenn's approval: her tail was wagging almost in a circle, and she was licking everywhere she could reach.

"Do you like her?" he asked, an idea striking him. He turned it over in his mind and couldn't see any disadvantage to it. Elenn liked the puppy. Elenn could have her. He wouldn't have to explain anything to anyone at all.

"She's wonderful," Elenn said.

Ferdia glanced back at the kennels. The dog woman was still safely inside. Some grooms could see them but not hear them. They were gone already, after all. "She's for you," he said.

"Oh, Ferdia!" she cried, so enraptured that he felt guilty. "She's the best present anyone's ever given me."

"I'm glad you like her," he said.

"I'll call her Beauty," Elenn said, looking from him to the puppy.

"But then when people call, you won't know if they mean you or her."

Elenn smiled, not her usual smile but a broad grin. "I'll work something out," she said. The puppy chewed the corner of her cloak. "No, Beauty, don't eat my clothes." She turned back to Ferdia. "How are we going to manage in the chariot?" she asked.

"I thought you could hold her," he said, realizing as Beauty squirmed how inadequate a plan it was.

"I need a box or something. I'll get one from the kennels."

"No!" Ferdia didn't know how he was going to stop her, but he knew he had to. He hated thinking quickly. "I just want to go now," he said.

Elenn's face softened. "I want to get away as well. But she'll escape and jump out and maybe hurt herself." Then she went back to cooing. "My Beauty, my beautiful puppy."

Ferdia looked at the pile of things in the chariot. None of them would do for a puppy. "When she's trained, she can run along beside a chariot," he said and sighed. "I'll go and find something."

"I'll go," Elenn said, looking up.

"You wait here and look after her," he said firmly and took a deep breath before plunging into the stables. The dog woman was crouching over the remaining puppies. She looked up as he came in. "I need a box or something, to carry her safely," he said.

"Of course you do," she said. "I didn't think. Now what—" She straightened carefully, a hand to the small of her back, and looked around the kennels thoughtfully. "I think I'll have to go over to the stables."

"Isn't there anything here?" Ferdia asked desperately.

"I don't think so. People don't normally take puppies in chariots." She frowned.

Ferdia knew what was about to happen. She would go outside and Elenn would still be cooing "My puppy" and the woman would know that Ferdia had given away her gift. The possibilities then started from his having to fight a champion of the woman's choosing, followed by fighting one of Elenn's, and ran right up to all-out war between Oriel, Connat, and Lagin. How could he have been so stupid as to think it could possibly work? Even if she didn't come out now, Elenn would say something to someone before they left and it would get back to her. The worst of it was that he really had acted dishonorably. It hadn't seemed like that at the time, because he hadn't really been thinking of the puppy as a gift, just as a nuisance, but now he could see what he had done.

"What's that?" he asked as his eyes lit on at a wicker basket in the shadows.

"It's just some apples," the dog woman said. "I brought it in from home so I would have some to eat here. It is the right sort of size. I don't know if it's strong enough."

"It looks strong to me," he said. "I'll help you move the apples."

He hardly dared to breathe, but she assented mildly.

The apples went into a sack. He barely managed to restrain the dog woman from coming out to settle the puppy in the basket. He came back out alone, imagining more disasters, but Elenn was sitting alone on a stone playing with the puppy. "Here, put her in this," he said, offering the basket.

At last, at long, long last, after Ferdia had died a thousand coward's deaths of fear of having his lies and ingratitude discovered, the three of them drove safely out of the lower gates of Ardmachan. Elenn said good-bye to the guards, but didn't mention the puppy. Ferdia drove past the stone where Darag's mother had died, past the turning to the woods where they had killed the swan, and turned south for Lagin by way of Connat. The puppy gave a few yelps, then when Elenn soothed her, curled up and went to sleep. Ferdia drove on, knowing now that the puppy was something he would never be able to explain to anyone. Five days to Cruachan, where he could leave Beauty and Elenn. If he had his wish, he'd leave them at the gates and never see either of them again.

# 5

## CONNAT

# —17—

## (CONAL)

The Isles had been good, Lagin had been better, Muin had been wonderful, only Connat lay between him and victory. Leary and Nid's chariot rolled along ahead, Darag and Laig came behind. The road rose and fell over rolling farmland, winter-brown now. Apart from the occasional pheasant, he hadn't seen any life for hours. A feeble sun shone now and then through clouds, and it hadn't rained all day. If it hadn't been for Emer's set scowl, Conal could have sung.

"What's wrong?" he asked when the silence had stretched too long, although he already knew what was wrong. She didn't want to reach Cruachan, to see her mother, for this journey to be over.

"For someone with parents like yours, you're very reluctant to believe in parents like mine," Emer said between her teeth, her eyes on the road ahead.

"But why do you think they won't let you go back to Ardmachan for the three months left of your time there?" Conal tried hard to sound reasonable.

"You don't know how hard it was for me to get away at all," Emer said. "And it's hardly fostering now that I am of fighting age. She'll say there's no use to it."

"Well, I don't think she'll be that unreasonable," Conal said hopefully. Emer gritted her teeth. "And even if she does, whatever she says, as soon as I get home I'll talk to Conary and my parents, then I'll have Conary send me back to ask her." His mother had half-agreed before they left, after all. Speaking to Conary about it wouldn't be easy, but it would be easier than it would have been before. As for his father . . . well, when he got back Amagien should see that he was a boy no longer.

"And what about this stupid half-arranged thing with Darag?"

"Everyone knows neither of you want that. And if . . ." he trailed off, not daring to say it. It was the most ill-omened thing you could do, to count on victory halfway around the course. "Whatever happens, I should look like a good alliance to your mother, and it won't be more than a year that you have to stay there," he said instead.

"You don't know my mother," she muttered. "I wish I was a champion of Muin."

Conal laughed in surprised recognition. "So do I," he admitted. "I've never had such fun in my life. Even exhausted. Even covered in mud and freezing cold and starving."

"They really know how to have a good time," Emer agreed, then giggled. "It *was* a good time, though, it really was."

"And not only that, but unlike all the contests in the Isles and Lagin, it was a good challenge, because it was actually something that does count for being a king," Conal said.

Emer raised her eyebrows and darted a quick glance at him. "Flying Leary's breeches like a banner from the top of the palisade is something a king needs to be able to do?"

Conal laughed. "Wasn't he furious! But you know what I mean. Not that specifically, not any of the specific goals, but organizing the watches, arranging the raids and the defense, even little details arranging how people eat so that nobody has to sit down with anyone they have a bloodfeud with, getting everyone working together. It's useful knowledge. I think it's a better way than Conary's, having the champions working together in watches like that, having rivalry between watches instead of rivalry between champions. I learned a lot doing it, from Samar and the others. Think how cheerfully Samar let me take her place as watch captain and make mistakes, and how she helped me."

"Once we'd shown we were competent." Emer was staring out at the road again. "It really felt like belonging, as if we had a place in the Heather Watch. As if they'd be there at our backs when we needed them. All of the rivalry and all of the goals were just part of that, and that was what was important. It was easier for me, of course. I didn't have to be organizing everyone, didn't have to be in charge."

"Even that was fun," Conal said. "Once I'd worked out how to ask, anyway." He grinned. "I don't think I'll ever forget the last month as long as I live." The road widened ahead of them, making a broad, straight track.

"I've never had such a good month," Emer agreed, smiling. "I just wish we could have stayed there forever."

"If I am ever king, I will organize the champions of Ardmachan into watches like that," Conal said. "And whatever else, next time it snows, whenever it is, I'm going to have another snowball fight."

"I'll be stuck on my own in Connat," Emer said, suddenly glum again.

"Not forever," Conal said. "I may have to go back alone, but I'll come and marry you as soon as I can."

"Come soon." He moved a little closer to her. "Everything rests on what happens in Cruachan now."

"What do you think they will arrange?" Conal asked.

"Before we went to Muin, I'd never imagined anything but contests the way we had them in Lagin and the Isles—racing, fighting, spear-throwing, hurley. But Maga will want to outdo Muin. I have no idea what she'll come up with. She will have had plenty of time to think. She will also have had time to hear that you won in Muin, Darag won in Lagin, and the honors of the Isles were divided between you. She may well have her own ideas about who she wants as the next king of Oriel."

"You can't mean she'd cheat?" Conal tried to speak lightly to disguise the fact that he was shocked.

"I don't know. I sometimes think she would cheat for her advantage unless she was afraid she might get caught," Emer said, lowering her voice, although there wasn't much chance of the others catching what they were saying. "She won't cheat directly. My father would catch her if nobody else would. But she's setting the rules, and that's somewhere she might try to give someone an advantage. Be very careful with her."

"Hoy!" Laig called, coming up on their left. "How about a race?"

The road stretched ahead of them straight and inviting, wide enough now that the three chariots could run abreast. Nid, ahead of them, dropped back a little so that they were almost even.

"We've been doing nothing but racing for months," Emer called, but she was smiling, and Conal could see that she was already tightening her grip on the reins. He saw Darag putting his hand on the side of his chariot, as if casually.

"We didn't race at all in Muin," Nid replied, indignant.

"But Lagin made up for it," Laig said. "I wouldn't normally want to risk the horses on strange ground, but this road could have been made for racing, and we're nearly there, aren't we?"

"Very nearly," Emer said, sounding despondent. "We're less than an hour from Cruachan here, coming in on the south road. But we'll get covered with mud, racing, and it's bad enough anyway." It was wonderful how she could sound like that with every muscle tensed and ready to be off, as if there was still a decision to be made and she was giving it consideration.

"We may be doing nothing but racing in Connat," Nid warned, her eyes on the road.

"Go!" called Leary unexpectedly, but the others were as fast off the mark as Nid.

For a little while, they were ahead, and Conal remembered the second race in Lagin, the one they had won. Then Nid and Leary came up on the side and pulled a little ahead. Conal looked to see where Darag was and saw that he was lagging well behind. As he looked, Darag signaled to him to let Leary go. For a moment, he frowned; then he saw it and began to laugh.

"Let Leary get ahead," he whispered to Emer. She did not turn to look at him, she needed her attention for the horses. She slacked off as he had asked, though, unquestioning, and Nid and Leary surged forward, far ahead of the others as Emer and Laig drew their chariots to a halt.

"I wonder how long it will take him to notice?" Darag asked, laughing.

"I wish I could see his face," Conal said.

"It was Laig's idea," Darag said.

Laig grinned. "He'll be thinking this time, this time at least I'm winning, and then he'll realize that this time doesn't mean anything, and then he'll stop and look round and realize—"

Up ahead, Leary's chariot drew to a halt, spraying mud.

"We should go up," Emer said seriously. Conal realized then that she hadn't been laughing with the others.

"Make them come back," Laig said, still laughing.

"No, Emer's right, we should go up," Darag said.

"What's wrong?" Conal asked quietly as they drove on.

"That wasn't funny," she said, giving him a quick sideways glance. "Think if they'd done that to us. Leary doesn't need to have it rubbed in that he can't win now."

"You're right," he said, immediately contrite.

But Nid and Leary were laughing helplessly when they drew up. "I'll strangle you," Nid said.

"Get you next time!" Leary chortled, taking a battle position with empty hands.

"Thought you'd like to win for a change," Laig said.

Leary stopped laughing. "Don't mind being fairly beaten," he said. "Do mind seeing the chance snatched away. I know I was a fool to make an issue of the hero's portion, been meaning to say that for a while. Know I'm not as good as you two, never have been. Amagien got on the wrong side of me. Don't want to be king anyway. But I'm not sorry now. I wouldn't have missed Muin for anything."

"Well said," Conal said. "And we don't blame you at all."

Leary grinned and Nid rolled her eyes.

"I've enjoyed it, too," Darag admitted.

"Well, let's get on with it, then," Laig said and twitched his reins.

They drove on, still abreast but no longer racing. The sun was buried deep in clouds now, and the light started to dim, the short winter's day almost over already. The road curved around between two hills and at last, Cruachan was in sight. Conal had spent a year here when he was nine. It had the strange familiarity of something known in childhood and not seen for years. It seemed both larger and smaller than he remembered. Nid gasped at the sight of the cluster of buildings nestling inside the palisade at the foot of the craggy hill.

"Do you all live down here?" she called to Emer. "What happens when raiders come?"

"There isn't room on the top for everyone to live," Emer said. "There's two halls up there, though you can only see one from here. That one's called the Upper Hall, or the Dun Hall, and we usually just use it for big feasts. The other is a storehouse. A few of the champions have houses up there. Everyone else lives down here in the village usually and they just go up in time of danger or for festivals. The hill is very steep, as you can see, and there isn't much flat space on the top, not like Ard-machan."

"How unusual," Laig said. Conal was quite sure that all of them were thinking how easy it would be to capture the village. Conal craned his neck upwards. He had stayed in the Lower Hall, down in the village. He had been to the Upper Hall, but he didn't think he'd ever been right up to the top of the hill. As best he could tell in the fading light, it seemed to be a desolate crag. Dark birds hung on the air around it, giving it a sinister feel.

Emer drew ahead of the others as they came closer. Her reluctance to finish the journey seemed to have been overtaken now that the end was in sight. The palisade seemed very sturdy, and two guards came out of a little hut behind the south gate when they drew up before it.

"Ap Allel," one of them greeted Emer cheerfully. "Both of you back on the same day without warning?"

"It's good to see you back," the other said. "What's this I hear about you taking up arms already at your age?"

"The priest said it was a lucky day, so I did," Emer replied.

"Luck has come of it, from what we hear," he said. "Ap Dair passed through singing about you and the Victor—is that him behind you now?" Conal squirmed inwardly at the name, but kept his face still.

"Indeed," Emer said. "Don't you remember teaching him how to hold a spear when he was here before?"

Conal had only hazy memories of it himself, and certainly couldn't recall the guard's name.

"There are so many children," the guard said. "Who can tell which ones will grow up to become heroes?"

"Ap Fial," said the other guard, at which they both roared with laughter.

"Ap Amagien, these reprobates are ap Roth and ap Nemed," Emer said, indicating. Conal bowed. Just then the other two chariots drew up and Emer introduced everyone.

"We had heard you were coming," the second guard, ap Nemed, said. "You are all expected, though nobody was looking for you today especially. Your sister didn't say anything."

"My sister? She's here?" Emer sounded dismayed. Conal wondered what had made Elenn leave Ardmachan early. Boredom seemed most plausible.

Ap Roth looked at Emer. "Your parents are in the Lower Hall. Do you want to take your guests there, or do you want to welcome them here?"

"Can I?" Emer asked, sounding surprised. Then she smiled. "I can. I hadn't thought, because I haven't been home since I've been grown up. I'd like to."

"Your mother will probably want to do it again in the hall, but no reason you can't give them the peace of Cruachan," ap Roth said.

"That way, the horses won't have to stand about," Emer said. Ap Nemed looked at her strangely, but he opened the gates and they all drove in. Ap Roth disappeared into the hut and came out while they were dismounting, carrying a plate of salted bread and a cup of ale. Emer took them from him and welcomed all of them individually to Cruachan, beginning with Conal and ending with Nid.

They all went to the stables, where Emer took much longer than usual fussing with the horses and arguing with the stable-master about their need for hay after the journey. Conal couldn't help picking up some of her nervousness, however hard he tried to speak lightly.

"As if there's any goodness in grass at this season," she muttered as she led them out again. Then she took Conal's hand and squeezed it.

She led them to the Weapon Hall, a small building that had no purpose but storing weapons, not a room in a storehouse as at home. Conal found himself reluctant to leave his sword here, although it had lain with his spears in the weapon room in Muin gathering dust the whole time he was there. It was the larger sword Conary had given him after he had outgrown the Jarnish blade.

The daylight was completely gone by the time they came through the lanes of the village to the Lower Hall.

The door guard wanted them to wait. "Say I have given them welcome already," Emer said to him. He raised his eyebrows at this. "Say that they have given their names already and accepted the peace of Cruachan. Tell them who is here," she said.

He went in to announce them. Emer shifted her weight between her feet. Conal stood still, not touching her. After a moment, the guard came back and they all followed him in.

Inside, by the light of candles and hearth fires, the hall seemed much like the Red Hall at home. The door guard led them to an alcove, where, to his astonishment, he saw Ferdia sitting with two other men. Ferdia was smiling but seemed a little nervous. The other two men were a young champion and a graying champion, one on either side of the fireplace, like older and younger images of each other, clearly father and son.

Emer rushed forward and embraced the older man. "Father!" she said. Then she embraced the younger man, more formally. He must be her brother Mingor. Conal's memories of him eight years before were of a gawky boy, nothing like the way he was now.

Then Allel turned to the rest of them. "I hear my impetuous daughter has given you all welcome to Cruachan already," he said, smiling. "But let me repeat that now in my name, and my wife's. You are all welcome, and may your quest prosper here."

"Where is Mother?" Emer asked.

"She is talking to your sister," Allel said. "She asked me to send you in to her as soon as you arrived." He smiled at the rest of them. "My wife has been separated from her daughters for such a long time. I'm sure you understand. Do sit down, there will be a servant with drinks in a moment, and we will eat later of course."

Emer looked at him, an unreadable mix of emotions in her face, then she went off into the shadows of the hall, leaving Conal feeling entirely bereft.

# —18—

## (ELENN)

They had been talking for only an hour when Emer scratched at the door and asked for entry. Maga called her in at once, and they both looked at her for a moment. She wore no overdress and her shift was bound around her legs. Her hair, as so often, was straggling out of its braids. She looked as if she had just come from the stables.

"Mother—" she said.

"Darling," Maga said, and opened her arms, just as she had done with Elenn an hour before.

Then Emer came to embrace Elenn, awkwardly. Emer had grown taller in the three months since Elenn had seen her.

Maga sat down again on the bed, which sent up a waft of the scent of heather and lavender. Smelling that again made Elenn realize that she was home at last. She felt the prickle of tears at her eyes.

"Now, girls," Maga said, lowering her voice confidentially. "Sit down, both of you, and tell me everything."

So it began again. Elenn had been telling her about their reception at Ardmachan and Emer's taking up arms. Now she would want all the rest. Emer and Elenn sat down on the stools on each side of the fire. Beauty wriggled closer to Elenn as she sat down, getting farther away from the white cat curled on the bed. She didn't make a noise, just nestled into Elenn's legs. She was such a good puppy. Elenn stroked her head. Ferdia hadn't exactly said he loved her, but why else would he have gone to all that trouble to get her Beauty? He probably wanted to talk to his father before saying anything official. He had behaved perfectly all the way from Ardmachan, paying her compliments but never touching her. He was so honorable.

Elenn came back to reality to see her mother and sister looking at her. "I'm sorry," she said, blood heating her cheeks. "What?"

"Why did you leave Ardmachan early?" Maga asked, leaning forward on her elbow.

"I wanted to come home. I was lonely," she admitted.

"You should have asked me," Maga said. "It might have been useful to keep you there a little longer."

"I'm going back until the spring," Emer said eagerly, almost bouncing off her stool. "I'm only here now because I'm Conal's charioteer, so whatever you needed Elenn to be there for, I'll be able to do."

"No, I don't think either of you need go back there," Maga said soothingly, as if she hadn't heard that Emer wanted to be there. She'd told her mother how much Emer had changed. But Maga would have to see for herself before she believed it. "As for being Conal's charioteer, you should have asked me about that. It would have been much better for you to have been Darag's."

"Darag and I don't get on," Emer said, bristling like a cat.

"Conary and I have been negotiating about you and Darag, you know that, darling," Maga said, sitting back and letting a touch of reproach creep into her tone.

"Conal's going to be the king of Oriel," Emer said defiantly.

"I don't think so," Maga said, and smiled her most satisfied smile. "That's certainly not what Conary intends, and really, he ought to know more about these things than you do, don't you think?"

"It isn't only Conary's decision. Conal would make a wonderful king. The Royal Kin of Oriel will see that. And if I were married to him—"

"You're only sixteen, much too young to be deciding about marriage yet," Maga said. Emer subsided and Elenn let out a breath she hadn't known she was holding. She hated it when Maga and Allel fought, and it had looked as if Emer was going to fight in just the same way. "You've both been away from me for so long, there's a lot you don't know about the way the world's going, just as I need to catch up on what you've learned while you've been away. You're much too young to be making alliances for yourselves yet, and I won't have you trampling across the ones I've already made. As it happens, I haven't quite decided what to do about Oriel. Maybe I will find some weakness, then we will go to war with them. Since you have been away, I have been making military alliances that will surprise you, I think. Your father is positively longing to fight. But if I were thinking about settling Oriel with a marriage, it would be Darag I'd be thinking of for you."

Emer drew breath to speak. Elenn gestured to her to be quiet. It was the wrong moment to interrupt. Emer ignored her. "Mother, I don't want to marry Darag. I love Conal."

An expression of pain crossed Maga's face, then she laughed. "I haven't taught you very much at all if you think that love has anything to do with marriage, or marriage with love. Most especially the kind of love you fall into when you are sixteen years old. That love may be very sweet indeed, and I would wish that for you both, but marriage is a serious business."

Elenn could have kicked her sister. Now that she'd ruined everything, there would be no careful bringing the subject around to an alliance with Lagin.

"But unless there is love in a marriage, there will be no children," Emer said, stubbornly insistent. She rocked forward and made her stool scrape on the hearth.

"Duty can be enough," Maga said. "And that is a different kind of love from what you are talking about."

Elenn's eyes met Emer's across the fire. For once, they seemed to be in agreement in trusting their love and their loved ones. It was too much to hope to get Maga to understand. Elenn scooped Beauty up onto her lap and held her. She could get around Maga, if left to get on with it. She tried to signal as much with her eyes, but Emer, heedless as ever, caught none of it.

"As well as love, it would make a good alliance. Conal is winning, Mother, really he is."

"Put it out of your mind," Maga said firmly. "Conal ap Amagien is not for you. If you truly will not marry Darag, well, I am considering other offers, ones that would make both of you a queen." Elenn blinked. Where was there for Emer to be queen of, apart from Oriel? Muin had a queen already, and the royal children there were babies. Lew ap Ross of Anlar was quite old, wasn't he? Not Lagin, surely not Lagin? She suddenly had the awful vision of Maga marrying them off to the wrong men, Emer to Ferdia and her to mocking Conal.

"I don't suppose either of you have given any thought to Tir Tana-giri?"

Elenn blinked. She certainly hadn't. She shook her head. From Emer's blank face, it was plain that the big island to the east hadn't crossed her mind since she left home.

"An alliance?" Elenn asked, knowing she had to say something, had to keep her mother talking about it until she came to what she wanted to say. What could Tir Tanagiri have to offer them?

"An alliance, perhaps, but with which side?" Maga smiled again and stroked the white cat, which rolled onto its back and purred. "Urdo ap Avren is High King, for as long as he can stay on top. He wants fighting folk, and in exchange, he offers gold and a marriage alliance. Would you like to be High Queen of Tir Tanagiri, my dear? But can we spare the champions to send across the water? He might lose in any case. As well as the Jarnish enemies he knows about, his sister, the Queen of Demedia, has been looking around in secret for alliances against him. She is sitting up there at the north of his kingdom plotting against him, and will rise when she is ready. She also has sent to me."

"What does she offer?" Elenn prompted.

"Gold, and a promise to fight with us in our need. Urdo does not offer that, it is his sticking point. If he did . . . well, with cavalry, war with Oriel would be practical. But the queen of Demedia does not have cavalry, whatever she says, and without that, what are a few Demedians more or less? And she can offer no marriage alliance. Her older son, the one who will be High King should they win, is married already, to some Jarnish princess." Maga rolled her eyes. "Her younger son is not yet ten years old, as if younger sons were good enough for my darlings anyway." Maga made her voice caressing.

"How old is Urdo?" Elenn asked, her heart sinking.

"Twenty-five or six. He's never been married. He was betrothed to one of the Crow of Wenlad's daughters, but she died in a plague. He is holding out for a good alliance, but he will not wait much longer, he has no heirs. He would be ideal for you, if only we could be sure that he would survive." Maga frowned a little.

"But I don't want—" Emer began, tears in her eyes.

Elenn decided to interrupt. All Emer would do was make Maga more and more set on a course that so far, however awful it appeared, was not settled policy. If Maga could be distracted, she might change her mind another day and forget about these suggestions as if they had never been mooted. Tir Tanagiri was far away from everyday affairs. If she became angry, she would never forget.

"You said war with Oriel," Elenn said, straight across her sister's voice. "Did you mean a raid, or a real war?"

Emer shut up and glared at her across the fire between them.

"That would depend, darling," Maga said. "Certainly a raid next summer, to test them. As for war, I think we're too well matched. Everyone will fight in a raid, but a war takes people who really care about it. Nobody minds dying in battle, but they like to be taken prisoner if they lose, not like in war. So I don't think so. Unless . . . did you notice any weaknesses when you were there, anything that would give us an advantage?"

"Mother!" Emer burst out. "You know you can't ask us that! We were fostered there. It would be enough to put us under the Ban, and you, too."

Maga trilled the laugh she laughed when she did not mean it, the laugh she had taught Elenn. Beauty cowered down on Elenn's lap at the sound. "Darling, despite what they may have taught you, the priests aren't quite so urgent about enforcing that sort of thing as you may think. You have to do considerably worse than that to be put under the Ban. Besides, who would ever know? What have you discovered, Emer?"

"Nothing," Emer said, looking down and biting her lip.

Maga raised her eyebrows. "Extraordinary. Elenn?"

Elenn could think of nothing anyway. She shook her head. "They don't always guard the lower gate at Ardmachan," she said, remembering Leary swinging on it. "But everything is at the top of the hill, and they always guard the upper one."

Maga didn't seem to be listening. She wasn't looking at her but at Emer, who was staring defiantly at the rushes on the floor. Maga got up, dislodging the cat, who hissed. Beauty scrambled down from Elenn's lap and stood between Elenn and the bed, as if to defend her from the cat. Elenn put her hand down onto Beauty's head, willing her to be still and quiet and not draw Maga's attention. But Maga did not even glance at them. She walked across to stand before Emer, who continued to stare downwards. Elenn stayed calm and silent, hardly moving, keeping her face tranquil, making herself untouchable inside herself even if Maga should turn on her. Maga put her forefinger on Emer's chin and tilted her face up. Emer met her eyes defiantly.

"What did you learn?" Maga asked softly.

"Nothing. I told you, nothing," Emer said. Her voice sounded too loud in contrast and was full of the stubbornness Elenn had come to recognize.

"Will you put your new friends above your own mother?" Maga asked, her voice now reproachful.

"I saw no weaknesses," Emer said.

"Then why this talk of the Ban, of a fosterling's duty? Someone has told you that, to stop you doing your real duty to me and to Connat. Who told you?"

"Nobody. Ap Fial taught me about the Ban when I was seven years old and he was teaching me the law."

Elenn had no idea what Emer was trying to hide, but it was completely obvious that she was keeping something back. Maga stared down at Emer for a moment. Elenn kept having to remind herself to breathe. She kept her hand on Beauty's head. Having her puppy with her helped to make her brave.

"I know you're hiding something," Maga said, anger creeping into her voice now. "And now I know there is something to find, I will find out what it is whether you tell me or not, so I will know anyway, but it will be the worse for you."

"No, Mother," Emer said steadily.

"Then there is something, some weakness that would let me conquer Oriel, and you are keeping it from me?"

"There's nothing," Emer said, passionately and emphatically.

"You're lying," Maga said, and caught hold of Emer's braids and pulled her head back by them, twisting them hard, so hard Elenn was afraid she might pull them out by the roots. Elenn's own scalp hurt in remembered pain. "I can tell you're lying to me. Tell me now."

"If I would ever have told you, I wouldn't now," Emer screamed, tears of pain and chagrin on her face. She stood up, wrenching her hair free. A hank of it stayed in Maga's hand, blood on the ripped-out roots. Emer's hand went to her waist where her sword would be if she was wearing it, and Elenn thanked Damona, Lady of Wisdom, for making the law that no weapons must be brought into the hall. She didn't trust Emer in this mood to remember that she would fall under the Ban just as much for kinmurder. Emer pushed Maga away from her, forcing her mother to take a step back. They were almost equal in height, and standing glaring at each other, they looked very alike.

"I see you have gone very far away from me," Maga said coldly. "I thought my daughters had come home, but I see I have been rearing snakes to betray me."

"I am your daughter, yes, but not your property," Emer said, taking a step toward the door. "It might be as well for you to leave me out of your schemes from now on, Mother."

"Where are you going?" Maga asked, her voice like ice.

"Back into the hall," Emer said.

"Oh, don't be such a fool," Maga said. "Do you think your father will take your part against mine?"

"If I tell him you wanted me to betray my foster-father? If I tell him I have a marriage alliance arranged with Conal and that Conal will be king of Oriel? He might."

Elenn looked at her sister with horror. Could Emer really be proposing to start another war between their parents? War between Connat and Oriel would be nothing in comparison.

"With Conal, not with his parents and his uncle?" Maga's tone ridiculed the notion.

"Sometimes, when I am away from you, I almost forget how impossible you are," Emer said. "If I have to run away with Conal and live in a ditch, then I will."

"His parents and his uncle will just adore that," Maga said, her voice dripping scorn. "If you are anything to him, it is as princess of Connat, as you would soon find out if you tried that. But you are my daughter, my blood. I bore you and suckled you and named you " Maga's voice softened. "If you truly want to marry Conal this much, if that's what all this is about, then just tell me what weakness you saw in Oriel and I will see what can be done."

"You should have said that before," Emer said. "What sort of fool and traitor do you think me?" Then she grabbed her torn hair from where Maga still clutched it and threw it into the fire, where it flared up quickly, filling the room with the harsh funeral smell of burned hair.

Maga did nothing, just watched the hairs shrivel and turn until Emer left the room. Then she sang her charm to make the fire stop burning. The room was very dark suddenly, with only the flickering candlelight. She reached down into the cold gray embers and took up what was left of the hairs. She shook her head over them.

"Ashes. But I'm her mother. Doesn't she realize I have enough of her hair and blood for anything I might want?" Then she looked at Elenn for the first time in a long time. The look made Elenn feel cold inside, made her wish she had stayed in Ardmachan even though she had been so lonely. "Go after her. And try to do better than you have for the last year at stopping her doing stupid things," she said. Elenn stood, her legs shaking a little. Then she stooped to gather up Beauty. "No, leave the puppy here," Maga said.

Elenn tried to speak and swallowed, finding her throat too dry. "But she's scared of the cat," she said. The cat's eyes shone very green in the dim light.

"Nothing but defiance on all sides," Maga said, shaking her head.

"Take her, then. But I take it you haven't told my secrets to anyone, or contracted any alliances, and aren't keeping any secrets from me?"

"Oh, no, Mother," Elenn said, hugging Beauty. It was true, she hadn't any alliance, only a hope. As for telling Maga's secrets, she'd have thought Emer's refusal to tell Oriel's secret, whatever it was, would have made Maga realize how unlikely that was.

"And you at least will do as I tell you?"

"Oh, yes, Mother," Elenn said fervently. Beauty was getting heavy and trying to lick her face, but Elenn held her tight.

"Then get after her," Maga said. "Find out what she knows about Oriel, if you can. Stop her going straight to Conal and pouring out my secrets along with her silly infatuation."

Elenn raised her chin and made for the door. She didn't have any idea how she was going to do it, but at least she'd be away from Maga and the chances were good that by tomorrow, Maga would be back to being sweet to her.

"Come back afterwards," Maga added as Elenn opened the door. "I want you to tell me all about this silly contest, how it was declared and what everyone thinks about it."

"Yes, Mother," Elenn said and went out after Emer, shutting the door quietly behind her and not sighing at all, not on the outside where anyone might see.

# — 19 —

## (EMER)

Emer was shaking. She had been through a battle and it hadn't made her shake the way she did after a quarrel with Maga. She stood and forced herself still, taking deep breaths. Her father would, as always, be drinking in the hall. She couldn't go to him like this. There was nobody around. These rooms belonged to the Royal Kin. She didn't know if one of them was still hers and Elenn's. She didn't want it to be.

It was dark and shadowed, the only light coming from the fires in the open part of the hall. Emer put her hands up to her head and loosened her hair. She shook it out around her head for a moment. She almost wished she could keep it like that, mourning her hopes. But she had known Maga would not be easy. Maga always got her way by being impossible. When you thought you knew how impossible she could be, she surprised you by seeming to be sweet and reasonable, only to twist around and be more impossible than ever. She made you lose your temper, or she co-opted you. The only way Emer could deal with her was to get right away from her. Emer pulled her hair back hard, ignoring the pain. Elenn said it was possible to learn a lot from Maga, and so it was. It was possible to learn by bad examples. She would be a mother and a ruler and never act like that, never.

She was old enough to fight back. She was a warrior. She wouldn't strike Maga unless she had to, but she wouldn't let her pull her hair and slap her face anymore either.

Deep, calming breaths made her feel more like herself. The horrible things Maga had said were still going around in her head. There was just enough truth in them for them to sting. Conal didn't only want her because she was a princess of Connat, but she had known her threat of running off to live in a ditch was hollow even as she made it. Conal wanted to be king of Oriel, and that meant everyone would have to agree. Why did Maga have to be so impossible? It was a good alliance, or it could be. Could have been. Emer gritted her teeth. She had lost a battle, but not the war yet. She would stand up to her. She would win. A year, Conal had said. A year! She had only been home an hour so far.

She wiped a last few angry tears from her face and took a few steps toward the hall.

Maga's door opened, and Emer spun around, expecting her mother. She would be cooing now, making any opposition sound like the sulks of a baby. But it was only Elenn, saying "Yes, Mother" as she closed the door. She was doing what Maga wanted, like always. She had a hound puppy in her arms. Emer had half noticed it in her mother's room but paid it no attention.

"I'm here," Emer said, not wanting her sister to fall over her in the shadows.

"Why do you have to be such a complete idiot?" Elenn burst out angrily.

Emer blinked. This wasn't the perfect princess act Elenn usually showed the world. "What do you mean?" she asked.

"Deliberately tightening all Maga's threads to breaking point like that. You're as bad as she is, worse, because she does use diplomacy and you just go head-on like a bull. If you want to marry Conal, you've gone exactly the wrong way about it, antagonizing her like that. You need to make her think things are her idea, or a good idea at least, or you need to get her so tangled up in the complications of several ideas that she loses sight of where the whole thing is going."

"But that's so dangerous," Emer said.

"Oh, and getting her furious so she loses control is safe?" Elenn must have been squeezing the puppy too hard, it gave a little whine of protest and Elenn set it down at her feet. "Or sensible?" she went on. "Or good strategy? Because when she gets furious, it makes her more and more set on what she wants to do, when otherwise she might change her mind."

"What got her so furious is my refusing to betray my honor," Emer said stiffly.

"You should have told her whatever it is. It's probably nothing, anyway," Elenn said scornfully. "What could you have found out that would really make a difference?"

Emer thought of Beastmother rearing up and her terrifying curse, and said nothing.

"All right, maybe you do have something," Elenn said after a moment's silence. "But whose side are you on?"

"Oh, stop trying to do Maga's work for her," Emer said. "It's disgusting. She may have no honor, but you do. They treated us well at Ardmachan, and you know how sacred the laws of fostering are. You know the Hawthorn Knowledge as well as I do, that breaking them is under the Ban."

"That's harming a fosterling," Elenn said uncertainly.

Maybe she didn't know the Hawthorn Knowledge as well as Emer. Emer had always found a certain fascination with the idea of cursing, and of the Ban in particular. There was something quite horrible about the thought of putting someone under a curse that stopped them reaching the gods at all, so that they could not even light a fire or clean their wounds or keep food fresh. It had always seemed worse than killing someone. And the things that could bring it on had a gruesome fascination as well, or they had when she had been a child. Maybe Elenn had shut her delicate ears to them.

"Yes, harming a fosterling, but also using anything you learned when fostered against your foster family," Emer said. "Think about it. It has to work like that or fosterlings couldn't be sacred guests, because they'd be little spies. Nobody could trust them."

"Harm, yes, but remembering what you've seen, whatever it is, and telling your mother can't possibly count," Elenn said. "What is it, anyway?"

"I'm not going to tell you," Emer said straight out. "And you ask anyone about the Hawthorn Knowledge. I'm not making it up. You ask ap Roth. Ask your friend ap Ringabur."

"Orlam's in Rathadun," Elenn said, sounding desolate. "Talking about the decision she made and whether she can be Conary's lawspeaker. Everyone was gone except me."

"Ask her when you see her," Emer said, feeling a little sorry for her sister despite everything.

"I will. But even so, you ruined everything defying her head-on like that. She won't let you marry Conal now, you know."

"Not right now, no, but it might seem like a better idea in a little while," Emer said as positively as she could. "When Conary sends to her about it. When Conal has won."

"You're the one of us who's supposed to be grown up," Elenn said. "Don't be so silly. You heard what Maga said, as if you didn't know already. Conary wants Darag to be his heir. This contest will only change anything if it goes the way Conary wants."

"It isn't up to Conary, it's up to the Royal Kin of Oriel once Conary's dead," Emer insisted.

"While he's alive, it's up to him, and he's not an old man. How long were you thinking of waiting?" Elenn asked. "I want to get married when I'm still young enough to have children."

"I didn't say anything about you." Emer was confused. The puppy came pushing against her legs; she put her hand down and petted it.

"If you were married to Conal, that gives her one daughter less to play alliances with."

"Who do you want to marry, then?" Emer had no idea. Elenn flirted with everyone.

But Elenn just sniffed. "If I told you, you'd do something to mess it up, and right now, your saying a word about it for or against would mess it up with Maga. She won't rest until she finds out whatever it is you're keeping from her."

"She won't," Emer said. Nobody who knew was likely to tell Maga. But if she crossed the border in arms, she would find it out soon enough.

"Whose side are you on?" Elenn asked. "You wouldn't fight Conal, would you? Would you fight Oriel?"

"I'm Conal's charioteer," Emer said, very sure. "I don't think I could, unless Oriel invaded us. When I marry Conal, I'll fight for Oriel against Connat if Connat invades."

"If mother finds that out, she'll never let you marry him," Elenn said, hardly above a whisper. "That's like saying you'd not make her alliance. If you had a choice of where to live, you'd pick Oriel, then?"

"Muin," Emer said and laughed. She wished she could see Elenn's expression. "Look, I'm going into the hall. I'm still absolutely furious with Maga, but you can feel sure I'm not about to kill anyone. I'm also never going to tell Maga or you or anyone what it would be dishonorable for me to tell, so you may as well stop trying."

"What are you going to tell Allel?" Elenn asked.

"Right now, in front of everyone? Nothing. But when I get the chance to talk to him properly, probably tomorrow outside somewhere, I'm going to tell him what Maga asked, and I'm going to tell him about my arrangement with Conal. He'll be on my side when he sees it, I know he will."

"You'd start a war between them?" Elenn asked.

"It's Maga who wants a war," Emer said, puzzled.

"Not between Oriel and Connat, between Allel and Maga!"

"They're always fighting," Emer said dismissively. "If Maga is going to be utterly unreasonable, then of course I'm going to go to father. Wouldn't you?"

"Life is completely impossible when they're really feuding, as opposed to just normal bickering, and you know it," Elenn said.

"Well, sorry if my desire to marry the man I love is getting in the way of your comfort," Emer said, entirely out of patience with her sister. "I'm going to the hall now. I want a drink."

"I'll come with you," Elenn said, ignoring everything else.

They had to greet a number of old friends on their way to their father. Many of them Emer was genuinely glad to see. Everyone said how much they'd grown, and most commented on Elenn's beauty and Emer's height. Old Barr, who had nursed them and Maga before them, tutted over Emer's scar. "I'm proud of it," Emer said. "It was a fair fight and a won battle, no shame to be wounded by Atha ap Gren."

"An honorable wound, sure enough, and healed well and clean. But it spoils your beauty," Barr said, touching her fingers to Emer's cheek.

Emer winced away, though it did not hurt and had not since the moment Conal healed it. "It's Elenn who has songs sung to her beauty," she said, trying to smile. "I am a champion, and have songs sung about my fighting abilities."

"Songs, is it?" Barr asked.

"Amagien the Poet did write a song about me," Elenn admitted.

Barr chuckled. "To think of my nurslings grown up enough for that already. And was it Amagien the Poet who wrote a song about you, Emer?"

"No, it was Gabran ap Dair," Emer said. "The song's mostly about Conal the Victor. I'm his charioteer."

Barr looked most impressed, and let them go.

Allel was still sitting in the alcove, drinking with Mingor and his guests. They all glanced up as she came in. She had thought she was getting away with appearing outwardly calm until she saw Conal catch sight of her. He rose half to his feet, then remembered himself and sat down again.

"Does our mother want me?" Mingor asked.

Emer suppressed the strong desire to snap that Maga must have wanted him more than anything once, but rarely since. "I don't think so," she said.

"Darag was just telling me about the contests," Allel said. He moved over a little and patted the bench on each side of him. She walked over with Elenn and sat down beside her father. Emer grimaced at Conal as she passed him, that being the nearest to private conversation they were likely to get tonight. She could read the worry in his eyes. She wished she'd been able to explain properly about Maga. But Maga's impossibility defied description.

She sat back, taking deep drafts of the ale when it came around. She listened to Leary giving a fair account of the chariot racing at Lagin, helped out by occasional comments from the others. Elenn's puppy moved among the company, sniffing everyone's feet in a friendly way. It seemed to know Ferdia already, and to be very taken with Darag, who rubbed it hard behind the ears with practiced ease. Conal kept looking at her inquiringly, but she couldn't say anything without everyone hearing.

After a little while, a servant brought supper—a pot of lamb stew with bowls for the company, and a ladle.

"Help yourselves," Allel said. "I thought it was unwise to serve you a roast, with the hero's portion in dispute among you."

There was an awkward laugh.

"A good hot stew is ideal in this cold weather," Ferdia said.

"As long as it's not served with a knife," Nid said. The laughter this time was much more heartfelt. Everyone knew the story of the champions fishing about in the stew with their knives and eating the first thing they managed to stab, and with the pot in front of them, it suddenly seemed even funnier than usual.

Emer got up to serve herself and managed to seat herself next to Conal when she sat down again. They still couldn't talk without everyone hearing what they said, but at least their knees could touch.

After they had eaten and Allel was just beginning to pester Emer to sing, Maga came to join them. She had changed her clothes completely and was wearing all her gold. Emer immediately felt travel-worn and dowdy. She wished she had worn the two arm-rings she had brought from Oriel, the gold one Conary had gifted her with after the battle, and the twisted copper-and-bronze one Conal had given her.

"No need to get up," Maga said after everyone had stood and bowed. "I am not really well enough to receive guests this evening, but I wanted to greet you. Cruachan is fortunate to have so many distinguished visitors in this season."

"They are here on a quest, my dear," Allel said cheerfully.

"I have heard of it," Maga said. "I have been thinking and consulting about it since I first heard that you three young princes would be coming here to compete."

"They had contests in the Isles and chariot races in Lagin and in Muin—" Allel began, but Maga raised her hand and cut him off.

Emer felt her stomach clench. There was not much Maga could do to cheat in a fair contest. Darag was very good, but so was Conal. But Maga was setting the rules of the contest, and that almost guaranteed it wouldn't be fair. But it wouldn't be too blatant either. Maga was quite shrewd enough to know when people were watching.

"I have decided that the fairest test would be for the three of you to go, unaccompanied, up to the heights of Cruachan tomorrow evening at sunset. There is a cave up there among the rocks. You will stay there, without going into the cave, for three nights and days, defending yourselves against anything that comes against you. Whoever does this will be awarded Connat's prize."

Emer stared at her mother as if she'd never seen her before. Nobody ever went up to the heights of Cruachan. Nobody dared. Even the Ward fires were lit from lower down. All the things Barr had said when making threats to get her to behave came into her head—the monsters, the ghosts, the lane to the land of the dead. They said there was something there that would come out to defend Connat, if it was called. Nobody went up past the bonfire mound except a new king of Connat, who had to spend one night on the heights. Emer had never liked spending the night even at the Upper Hall. Sending them up there for three nights was terrible. Maga ought to know what was there, she was the king, but Maga wasn't trustworthy. She wished she could be sure Maga wasn't sending the three of them to certain death. What could Conary do if they all died after all, other than complain? He could go to war to avenge them, even if Maga said it was an accident, but it wouldn't make them alive again. Maga wasn't bound by the things that bound other people—the web of honor and fear and trust that made the world safe.

Leary drew breath to speak, but Conal got in before him. "What lives in the cave?" he asked.

Maga laughed. "Some say one thing and some say another. It is an unchancy place."

"And if we all complete the quest?" Leary asked.

"Then I will have to devise another test," Maga said, sounding as if this were a very unlikely contingency. Emer agreed with her for once. She would have been more inclined to ask what happened if none of them were ever seen again. Darag said nothing, just stared into the fire.

Maybe he had a better idea about the top of Cruachan than the others.

Maga sat down then, between Darag and Leary, and made herself as agreeable as she could be, which was sufficient to make both young champions unbend.

Elenn was sitting stroking her puppy and talking to Ferdia. Allel was drinking amiably. Emer turned to look at Conal. He was as beautiful and as beloved as ever, and she longed to hold him. "I've never been to the heights of Cruachan," she said quietly, but not so quietly as to be accused of whispering. Nid could certainly hear. "Everything I know about it I learned from my nurse when she wanted me to be good. I have heard that it is a strange and dangerous place, maybe a gateway to the land of the gods, a haunt of monsters, god-touched, a place where time acts strangely. I don't know what is true about it. Be careful. Keep close track of time."

Conal smiled, undaunted. Emer tried hard to smile back.

# — 20 —

## (FERDIA)

He had been longing to leave, but now he had to stay until the contest was over. He just had to. Darag understood, of course. Strangely enough, Maga didn't seem to have any problem understanding either. She just smiled, assured him he was welcome, thanked him again for returning Elenn to her, and said that it would be more than flesh and blood could bear for him to leave now. She was much nicer than he had expected. He wondered if his father could possibly have misjudged her.

Everyone in Cruachan went out to watch them go. It was strange to see three champions setting out on foot with swords and spears and waterskins. Their charioteers seemed to think the same and kept fussing over them until the last minute. They were to ascend in order of age, the next to follow when the first was out of sight. Ferdia didn't see what good it would do, considering that the top of the hill could hardly comprise half a mile of craggy land and that they'd all been told how to find the cave.

Conal left first, as the sun began to slip behind the shoulder of the hill. He embraced Emer fiercely and set off among the rocks. Emer did not go back to her parents but stood still, watching him out of sight.

"Do you want to take my cloak as well?" Laig asked.

"This one was warm enough on night watches in Muin," Darag answered with commendable patience. It was chilly and damp, typical winter weather, not terribly cold.

"You had hot drinks then, and somewhere warm to go before and after. Three nights and days outside at this time of year is a challenge in itself. It would have to be midwinter." Laig shot a furious glance at Maga, as if to hold her responsible for the season.

"Just past midwinter," Ferdia said and smiled at Darag. He had no doubt of his friend's powers of endurance.

"At least it isn't snowing," Darag said and won a reluctant smile from Laig.

Then the priest, ap Fial, called to them that it was time for Darag to go. He embraced them both swiftly. "Good luck," Ferdia said. "But I'm sure you will win this." Darag just smiled, turned, and walked uphill with an even stride, not looking back.

When Darag was out of sight and Leary began to make his way up, Ferdia turned back to the others. Elenn, the wretched puppy at her feet, was standing with her parents and brother, most of the people of the court and village around them. Ferdia and Laig went to join them. Emer was still standing alone where Conal had been. Nid went to her and said something quietly, and they walked back to the Upper Hall together, just ahead of Ferdia and Laig.

"What do you think is in that cave?" Laig asked Ferdia.

"I don't believe any of the stories about monsters," Ferdia said as decisively as he could. "And it can hardly be wolves up here. Maybe a bear?"

"Darag could deal with a bear," Laig said, made more cheerful at the thought. Ferdia wondered if he had ever seen a bear. "He has his spears. Anyway, a bear would be snoozing at this time of year. I'm more worried about the cold than anything. It might snow in the night. He'll have to sleep sometime."

The Upper Hall was smaller but more sturdily built than the Lower Hall. There was a boar roasting over the fire. Ferdia wondered for a crazy moment if there might be boar in the cave, in contradiction to everything he had ever learned about the habits of boar. He was glad they would be staying up here, nearer the heights.

That evening they feasted, drinking to the three princes of Oriel and their ordeal. It was strange to be warm and well fed, sitting in the light hearing music and conversation, knowing that Darag was not very far away but outside in the cold and the dark. He sat in an eating alcove with Allel and his children and some of the champions of his household. Nid and Laig were sitting with Maga and some of her women. Ferdia heard occasional loud laughter from Laig and worried that he would get very drunk and disgrace Darag. Laig was a good charioteer, and undoubtedly devoted, but sometimes he disgusted Ferdia.

The next day was bright and clear and very cold. Laig looked the way Ferdia had felt after the Feast of Bel. He swore, not for the first time, that he would never drink again, and said that Maga kept asking questions about the security of Oriel, which he knew better than to answer, drunk or sober. Ferdia wondered if she was really planning a war against Oriel. It would be something to ask his father when he was home. Maybe knowing what she had asked Laig would be information that would help his father put together a picture of what Maga was doing.

After breakfast, Mingor led out a hunt. Ferdia went with them. There seemed little chance of anything happening on the heights the first day. There was nothing to watch, after all, and hunting was always a pleasure. But when they came back in the twilight, pleased and tired, having killed two hinds and a stag, Leary was sitting beside Maga in the hall, a cup of hot ale in his left hand. His right arm was bandaged.

"What brings you back so soon?" Ferdia asked. He hadn't thought Leary would give up, even if he couldn't win.

"To save him wearying of repeating it, Leary will tell us all his story after dinner," Maga said. Leary smiled sheepishly. They contained their curiosity while they ate. Tonight Maga seemed to be devoting herself to Leary. He wondered if Leary would let slip any secrets about Oriel's defenses. He sat with Elenn and Laig and some champions of Connat and talked mostly about the hunt.

After dinner, Emer took up the harp and sang the old song of Manan and Rhianna declaring their love for each other while dashing about the field dispatching their enemies in the Battle of the Towers. Ferdia thought it exactly the song one would expect a charioteer to choose.

Then Leary came forward and took the musician's stool. "Mine's not much of a story," he said, and was met with sympathetic laughter. "I went up the hill last. Found the cave easily enough, but there was no sign of the others anywhere. I settled down to keep watch, and watched all night, with no sign of anything. The sun came up at the usual time, though it felt like forever. The day passed uneventfully. The only odd thing was where Conal and Darag could be. I walked about a bit looking for them. I didn't go in the cave. The second night, I must have dropped off for a minute. Something came out of the cave, a great dark shape, I couldn't see it properly. It attacked me, and I fought it. That's when I got this scratch." He indicated his bound arm. "I didn't kill it, it fled back into the cave. I slept a bit more the next day, had some strange dreams, too. The third night, three armed warriors came out of the cave, but I was ready for them. At least one of them went down, but by the time it got light, her body had vanished. I came back down at sunset today." He spread his hands as if to say that was all there was to it.

There was a silence. Ferdia was baffled.

"It's only been one day," Nid said at last.

"Maga told me that," Leary said. "Very strange indeed. No accounting for it. Doesn't make sense."

"It may yet be that Leary will win the contest," Maga said, her voice smooth and assured.

When Ferdia went off to bed, Leary was leaning on Maga, looking deep into her eyes. It looked almost amorous. Allel was across the hall taking no notice at all. When Ferdia passed them, Maga was smiling in a very pleased way and saying something about Beastmother, so he must have been mistaken, it must have been a religious discussion. No wonder Leary wanted to drown his troubles, really, after three days turning into one like that.

The next day was even colder, with a few flakes of icy snow blowing about. Ferdia managed to forestall Laig by assuring him right away that he thought Darag's cloak would be warm enough even for this weather. He couldn't help looking up to the icy heights and worrying. It was waiting that was so difficult, not doing. Late in the afternoon, he managed to evade Elenn for a little while. She was so persistent in her attentions that he wondered if Maga had asked her to keep watch on him. For a girl who had wanted to be home so much, she seemed to have nothing to do now she was here except get under his feet. She had never seemed this irritating at Ardmachan.

He wrapped himself in his cloak and walked up to the bonfire height, where he had stood to watch Darag leave. He wasn't entirely surprised to see Emer up there, shivering. They greeted each other and then stood in their separate silences. The snow was thickening, and as it began to grow dark, Ferdia was ready to suggest they go back together. Then a figure appeared, making his way down among the rocks. He couldn't tell for a moment which of them it was, which was ridiculous considering how much taller Conal had grown this last year. When he saw that it was Conal, he felt a great relief. He slipped away, leaving Emer to greet him. They wouldn't have wanted him there any more than he wanted to talk to them. When he came into the hall, brushing the snow off his shoulders, Elenn was there again, waiting for him.

"Conal's back," he said.

She smiled. "You never doubted Darag would win, did you?"

He hadn't, really. He didn't like to say that Darag would likely win anything that touched the world of the gods. Darag so hated feeling the weight of that. He wouldn't want everyone knowing. Nor did Ferdia want to claim victory until Darag was back and risk ill-wishing him. "I have never doubted that he is the best," Ferdia said. He let her take his wet cloak.

Emer did not sing that night. Conal told his story straight after dinner. "I have been away two nights, but to me it felt like three," he began. "The first night, I went up first and alone, and saw no sign of the others coming to join me. The cave mouth was very dark when I reached it. I did not go inside but walked to and fro outside the entrance. For hours, nothing happened, but I kept moving, doing some exercises to keep warm. Then, in the depths of that first night, a creature came out of the cave. I have heard talk of monsters, and I suppose it was monstrous, yet it seemed to me somehow beautiful as well. It was like a huge black cat, bigger than I am, with claws like swords. I fought it all over the heights. At last, I slew it among the rocks on the very summit. I went back to the cave mouth, and after a short time, a troop of armed warriors came out. They did not see me at first and I heard them talking, using a language that was completely strange to me. They were strangely armed, too. Most of them had only short spears which they carried against their shoulders."

Conal paused, staring into space. "I hadn't been told to kill anyone that came out of the cave, only to defend myself against attack, so I followed them. They went over the hill, talking quietly. There were twelve of them, too many for me to fight alone, but not a whole army. I saw a woman who seemed to be their leader, and I thought she was explaining to them how they would ambush something. They were folk like I have never seen. I followed them until they seemed to melt from one minute to the next as they came over the crest of the hill near where I had slain the beast."

"Do you think they were the spirits of our ancestors?" Allel asked. "Maybe the woman was Crua, who founded this dun?"

"Maybe," Conal said, but he shook his head. "I only saw them in the darkness. They usually took good care not to be seen against the sky, as if they were hiding from someone. But I thought they had short hair. I would be very interested to talk to the priests about them. In any case, I went back to the cave mouth, my mind full of speculation. I watched for the rest of the night, and watched the sun come up. There was a chill mist clinging to the top of the hill. I saw ravens now and then throughout the day, but nothing else. I ate some of the provisions I had brought with me, and I slept a little, around midday when it seemed safest. I also went up to the top of the heights, to examine the body of the beast in daylight. It was gone, there was no sign of it. Nor could I find any prints of the people I had been following, nor even of my own. The ground was hard, but the thin winter grass did not even seem bent. The night came soon enough. That second night, I was attacked almost as soon as the sun was down. Bats came streaming out of the cave like smoke. I say they were bats, but they were not like normal bats for they came towards me plainly intent on attack. I fought them for a long time in the darkness, trying to protect my face from them." He shuddered, and Ferdia shuddered in sympathy. He had never liked bats.

"Towards morning, they left and I saw people again, two men who attacked me as if they knew and hated me. I think they called my name. I fought and killed them both, but when dawn came, their bodies were gone. The day was damp and misty again. Unlike the day before, I did not sleep at all. I found I had some tiny bites from the bats, and sang charms over them. When night came, I tied my hair back very carefully in case more bats came. There were no bats. What came out was a troop of four huge horses.

"The first horse carried a woman slumped over the saddle. The second carried a warrior. The third carried a man who seemed to be me, and the last carried a woman who seemed to be my charioteer, Emer ap Allel. I called to her, but they all rode on as if they could not see or hear me. I ran after them, but however fast I ran, I could not gain on the horses, though they were only walking and I was running as fast as I could. I could not catch up, but as I went back towards the cave, I saw the man I had thought was me, walking now. I saw that he was badly wounded. He kept murmuring for water, but when I tried to give him my water bottle, he didn't seem to see me. At last, I went back to the cave, walking to and fro quietly, reciting poetry inwardly to keep myself calm and awake."

Conal smiled reassuringly at Emer, and then looked around at the puzzled faces in the hall. "I don't understand it either," he said. "I'm nearly finished. Near dawn a huge man came out of the cave carrying an ax. 'Conal ap Amagien,' he said, 'let us have a contest. Kneel, and I will strike off your head, and then you may do the same for me.' 'Let me rather strike first,' I replied. 'And let me know your name, for it seems you know mine.' 'I am called Bachlach,' he said and laughed, so that I knew his name meant something, though I had never heard it before. He then handed me his huge ax and knelt before me. I hewed as hard as I could and chopped off his head. He then stood, picked up his head, put it under his arm, and bowed to me." Conal hesitated. "I think he went away, back into the cave. Perhaps I fell asleep. The next thing I knew, it was morning, a wintry morning with some snow in the air. I waited all day and returned here at sunset, to find that only two days had passed, and not the three I had experienced."

There was much muttering about Conal's story, especially about the strangely armed people and the huge man, Bachlach. Elenn seemed especially concerned about Conal seeing Emer on a horse and kept asking what it could possibly mean.

"His death, do you think?" Mingor asked. "Seeing himself as an old man wounded and looking for water?"

"I'm glad I never have to go up that hill," Elenn said.

"Kings only have to spend one night," Mingor said, not sounding very happy about it.

Ferdia was glad the kingship ritual of Lagin was nothing so unpleasant. He didn't see why Maga had thought this an appropriate test, unless she had also wanted to make sure Darag would win. He wondered what Darag was seeing, out there beyond the walls of the dun.

The next day was bright and very cold. At sunset, everyone gathered again at the bonfire height. Ferdia and Laig were there first, and the others came by ones and twos until the hillside was full, the way it had been when they all left. Maga and Allel were both there, dressed in their finery. Conal looked better for his night's sleep, and Leary's arm was evidently healed enough that he did not need it bandaged anymore. Elenn came over to stand with him and Laig. Ferdia wished she wouldn't take the puppy with her everywhere, or at least that she would train her to wait quietly. The puppy ran about, chasing smells. At least she showed no sign of trying to go up the hill. Laig talked to Elenn about how she should train her, most of it sensible advice that he doubted Elenn would follow. They waited until it was much darker than it had been the night before when Conal came down. The conversation died down as sunset passed.

"What happens if he doesn't come until tomorrow?" Laig asked. The thought had crossed Ferdia's mind, too. Was four days closer to three than two? Past that came the thought he did not want to think at all—what if he never came? What if the dark world he feared claimed him entirely?

"There he is," Elenn said, pointing. And there was Darag, making his way slowly down.

"Greetings, Darag, first among the young champions of Oriel," Maga said as he came down among them.

He looked dazed. He ignored her entirely and went up to Ferdia, who let him lean on his arm. "Get me to where I can sleep safely," he muttered.

"Darag's very tired, he needs to sleep before he talks," Ferdia said as loudly and decisively as he could. Nobody argued. "Are you wounded?" he asked quietly.

"Nothing to make a fuss about," Darag said. "I just need to rest."

He and Laig supported Darag back to the hall. They took him to the room where they had been sleeping and undressed him. He let them do it, he was almost asleep already. He was cold, and wounded in several places by what seemed to be teeth and claws as well as a sword. Laig insisted it was his place as charioteer to sing over the wounds, so Ferdia let him. They wrapped Darag in warm blankets, and Ferdia lay down beside him so he could share his warmth with his friend. Laig lay down on Darag's other side, and they all three stayed like that all night, not going into the hall to eat.

In the morning, Darag woke very early, in the first light of dawn. He woke Ferdia by laughing.

"There can't be anything much wrong if you're giggling like that," Ferdia said, deeply relieved.

"You were snoring low and Laig was snoring high," Darag said. Laig was still snoring, proving Darag's point.

"So what happened?" Ferdia asked.

"Oh, lots of strange things," Darag said dismissively.

"You'll have to do better than that when you tell your story in the hall," Ferdia said.

"Nive's hair, is that what she's making us do? What happened with the others? I know I was last down and won. I wasn't quite so far out of it as that."

"Leary lasted one day, Conal two. They both thought they'd done three. Leary fought a monster and some warriors. Conal had some very strange adventures, including seeing himself as an old man and meeting an ogre who cut off his head," Ferdia said.

"Bachlach," Darag said. "He cut off mine, and I knelt for him to do it. I'll mention him. There's ever such a lot I won't say, though, daren't say to Maga." He yawned. "I think I'll sleep a little more now. I didn't sleep a wink for three days. I'll tell you all about it when I wake up again."

He put his head down and was asleep again almost at once. Ferdia lay propped up on his elbow, feeling happy and proud, watching over Darag as he slept.

# 6

# THE SUITORS

# — 21 —

## (CONAL)

Conal took a deep breath and smiled pleasantly. Nobody was looking at him except Inis, but he had to be ready for Maga. It was half a month before the Feast of Bel and he was back in Connat again, trying to prevent a full-scale war after four anguished months at home. It had taken all his powers of persuasion even to get Conary to agree to let him come.

Orlam was pacing all around the little house where the four of them had been left to wait. "They can't do this to us," she said, touching her hand to the green leaves on the spray of beech pinning her cloak together. Conal glanced down at his matching one for a second.

Ap Carbad, who, as senior herald, had carried the large branch all the way from Ardmachan, shook his head. "If word goes out that Maga has abused heralds, she will lose her allies, and if she were to kill us, Conary would in honor be bound to invade Connat," he said. "But we are only being kept waiting, not abused so far."

"Her allies might not take any notice," Conal said. "They're panting at the prospect of carving up Oriel." He would never have believed things could be so bad. A year ago, he had fought off Atha's attack. Now Atha was their only ally, and depending on what Beastmother's threat had meant, Oriel might be about to be destroyed. Suffer, he thought for the thousandth time, turning it over in his mind. Suffer as the mare suffered. The mare had *died*. Would they all die in the first battle? Or die as soon as the border was crossed? Or would they all be in some way struck down, transformed and helpless as his dreams told him? In some ways, that would be the worst of all.

Ap Carbad sighed. "Can a kingdom be carved up like a cow?" Immediately, Conal's overactive mind offered up the image of Amagien carving the cow at Edar. The first among the young champions. His father would never forgive him for losing, never. He would never forgive himself. He felt sick at the memory. "Would the gods allow it?"

Inis looked up. "Kingdoms can be lost. The victors make a new peace with the gods of the land. This is how our ancestors took Tir Isarnagiri. It isn't even difficult. A man and a woman lie together on the earth and call on the gods to answer, and the world changes, names change. The land gods listen to the king, whoever the king is, and that is one way to make a kingdom."

"But the law prevents such wars," Orlam said gently. "Unless there is cause for a bloodfeud, and there is no such cause here. No cause at all."

"The law is what we have come to call on," ap Carbad said. "We will tell Maga that she will be placed under the Ban if she takes advantage of our weakness to invade for her own power."

"It will be enforced," Orlam said. "It might be little comfort to us afterwards, but they are sure at Rathadun. And the threat of the Ban ought to be enough to prevent Maga from this course."

"Or anyone," ap Carbad said. "Why do people risk such wars, dead against the Ward?"

"Feuds, or invasions of strangers," Inis said, and his eyes had that glaze that meant he was looking across the worlds. "Or the Ward may be broken. All these things are coming, too. Soon, but not yet. Maga is enough for now, and set on her purposes."

Conal had about a thousand questions, but he knew better than to ask his grandfather. "That's not cheering news," he said. Inis grinned.

Ap Carbad frowned. "That Beastmother is ready to destroy all of us for breaking our covenants with the animals is hardly cheering news either," he said sternly. "Don't make remarks like that to Maga. I told Conary you were the wrong choice for this mission. Too young and frivolous." He sniffed.

"My father said the same," Conal said and smiled.

Orlam whirled around. "Can we stop having this stupid argument? We're all heralds of Oriel. We need to be united. Conal is here and will do what he can. Conary wanted to send a nephew. Darag is . . . busy, and my brother would hardly be appropriate."

Being as it was all Leary's fault that Maga knew about their weakness, to be sure. Conal would have replied with an attempt to conciliate ap Carbad, but the door opened and a champion of Connat came in. "Come to the Lower Hall, Maga will see you now," he said, bowing.

They followed him out in silence.

The Lower Hall was crowded. Maga and Allel sat together on a bench at one end, their three children standing behind them. Conal didn't look at anything else for a while, for there was Emer, Emer at last. His heart rose at the sight of her after so long. She looked tired and sad, and her face was pulled down where her scar was. He longed to hold her, to smooth her cheek, to get into a chariot with her and drive far away. She smiled when their eyes met, which was enough to let him know that everything was all right. Then she looked away.

To her right stood two priests, one middle-aged, his shawl folded tidily, the other very old, her white hair so thin that it hardly showed where it was cut for the gods. Her eyes were very dark and alert, moving over the crowd. To Maga's left stood a man who must be her lawspeaker. He was smiling at Orlam. Next to him was ap Dair the Poet. Conal looked over the crowd and was surprised to meet Ferdia's eyes. He looked bemused, as so often. Conal felt a little sorry for him. Next to Ferdia was his father, Cethern of Lagin. He was looking at the heralds appraisingly. His uncle Lew of Anlar was there, too, dressed in armor, avoiding Conal's eyes. Things were very bad if even Anlar had deserted Oriel. Yet Lew's being here in the hall might be good. All of the leaders of Maga's allies must be here, and some of their champions as well as most of hers. Perhaps it would be possible to shame her in front of them.

After they had been given heralds' welcomes and safe-conducts, ap Carbad spoke first as they had agreed, holding up his big beech branch.

"We have heard that you intend to make war on Oriel, and King Conary would know why."

Maga smiled. Conal didn't like to look at Maga. He had expected her to look like Elenn, but she didn't. When she smiled like that, she looked like a twisted version of Emer. It was painful to see. "That's easily answered," she said. "We do not intend to make war."

Ap Carbad was silent for a moment, clearly taken aback. "Then we have been misinformed," he said in a tone of doubt.

"And all these military preparations we saw as we came south?" Conal asked, his tone one of polite inquiry.

Maga laughed. Conal looked away from her. Elenn, he noticed, was looking into the crowd. Mingor and Allel both looked at Maga with approval. Emer was frowning and staring at her feet. "We are planning a cattle raid," Maga said, spreading her hands. "You see, my husband has a wonderful bull, and I would have one to match it for my herds. I have heard that Amagien the Poet has a truly wonderful bull, famed in song, at his farm of Edar." Her eyes rested on Conal for a moment, full of contempt and triumph. "We have decided to go raiding up through Oriel until we should reach our prize or be stopped. There is nothing in the law against that, is there, lawspeaker?" She was so smug she was almost purring. A ripple of laughter ran around the court. Most of their arguments were demolished by this outrageous claim. A raid was different from a war.

"Not if you keep the law," Orlam said evenly.

"Of course we will keep the law," Maga said. "But if we were to find our way undefended, then we might keep what we had taken. This would not be against the law. It would not be a feud where all must die and no prisoners be taken."

Conal could see it already. They were as good as dead. Or, possibly, enslaved if the curse did not kill them. But Inis turned to him and winked.

Then Inis took a half-step forward. He took off his shawl, shook it, and settled it again on his shoulders. There was something about the way he did this which was compelling. Conal darted a glance away and saw that almost the whole room was watching Inis. The other priests, both of them, rearranged their own shawls. Nobody else moved at all. With one hand on his herald's branch and the other outstretched, palm downward, Inis spoke at last.

"Will you send many against one?" he asked.

There was a silence. "Of course not," Allel answered, glancing sideways at Maga, who looked uncomfortable but stared at Inis with the rest.

"Will you skulk in the woods and go around defended roads?" Inis asked.

"Never," Allel answered. "We will fight by the rules of war. Do you think we have no honor?"

Inis swayed a little as if he were absorbing the force of the direct question. "You have honor, Allel ap Dallan, but does your king?" he answered. "Will she stand by your words?"

"Allel is my war-leader," Maga said. "Such choices are his."

"Do you stand by his words, Maga ap Arcan?" Inis asked.

"Yes," Maga said. "We will not send many against one. We will not go around defended roads. Not that I think there will be many defended roads."

"There are only two roads from Connat into Oriel," ap Carbad said, stating the obvious.

"One with deep water and the other lined with thorns," Inis agreed, which was more poetry than sense. Conal had come by the one with deep water this time. The ford had been very pleasant in the sunshine. He had gone home by way of the one lined by thorns last time, and found it an ordinary wooded road.

"Two will be enough," Maga said.

Conal was afraid she was right. But Inis looked insanely cheerful, so maybe it had not been enough in other worlds. He couldn't see how. Even if they had two people who could fight, who could fight all these champions, even one at a time? Maybe Inis was just too crazy to care.

There was a feast for them that night. Conal kept trying to speak to Emer, but he couldn't get near her. He was seated with Inis and Maga and Elenn. Emer was off in the opposite alcove with her father and Orlam and ap Carbad.

"So nice to be able to talk to you again, ap Amagien," Maga said as she served the meat. "How very kind of Conary to send a nephew, even if he couldn't spare his heir."

Conal wondered if Maga could possibly know what Darag was doing right now. He smiled at her as best he could. "I will have to suffice," he said. He glanced over at the opposite alcove. There was an advantage to this seating. Ap Carbad couldn't possibly hear anything he said. "Besides, I had another reason for wanting to come. I want to negotiate with you about my marrying your younger daughter, my charioteer, Emer." He took a bite of his venison and smiled at her around it.

"Does Conary agree?" Maga asked.

"He does," Conal said. It had been a hard fought battle, and he had often wished Emer was there to help. Conary liked Emer. "He has written to you ceasing the negotiations for her to marry Darag and asking about this. Have you not received the letter?"

"And what about your dear parents?" Maga asked, sidestepping that question entirely.

Conal would rather not have been asked that. "They will raise no objection," he said, stretching the truth a little thin. They would raise no more objections if faced with an actual marriage, anyway. At least he hoped not.

"Then it is a pity," Maga said, biting her lip as if she meant it. "Only this past month I have agreed a different alliance for Emer. I thought that since Conary was no longer offering Darag and since an alliance with Oriel didn't suit my plans, I should look elsewhere. Might you be interested in Elenn instead?" She gestured to Elenn, who was eating neatly. She was dressed beautifully, as always. She gave him a look that had daggers in it, but said nothing.

Conal raised his eyebrows to indicate that he didn't believe a word of what Maga said. "You astonish me," he said. Inis let out his high-pitched cackle.

"What, ap Amagien, with the news that it is my ugly daughter and not my beautiful one who is first betrothed?" Maga asked. "But Elenn has not yet taken up arms."

Conal was so furious that he was almost glad to be freed of the constraints of politeness. "Why, you wrong yourself and the daughter who inherited your looks," he said. "Elenn is something out of the ordinary, of course, hair like black night and eyes like stars as my father's poem puts it. But Emer is not ugly, indeed she is better than plain. As you also must have been when you were young."

For a moment, he saw that he had really angered Maga, and rejoiced. Inis sat contemplating them, a smile on his lips. Elenn was shrinking back against the wall as if to avoid a blow. Then Maga leaned forward toward him and smiled. "Conal," she said, and hearing his name on her lips was shocking, showing they had left behind even feigned politeness. "You have made me an offer. Now tell me what it gains me to marry my daughter to you?"

"Peace with Oriel," he said.

Maga laughed scornfully. "That is not something I wish to gain. She could be a queen. She could give me a kingdom."

"She could yet be a queen married to me. The choice of the Kin of Oriel has not been made. There are many chances in the world." Even as he said it, Conal realized that he didn't believe it anymore. Darag would be king, and his sons after him. Nothing he could do would be enough.

Maga raised her eyebrows in scornful doubt. "Is that the best you can offer?" she asked. "Then listen to me, Conal. Oriel is doomed. You're clever enough to see that. It is mine already. It isn't even going to exist when my cattle raid is over. Come and join me. You can be one of my champions, fighting for me and for Connat, living in my hall. This isn't very much gain for a daughter, but I am prepared to accept it."

Conal looked away from Maga's eager face. Inis was staring into the invisible distance. Elenn's lips were parted in astonishment.

He couldn't possibly agree. He could hardly believe she thought he had so little honor that he might take her offer seriously. Nobody would. Still, saying that would gain him nothing. He looked across the room. Emer was talking to Orlam. He glanced at Inis and saw that his grandfather was bright eyed again, watching him. He took another bite of his venison, chewed and swallowed, then looked back at Maga.

"I will say nothing now to your proposal. Let me talk to Emer."

"Then talk to her," Maga said. "But this offer is made reluctantly and at her request."

"She has done nothing but beg to be allowed to marry you since she came home," Elenn said. Maga spared Elenn an irritated glance and looked back at Conal.

"You can speak to her after dinner," she said.

They continued their meal in silence, broken only by Inis's occasional humming. When Conal got up to go to Emer, his grandfather put his hand on his shoulder. Conal looked at him, but he said nothing, just let him go again.

The musicians were getting ready to sing, and servants were pouring out more ale as Conal crossed the room. "Your mother said I can speak to you," he said, leaning on Emer's shoulder. "Where can we go?"

"Outside," Emer said, rising at once.

Allel smiled at them benignly. Ap Carbad frowned and muttered something quietly to Orlam. Conal bowed and followed Emer out of the hall.

Emer greeted the guard at the door and led Conal through the village toward the stables. The night was overcast and damp and the ground was muddy. It wasn't easy to see where they were going. They walked in silence.

It was even darker inside the stables. There was a smell of horses and of hay and damp springtime, and then Emer was in his arms and he was intoxicated by the scent of her. They held each other for a long moment, murmuring nonsense and affirmations.

"Did Conary agree?" Emer asked after a little while.

"It wasn't easy, but he did in the end," Conal said. "And I see you got your mother to agree to something, but it isn't something I can possibly consider."

"My parents have been fighting about it," Emer said. "That you become a champion of Connat is supposed to be a compromise. I know how impossible it is."

"I feel terrible for having left you here all this time with them," he said. "I didn't realize until tonight how awful she is. We'll have to run away. I think we could go to Muin. or, failing that, right away across the sea to seek our fortunes in other lands." The thought was enticing. Traveling together had been a joy. He wished they could start at once.

Emer hugged him tighter. "I never thought you'd say that," she said, so quietly he could hardly hear her. "But we can't, you know we can't. Not now. Maga won't turn aside for anything. You can't desert Oriel now, and it would be the same if you agreed to Maga's offer or if we ran away. You couldn't live without honor."

"You're right," Conal said, his heart sinking. "Well, if I must die, at least you should know that I love you more than breath."

Emer kissed him, and if he had to die, he wished he could die in that moment. "I don't think you need to die," she said breathlessly. "I have been talking to ap Fial, our priest, and he seems to think that the most likely thing is that all the fighting folk of Oriel will fall sick for a span of time, three days, or maybe six or nine days. After that, they will be well again. And Inis ap Fathag, may the Lord of Healing let him see many more summers, has made Maga say in front of everyone that she won't cheat. So it ought to be possible to hold the roads for that long."

"Who could?" Conal asked. A horse shifted nearby and another sent out a whuffle that sounded inquiring

"You and me, if you can fight. But if not, anyone who will fight. I've been thinking about it. There are bound to be exceptions. Probably it will only strike champions. Maybe the farmers will be able to fight. And then there are people like your father who would hardly count as fighting folk of Oriel but who can fight. And . . ." She hesitated, then kissed him again.

"Ap Fial might be wrong, but he seemed to think that Darag would be able to fight because his father is a god."

"Darag's father?" Conal asked blankly.

"They're calling him Black Darag here because of the way he was black with blood when he came down from the heights," Emer said.

"Why does ap Fial think his father was a god?" Conal's voice seemed to echo in his ears in the darkness. He clutched at Emer as if he were drowning.

"I expect he saw it across the worlds," Emer said. "You should ask Inis. But he thinks Darag will be able to fight and hold one of the roads."

"And Atha can hold the other," Conal said.

"Atha? Can you trust her that far? She might take the whole country if nobody can stop her."

"She's married to Darag. While we're down here. Today, in Ardmachan. It should be done by now. She won't be bringing troops from the Isles, her mother won't countenance it, but she'll be there herself. But could anyone hold a road for nine days? Against everyone, even one at a time?"

"I will go and help," Emer said. "As soon as the war starts, I will run away and find you, and help hold the road."

"Maga will be furious with you," Conal said.

"I will do it in disguise, so she doesn't know who I am. If she did, she's perfectly capable of kidnapping me, to stop me. Then afterward, when Oriel is safe, we can go right away and change our names and leave everything behind. We could go to Tir Tanagiri, to King Urdo. My mother has told me that his sister is plotting against him, we could tell him that and warn him and he might accept us as champions. After three years, we can marry without needing our parents' blessings."

"Come away with me now," he said. "When we leave tomorrow. Don't stay here with her another day."

"She would call that an abduction and cause for a feud between Connat and Oriel," Emer said sadly. "But once the war has started, she won't miss me in the daytime as long as I am here to eat at night."

They held each other for another long moment. "You are so brave," Conal said, already feeling the pain of the thought that she could die holding the road for Oriel. "I will always love you," he said.

"I love you," Emer said. "What will you tell Maga?"

"That I cannot in honor desert Oriel now, but that we shall see what time brings." Conal shrugged. "It is not a lie."

"You must get Conary to bring his fighting folk south before the Feast of Bel, so that after the three or six or nine days, they will be there where they are needed," Emer said.

"Unless it is thirty days, or ninety," Conal said. "Even nine days is a terribly long time."

"On the other side of it, we will be together," Emer said. He squeezed her in silence, trying to believe in another side of the perilous gulf that lay ahead of them.

# —22—

## (ELENN)

It should have been lovely. They were going to defeat Oriel, but Lagin was allied to them. Ferdia was here. The good thing about everyone in Oriel being struck down by the curse would be that nobody got hurt. They had a big army ready, her father said, in case the farmers came out to fight. Her mother said the big army was to keep their allies happy and to glorify Connat. But in any case, no champions of Oriel were supposed to die, and none of Connat either, none of her friends, none of the people who she had smiled at when they opened the gates for her. The army went out of Cruachan on the morning after the Feast of Bel, all in a long stream, chariots ahead and farmers following along behind in little clumps. The champions were painted and armored for war. Many of them had banners flying. Most of the banners were the naked man of Connat, black against blue, but among them flew the bramble of Muin, red on black, the raven of Anlar, black on white, and the green hill of Lagin. War seemed a splendid thing when she stood at the gate of Cruachan and waved them off.

But it was all wrong already. By sundown, they were not even across the border of Oriel, and they had thirteen bodies to burn and sing the Hymn of Return for. She hadn't known it, but it had all gone wrong from the moment that Inis tricked her mother into agreeing not to go around the two roads. That meant there were only two ways they could get into Oriel. That shouldn't have mattered, but both roads were held against them. They were astonished when the news was first brought back to them.

First they heard that the road through the woods was guarded by Atha ap Gren. It wasn't such a surprise as it might have been, because they'd had the news that she had recently married Darag in a great hurry. The Isles had promised not to send support even so, they knew Connat was going to win. But Atha was there, and not alone.

Allel told them about it at dinner. The family were eating in a tent
out near the border, where the whole army was encamped. They were
alone in the tent except for the champion Nandran ap Roth. Dinner was
scant, bread and cheese brought up hastily from Cruachan. Maga had
expected to be halfway to Ardmachan by now, living off the land.

"They waited, hidden in the woods, until the army of Connat and its
allies advanced onto the soil of Oriel. Then we heard cries, letting us
know that the curse had fallen on the waiting folk of Oriel. But even as
we rejoiced, Atha and her companions fired their deadly slingshots and
some of our champions fell to the ground. Others had to stop as chariots
up ahead collapsed as their horses stumbled, legs broken. Then Atha came
out in her chariot, with a charioteer. I asked her why she was there fighting us, when we had no quarrel with the Isles. She said she was married
to Darag. I asked about her charioteer and companions. She laughed and
said that every bride may bring her handmaidens from home. She said she
had brought twelve handmaidens, all chosen for such fine womanly skills
as she had thought she might have need of in Oriel."

Allel sounded almost admiring. Nandran had a smile on his face, too.
Mingor shook his head a little. Elenn didn't see what was so good about
it.

"What did you do then?" she asked.

"Oh, she waited in the middle of the road and called out for honorable
single combats, one against one as we had promised ap Fathag. My nephew
Bran demanded the honor of fighting her, which I granted. He went
forward to fight her and died almost at once, a spear through his heart."
Allel paused. "Then a champion of Muin came forward and fought her,
a woman called Samar ap Ardan, one of the war-leaders, very experienced,
with many heads on her chariot, but old for a champion, with gray in her
hair. They fought for quite a while before Atha killed her. This was dis-
couraging for the rest of our champions. Atha has a formidable reputation.
Nobody was pressing to come forward to fight against her. I decided to
leave half the army there to keep her there and take the others to the
other road."

"Dithering," Maga snapped. "Showing weakness."

"It should have worked," Allel said mildly. "We went on until we
reached the ford on the other road. On the far side of it were some folk
of Oriel, standing beside the road looking very weak and unhappy, and
in front of them was Darag, fit and well, in his chariot. His charioteer was
disguised, a scarf over her face. There was no way of telling who she was,
not even by the way she moved or stood. She did not speak."

Emer opened her mouth, but closed it again when her father gave her a stern look. Elenn wondered who it could be and why she would need a disguise.

"We were astonished to see Darag, much more than Atha. Atha belonged to the Isles when the curse was spoken, and maybe even now. But Darag is unquestionably one of the fighting folk of Oriel. I asked him why he was here and not laid low. He answered that it seemed he had his father to thank for that, whoever his father might be."

"Who is his father?" Nandran asked.

"Nobody knows," Maga said. "His mother was unmarried, and he was born at the Feast of the Mother. Nobody ever knew Dechtir to care about any man except her brother Conary."

Elenn didn't want to say anything; she especially didn't want to make Maga angry, but she couldn't help remembering Darag's face when he'd talked to her at the Feast of Bel last year. "Everyone knows the gods go to the festivals sometimes," she said quietly. "If he's not been struck down, it's more likely because his father is a god than anything unnatural."

"Incest is hateful to the gods," Nandran agreed. He looked at Elenn worshipfully. She smiled at him. He was only two years older than Mingor, but already he was acknowledged the greatest champion in Cruachan. He would have been handsome if it hadn't been for his scars. A few years ago, she used to think he was wonderful. It was nice that he looked at her like that even though she must look a mess. She still had her hair straggling loose around her face from the funeral.

"Go on," Maga directed Allel.

"Darag demanded single combats, exactly as Atha had. Eleven men went against him before the light went, eleven champions, and all of them he killed or wounded. Only one of them struck him, wounding him in the upper thigh. He recovered from it rapidly."

"So what tomorrow?" Mingor asked.

"The same," Allel said.

"The same except that someone will kill Darag or Atha, and the army will move forward as we planned," Maga said impatiently.

"Atha is a famous warrior in the prime of her life," Allel said. "Darag is young and relatively untried, but he did remarkably well today. Even though they are fighting alone against us all, we must fight them one at a time, so it might not be as easy as you think to get past them."

"I have heard that Darag once played hurley alone against all of the children of Ardmachan," Mingor said.

Maga frowned at him. "We have such a large army," she said. "Some champion will bring them down. Let us send champions against both of them until one of them falls."

Allel looked at Nandran, who looked away. Elenn waited for him to say that he would kill Atha. She hoped it would be Atha, who was loud and rude and thought herself better than everyone else. She liked Darag. She realized abruptly that war was horrible when it came to killing people. She remembered the Ward, the vow that Maga had renewed only yesterday. How could you have strife without bitterness if you were killing people, one against another?

She wanted Connat to win, of course, but her cousin Bran was dead. Dead, never again to laugh and flirt with her or try to get her to go for walks with him outside the dun. Even now, his soul would be moving through the underworld, giving back his life, ready to come out and be reborn. He'd have to go through childhood again somewhere else, as someone else. It would be twenty years before he was again as old and wise as he had been this morning. He would never again be Bran of Cruachan, or know that he had been. His soul was passing through the underworld and all his memories were being given back with his name. Poor Bran. Or worse, maybe Atha had taken his head, and one of his souls would live on trapped inside it as one of her protectors. Either way was terribly sad. She wondered suddenly how Darag felt. Atha had killed people before, but Darag hadn't.

Nandran had still not said anything, and the silence was becoming awkward. "What's it like to kill people?" Elenn asked. Everyone turned to stare at her. Nandran looked embarrassed. Maga looked curious. Allel looked tired.

"Easier than you would think," Emer said. "Like in practice, only doing it for real."

"I didn't mean that," she said, not able to say what she meant, knowing it was a childish question, an unanswerable question, something she shouldn't have said. Maybe it was even one of the things that had been explained sometime when she had been sitting dreaming with her ears turned off. She struggled to explain. "I was thinking about Bran, so alive this morning, dead now. What it is to do that to someone."

"When you're in battle, you know they'd do it to you unless you do it first," Emer said.

"And there's usually no time to think anyway," Mingor said. "That's what Emer means about it being like practice. You know what to do, you do it, you don't think. Especially you don't think about that sort of thing, that they are alive and so are you, and soon one of you will be dead, good-bye to everyone, down into the dark and everything to learn again."

"Did Atha take his head?" she asked, wanting to know now.

"Yes," Allel said.

"I took the head of the man I killed at Edar," Emer said. "It is protecting Conal's chariot even now. His family wanted to ransom it, but I wouldn't."

"I don't know how you could," Elenn said.

"Your older daughter is as gentle as she is beautiful," Nandran said to Allel. "If you will let me marry her, I will kill Darag for you."

Elenn went cold all through. She liked Nandran. But she loved Ferdia. Surely Maga wouldn't agree, surely she couldn't. She had told Conal that Elenn could not marry before she had taken up arms. But she had been negotiating shadow marriage alliances all spring.

Allel looked at Maga uncertainly.

"Do we need to bargain with our champions now?" Maga asked, looking down her nose.

"Darag killed eleven of your champions today," Nandran said. "People fight because they want to win. Let me put it the other way around—if I kill Darag and open the road to Oriel as an offering to lay at her feet, might I hope to marry your daughter?" He smiled shyly at Elenn, as if it were all agreed between them and they had only to convince her parents. She smiled back, chilled at heart but unable to say anything.

"Kill Darag and I will entertain your suit," Maga said.

Elenn did not faint. She continued to sit and smile for the whole evening. She went to bed, keeping Beauty with her in the tent, which wasn't allowed now that Beauty was bigger. She knew Emer would not complain about it. She hardly slept all night, even with the comfort of Beauty's presence. She didn't know what to think. She tried to console herself. Marrying Nandran would not be such a terrible thing after all. She liked him. She could stay at home. But in the dark hours, she realized that this was not what she wanted. She wanted to leave Cruachan, to get away from Maga.

When she did fall asleep, her dreams were confused nightmares. She kissed Nandran before he got into his chariot, boasting he would kill Darag and marry her. She kissed his cold lips when they brought his body back. He became an empty armor coat, which she feared and loathed, but Maga laughed when she saw it. She was hunting through a press of people on the top of Ardmachan, looking for Ferdia. At last she saw him through the crowd, but when she pushed her way to him, she found that he was hollowed out from within and there was nothing inside his skin.

She woke to find it still dark. Emer was asleep and snoring gently. She dressed quietly in the darkness. Beauty was asleep, too, but woke quickly when Elenn roused her, making hardly any protest, her tail thumping enthusiastically. They crawled out of the tent. It was not long before dawn. A chilly wind was blowing, she clutched her cloak around her. People were sleeping everywhere, in tents or wrapped in cloaks, but nobody else seemed to be awake. She could walk away, pick her way between the sleeping champions, walk right away from Nandran and Maga and everyone. Emer would be so surprised when she woke up. But where would she go? Where was there a place for her in the world?

Beauty pushed her nose into Elenn's hand. She hardly had to jump up at all now, she had grown so much. She was half her full size already. Elenn stroked her head absently, staring into the darkness. There wasn't anywhere to go, nowhere out in the wide world for a princess and her dog. Worse, Maga didn't mean well for her. She couldn't be trusted. Maga always said she knew best, and Elenn had believed it, or tried to believe it. Maga loved her, of course she did. She pulled Beauty's ears, making the dog wriggle with delight. She couldn't say no to Maga, she knew she couldn't. It was bad enough for Maga that Emer was defying her all the time since they came home. Elenn had to do what she said. But that meant she was in Maga's power, for good or ill. Maga had said to Conal that a champion was a small gain to her for the loss of a daughter, which made it seem as if to Maga her daughters were something to be spent. She didn't want to be spent for her mother's goals.

She wondered if she could go out into the night and find Darag and persuade him to make peace. She had no sooner thought it than she knew how ridiculous it was. He hadn't sought this war. Maga had. Her mother and father and everyone else thought it was a wonderful idea. They could stop it if they changed their minds, but Darag couldn't. They had talked about the wealth of Oriel, the gold and the weapons—and the real wealth of course, the cows and the land. Darag was only defending his home.

The sky was growing a little paler. Day was coming. Maga never changed her mind once she had really made it up. There was nowhere to go, and besides, her mother needed her. She should go back to the tent and sleep so that she would not look terrible when she waved the army off again in the real morning. She kept telling herself this, but she didn't move, just stood there with Beauty as if she thought something was going to change.

# —23—

## (EMER)

The streaming clouds in the western sky were red-lit as the sun slipped down between them. On the other side of the stream, Darag was taking an ax to the throat of Trivan ap Cunegan, whose mother was Allel's charioteer Iross. Maga had never liked Trivan. For once, she would be pleased at another day's delay, assuming Atha had held her road.

Emer felt as if she had been beaten all over. She could hardly drag herself out of the chariot to stretch. She was covered in bruises and healed wounds. The grass under the trees looked temptingly soft. She could have flung herself down on it and slept for three days without waking. She stretched, loosening her muscles, but the ache went bone-deep.

She was sickened by the whole thing. She had not thought what it would mean to be killing her friends and kinfolk, or rather, helping Darag to kill them. Trivan had fought Atha on the second day and survived, badly wounded. As soon as she was fully recovered, she had come against Darag, wanting the glory. The cold comfort in seeing Trivan dead was knowing that at least one of the champions who had come against them today had not done it dreaming of Elenn. Far too many of them seemed to have taken up the cult of Elenn's perfection and longed to die for her or win her. There was something unwholesome about it, especially the delight Maga took in it.

She wished she could have warned Trivan how good Darag was. Trivan was ten years older than Emer. She had been a fire hurley player. Emer had always been a little in awe of her. She had spoken up against Maga in council. She was one of the Royal Kin of Connat. Her grandfather was Allel's father's brother, she was a cousin. If Emer had killed her, it would have been kinmurder. All she had done was hold the horses steady; Darag had killed her with his first thrown spear. In any normal situation, even if they had been fighting on different sides of a battle, she wouldn't have gone against her cousin.

Darag smiled up at Emer as he waded back across the stream. The Oriel side was higher than the Connat side, and fringed by willow trees. This was to their advantage when they were waiting; it gave them shade and some relief from the flies. He climbed out up the side of the ford. "You look tired. I wouldn't wonder if we feel as bad as everyone else tonight, and nobody is envious of us."

She smiled back feebly. "I can't come back with you now, there's no time," she said.

Darag glanced at the sun and then over at the massed champions of Connat, who were clearly milling about preparing to go back to camp. Trivan's charioteer was carrying her headless body towards Allel.

"She was the last challenge of the day," he said, swinging Trivan's head by its hair. "You could spare an hour. It cheers Conal so much to see you."

Emer couldn't say that it didn't cheer her to see him, though it was the truth. She could never have imagined strong Conal struck down and made feeble, groaning in pain, hardly able to stand. Still less would she have imagined her own squeamishness. She could bear battle and death, but sickness and pain were different, especially Conal's pain which she could do nothing to help. Seeing him on the other nights had been terrible. His face was drawn and lined, and every so often he drew in his breath as he endured another pain. He said it felt like being knifed in the belly, but it ran through him like cramps. The whole host of Oriel was in the same state. Finca seemed to take it best of all of them, hardly wincing even when the pain was so bad she had to hold on to a tree in order to stand up. Emer didn't want to see them again. Today had been bad enough already. Until she could see Conal restored to himself, it was unendurably painful to see him at all.

"They will miss me at the camp if I don't hurry back," she said, although there had been no sign so far that they had missed her.

"I do really appreciate your doing this," Darag said. "I know Conal does, and Conary, too. All of Oriel."

"All of Oriel doesn't know, and needn't if all goes well. Don't thank me yet," Emer said, looking resolutely away from the head in his hand. She was glad of the scarf over her face, hiding her expression.

Sometimes, fighting with him, free from the thought of having to marry him, she could almost like Darag. Other times, he still made her skin crawl. He knew who Trivan was, he knew she was Emer's cousin, but still he stood there swinging her head as if she were nothing more to either of them than another guardian for the chariot. It had plenty of them already, too many of them people she had liked.

"We've got through three days," Darag said. "Ap Carbad said we'd never do that. Maybe it will end tonight. But anyway, I'll see you here in the morning?"

"Of course," she said. She had promised Conal she would do it, even if she had not thought what it meant to belong to both sides at once. They would put her name in the lists as a traitor if this were ever known. If the curse were over tomorrow, she would hear it from Darag. She did

not believe it would be. Some part of her did not believe it would ever
be over. Life would keep this pattern, killing her own people day after
day, and she would never have enough rest.

She spat on the ground and called on the Wise Lady's help against
self-pity as she came under the shade of the trees. She changed out of her
armor, leaving it there for Darag to retrieve for cleaning later. At least
there were plenty of hale people to do that. She tucked the scarf inside
her helmet. Then she dressed in the clothes she had left bundled up that
morning. She made her way through the trees downstream to the other
crossing point she had found lower down.

When she slipped into their tent, Elenn was combing her hair. Beauty
was sitting at her feet. They both turned to look at Emer as she came in.
"Where have you been?" Elenn asked.

"Around," Emer said, lying down on the comfortable mound of
heather that was her bed. She didn't need to change her clothes, they had
hardly been worn. "Do I have time for a nap before dinner?"

"No!" Elenn sounded impatient. "Get the leaves out of your hair. If
you've been in the woods all day, you won't have heard, but can't you
even see what I'm wearing?"

Emer opened her eyes and looked. Elenn's overdress was one of
Maga's, a very pale yellow. On her shoulders she was settling a tightly
woven shawl, the warp red and the weft yellow. The effect was bridal
orange.

"She's letting you marry Ferdia?" Emer asked, bouncing up off the
bed and feeling the stiffness in all her bones.

Elenn's face closed up like a flower at sunset. "No. Neither Ferdia
nor Cethern have asked. A new alliance."

"I didn't think she'd go as far as marriage unless someone actually
opened the road into Oriel," Emer said, then regretted it at once as the
calm mask of her sister's face cracked and for a moment, she saw the
anguish beneath.

"Neither did I," said Elenn, and her voice had tears not far behind it.
She swallowed. "But Firbaith ap Gren has come, come by sea. Maga thinks
Atha will have to withdraw if her brother tells her to."

"That's nonsense," Emer said. "I met Firbaith when I was in the Isles.
I got the feeling he'd make a fine king one day, because unlike Atha, he
can do things other than fight. He'll probably make you an excellent
husband, though I suppose he must be nearly thirty. But the thought that
Atha would listen to him, or to anyone, is nonsense."

"But it's Mother's kind of nonsense," Elenn said, picking up the comb
again. "It is an alliance, and of the kind she most wants. At least I'll get
away."

"And it means she'll have to stop promising you to people as a sort of prize for killing Darag," Emer said.

Elenn ran the comb through her hair, though it was smooth and shining already. "Firbaith has promised her that as well as the alliance, he will open a road into Oriel. If Atha won't obey, that means he'll have to fight Darag."

"How awful for Darag to have to kill his wife's brother," Emer said without thinking, Trivan's face in her mind, dangling by the hair from Darag's hand.

"You might consider that he could win," Elenn said, flinging the comb down. Beauty whined and put her nose in Elenn's lap. "Do you think I like the thought of being married to someone who is about to die?" she asked more quietly.

"Yes, of course he could win," Emer said quickly. "He's not as noted a warrior as Atha, but Atha would tend to overshadow anyone. Firbaith has a good reputation." She was surprised that he'd agreed to anything so silly as opening a road; his reputation was for good sense. Darag was so terribly good, almost inhumanly good. Even though she had practiced near him and seen him in contests all the last year, it was only now she was driving his chariot that she saw how good he was. It would be disloyal to think that he was better than Conal. But he was awfully good, and it seemed to come to him so easily. No wonder Conal resented it.

She pulled the leaves out of her hair, looking at her sister thoughtfully. Maybe, though she'd never say it, Elenn would be glad if Darag killed Firbaith, so she could marry Ferdia. But she didn't think so. Elenn's sense of duty was much stronger than that. Besides, Firbaith was a handsome man, and much more sensible than Ferdia. She had never been able to understand how it was that her sister had got so besotted with the sulky idiot in the first place.

Elenn tutted at Emer and put on the pearl circlet Orlam had given her. It looked magnificent. "It's almost time," she said. "Your hair will do."

"Time for the funerals?" Emer asked. "Darag killed Trivan, did you know?"

"Nobody told me, but somebody would have told me if she'd managed to kill him and open the road, so I suppose I knew. And right after the funerals comes the wedding."

"The actual wedding?" Emer was shocked. "Now? Tonight? Not just a betrothal?"

"Would I wear the shawl for a betrothal?" Elenn asked, smoothing it on her shoulders. The bridal color did not suit her as much as the colors she normally wore.

"People often do. Betrothal is a sacrament, too."

"Well, anyway, Firbaith wanted the real wedding tonight. After all, Atha is married to Darag. It'll give him moral authority talking to her." Elenn was clearly repeating something she'd been told. She stood up, stooping because of the tent, and Emer realized that she was shaking a little. Beauty stood, too, and paced beside her mistress.

"It'll be all right," Emer said clumsily.

Elenn put her hand out to Beauty, who licked it. She fussed at the dog, pulling her ears, not looking at Emer as she spoke. "I keep wishing Orlam could be here," she said. "I wanted to ask . . . have you and Conal . . ." She hesitated. "I mean, I've never . . ." she began, and trailed off again.

Emer felt like an old woman, immensely older than her sister, decades and centuries older. "Yes we have," she said. She stopped and looked for words for something which was mostly a wordless delight. "It's just as good as everyone says. It's a bit awkward at first, but then it's lovely. You just need to pay attention to how things feel and not be afraid. You think about making him feel good—and don't worry about asking if you're not sure. Then making you feel good is up to him. Most likely Firbaith knows all about it and can show you."

Elenn still wasn't looking up. "Thank you. That is a help. Ap Fial blessed my womb and told me about childbearing, but I didn't like to ask about that."

"What did he tell you about childbearing?" Emer asked, suddenly intensely curious. "I've always wanted to know."

Now Elenn looked up, her beautiful face sealed shut. "It's a mystery of the Mother," she said. "The sun is nearly down. We should go."

Emer followed her sister to the funeral pyres. They were in the same place they had been the other nights, just outside the camp. She tried to think of the fallen, but repetition had made the ceremony seem almost routine. Her body was exhausted but her mind could not be quiet. Even as they sang the Hymn of Return, it kept darting off to Conal, stricken, to love and death and the nature of betrayal. Afterwards ap Fial and their parents came over to them. Allel thrust a bough of blackthorn into Emer's arms. It was heavy with pink blossom, the heady scent hung on the air. He was carrying birch, and Maga silver fir.

"Where have you been all day?" Maga asked.

"Emer ap Allel has been helping weave the gods' will," ap Fial said, almost before Emer could wonder how to answer. Ap Fial frowned at Maga and drew his shawl tight around him.

"Well, you'll have to manage without her tomorrow," Maga said. "I need her."

"She must help daily while we stay here," ap Fial said, still looking very severe. "Without her, we would all be less than we could be."

Allel patted Maga's shoulder warningly. Maga looked as if she wanted to say more, and even question the priest. She looked angrily around. "The bridegroom is waiting," she said.

Emer went through her part in the ceremony as if in a dream. If she was doing the gods' will, then what could the gods possibly want? Beastmother had struck Oriel down. It didn't make sense. She had thought she was thwarting the gods. But then, she hadn't thought Maga would notice she was missing. As for ap Fial, how did he know? Oracle-priests could know anything, but did that mean she did this in other worlds? And was he betraying Connat in protecting her? The oracle-priests had their own loyalty, to the gods and the worlds, but he belonged to Connat as Inis belonged to Oriel.

Emer threw down her branch an instant after she should have, but Firbaith trod it down just as he should. It was a terribly rushed wedding, but all the omens were good, and at least Elenn would not be stuck here with Maga. If Emer was in Oriel, she could go to the Isles and visit sometimes, and Elenn and Firbaith would be bound to visit Atha and Darag. Emer could not make these thoughts more than empty wisps of plans that she knew would never come to be even as Firbaith kissed Elenn. He was as good as dead already, whether he knew it or not.

The feast was held out of doors around the campfires in the dusk. It was like a festival, everyone eating in sight of everyone else, except for those who were part of bloodfeuds who ate carefully apart, as always. Bloodfeuds were suspended for festivals, so anyone could eat with anyone.

Emer ate with her parents, Elenn and Firbaith, and Lew ap Ross of Anlar. She had no idea why Maga had singled him out for attention, but she was glad to see him; he seemed almost like an ally. His smile reminded her of Conal. They talked for a while of the contest and the journey she had made with the three princes of Oriel. She longed to ask him why he had abandoned his long-standing alliance with Oriel, but dared not. Maga seemed pleased that Emer was entertaining Lew and spoke mostly to Firbaith. Emer was glad to be overlooked again. She didn't want to have to lie about what she had been doing all day.

Firbaith and Elenn shared the traditional loaf, but everyone else ate griddies hot from the campfires. Maga had spared one of her herd for the feast, giving Firbaith the champion's portion. The meat was stringy and limited. Emer heard some muttered complaints from the champions. At least there was plenty of ale, and everyone drank deep. There was much laughter. Although it was war and their friends were dying, there had been no great battles. The host seemed ready to be amused after three days waiting around achieving nothing. Every moth that blundered into the fire aroused laughter, every joke made people roar. Even those pining for love of Elenn, or saying they were, seemed to think Firbaith a fair match for her. Ferdia seemed to be drinking sparingly, but cheerfully enough as far as Emer could tell. People were talking as if it were a settled fact that the road would open tomorrow.

During the singing, Elenn leaned close to whisper to Emer. "Sisterly secrets!" bellowed Firbaith, laughing and downing another cup of ale.

Lew smiled. "Don't they make a pretty picture heads together like that?"

Emer felt apprehensive. What could Elenn want to ask now?

"Will you look after Beauty tonight?" Elenn asked urgently. "She's used to sleeping with me, and she might come and look for me. And if I tie her up, she'll howl. There aren't any other dogs here or I'd leave her with a kennel master. She's used to you. She won't mind."

Emer looked down at the hound. Beauty was more than half grown now, not a puppy anymore. She liked dogs well enough, in their place, out hunting. "Of course I will," she said. Elenn knelt and hugged the dog, whispering in her ear as she had whispered in Emer's. When she rose, she had tears in her eyes. They were gone before she turned back to the others.

Then Elenn and Firbaith went off to the specially prepared tent, everyone calling out traditional bawdy blessings on the marriage bed. It occurred to Emer that this was probably the first wedding she had ever been to where the bride and groom really were consummating not just their fertility, but their relationship. Some of the jokes were ones usually heard at betrothals. Harps and drums struck up tunes and half the camp began to dance. Emer kept her hand on Beauty's neck, holding her from going after her mistress. She drew the dog with her through the crowds toward her tent and her bed.

Maga came up to her as she left the circle of the firelight. There was a tremendous noise from the music and the dancing, but nobody was paying them any attention. "That went well," she said. Emer smiled her agreement. "Tomorrow, I shall betroth you to Lew ap Ross of Anlar."

Emer stood still for a moment, chilled through. Then hot anger warmed her. "You will not," she said. "Have you forgotten what I said to you when I came back from Muin? Have you forgotten all I have said to you since?"

"Conal is a fool and has taken so long considering that it amounts to refusing my offer," Maga said. "I have had enough of your obstinacy. Lew is an allied king. He likes the look of you, and has done so since he first saw you. You were talking to him happily at dinner, so it is clear you do not dislike him. He wants a wife who will guide him and make him a strong alliance, he has said as much to me. As for you, you will be a queen immediately. What more could you want?"

Emer remembered Anlar, the cobwebs in the hall and the dogs lying down among the champions. She thought of Lew, good-hearted but nearly forty years old and weak-willed. "While Conal the Victor lives, I will never marry anyone else," she said.

"He won't live very long once we open a road to Oriel," Maga said and smiled.

"If you hear news he is dead, talk to me of your matchmaking," Emer said. "You cannot make me marry against my will."

Maga looked at her impatiently. "What will you do?" she asked. "Kill yourself like a cowardly Vincan and set yourself against the pattern the gods have woven for your life? 'Her father brought bold Drusan to her bed, but there they found fair Elenn lying dead,' " she sang. Beauty raised her hackles and growled at Maga. "Life is not for throwing away like that."

Emer was ready to fly out against her mother, to rail and shout and object again. As she drew herself up to do it, she felt all the aches of the day again. "I am too tired for this nonsense," she said evenly. "I have said everything I am going to say about this many times already. I told you I am not your property."

"I gave you life," Maga said. "I gave you breath itself. And no thanks, just ingratitude. I am your mother and your king and you owe me obedience."

"There's more to being a mother than that, or a king either," Emer said. Then while Maga stood speechless, she walked on toward her bed, taking her sister's dog with her.

# — 24 —

## (FERDIA)

Just as Ferdia was about to make his second cast at the target, a hush spread among the other young warriors who were practicing with him. He threw, making his neck shot, then turned to see. Maga was stepping down from a chariot close behind him. She was wearing all her finery, gold torcs and arm-rings, and brooches set with pearls, and long chains of amber. She smiled at him but did not speak, waiting politely for him to throw his third spear. He turned away from her, took a calming breath, and threw. The spear flew straight for the heart of the target and his companions stamped their feet in praise. His face heated as he turned back towards them.

"Well thrown, son of Cethern," Maga said. "I am going to Cruachan with the carts to bring back ale and food for feasting. Will you come with me to drive my chariot and protect me from dangers we might encounter on the way?"

Ferdia just looked at her for a moment. Who would attack Maga's chariot, when all the fighting folk of Oriel were laid low by a curse and everyone else in the island was allied to Connat? And he knew she could drive a chariot herself. She had just driven it across the camp, after all. Or, if she had wanted a champion to go with her, the whole might of Connat was drawn up here with nothing to do. After seven days of it, they were becoming so restless they were beginning to fight among themselves. All the same, however ridiculous her request was, he could not in courtesy refuse her. Besides, everyone was listening.

"I will come with you, for what little I might do," he said and bowed.

Maga narrowed her eyes. "I am sure you could do great deeds if you were called upon to do so," she said and bowed in return. Her gold flashed as it caught the sun when she straightened. She turned and mounted the chariot, holding the reins to Ferdia. He took them and climbed in beside her. The looks the others gave him were envious. He would gladly have changed places with any of them.

The ponies, both dusky black mares that looked as if they had no staying power, were lively and ready to be off. They drove in silence until they were out of the camp. Ferdia had to concentrate on steering wide of tents and groups of people running about. Most of them seemed to be sharpening weapons or practicing, but there were big groups gathered around people telling stories. Nobody seemed to want to move out of his way. He was glad when they were past the press of people. The carts were waiting, drawn up on the road to Cruachan under a stand of alders. There seemed to be a great number of them.

"We will lead the way," Maga said, waving to the carters. "Go slowly and let them stay only a little way behind. We are here for their protection."

There was nobody now to hear anything Ferdia said. "What are we to protect them from?" he asked.

Maga looked at him and smiled, a smile he did not at all like. "Mostly from their own fears," she said. "But we have taken up arms, and long ago I made a law that in time of war, all supply carts will be accompanied by a chariot. It has many times saved food that we needed from being taken by the enemy."

"This is not war," Ferdia said, almost before he could think what he was saying.

"It is most like war," Maga said.

Ferdia thought it wisest not to reply to this at all. His father kept the distinction very clear.

They drove on slowly for a little while. They passed farmhouses and tilled fields and here and there a wooded spinney. The land was much like Ferdia was used to in Lagin. It would have been a pleasant drive, except that he was very aware that Maga was watching him.

"You are a fine young champion," she said after a while.

"Thank you," Ferdia replied, horribly embarrassed.

"It seems to me that you would do well against one of the Keepers of the Roads. You throw your spear straight, even when you have been surprised. You are young and strong and well trained. Yet you have not gone against them. Why is that?"

Ferdia stared between the horses' ears. She should not have asked. He could not say that he had no desire to die. "Darag is my foster brother," he said. "It would be the greatest impiety to fight him."

"Oh, yes, that little stay in Ardmachan from which we all hoped for so much and yet gained so little," Maga said, her voice gentle. "I was against it from the start, but allowed Allel to overrule me. If Darag is your foster brother, you must know him well."

"Very well indeed." The road was rising to go over a little hill, and a dark cloud covered the sun.

"We all know he is good with a spear, but so little else about him." Maga hesitated as if she wanted Ferdia to say something.

"I can tell you what he is like, but you met him when he came to Cruachan in the contests after Amagien's Feast," Ferdia said.

"That was for such a short while, and besides, he was on the hill or asleep for most of the time. And such strange things he fought, too, three-headed dogs, headless ogres. Is it true that his father is a god?"

"I have heard it said," Ferdia said cautiously. "It would explain how it is that the curse has not laid him down."

"Such a strange curse," Maga said. "And who knows how long it will last? But if he is the son of a god, which god would it be, do you think? Or has he not confided that even to his foster brother?"

"He doesn't know," Ferdia said. "Many of the gods come to the festivals, it is said."

A soft rain started to fall. The first drops of it sent up a fresh green smell from the dust of the road. Maga drew a fold of her overdress over her head. "How curious that the god should protect him without revealing himself."

"I don't know if he's protecting him," Ferdia protested. "It could just happen that way, because of who his father is."

"If his father didn't take notice, he wouldn't have seen the three-headed dog," Maga said as if she were perfectly sure, as if the gods took her into their confidence about such things. "No, he must know and be keeping it to himself."

Ferdia thought about what Darag had said about the strangeness. He was sure Darag had been telling the truth. He didn't want to say that to Maga. He just shook his head, feeling the dampness of his hair as he did.

"Also, some divinity must be protecting him both from the curse and from our spears, and guiding his spears to kill our champions," Maga went on in the same tone.

"He doesn't need his spears guided by the gods," Ferdia said. "He is uncommonly good—fast and accurate, with good judgment as well as a good eye."

"I begin to understand why you don't want to fight him," Maga said.

Ferdia felt heat rising in his cheeks. "He is my foster brother," he repeated, and turned his face away from Maga. The rain was heavier, but he welcomed it now. He realized he had unintentionally put on a burst of speed and he slowed carefully so the carts could keep up.

"Do you think my daughter Elenn beautiful?" Maga asked. Her voice was soft and confiding now.

Ferdia wondered how many men she had beguiled to their deaths with that question. Four at least, whom Elenn had married, one every night for the last four nights. Nobody would ever know how many others had gone to death hoping to clear the road and win Elenn's fabled starry eyes and midnight hair. "Very beautiful," he said. "One of the three most beautiful women of the Island of Tir Isarnagiri, as the poet has it." Anything else would have been rude. Besides, nobody could deny that Elenn was beautiful.

"And do you not desire to win her for yourself? She loves you already."

That wretched dog, he thought at once. He was not going to die for a foolish mistake like that. Then he realized Maga could be lying, could say that to all the men as well as asking about Elenn's beauty. "My father has different marriage plans for me," he said cautiously.

"And you are such a dutiful son that you would give up your own desires? Lagin is allied to Connat. A closer alliance would please Cethern now, whatever he said before. Besides, he is sentimental. He would put your happiness before expediency."

Ferdia was by no means as confident of that as Maga seemed to be. But in any case, it wasn't the point and she clearly wanted to force the issue. He could not get away. Cruachan was not yet in sight. The land seemed green and gentle, all hard edges softened by the rain and low cloud. "I do not want to marry your daughter," he said.

Maga was not smiling now. Her eyes were very bright as she peered out beneath the fold of cloth. "You do not? What a strange man you are, Ferdia ap Cethern. You do not want Elenn, when all the other champions of the island want her. You will not fight Darag because he is your foster brother. As for Atha, you doubtless have some equally strong but undisclosed tie that prevents you from fighting her?"

He could say nothing. He drove on, staring forward at the endless road, up and down, the fields, the green and dripping trees.

"Has the Great Cat taken your tongue?" Maga asked at last. "No ties to Atha?"

"No," he admitted.

"Then why would a bold young man like you refuse to go against her?"

"You cannot make me go to my death for nothing," he said, finding words at last. "Atha is the greatest champion of our age. I took up arms only a year ago. I am willing to fight in battle, eager. But going against Atha would be certain death. It would clear no roads for you, and leave my family grieved to no gain."

"There are worse things than death," Maga said. Incredibly, she was smiling again. "Do you know ap Dair the Poet? He is in the camp."

Ferdia did know him. He found him annoying. He had been the one to negotiate Cethern's alliance with Maga, against all Ferdia's advice. He kept bringing Maga's messages, and when Ferdia reproached him with running her errands, he said that running Maga's errands was inspiring. He said nobody could ever have imagined this war and that poets would be writing about it for generations. He was protected as a poet; nobody could kill him and so he did not fight. He talked and laughed as much as someone who had the right to boast of his deeds.

"I know him," Ferdia admitted.

Maga put a finger on Ferdia's chin, forcing his head up. "Look at the road, young champion," she advised. The worst of this was that despite her impertinence she was right. It was dangerous not to pay attention, especially now that the road was slippery in the rain.

"Sorry," he said between gritted teeth.

"Ap Dair will make whatever song I tell him," Maga said. "If I tell him you are a coward, he will sing that. If I tell him you gave a pledge to Elenn and then refused her love, he will find that material for a fine song. It will not kill you, but he is a poet of renown. You will hear it all your life, and every day you do not hear it, you will hear in every silence the certainty that people have just stopped singing it because you came along."

"How can you so insult my honor?" Ferdia asked, furious.

Maga laughed, throwing back her head and letting the fold of cloth fall so that her hair was free in the rain. "You cannot speak of honor," she said. "You are a coward and a pledge-breaker. It is nothing but the truth."

"What do you want from me?" Ferdia wondered if he could possibly kill Maga right now and say they had been attacked by bandits, or even that she had been struck by lightning. Then he remembered the carts following along behind. They were private, but in plain sight. Maga knew what she was doing. She was always so very clever. Ferdia knew he could never hope to outsmart her.

"I want you to fight Darag and clear a way into Connat for me. The gods are protecting Darag. Putting great champions against him seems to be doing nothing but killing the champions. Maybe if he saw his friend and bedmate before his spear, he would hesitate and let you kill him. Or if not, maybe if he kills his foster brother, the gods will take their hand away from him afterwards, for the impiety of the act."

It took Ferdia a moment to understand what she had said. "You are a fine one to speak to me of honor," he said.

Maga smiled. "Neither of us have honor, so we can understand each other."

"Then why don't you send troops through the woods and leave them guarding the roads for nothing?" Ferdia asked. "It is only honor that constrains you to go against them one at a time on the roads."

"*I* am not going against them," Maga said. "You are. And that is why I cannot. Honor is all in appearance. Inis ap Fathag was very clever when he made me promise before everyone that I would not go around unguarded roads. If I did, everyone would know I had no honor—and that would be if I could find enough people who would follow me without honor, which is doubtful. You might, little champion, but would your father? There are not enough of my folk who would, unless I were to make them very drunk, and maybe not even then. They fear the Ban. I cannot control Rathadun, much as I would like to."

Ferdia could not suppress a gasp of horror at the very idea. It seemed blasphemous even to think of controlling Rathadun of the Kings. He looked at Maga, at her gold and jewels and her damp hair. There was nothing to show of the horrors inside her except a gleam in her dark eyes. If she could think these things, who else might?

"How many people are like you?" he asked, hardly knowing how he dared ask.

"Shocked, little champion?" she asked.

"Yes," he said baldly. "I meant how many people are like you and set the show of honor above the real thing?"

"You yourself are like me in that, Ferdia ap Cethern," Maga said. "And so you will go out and fight to open the road for me."

She was right, he thought. He had no honor. He had taken the gift from the dog-woman and given it to Elenn. He was afraid to fight Atha. It would be better to die and take the name of honor down into the dark with him than to live with Maga and ap Dair singing satires about him.

"I will fight," he said. They came around the curve of the hill of Cruachan as he said it, and he saw the gates across the road no great way before him.

"Good. Then the supplies we will take back to the camp now will be for your wedding feast tonight."

"No," Ferdia said, determined. "It seems you can send me to my death, but you cannot make me marry your daughter."

"Elenn loves you," Maga said. "And you gave her the dog as pledge. What is one night, to make her happy?"

"Dead men father no children," Ferdia said. It was a proverb everyone knew. Spending one night married to her and dying would not give him an heir. "And I might yet live," he finished, not believing it, and slowing the chariot to give himself time to finish what he needed to say before they reached the gates.

"And would it be so terrible to live and be married to Elenn the Beautiful and be the envy of all men?"

"No. But it would be unendurable to have to call you mother," he replied.

Maga laughed, sounding genuinely amused for the first time since he had known her. "A betrothal, then," she said. "A betrothal you can break in a little while if you survive, but which will not break her heart if you die. I am speaking now not for policy, but for my daughter's happiness."

They were nearly at the gates. Ferdia lowered his voice. "Much you cared about Elenn's happiness when you married her to four men the last four nights."

"She still believes you are an honorable man," Maga said. "If you go out to fight without at least a betrothal, she will see that you are not, because you have broken your pledge. I might even have to inquire where that dog came from and why you gave it to her."

Maga spoke to the gate guard and they swept inside the dun, the row of carts following. Ferdia drove in silence as Maga directed him toward the storehouses. He could see it all now. Even dead, the dog could confound his honor. It was just like the stories of Lew or Wydion; curses set on a hero, the one mistake he had made had the power to overset everything else.

"You will have to speak to my father and explain it to him," he said.

This time, Maga's smile was triumphant.

# 7

# THE BATTLE AT THE FORD

# — 25 —

## (CONAL)

Darag came walking down the road alone. She hadn't come again tonight.

Conal turned and signaled to the boy waiting, who set off at once back to the camp at a run. He braced himself against the bole of an elm as the pain came through him again. He tried not to tense, to relax against it as his mother had told him. He was the best Oriel could do for a sentry right now. While he knew it was a very poor best, he would do what he could, always. He had argued against giving the duty to the children and servants, or even to Amagien and Orlam and Inis, though Orlam had volunteered. It was necessary to have someone there who could run at need, as the fighting folk could not, now. He had agreed to keep one of the children with him, and it had proved useful.

Even without being able to run, or fight, or do anything much, it was right that a champion be here, at the edge of the wood, waiting. Even on a damp afternoon like this, he was glad to be here. It got him out of the camp and away from the others, which he found a blessing. When Conary had suggested that the children could have the duty alone, Conal had said it made him feel better to be doing something. The other sentries had agreed. He wondered if they also spent their days thinking that they would be the first to fall to the enemy spears if Darag or Atha failed them and let the whole host of Connat through.

Conal drew breath as the pain left him for the moment. "Was it a good day, cousin?" he called.

Darag came nearer. He was black with blood again. His armor coat must have got drenched with it, and his face and legs were spattered. He raised his hand in greeting and grinned cheerfully. It was hard not to show that he hated him. Conal could have laughed to think of the reasons he had hated Darag before. Now none of the other reasons mattered. It was hard not to hate anyone who was well, even the servants who had not fallen to the curse, let alone Darag. It was probably good that Emer had not come. She might have seen resentment in his eyes. Maybe she had seen that on the first two nights and that was why she had not come back since. If only he didn't miss her so much.

"I held the road a seventh day," Darag said as he came close enough for conversation.

They stood a moment and looked at each other. They had already made all the jokes that could be made, on the days that had come before. Then the pain took Conal again, and he looked away, staring hard at a fringed piece of creamy fungus at the tree's root and just trying to breathe deeply, not giving in to the pain. Plenty of strong champions back at camp were screaming when the pains took them. He had screamed only once himself, when it came on him unexpectedly between one stride and the next, tearing through his guts like a jagged knife. He had fallen awkwardly, and the jolt from the fall bruised him and took his defenses. Screaming hadn't helped. It may even have made it worse. He was bitterly ashamed of it, most of all because his father had been nearby at the time. He had nearly knocked Amagien off his feet. He would not scream again, and certainly he would never scream in front of Darag. As the pain passed off this time he leaned into the tree and panted for a moment. His lips were bitten ragged already. Where he had not been clutching it, the bark was still spotted with cool water from the rain that had fallen an hour ago.

"Is Emer well?" Conal asked when he could speak again.

"She took a spear in her arm," Darag touched his own arm, just above the elbow. "But the spear was there, we could heal it without too much trouble. It wasn't a bad wound that would leave a weakness. Apart from that, she's fine. She's tired from all the fighting, of course. She sends her love to you, but she said she had to get back before they missed her."

This was what she had said every night since the third. Conal was surprised how much it hurt to hear that she had been wounded again. He buried his disappointment, pushing his sense of his own helplessness down with it. That sort of pain he was good at hiding. He just wished he could talk to her. "Did she say if she was having trouble with Maga?"

"She didn't say anything about it," Darag said. "She doesn't complain. You are fortunate to have her as your charioteer. As soon as this is over, you must marry her right away, if we all live. I will support that before Conary and your parents."

"Thank you," Conal said, dumbfounded by this support. "If that isn't possible, we have talked about running away together."

"What worse could Maga do to Oriel than this?" Darag asked, waving a hand that seemed to take in his blood-soaked coat.

"Were you wounded?" Conal asked.

"Only little wounds that are healed already," Darag said.

"It's not your own blood you've been wading in, then?"

Darag frowned, then looked down at himself in mild surprise. "No, this is the blood of Laran ap Noss, a champion of Connat. His head is on my chariot now. My sword took him in the throat and the blood went everywhere."

"Your sword?" Conal echoed and raised his eyebrows.

"Not my best weapon, I know." Darag shrugged. Conal had almost always been able to beat him with the sword, though that didn't stop Darag trying. Nothing stopped Darag trying. He'd never admit he was beaten. "It was quite a long fight, very tiring. I don't know why you like swords so much. But he was another husband of Elenn's. Emer had eaten with him last night. She didn't feel comfortable going against him. So when he came up and made his boast, I asked if he would fight me on foot and he agreed."

"He didn't know who Emer was?" Conal asked quickly.

"He didn't. But he was an honorable man, with an honorable charioteer, and they agreed at once." Darag sighed. "I have killed four of the poor girl's husbands now, starting with Atha's brother. How long can this go on?"

"Until Maga stops attacking, or until Beastmother lets us come and join you," Conal said. As he raised his hand to his head to make the Beastmother sign, he could feel the pain beginning again, slowly this time, building up as it ran through him like a cramp. He bent forward and rested his forehead on the cool, damp tree.

"Wouldn't you be better lying down?" Darag asked. The concern in his voice made Conal grit his teeth. To his surprise, gritting his teeth, combined with calm breathing, actually seemed to help a little.

"Lying down is much worse," he said as soon as he could, fighting to make his tone light. "I have even been sleeping, as much as I can between pains, sitting up leaning back against a tree."

"I haven't been sleeping much either," Darag said. "I can lie down in comfort, but the screams come so often and sound so terrible."

"You should sleep," Conal said awkwardly. "We all need you to be well."

Darag smiled, almost a grimace. "I am glad I can keep the road. But it makes me feel so cut off from the rest of you."

"You've run mad at last," Conal said, rolling his eyes. "How terrible, all the champions of Oriel are struck down by a curse except one, and that one is as crazy as an oracle-priest."

Darag laughed. The pain came to Conal just as he finished speaking, not a very bad one this time but much too soon after the last one, when he was still weak from it. It seemed to him that the pains were growing closer together. This one ran through his belly, both a gripping and a cramping, as if he had eaten too many green apples. It would not have been too terrible, except that it had been going on for seven days without a break. It was hard to bear Darag's laughter. He bit his lip and set himself to endure. If he had been well, he might have fought Darag now, for the thousandth time. But if he had been well, they wouldn't all need Darag the way they did. In some ways, that was the worst of this—not only was he helpless, but that Darag should be the one who wasn't.

"Don't worry," he said lightly as he straightened up. "My mother says it is no worse than childbirth."

"Lots of the women are saying that," Darag said a little uneasily.

"My mother said that's why she decided not to have any more children," Conal said, waving his hand airily. "But it's like seasickness. Nobody dies of it, they just wish they would."

He had expected Darag to laugh, but he frowned instead. "I always heard that childbirth hurts, but it is a mystery, that the woman is in the hand of the Mother. But then I heard of a woman in Muin who died having a baby once, in our great-grandfather's time."

"Died?" Conal was astonished. "I never heard that. Who told you?"

"Samar ap Ardan," Darag said. "She said there was a young wife living out in the woods whose husband had been killed by a falling tree, and she started walking towards Muin and the baby came, and she was alone and didn't know the right prayers and too afraid to call on the Mother without prayers, maybe, so she just . . . died of the pain."

"Maybe a wolf—" Conal began. He was going to add, "or a bear," but the pain came down hard and this time, he couldn't trust himself to speak through it.

When he could look at Darag again, Darag was staring at the sky. "Maybe a wolf or a bear got her on the way," Conal said, keeping his voice low. If Darag hadn't been there, he would have rocked to and fro a little; that sometimes helped. "Or maybe it is just the sort of story people tell late at night on watch to scare each other. Inis might know. But in any case, this isn't childbirth."

"Childbirth doesn't usually last this long," Darag said. "Aunt Elba was two days with Orlam, one night with Leary, and half a day with the twins. She says your mother was a day and a night with you, and my mother was three days with me." He lowered his voice a little at the end, as always when he spoke of his mother.

"You've really been thinking about this," Conal said.

"Maybe because I'm not suffering it," Darag said. "I asked last night. Aunt Elba said that it was just this sort of pain, but it was all worth it because you knew you would have a child at the end."

"Well, maybe that just might make this all worthwhile," Conal said and laughed, which was a mistake because it brought on the pain again.

"But what could you be giving birth to, if you were?" Darag asked. Even if Conal had been able to speak, he would have had no answer.

"She said we would suffer as the mare suffered," Conal said after a short eternity which was only the pain. With automatic piety, he touched his hand to his head in the way that symbolized Beastmother as he spoke of her. Darag echoed him, looking more worried than ever. "Grandfather thinks that means for a term of days, and so does the oracle-priest of Connat, ap Fial. But we have passed three already, and six. What if it never leaves us? The mare died."

Darag hesitated, drew breath, thought better of it, then spoke at last. "I don't think so. I think that if what we saw in the Cave of Cruachan means anything, it means we will survive this." He drew breath again, carefully. "Besides, the reason I have been wondering about birth is because I had a dream about the first times. About the building of Ardmachan. In my dream, the mare gave birth as she was killed, and Beastmother—" again he touched his head "—spoke through the filly that was born. And all the folk of the dun lay on the ground in pain that was very like the pain you have."

Conal looked at him sharply. "Have you told Inis?"

"You know how hard it is to ask Inis anything," Darag said guiltily. "I had this dream before you killed the mare, before any of this happened. But I had it over and over."

"Inis was always asking us about dreams like that," Conal said accusingly. Then the absurdity of it struck him and he smiled. "Of course I never told him my dreams either, and no doubt we had the same reason."

"You have dreams?" Darag asked, shaking his head. "Then they could have made oracle-priests out of both of us and left the kingship to poor Leary?" He grinned at Conal.

It was difficult to do, because the pain was coming again, but Conal managed an answering grin. He let the pain flow through him, trying not to be impatient although he knew what he wanted to say and could not say it. He knew better than to try to talk across the pains. He had heard other people trying. Talking came too close to screaming. The pain felt like lightning striking through him, slowly. He clenched and unclenched his fists. Darag kept standing there waiting for it to go, not showing any impatience. Hatred welled up in Conal like bile in his throat, but he swallowed it back. He could have clutched it to him like a familiar cloak on a cold night, but instead, he pushed it away. This wasn't Darag's fault, he thought for the first time. Not everything was. It had taken this to make him see it, but it was true.

"Remember how we let Leary win the race on the road to Cruachan?" Conal asked as soon as he had breath. Darag's grin had recalled Muin, where their rivalry had for a little while seemed a wholesome thing. "Leary would make a terrible king of Oriel."

"You wouldn't," Darag said warily.

"You wouldn't either," Conal said, and they looked at each other tentatively for a moment, on entirely new ground.

Darag looked down. "In the cave on Cruachan, I saw you avenge my death."

Conal went cold. "Were you king of Oriel then?" he asked.

"I was. But we were not old men, we were hardly more than ten years older than we are now."

Conal thought of the way he had seen himself crawling forward, looking for water, clutching a helmet in one hand, the other arm hanging loose from his shoulder. How hard it was to judge time. He had not been wearing a king's colors. There had been some gray in his hair. He had been wearing a herald's spray pinned to a short cloak. He shook his head to drive the vision away. "Inis says nobody can know our real future, which is always changeable. He says we can only know how things have been in other worlds."

"I think you avenge my death in all the other worlds," Darag said.

"What else did you see in the cave, really?" Conal asked, wanting time to think about the implications of what Darag had said, and about the new way they were talking.

"Apart from you avenging my death? You returned my head to my body, to give me release." Darag's smile was strange. "Well, I saw my death, of course, bound to a stone, too weak to stand without support but fighting to the very end. And I fought monsters, as I said in the hall, and met the god who called himself Bachlach and took his head, and let him take mine."

The pain had come over Conal again as Darag was speaking, and he kept his eyes fixed on his cousin's face, seeing it clearly, the curl of his nostril and the angle of his dark eyes. He had hated him for so long that it was a hard habit to break. He had denied all the good things about him to do it.

"I knew he might kill me, of course, but I had already seen my death, and what could be worse than that?" Darag went on, not looking at Conal, staring off into the trees. "When he handed me back my head I asked him the way to the third day after I had come up the hill, and he pointed out the path to me. Somewhere on the way down, my head went from being under my arm to being back on my neck again."

"I thought—" Conal began, but the word came out on a squeak, so he began again, husking the words. "I thought it was because you did not sleep."

This made Darag look more cheerful. "That would be a worthy reason," he said. "I thought it was because the gods take an interest in me, and because I am not afraid to ask them for help."

"That isn't an unworthy reason," Conal said reluctantly. Their eyes met. "You won the contest," Conal conceded, for the first time.

"I always thought you hated me for things I can't help," Darag said.

There were a lot of easy answers he could have made that would have turned that away. But Conal understood what he meant. He swallowed awkwardly, and suddenly he felt the way he did in his dreams, the way Inis talked about feeling, as if the choice he made next would change worlds. The easy way would be to lie and go on striving futilely against Darag. But the hard way—

It was only recently that he had realized there were ways of living honorably that did not involve becoming king of Oriel. He had told Emer that there were things more important, but he should have put it like that. She would understand, and he wasn't sure Darag would. He thought how brave Emer was, to stay in Connat, eating with her mother every night, and every day coming to the ford to fight for them, holding the road at least as much as Darag was. There was no honor in taking the easy way, none at all.

"I hated you because you always made me second-best," Conal said, stumbling over the words. "I hated you because you were better than me."

"I never hated you," Darag said. "I just reacted to you hating me. And you are better than everyone else. It's not surprising you wanted to be best of all."

"I don't think I hate you anymore," Conal said, not quite sure whether it was true or what it meant, or even that he would really say it until the words were hanging in the air.

"Are you offering me friendship?" Darag asked, incredulous. There was warmth in his smile. Conal almost . . . no, Conal *did* like him for it.

He could feel the distant warning that the pain was coming again. "Friendship, loyalty, my house to yours," he said as briefly as he could.

Darag put out his arms to embrace Conal as kin. Conal moved forward to return the embrace, and as he did, the pain took him, skewering him right through. If Darag had not held him up, he would have fallen. He breathed hard and did not scream. He was sure the pains had not been this close together even yesterday, not even this morning.

When he could stand alone, Darag let him go, and they looked at each other warily. They had known each other all their lives, but they had never before been friends.

"You should go back to camp before Atha comes looking for you," Conal said.

"The boy will have told them I held my road," Darag said. "If she had not held hers, we would know by now. Your relief should be coming soon. I'll wait here a little while longer with you."

# —26—

## (ELENN)

Elenn was sitting in front of her tent when they brought Laran back. She was staring aimlessly across the camp, but she would have denied to anyone else that she was waiting. She could not deny it to herself, not the fourth time she had done it, the seventh morning of the war.

She had dressed that morning in her new slate-blue overdress, a wedding gift from Laran. She had bound up her hair with Orlam's silver-and-pearl circlet. She had kissed her new husband farewell and wished him luck, in front of her parents and half the camp. Then she had taken Beauty to the master of hounds, who was here without his dogs and only too glad to have Beauty to train. She had come back here alone. She could not bear to be with anyone, and the comfort Beauty offered was too painful. After four days of sending husbands off to fight Darag, hope was something she would have liked to feel. Laran ap Noss was a good man and a fine champion, one of the Royal Kin of Muin. She had liked him, and he had adored her. Their night together had been delightful. She had wept silently in the darkness, after he fell asleep, struggling to hold back sobs that might have woken him.

His charioteer, Semion, drew up in front of the tent. He and another of Laran's followers lifted Laran's headless body out and set it down on the ground in front of Elenn.

Now that she was expected to weep, tears seemed far away. She rose to her feet in one movement and stood grave and still. She reached up and removed the circlet from her hair and ran her hands through it, letting it fall into the disarray of mourning.

"Bring me water and cloths," she said. She set the circlet down just inside the tent, where it would stay dry. Then she knelt beside Laran's body and let her hair fall forward over her face. She gave the traditional three howls. As she did, the tears came, as they had every time. She let them fall unchecked.

A servant brought a bowl of water and some strips of cloth. Elenn straightened up and pushed back her hair. She did not wipe her eyes. It was good that her tears should be seen. Tears were said to ease the dead on the first part of their journey. She would have done anything she could to make it easier for Laran. It was the least she could do. After all, whether she wanted him to or not, he had died for her.

She took the bowl, then motioned the servant away. A circle of people had gathered. She wished they would not. She knew this must be done under the sky and before any who would watch, but even so, she would have preferred to be alone. Alone with Laran one last time, if he cared for that now. Dark clouds covered the sun. Soon it would rain, but she could pay no attention to that.

Semion brought a length of fine white linen, as fine as the blue Elenn was wearing and doubtless also woven by Laran's mother. Elenn took it and set it down carefully. She wished there had been time for her to weave a winding-sheet herself. Even the poorest farmers wrapped a little strip of woven cloth around their dead, binding it around a wrist or a forehead. However much or little, the cloth was always made by those closest to the dead—a parent, or a spouse, or a child. She wished there had been time for her to know Laran's mother.

The charioteer hesitated for a moment, looking at Elenn with grief on his face. "Shall I help?" he asked. Elenn shook her head. She did not want the distraction. She knew what to do. She had always done it alone before.

She pulled off Laran's soiled and bloody shift and clout and piled them together behind her. She dipped a clean cloth in the water and began to clean off the blood. The water wasn't really warm enough, but Elenn didn't want to call for more. She'd have to talk to someone. She worked steadily, washing him as gently as if he had been alive and able to feel her touch. She remembered her father washing and binding up her scrapes and scratches when she was a child. One day she might wash a baby, or perhaps even wash and bind the wounds of a living husband. She hadn't found the death wound yet. Darag had taken his head and his armor, as usual. She wished she could ransom the head, all her husbands' heads. She had asked Maga about it, but her mother had said that she had nothing Darag wanted.

It took hours before Laran was clean. The rain came long before she had finished, but she worked on. Without a head, she could not possibly remove all the blood, but she had done her best and he would not come before the Lord of the Dead disgracefully dirty. She commended him to as many gods as she could, calling out loudly and holding up her hands in the rain. She had no idea whether any of them heard or cared. She doubted it. When she bent to wrap him in the linen, she felt despair. If any gods paid attention to people, they were away on the roads, helping Darag and Atha hold off the might of the island and kill her husbands. None of them cared for the mourning cries of Elenn ap Allel, alone in the center of the camp of Connat. All the same, she sewed up the linen in the ritual way and whispered a last prayer to the merciful Queen of the Dead. She pricked her finger with the needle and blotted the blood carefully onto the last damp stitches. Now he was ready to have his body burned and his name given back in the Hymn of Return at sunset.

She tucked the needle back into her sleeve. She bent forward over his body for one last moment, then straightened up and stretched, alone in a little circle of quiet among the waiting people. It was only afternoon yet, there was all the rest of the day to live through before the next. The rain had stopped and the clouds were scudding fast across the sky.

Semion came forward and bowed. "I shall take him now," he said. Elenn bowed in return. Semion's face was cold as he lifted the burden into the chariot one last time. Elenn wondered if he hated her for causing Laran's death. They had been very close. Last night, Semion had eaten with them, smiling and congratulating them. All her husbands and their charioteers were sure they would be different, would be the ones who would kill Darag and live on past the fight at the ford. She wondered what would happen when she stopped being able to pretend to believe them.

She looked at the crowd then, expecting to see her mother come with news of who she must marry tonight. But Maga wasn't among the watchers today. The person who came forward as Semion took Laran's body away was Ferdia's father, Cethern of Lagin. He was a man in vigorous middle age, broadly built like his son and dressed as a king in red and green. Several other people also stepped forward, but he raised a hand to bar their way. "I have business with the Lady Elenn that won't wait," he said, frowning at them until they gave way and retreated before his authority.

"May I sit down?" he asked politely, coming forward. The people waiting moved farther away. Some of them left altogether.

Elenn raised her chin, confused. She had never had much conversation with Cethern, although he had been at Cruachan for a month before the war began. She could not think what his business with her could be, unless possibly he had come to speak for his son. Her heart gave a great leap, and then a lurch as she understood what it would mean. "You are welcome, sir," she said automatically. "Can I offer you refreshment?"

Cethern sat down on the drier grass where the tent had partly sheltered it. "Not now, thank you," he said quietly, so only she could hear. "You must fast until sunset, and I would not eat before you."

Elenn smiled, hiding her feelings. She moved Laran's bloody clothes into the tent, out of the way for now. Then she settled herself next to him on the cushion she had used before, straightening her skirts carefully. The leather of the cushion was wet. "So, why do you honor me with your company?" she asked.

He looked at her shrewdly and shook his head, gesturing to the people around them. Ap Dair the Poet was among them now. He smiled at Elenn as their eyes met. "This is about as private as we can get without going out of camp, which there isn't time for. And I'm sorry, but there's no polite way to say this. Your mother wants my son to marry you. I'm against it, not for any harm you've done me or anything against you yourself at all. You're beautiful enough in all truth, but I don't like this business you and your mother have been doing between you. The last thing I want is for my son to get killed tomorrow morning because your mother is holding you out as a prize in a game and he's gone daft enough to try to win you."

"Neither do I," Elenn said, and to her dismay felt her voice quaver in the middle. The thought of Ferdia brought before her dead and headless was unbearable. She swallowed hard to avoid tears. "Not in the least. Do you think I like having my husbands brought before me cold and dead? Can't you see it would be ninety times worse if it were Ferdia?"

"So it's true what your mother says?"

"What does she say?" Elenn asked, getting her voice back under control.

"She tells me you are in love with my son. She says he is in love with you, too, and gave you a dog in pledge of this before you both left Ardmachan. Is this true, or one of her fabulations that she has put together to ensnare me? And if it is true, how is it that you have allowed yourself to be married off to four other men night after night and seen them each killed in the morning? Are you the most heartless woman in Tir Isarnagiri, as well as the most beautiful?"

Elenn looked down, knowing her cheeks were heating with anger and embarrassment. How she had gloried in being called one of the three most beautiful women in Tir Isarnagiri, and how it hurt now to be called the most beautiful. "I am not heartless," she said quietly, keeping control of her voice only with an effort. "And what my mother says is true. I love Ferdia, and he gave me a dog. The dog is with the master of hounds now, but you may have seen her with me."

"I've seen her," Cethern admitted. "But then why did Ferdia never mention this to me? Even now, it was your mother came and told me, with him just standing by saying yes and no at her side. I'm not such an ogre as all that. He's a grown man now, and he isn't afraid of me usually, though he has been very close with his counsel since he came back from Oriel."

"I think he thought it wasn't policy," Elenn said, looking up again, to see him frowning at her. "I knew it wasn't my mother's policy."

"You're telling me two young people in love put it aside without mentioning it for considerations of policy?" Cethern sounded frankly disbelieving.

"I certainly mentioned it to my mother," Elenn said. She held Cethern's skeptical eyes with an effort. "My sister came back from Oriel screaming and shouting that she was to marry ap Amagien the Victor, and my mother took it very badly. So I didn't press her about Ferdia. I thought there was time and she might see the advantages later. Then . . . I know it sounds terrible, but Ferdia was here and he didn't say anything and you didn't, so I didn't know what to think. He hadn't exactly said that was why he was giving me the dog, though it seemed clearly his intention at the time. He wasn't breaking any specific promises if he didn't want me anymore. It was all things unsaid. Sometimes I wondered if I'd made the whole thing up. He's been avoiding me since you've been here. And I knew it might not be what you wanted for Lagin, I thought you might have told him a definite no. Then Maga had made arrangements already and she didn't give me any choice, and they were all men I liked, even if they weren't Ferdia. My mother told me the kind of love you feel as a girl is sweet, but marriage is something different. I tried to put Ferdia out of my mind. I would have been a good wife to any of them, if there had been time."

"You're a biddable girl for your mother's daughter," Cethern said, biting his lip. "Well, I suppose there's no reason why you shouldn't be, and I can see you're telling me the truth as you see it. Your side of it seems clear enough. Poor girl, you're as much the victim in this as anyone. But that doesn't explain why Ferdia didn't say a word about it after he left Ardmachan, to me or to you."

"I don't know," Elenn said, furious. "You should ask him. And I am *not* a victim or a biddable girl. I have made my own choices."

"Choices you didn't have many options in, from the sound of it," Cethern said. A watery sunshine was coming through the clouds. It caught the silver streaks in his beard.

"I would have said no if my mother had suggested anyone I could not bear," Elenn insisted. Cethern looked pityingly at her, and she smiled to avoid gritting her teeth. She wanted to growl in the back of her throat the way Beauty did when she was forced to keep still. She hated pity. She hated being treated as a child. "I will refuse to marry Ferdia tonight," she said.

"Maybe you are your mother's daughter, if you'll spite your heart out of pride," Cethern said. "Besides, a marriage has not been arranged. You are men and women grown, if very young and foolish ones. You don't need my consent for a marriage. Whether I would still call Ferdia my son if he married without my consent is another matter. An alliance is a different thing, and your mother is talking about an alliance. That's what she wants, whatever you want. She wants one that will hold even with Ferdia dead. I said I'd not even begin to negotiate one until I'd spoken to you." He sighed. "Even if I give consent, what Ferdia wants now is a betrothal, with a marriage to happen after the war, all being well."

"He is the cleverest, most admirable champion on the island of Tir Isarnagiri," Elenn burst out. Cethern raised a warning finger, and she went on more quietly. "Then he *won't* be killed trying to open a road, and I won't have to marry another champion every night." It did cross her mind that Ferdia might have thought of this several days ago and spared her considerable anguish, but she banished the thought in the general relief. She could have embraced Cethern. If he was to be her husband's father, he would be kin and she could. But not now, not with people watching.

"That would be if I agreed to a betrothal, which I haven't," Cethern said. "I haven't yet," he softened it, looking at her. "And in any case, according to your mother, he insists on fighting Darag tomorrow whatever happens."

Elenn stared at him in consternation. "Fighting Darag?" she asked.

"Hush, not so loud," Cethern said. "They may all guess what we're talking about, but let's not make them sure of it. Fighting Darag, yes, when every other sentence out of him has had Darag in it since he came home. And when he's told me ninety-nine times that Darag is the best fighter of the generation, even before he started killing all comers. I can't see any sense in it."

"Are you going to stop him?" Elenn asked, leaning forward, her voice only just above a whisper.

"How can I?" Cethern's voice was barely louder than hers. "I can refuse consent to a betrothal or an alliance, but I can't stop him fighting Darag if he wants to. I can counsel him against it, but if he really is decided on it, then he is. He's a grown man, not a babe. He's taken up arms even if he isn't the best champion there ever was, the way he says Darag is. He can fight if he wants to. Lagin is on this side of the war, much as I may regret it now. We've lost two champions already, one against Darag and another against Atha. My people wouldn't stand for it if I took them away now. It might be different if Ferdia were the only heir to Lagin, but I have another son and two daughters, not to mention all my nephews."

"Then if Ferdia has decided to fight and you can't stop him, why are you talking to me at all?"

"I wanted to get to the bottom of things. I was hoping it was all a lie, though I can see it isn't. If you love each other, it makes a difference.

It may be that your mother isn't about to give up using you as a prize to make men fight, and she's told Ferdia he has to fight if he wants you. That seems most likely to me. I was hoping that if I could forbid the betrothal clearly and permanently, and with good arguments, he'd change his mind about wanting to fight. I wanted to say you were a pretty face who didn't care for him and a bad alliance, issues of policy—as you said, policy does come into it when you're a king's son or a king's daughter."

"I know," she said, and though she wouldn't have thought there were any tears left inside her, she had to blink some away. "Tell him that. Tell him I don't want to marry him. Anything to save his life."

Cethern leaned forward urgently. "Will you speak to him? Will you tell him that? Will you tell your mother that?"

Elenn took a deep breath and thought of Ferdia, dancing with her at the Feast of Bel, so polite, so kind, never pressing her as so many men did. She thought of him giving her Beauty, his diffidence, the brightness of his smile as they left Ardmachan and were alone in the chariot. She loved him. She could be brave for him. She could give him up to save his life.

"I will," she said, thinking hard about Ferdia to avoid thinking about Maga and what this would mean to her. "Come with me now, let's find them together."

# — 27 —

## (EMER)

The camp was bright and bustling in the glitter of sunshine after rain. There were friends and strangers everywhere in little knots, talking, singing, practicing, even wrestling. They had the restless look of people trying hard to amuse themselves when they've been kept waiting too long. Emer wished them all far away. She could hardly put one foot in front of the other. Healing always made her feel distant, not properly connected to the world. There had been no time to rest today after Darag drew out the spear. If she could reach the tent without anyone stopping her, there might be time to sleep a little before tonight's funerals and wedding. If she could sleep for even a few moments she would be able to bear it. If Elenn was in the same mood she had been in for the last few days and didn't want to talk, she might manage it. She edged carefully through the crowds and into the welcome dimness of the tent.

Elenn was not there. Just inside, she almost tripped over a wad of bloody and befouled garments. Next to them on the ground was her sister's silver circlet. Emer picked it up and frowned at it. It wasn't at all like Elenn to be so untidy. Something must be seriously wrong. Though what could be worse than what Maga had been doing to Elenn the last few days, she couldn't think.

She turned the circlet over in her hands for a moment. It might be nothing, some sudden summons. Or it might be something terrible. Elenn had been so quiet and obedient; she hadn't wanted to talk at all. Emer had suggested that she could go to Atha and claim her protection after Firbaith died. Elenn had just shaken her head and smiled and said she did not mind the new marriage Maga had found her. It was as if she were sitting in the middle of one of the pearls on her headdress, smiling and beautiful and distant, protected from everything happening around her. Emer had no idea what the consequences might be if something had broken through that.

She looked longingly at her own blankets, set the circlet down carefully on Elenn's, and went in search of her sister.

Several people had seen Elenn leaving with Cethern of Lagin and marked the direction, so it wasn't long before Emer came up with them. Maga was standing near the pyres where today's dead were waiting for sunset and the spark of fire to send them on their way. She was smiling in a way Emer recognized as triumphant. At her side stood Ferdia, looking sullen and unhappy. Cethern was beside him, frowning. Elenn, on his other side, was almost incandescent with anger, though she might have seemed calm to someone who didn't know her. Emer had never seen her sister so disheveled. Her hair was loose for mourning, and her blue dress was stained with grass and blood. The poet ap Dair stood between Elenn and Maga in an attitude of rapt attention.

Maga was speaking when Emer came up to them. "Most kings wish their sons to win renown," she said

"Most women wish their husbands to survive," Elenn said passionately.

Emer eased in beside Elenn. Ap Dair bowed as he made space for her. Maga smiled a welcome. Elenn ignored her. Cethern gave her a quick glance, then returned his attention to Elenn. Ferdia didn't even seem to see her.

"I am going to fight anyway. Honor requires it," Ferdia said, darting a look at his father that seemed almost guilty.

"Oh, Ferdia," Elenn said. "It isn't necessary. Someone will open the road or they won't, but it needn't be you. If our parents will agree, let us be betrothed now and married later, after the war, and after the details of an alliance have been worked out."

"You will have plenty of chances to distinguish yourself in battle without going up against Atha ap Gren or Black Darag directly now, when you are still a young man," Cethern said.

"I am going to fight anyway," Ferdia said, staring straight in front of him.

It was clear to Emer that Maga had got at him somehow. Maybe it was clear to Cethern as well, from the way he was frowning.

Elenn looked on the edge of tears. "I won't let you die for me," she said.

Ferdia looked at her sternly, almost with dislike. "I am going to fight anyway," he repeated doggedly.

"Why?" Emer asked. Everyone looked at her. "Why are you going to fight?" she asked again.

Ferdia stared dumbly at her for a moment.

"Yes, why, son?" Cethern asked eagerly.

"It concerns my honor," Ferdia said at last, looking at ap Dair.

"Nothing could dissuade you," ap Dair said, as if quoting something, or perhaps making something up.

"Nothing," Ferdia echoed gratefully.

Nobody could say anything to that, of course. Elenn drew breath to speak, but thought better of it and sighed instead. Emer wanted to shake Ferdia. He would be killed. It would break Elenn's heart. Worst of all, she would have to help, or stand by and watch Darag kill him. It was only then she realized how bad things were. It would break Darag's heart even more surely than Elenn's. Indeed, it might distress Darag so much that he could not keep fighting. Her breath caught on that. It didn't bear thinking about, because if Darag couldn't go on, then the army of Connat came forward into Oriel. This didn't seem like chance. This seemed like a plan. Emer looked at her mother, the master-planner. She was smiling sweetly at Cethern. Emer looked back at Elenn. A tear had escaped her brimming eyes and was trickling down her cheek. There was something terrible and relentless in this, something far beyond ordinary cattle-raiding, or even ordinary war.

There was only ever one way to stop Maga, one person who could stop her. She had to find her father. Maga's smile reminded her only too well of the last time their parents had been at war with each other. Allel could stop her, though it wouldn't be easy even for him.

"Do we have a betrothal tonight?" Maga asked at last.

Cethern let go of his beard, which he had been tugging gently. He looked at Ferdia, who was staring at the grass at his feet. Cethern did not quite shake his head. He turned to Elenn, who was standing perfectly still and quiet but whose face was now running with tears. "We do," he said, and he sounded thirty years older than he had before.

Elenn bowed to Cethern, who bowed back gravely. Then she put out her hand to Ferdia, who took it and held it tightly.

"Tonight after the funerals, then," Maga said.

The sunset, the funerals, and the betrothal passed in a haze for Emer. Allel was there, but she could not hope to have him alone for a moment. There was plenty of food afterward, for once; fresh supplies must have come from somewhere. Ferdia did not seem to have much appetite. Elenn kept looking at him, but he rarely met her eyes. Allel too kept very quiet, drinking with Cethern and Lew of Anlar, who seemed to be a permanent addition to their dinner group now.

Elenn and Ferdia led the first dance. Most people seemed to be wild and enthusiastic in the firelight. Emer waited until the second dance, which was one anyone could dance, men together, women together, even children with parents. She grabbed Allel's hand and pulled him up. "Dance with me, Father," she said. Their eyes were on a level now, as they had not been when last they had danced together.

"There are plenty of younger people who would be only too pleased to dance with you," he complained and gestured to Lew, who smiled. Lew could hardly be used to being called young.

"Oh, please, come on," she said, not letting go of her father's hand.

Allel sighed and shrugged and followed her as if he had no choice. As soon as they were far enough away from the others, with enough dancers between them and Maga that they couldn't be seen or heard, she stopped and took both his hands. "You must stop Mother doing this to Elenn."

"I can't," he said, freeing his hands and gesturing with them as if to ward her off. "I promised."

"Promised who? What? Why?"

Allel looked wretched. "Promised Maga I wouldn't interfere."

"Wouldn't interfere with what?" Getting him to talk tonight was like teasing out a sea anemone with a piece of seaweed.

Allel sighed and looked around as if for help. Everyone around them was moving in the dance. Nobody was even looking at them. "I shouldn't tell you."

"I have kept your secrets before, even at cost to myself," Emer said, which was a truth Allel had to acknowledge. "I can't see what you can have promised that would stop you helping Elenn."

"Well, but make sure this doesn't go any farther," he said. "Maga said she could bring the whole island together to conquer Oriel, and conquer it, right to the northern sea, before the Feast of Lew and the harvest. If she does, she has dominion over me, and if she does not, I have dominion over her—no more fighting between us in either case. But I must not interfere. I promised I would leave her alone to do what she wanted to arrange it."

"This entire war, all this craziness, is a war between the two of you?" Emer's voice shook with anger. She felt almost drunk with it.

"I didn't think she could possibly do it," Allel said. "You know what she can be like."

"I know what she can be like, and if you can't resist her, how much less can we? Have you thought what this is doing to Elenn?" Emer glared at her father.

"They have all of them been good men, and good marriages," Allel said. "Maga is trying to win, yes, but she has a care for you children as well. She wouldn't hurt you to try to win."

"I don't know how you can be so blind and stupid," Emer burst out. "Do you know she has been trying to marry me to Lew ap Ross?"

"He is the king of Anlar, and he has no heir," Allel said uncertainly.

"He is forty-five years old at least, and he is Conal's uncle!"

"I spoke to her for you, for Conal," Allel said, much more confidently. "She made him an offer and he wouldn't take it. She may have suggested Lew, but she hasn't forced him on you. He wouldn't be a bad match in many ways. Yes, he's older, but he's a good man."

What Emer wanted to say to that would have taken all night, and it was irrelevant anyway. "I am not going to marry him. I am going to marry Conal. But what about Elenn? Do you know she loves Ferdia, and Ferdia doesn't love her, and Maga has somehow forced him into fighting, even though he is young, Darag's best friend, and nothing like as good as Darag?"

"I didn't know he didn't love her," Allel said. "But—"

"She has seen four good husbands die for her, and three dozen good men die trying to win her, and now she is going to see the man she loves die just like them, under Darag's spears. You have to stop this. Whatever you promised, you have to stop Maga. She is completely out of control, and nobody else has ever had any way of checking her."

"I promised," Allel said, moving aside to let a pair of hurtling dancers pass them. "If I get in her way, she will call it interference and call the whole thing off. She hasn't forced you or Elenn to marry anyone. Ferdia is Cethern's son, not mine. It's not my responsibility if he's fighting people who are better than he is."

"And you'll let Elenn break her heart like that?"

"She has agreed to it, and so has he. Maga may have suggested these men to Elenn, but Elenn has accepted them. Making marriage alliances is a reasonable thing for a king to do." He hesitated. "Or a queen."

"She's agreed to let you be king if she loses?" Emer was horrified.

Allel looked uncomfortable. The music stopped, but he led Emer out of the way as another couple-dance began. "I'm of the Royal Kin the same as she is. We were both chosen, in a way," he said, in a tone of justification.

Emer had been taught by Inis for a year, and by ap Fial for years before that. "You know better than that, Father," she said. "Kingship is not something to be passed from hand to hand like an arm-ring. It is a sacred trust, and what's more, she just won't give it up."

"She swore she would, if she lost."

Emer was silent for a moment, amid the noise of the harps and drums and dancers leaping in the firelight. "Then maybe she will," she said. "But she should not. The gods will not permit it."

"The gods are showing every sign so far of being on your mother's side," Allel said.

"I'm sure Damona the Just isn't," Emer said, stretching her fingers as she said the holy name.

Allel frowned. "They are not my concern. If I come to be king, I will stand between them and the people then. Now, that is for Maga."

"Is the chance of kingship so much for you that you will risk my happiness and Elenn's and Mingor's, if need be, for the chance of it? You know there are no children in marriage without love. And all of this is hurting Elenn more than she can bear."

"It's not your happiness, and love grows in marriage," he said uncomfortably. Emer knew then that this was hopeless, that he would not help her. He could be as stubborn as Maga when he was put to it. He had always resented Maga for being chosen king when he was the war-leader. "It is my promise. Anything I say she will see as interference. And besides, you exaggerate. Elenn is very young. She will recover. Or maybe Ferdia will beat Darag and open the road."

"I always thought I could trust you," she said, feeling that assurance slip away. The world seemed colder without it. As a child, Maga had never been fair, but Allel always had, when she could attract his attention.

"I haven't told her you're driving Darag's chariot," Allel said, smiling placatingly.

"You know?" This was another, even colder, shock.

"Did you really think a scarf would hide you from your own father?"

"Who else knows?"

"Nobody." Allel smiled. "I haven't told anyone, and I have stifled speculation whenever I can. When people have talked about it, I have suggested that it is ap Ringabur the lawspeaker, in disguise because she should not stand among the fighting folk of Oriel."

"And why didn't you tell anyone?"

"I wanted Darag to hold. I don't want Maga to win." Allel laughed.

"Then you are not even keeping your promise," Emer said, despising him. There had to be another way out, even if he had failed her.

"Not telling isn't intervening. She can't know I knew, and even if she did, it isn't the same as trying to stop her plans," Allel protested.

Emer looked at him and saw not her kind and powerful father, but a tired, greedy man, past middle age, his hair thinning on top. "Elenn thinks that those people are dying for her," she said. "She'll live with that burden her whole life. I am helping Darag to kill them, and they are my kin and my friends. I will have to live with that. But you don't understand, and you should. They're dying for you, you and Maga are killing those good people. And the same would hold if there had been no curse, if there had been a war with battles in the normal way of things. The weight of the souls of everyone who dies in this war falls on you and Maga because you are both so selfish and so caught up in your own personal war that you can't see how terrible it is to fight that war with other people's lives. If words were not wounding enough, could you not have taken up swords, or staves, or snowballs in winter as we did in Muin, or wrestled in the mud for supremacy? It would have better become the dignity of the kingdom of Connat than this."

Allel stood speechless as she turned and walked away. She was shaking with anger and tiredness, and she went back toward her tent. She did not know if Elenn would be sleeping there tonight or if she would go with Ferdia. She hoped her sister might at least have one good night with the man she loved to remember afterwards. Thinking of Ferdia's face, she did not think so. If he loved anyone, it was Darag. Maybe Elenn loved him because he didn't love her, he didn't press her to love him, like all the others. She hoped he would be kind. He would die tomorrow, there wasn't any way around it. He would die, and Elenn and Darag would break their hearts, and she couldn't do anything to stop it, because the only alternative was Darag dying, with Conal and all the folk of Oriel after him.

As she went into the tent, she tripped over the pile of bloody clothes. She pushed them outside wearily. Then she went out again and put them carefully out of the way, at the side of the tent where Elenn would not trip over them coming back. It wasn't much to do for her sister, all things considered.

Inside the tent once more, finally able to close her eyes, she was too

tired to sleep. She kept running over the argument with her father, thinking of better things she might have said, hearing again his denial of her
happiness as a thing of importance compared to his own power. She had
always loved her father. Still, she had Conal. Conal had said he would go
away with her. He did not care more about power. He could be trusted.
She tried not to think of Conal's face riven with pain, but to remember
the feel of his arms around her. She remembered the nights they had had
together, just sleeping, the comfort of the warmth of his body. She
counted them, recalling the feel of each, in Edar at the Feast of Bel, in
the Isles, on the road, in Muin, the whole blessed month in Muin. Recalling Conal in Muin, at last she felt sleep close over her head like deep
water.

Sometime later, she became aware that Elenn and Beauty had come
into the tent, and that Elenn was weeping. "Elenn?" she asked, trying to
pull herself up out of sleep.

"Go to sleep," Elenn said, her voice full of misery and resentment.

Without opening her eyes, Emer turned and reached over to her sister.
She opened her arms and embraced Elenn, who was stiff for a moment
and then hugged her back. For a little while, they held each other as they
had when they were tiny children and their parents had been quarreling.
"Go to sleep," Elenn said again at last, this time affectionately. "I think
you are still asleep."

"Mmm," Emer agreed. "You go to sleep, too." She let her sister push
her into her own space and pull the blanket up and held sleep off until
she heard Elenn lie down. Then she went back to sleep, a wonderful
healing sleep that brought her the dream that showed her the way out she
had thought impossible.

# —28—

## (FERDIA)

The sun was shining, the trees were green, and under them was a
twilight-blue haze of bluebells, scenting the air even out onto the
road where Ferdia's chariot was hurtling at what felt like breakneck pace
towards the ford. He wished they would go even faster so he really would
break his neck before they got there.

Ferdia was ready to die, but he wished he could do it without having
to see Darag's face. He couldn't pretend Darag wouldn't mind killing him,

however many other champions he had killed. He straightened himself with a hand at the side of the chariot. The banner of Lagin with its green hill spread out behind him. His spears were ready to his hand. It should have been a glorious first ride to war. When they sang about it afterwards, nobody would be able to tell he was only here because he was afraid.

His charioteer shot him a quick glance. "It's not too late to change your mind," she said. He shook his head at her. She was not really his charioteer but Cethern's comfortable old Pell, who had first taught him to harness horses and how to stand in a chariot.

"Oh yes it is," he said, glancing behind them. They were leading the way. Behind them came the other people who planned to challenge Darag that day, after Ferdia fell, and behind them, that part of the army of Connat and the allies who wanted to see the day's sport, along with those few confident folk who thought that Darag might still be defeated. Less than a third of the champions were there, along with a handful of the farmers. Cethern was there, and Allel, and ap Dair. It was quite enough people to remember it forever if they had seen Ferdia ap Cethern retreat from what he had said he would do. "What I was thinking, though," he said hesitantly, knowing he should have suggested it before. "They say Darag's charioteer always fights disguised."

"Nobody know who she is," Pell confirmed. She lowered her voice, even though they were out ahead and nobody could hear them. Pell was no different from the way she always was, even though she knew he was going to die. She always knew all the gossip and loved passing it on. "Some say she is a lawspeaker, and others say she is one of Atha's women. Atha has lost three charioteers in seven days, but Darag has kept this same one, as far as we know. But even though she's disguised, if she'd been killed and replaced, someone would have seen her go down. I think it's the same one, whoever she is. After all, he has the advantage of the water, which makes a difference. The road is higher on the Oriel side."

He had seen the ford on the first day, and the terrible sight of Darag's single chariot standing alone to defend it against all the might of the army.

"I was wondering if I could fight disguised," Ferdia said.

Pell laughed. "Because you are too new a warrior for your name to put fear into anyone? It might do for a charioteer, but not for a champion. You must give your name to make your boast. Only a fool would fight an unnamed champion at a ford."

Ferdia had forgotten the boast. "It is just that Darag is my foster brother," he said apologetically. In some ways, it was best that Darag recognizing him would be the worst thing. It would be over quickly, right at the beginning, and dying would almost be easy after that.

"Your father told me to keep reminding you that you could turn around at any time," Pell said. "I told him you wouldn't, young men are fools. But you could turn around now and in fifty years' time, think back on riding this far as youthful folly."

"I wish you wouldn't keep saying that," Ferdia muttered. Nothing would have pleased him more than turning around. Nothing was less possible.

Pell pursed her lips but kept driving on, barely slowing for the bends in the road. She was good, but then, she had been a charioteer for thirty years. Three of her four children were here with the army. "Yesterday Darag chose to fight with swords first," she said. "He talked with Laran ap Noss about it a while across the ford, asking if he would do that. Then when Laran agreed, they fought on the far bank. He might do that again."

"I have a sword," Ferdia said.

The road passed through a belt of alder and willows, then came out into the open space with the river ahead of them, and the ford. Darag's chariot was standing on the farther bank, just as it had the first day, and no doubt every day since. He looked at it and looked away. His stomach turned over and he swallowed hard. There was nothing else now. He was here to die and he would die. He wondered if the garlanded animals at the feasts felt like this when they saw the knife.

Pell slowed, and he realized that everyone following them was stopping. They drew to a halt just by the ford. Ferdia braced himself and looked up. Darag wasn't looking yet; he was in intense conversation with his mysterious charioteer.

"Give your boast now," Pell urged. He didn't know what to say. How could he boast, he who had no deeds to boast of?

When in doubt, go with what you have learned. He had a name to give, at least. He shut his eyes. "I am Ferdia ap Cethern," he began, and rolled out his ancestry as he had learned it, one after another—his grandfathers and great-grandfathers back through the generations—until he came to the end, or the beginning, the founding heroes of his line. ". . . ap Galian, ap Liath, ap Lethan. I am a prince of Lagin," he said, raising his voice a little, because it was here that his own deeds should have gone if he had any. He opened his eyes. Darag was standing as still as a stone and staring at him.

"I am here to challenge you for passage of this ford. Will you yield to my might and let us pass?"

He kept his eyes resolutely open. It was about as bad as it could be. Darag leapt out of the chariot and ran down the bank toward the water. "Ferdia ap Cethern?" he called. "How can this be? Ferdia ap Cethern is my friend and my foster brother. Surely you are some imposter abusing his name to challenge me."

"No, it really is me," Ferdia said miserably, but beginning to be aware that there was something strange about the way Darag was talking. Something unnatural. He sounded as if he were playing a part, not like himself at all. Maybe it was the shock.

"Then why do you come against me, my brother?" Darag demanded.

"Honor demands it," Ferdia said, falling back on what had worked before. He wished he could explain to Darag, who, alone of everyone he knew, might have understood. But of course it wasn't possible. There were too many other people here. In any case, Darag was honorable, he wouldn't understand how Maga had a hold on him. Ferdia could never tell him about the dog.

"We have been brothers, must we now be enemies?" Darag asked sadly, spreading his empty arms.

Despite Darag's unnatural tone, Ferdia choked on a sob and felt tears burning in his eyes. Pell put her hand on his arm. "You really could back out now," she advised. He shook her off fiercely.

"I must challenge you for the passage of the ford, so we must fight, but we need not be enemies," he managed to say clearly.

"Then come here and embrace me for the last time before we begin," Darag said.

Ferdia looked at Pell for guidance and was astonished to see that she was dashing away tears from her eyes. "Go, go," she said. Then, as he was climbing out of the chariot, she added, "It's like a story. They will sing of this for as long as there's anyone on this island to sing."

Ap Dair was somewhere in the crowd behind them. Ferdia had almost forgotten.

He walked down to the edge of the water and waded across. It was cold but not unpleasant. The other side was steeper. Darag offered his hand to help him out.

They stood there for a moment, looking at each other. Darag's face, up close, did not look sad but full of suppressed excitement. They embraced, and he whispered fiercely into Ferdia's ear. "Emer told me. You have promised to fight and challenge me for the road. You haven't said you'll try to kill me, and neither have I said I'll try to kill you. You said we're not enemies. We can fight here all day, the way we have other days. Practice, I mean. Say what we're going to do, so we can block. Make it look good."

"Emer?" Ferdia whispered, completely confused. Darag's eyes went to his charioteer. Once Ferdia knew, he wondered how he had not recognized her before. He didn't understand why she was here, when he had seen her in the camp of Connat last night. She was betraying her own land, her own family. He blinked at her.

"Do you agree?" Darag asked.

Ferdia thought it through for a moment. Pretending to fight opened up a possibility he had thought lost—life opening up beyond today, with honor. But was it honor, truly? "I promised Maga I would fight you," he said.

"Did you promise to try to kill me?" Darag asked.

"No, but I promised to try to open a road into Oriel, which is the same," Ferdia said wretchedly. He pulled back from the embrace, and they stood looking at each other. "You just heard me say so," he said, as if it would help.

Darag looked uncertain now. He frowned. "Tomorrow will be the ninth day since this began," he said. "Inis ap Fathag said that the sickness that has fallen on everyone else would last three days, or six, or nine. So tomorrow, it should be over. Why don't we fight here today in show only, and then tomorrow you can fight anyone you want for the road to Oriel, and I'll fight to stop your army, but we needn't fight each other."

"Yes," Ferdia said. That was honorable. He smiled at Darag, and wanted to embrace him again. But everyone was watching. He bowed instead.

"Swords first?" Darag asked, bowing. "I should think we can change weapons several times, and have rests between. Usually I rest while people are taking away the bodies and making their boasts. You wouldn't believe how tiring it is fighting all day, day after day."

"We could stop for meals," Ferdia said and giggled.

"Don't forget that people are watching," Darag said. "They can't hear us saying what we're doing if we keep it low, but they can certainly see everything."

He drew his sword, and Ferdia did the same. Absurdly, he remembered all the reasons against practicing with real swords. "Be careful. It would be terrible if we killed each other by accident," he said, but this time managed not to laugh, even though the nervous relief he felt was greater than it had ever been before. He could live past this day. He could live and still be friends with Darag. The sun was shining and sparkling on the water of the ford, and he was alive and might remain so. He could have sung with joy.

"We have to make it look good," Darag said, and leaped towards him, sword high.

They fought hard, moving up and down the clear space before the water. After an hour, they rested, and after another hour of close sword-work, Ferdia went back to the chariot for the spear-fight, sweating and bleeding from a few scratches where he hadn't brought his shield up quickly enough. Pell looked frankly admiring as she blotted and sang charms over the scratches as he rested. "You have lasted longer against him than anybody else," she said. "They must have good arms-masters in Oriel. It's clear you and Darag learned from the same one." Ferdia looked at her sharply. Had she guessed they were going through practice forms? But it hadn't all been routines; he thought they had varied it enough.

They exchanged spears several times. Ferdia was surprised how much skill it took to throw the spear and try not to hit, even when they had arranged in advance which direction they should duck. Darag's spears all struck the chariot. Ferdia's first throws went wild, and one of his later ones went too close and wounded one of Darag's horses. "What a song this will make," Pell said when they agreed to go back to swords.

At the end of the day, Ferdia was so exhausted he could hardly stand. He was back in his chariot. Darag held up his hand for them to speak.

"The day is drawing to an end," he called. "We cannot fight in darkness. We should lay down our weapons now until dawn brings a new day."

Ferdia looked at Pell for advice. "They will sing of this all over the world," she said. "Yes, tell him you will leave it until the morning."

"I will agree to that," Ferdia called. "Tomorrow we will fight again." There was a loud murmur from behind him, and a drumming of feet in approval. He turned to look and saw that the space between himself and the trees was packed. Almost all the champions were there.

"They have been coming up all day since they heard you were holding," Pell said.

Ferdia turned back to Darag. "Farewell until the morning, then," he said.

"Hold," Darag said. "Let us spend this night together as brothers, sharing our food and blankets for a last time."

"Can I?" Ferdia asked Pell.

"Do you want to?" she asked.

It was only then he realized how much he did want to. He would give anything to spend the night with Darag instead of having to bear again Maga's demands and Elenn's expectations and his father's anguish. "Oh, I do," he said. "But will they think it strange?"

"Strange, yes, but this whole day has been strange. Go. If he kills you in the night, the army will avenge you," Pell said. "Not that I think for a minute he will."

"I will spend this night with you," he said and climbed out of the chariot.

Cethern was there. Had he guessed? There was no hint of it in his eyes. "I am so proud of you, my son," he said and embraced Ferdia.

"Forgive me, I didn't realize you had a real chance against him. Now I understand why you wanted to fight."

Ferdia could say nothing. He couldn't tell his father he and Darag hadn't been trying to kill each other. He couldn't say he looked better than he was because Darag was so good he could do things that made him look good. So he just smiled awkwardly. "You don't mind me spending the night here?" he asked.

"It's little Elenn who will mind," Cethern said. "But I'll try to explain. Coming back and going out again would be very hard."

Ferdia raised his chin in acknowledgment. After a few more words, Cethern left him to go back to the camp before sunset. Ferdia realized there would be fewer bodies to burn tonight, only those Atha had killed. As well as surviving himself, he had saved the lives of several other champions.

He waded back across the ford to Darag. "Emer has gone off," Darag said. "She has to get back before they notice she's gone. It was her idea that we did not need to kill each other. I'm so glad she thought of it, because it might not have occurred to me until it was too late."

"I'd never have thought of it at all," Ferdia said. "I couldn't see any way out."

"How did Maga make you fight?" Darag started to stroll along the road into the trees.

"She said she'd tell ap Dair I was a coward, and ap Dair would make a song about it to shame me. She said Elenn was in love with me and she'd tell everyone I'd spurned her."

"Emer said you were betrothed to Elenn," Darag said. "Congratulations."

Before Ferdia did anything stupid like explaining about all that, he remembered that Darag had been a little in love with Elenn. So he just smiled, as if he wanted to marry Elenn, as if he were glad.

Just then they came to the end of the trees, and someone was there, supporting himself against the trunk of a tree. With a shock, Ferdia realized that it was Conal. All the arrogance of his posture was gone, and most of his good looks. He looked haggard and old and battered, like someone who had been badly wounded and the weapon taken away so there could be no healing. He twisted his face into a bitter smile of greeting.

"Have you come to join us at last, Ferdia?" he asked.

"Ferdia and I have been fighting all day. He has come to spend the night with us."

Conal looked incredulous, which wasn't surprising. "I see," he said, frowning and taking deep breaths. Ferdia had heard that the folk of Oriel fell on the ground and cried out when the pain came over them, but Conal did nothing but lean his head gently against the trunk of the tree. Probably it wasn't as bad as everyone thought.

They waited for the spasm to pass, so Conal could speak again. After a little while, they both looked away. It was that bad, after all. Ferdia didn't like Conal, but it was horrible to see anyone suffer like that. After a moment, Darag gave a great hail and raised his arms. "Atha!" he called.

Atha was coming along the road from the camp. She was still dressed for battle—naked, and painted for wild defiance. Ferdia could well believe the stories about strong champions fainting just at the sight of her. She was blue all over, with rolling eyes painted on her nipples and a fanged mouth on her stomach. She had the Eye of the Isles in the center of her forehead, and over her eyes was the Oak Branch of Oriel. Below that were lines and spirals in white and black, so it was impossible to read any human expression on her face. As if that wasn't enough, her hair was limed so it stuck straight out from her head in points that looked sharp enough to do damage, and she had dipped the very ends in red. It was similar but not identical to the way she had been painted on the first day she came out to hold the road. Ferdia wondered if she managed to make it different every day.

"The boy said you were back, and I was already at the camp, so I came looking for you in case you'd decided to stay out here for hours like last night," she said, embracing Darag. She was still considerably taller than he was.

Ferdia looked away. It wasn't that he had forgotten Atha, or that she and Darag were married now. He just hadn't exactly been thinking about it when he had agreed to spend the night here.

She bowed greetings to Ferdia and Conal, along with a slight inquiring look at Ferdia, but it was clear she could hardly wait to speak to Darag. "How many?" she asked eagerly.

"Oh, you win easily today," Darag said. "Not one. Ferdia and I fought all day with scarcely a scratch for either of us."

"You are just in time to hear them explain how this amazing feat occurred," Conal said, recovered and as sarcastic as ever.

Ferdia's cheeks heated. "Tomorrow, if you are not restored, Darag and I will fight in earnest," Ferdia said, gritting his teeth. It would be a pleasure to fight Conal.

"So you were not fighting in earnest?" Atha asked.

Darag laughed. "It was Emer's idea. We were bound to fight, since Ferdia had been forced to challenge me. But why were we bound to kill each other? I held the road. He fought me. Tomorrow, as he said, when everyone is restored, he can fight someone who is not his brother. Tonight he is spending with us. Everyone agreed."

Atha's face remained unreadable. Conal frowned. "If we are well tomorrow, that will be well," he said. Then he clutched the tree again, gritting his teeth audibly.

"Everyone will want to speak to you in the camp," Atha said.

"I ate with Maga yesterday. It can't be much worse," Ferdia said.

"You haven't seen our camp," Darag said. "I wish we needn't go back there. I wish we could just all stay out here in the woods for the night. All that screaming and talking between is so difficult."

"It's ridiculous to feel guilty for being fit," Atha said gruffly. "But we needn't go back if you don't want to. I could bring out some food and we could do that, sleep by the ford. Why not?" She turned to Ferdia. "Unless you specially wanted to see the others? Conary, or maybe Inis?"

Ferdia felt as if he were being dragged along on a current he hadn't expected. He would have liked to spend the night with just Darag, but he couldn't possibly say so to Atha. "Yes, I mean no," he stammered. "I'm not sure what I want. I'm so tired."

Atha laughed. The normal pink of the inside of her mouth looked strange with all that paint around it. "You don't know what tired is, after only one day," she said.

"I'll never call one-day-tired tired again," Darag agreed.

"And tired just doesn't compare," Conal put in, his voice sounding normally sardonic, only his face belying his tone.

Atha turned to Darag. "I'll go to find some food and bring it to the ford. Better if you don't go back at all to have to deal with questions. Nobody will bother me. Elba and Finca are frightened of me." She curled her lip.

"You're so good at dealing with people," Darag said admiringly. "Bring some ale as well."

"It's no use trying to drown troubles, they can swim," Ferdia said.

"Sometimes a little ale is good for sleep," Atha said. "I'll bring some. And I'll tell everyone about your day." She went off down the path, raising a hand in farewell. Ferdia couldn't help but be glad to see her go.

"I'll tell them, too, when I go back," Conal said. "But tell me, how is Emer?"

"Very well," Darag said. "She even got to rest today. A lot of the time, Ferdia and I were fighting with swords, because it was safer." He smiled at Ferdia. "I told you this was her idea."

"Is she coming tomorrow?" Conal asked.

"She said she would come in case," Darag said. "But surely tomorrow you will all be well and I will be the one to lie at my ease while you protect me." Ferdia was disconcerted to see that Conal didn't look as sure as Darag did.

They made their way back to the ford. Someone had seen to the horses already. The Connat side of the stream was deserted now and looked untidy, trampled and strewn with leftovers, bits of food the crows were picking over. "They're probably disappointed there was no blood today," Darag said.

"I was thinking it's strange to see the sun set without being at a funeral," Ferdia admitted. Darag shuddered. "Is it awful?" Ferdia asked tentatively.

"Atha and I make a game of it, counting heads. But yes, it's awful." Darag shook his head and stared across the stream. Ferdia put his hand on Darag's shoulder, and Darag leaned back against him. "Today was the last of it," he said. "And may all the gods bless Emer for finding a way to spare me killing you."

They were still sitting like that, quietly, when Atha came back. She was still painted for war but carrying a basket of food. Ferdia would have moved, but Darag put out a hand to stop him. Atha sat down on Darag's other side without comment. She shared out the food. They ate and drank, talking about fighting, about people you would want at your side in battle and people you would not. To Ferdia's surprise, Atha had a good opinion of Conal. As it grew dark, he felt the ale going to his head a little. The conversation became more relaxed. Later, Atha spread out the blankets she had brought. Without discussion, she made one bed for the three of them. Darag lay in the center and embraced them both.

Ferdia's head was spinning. "She is your wife," he whispered to Darag. He meant that wives were women, not girls, their wombs had been opened with the Mother's blessing, they were fertile ground that could bear children and should be planted with seed from nobody but their husbands.

He wasn't quiet enough. Atha laughed. Ferdia sat up abruptly, the blanket falling off. "Shall we tell him our big secret?" she asked.

"Yes, tell him," Darag said, drawing Ferdia back down.

"It's safe, I am pregnant already," Atha said. "As long as I keep thinking good strong thoughts of wanting him and don't let him slip away, the way so many silly women do, I will bear a son at the Feast of the Mother. Unlike most such, mine was begotten by my husband." She laughed again.

"And you're still fighting?" Ferdia asked, before realizing how stupid he was being. "Forget that," he said quickly.

Atha embraced him. "You are my husband's brother, and you are welcome in our bed," she said.

It was strange, the three of them together, sometimes unexpectedly awkward, but in the end, strangely satisfying. He was happy when he slept, curled up, with Darag again between himself and Atha.

Orlam ap Ringabur woke them. "Bad news," she said. "The sun is risen and the curse still holds."

Ferdia's heart tried to find a way out of his chest.

"Icy water on the neck would have been kinder," Atha said, sitting up without regard for her lack of clothes. The designs on her paint were smeared.

"I have said I will fight," Ferdia said, despairing.

"I can't," Darag said, not moving at all.

"I have come to say I will fight in your place," Orlam said. "I can fight to defend my homeland."

"But it's sacrilege to kill you," Ferdia protested.

"We have talked about this and we don't even know if it would count as the road being defended," Atha said. "Darag will fight."

"I will?" asked Darag. A crow across the stream made a derisive noise.

Ferdia felt as if a heavy weight had been dropped onto his shoulders. He stood up and reached for his clothes. Yesterday morning he had been ready for Darag to kill him, almost resigned. Now it was a fresh horror. Life was sweeter, it had more to offer him. It could still be snatched away like this?

"We could do what we did yesterday," Darag said, without moving.

For a moment hope rose again, then Ferdia shook his head. "For how long?" he asked. "No, we have to fight."

"Inis said it may be your doom," Orlam offered.

"Trample my doom in the mud with the pigs," Darag said, sitting up at last. "I will not kill my brother because of doom."

"Then I will, or he will kill me," Orlam said. She smiled at Ferdia. "No hard feelings, I hope?"

"This is crazy," Darag said. "Ferdia, go away. Go off into the woods. Let me fight someone else."

"Go away and do what?" Ferdia asked.

"Live," Darag said. He groaned.

"You can't ask him to live without honor," Atha said as someone stating an obvious truth.

"Is it even worth fighting to protect everyone if they are going to be in that state forever?" Darag asked. "Is it a life worth living? And how long can we go on without making a single mistake anyway? One mistake from either of us and we all die. It's amazing we've made it eight whole days. We can't keep it up indefinitely. Nobody could."

"We're very good," Atha said.

"Even so," Darag said. "My grandfather said three or six or nine days, and this is the ninth and still it goes on."

"Maybe tomorrow," Orlam said, but Darag made a gesture cutting her off and she was silent.

"Maybe twelve or fifteen or a hundred and forty-four," Darag said.

"Not even Necessity knows all ends," Atha said. "Maybe it is doom."

"I hate doom," Darag said emphatically. "I always knew it would be something like this, some horrible position where everything is wrong and whatever I choose leads to disaster. What next if I kill Ferdia? Killing you? Killing my shadow? Killing everything I care about in myself? There comes a point to say no, and this is it."

"I have said I am ready to fight in your place," Orlam said.

Darag flung off the blanket and walked off naked into the trees. Nobody said anything as he walked away.

"I should cross back over the stream," Ferdia said after a while. "They will be here soon."

"I need to paint myself and go to my own road," Atha said. She hesitated, then embraced Ferdia as kin. "Your name in my heart," she murmured, quietly so that Orlam would not hear. He whispered the same back to her.

"And tell Darag," he said.

"Darag knows," she said, shaking her head at the trees where he had vanished.

Orlam bowed to Ferdia. He waded back across the stream. It was another beautiful day, the mist was burning off already. He sat on a rock, his whole heart yearning to run after Darag, but knowing he must wait. He had never seen Orlam fight. She might not be as good as Darag. She might not even be as good as Ferdia. But she was a lawspeaker. If he killed her, he would fall under the Ban. Nobody would eat with him or speak to him. The gods would turn their faces away from his prayers. He would be an outcast. He would not exist in the same world as other people. Yet it would be cowardly to just stand there and let her kill him. He wondered when Pell and the others would arrive. He felt as if he might have been hungry at any other time. He went down to the stream and drank, which, horribly, made him feel a little better.

Emer came first, coming out of the woods. Then a servant brought up Darag's chariot and the horses. Orlam spoke to Emer for a little while, too softly for Ferdia to hear what they said. Then he heard the sound of chariots coming along the road from the camp. Before he could move, Darag stalked out of the woods. He said something to Orlam, then picked up his scattered clothes and armor and put them on. Orlam stepped out of the chariot and went back along the road toward the camp of Oriel.

Ferdia stared at his friend across the river. What had brought him back? Doom? Duty? Honor? Fear? Then Pell was there with his father's chariot. Behind her was the full might of Connat and the allies. It looked as if absolutely everyone with arms had come to see him die.

"Are you ready to start again?" Pell asked.

"I have to be," Ferdia said, climbing in and checking his spears. One of them was barbed. He looked at Pell. "Where did this come from?"

"Maga," she said, grinning. "Cruel-looking thing, isn't it? What they call a belly-spear. Goes in straight and can't come out."

"It's horrible," he said. "I'd rather have another ordinary one."

"The king of Connat gave you this one for your valor yesterday," Pell said.

Had Maga guessed they hadn't been fighting in earnest? Probably she had. Even if he were trying to kill Darag, he wouldn't want to hurt him that much. He wouldn't want to use that thing on his worst enemy. He would throw it first, casting it wide to get it out of the way. Maybe Darag would call for swords first again.

He did not. There was no need for a boast. When Ferdia was ready he looked over, and Darag was standing ready in his chariot, the heads bobbing on the back as Emer guided the horses slowly forward.

"Ready?" Darag called.

"Yes," Ferdia said.

He turned to Pell. "Drive straight forward, into the water," he said. She obeyed without question. Even before they reached the water he aimed and threw the first spear, the barbed one, carefully wide. Then, as they splashed into the ford, Darag's three spears came thudding across with hardly a breath between them. The first one wounded a horse, causing the chariot to swerve violently to the side before Pell brought it under control again. The second killed the other horse stone dead as they hit the water, bringing the chariot crashing to a halt in the water. Ferdia almost fell as he took aim with his own second spear and had to clutch the side of the chariot with his free hand. Then Darag's third spear came through the air and took Pell in the chest. The fourth spear was a surprise. It was the one Ferdia had thrown, of course. Darag would hardly have had time to look at it, pulling it out of the ground and sending it back. It took him in the belly, as it was meant to, twisting and spilling his guts out. He would have expected it to hurt, for the blood was coming out in waves, but there was only pressure.

Darag leaped the stream and came to a splashing halt at his side. "Ferdia ap Cethern, the valiant champion is wounded and his charioteer is down," he called. "I will draw out the spear and bind up his wound. He can withdraw in honor and I will fight the next challenger."

Nobody questioned this. That was why he had killed Pell, of course. Darag must have thought he could draw out the spear quickly and heal Ferdia with the help of strong spells and the weapon. Everything seemed to be turning red, which was unusual, but there didn't seem to be anything he could do about it. He couldn't move, the spear-point was pinning him to the chariot. There was water around his legs. If it had been an ordinary spear, it would have been a good idea, serving honor well. Darag was clever. He would never have thought of that.

"Your name in my heart," Ferdia said, or tried to say; his mouth didn't seem to be working well. He knew that when Darag pulled out the spear, he would die, before any charm could take effect. He hadn't expected that it would hurt quite so much, or for quite so long, before the merciful dark.

(THE SONG)

Under the willows
didn't I see Darag
armed and alone
defending his people.

Beside the ford
didn't I see Darag
battle-ready
arming with spears.

Into the rushing stream
didn't I see Darag
pride of Oriel
advancing with weapons.

Deep in the water
didn't I see Darag
the fearles warrior
slaying the champions.

Out in the flood's heart
didn't I see Darag
tears on his face
killing his companion.

Wild-eyed and weary
didn't I see Darag
black blood his garment,
mourning his enemies.

# 8

# TAKING RESPONSIBILITY

# — 29 —

## (CONAL)

If she came today—which he would not hope, because hope hurt too much—but *if* she came, he would be able to explain to her that she was wrong. Pain interrupted once more. Conal breathed hard through it but held the thread of thought. There was no time now when pain was not, but there was rhythm still, ebb and flow of the pain-tide. He could hold a thought through to the ebb, and even speak it after. Last night, at least, he had been able to speak it. Now, every whole thought held was a victory. If she came, if, he would tell her Amagien had not been cruel to make him face the bull when he was afraid. If he had not faced him, if he had not faced his fear, how could he have held through this?

He breathed. The sun was shining. The elm, which by rights should have been crushed by the force of his grip, remained straight and tall and utterly indifferent. Birds were singing in the spring sunshine. The pain was not in any one place. It moved through him like breath, like the breath of an enemy contesting for mastery. He would not give in. He could gain very little by standing here in defiance of the pain without moaning or screaming or weeping, but what little there was to be gained was hard-won learning, and he embraced it.

As soon as he heard the chariot hurtling down the road towards him, he turned and signaled the waiting child. It was a girl today, ap Casmal, not yet twelve years old. She did not hesitate but pelted off, her short braids flying up behind her. The camp would have some warning, for whatever good it would do. Conal was one of the strongest of them this morning.

Emer was alone in the chariot, a scarf bound about the lower part of her face. She turned in a tight circle and drew to a halt beside him. He took a step toward her, and another step. He breathed. The pain, its tide rising, breathed through him. He took another step despite it. He could endure this. He could endure anything he set himself to endure. He reached the chariot and realized he would have to climb in.

Emer was saying something about Darag and Ferdia. He could not attend yet. He needed to be in the chariot. He needed to be in the chariot now. But while he could make himself stand upright and even walk, his body balked at climbing.

"Help me in," he said. Even speaking was an effort.

"I knew you would come back with me," she said, satisfaction clear in her voice. "Quickly." She was there, and the touch of her arms was a comfort, but she could not lift him. The horses were fresh and would not keep still without her hand on the reins. They shifted uneasily, making the chariot bounce. Conal did not scream, held on to not screaming. At last he made it in and stood there trembling.

"Back to the ford?" she asked, and took his silence for assent. She took up the reins again and set off once more at racing speed. He could only clutch the side of the chariot and breathe, trying not to pant. The chariot jolted and lurched and he could not move in compensation, so every jerk went through him with a wave of pain, setting the waves at angles to each other so that they eddied and crashed over him in a series of crests without rhythm. After a little while there came an ebb at last. They were almost through the little belt of woodland, they would be at the ford in a moment. Emer's eyes were hard as flints, she stared out over the horses' heads as a charioteer should. They came out from the shade of the trees and Emer checked the pace of the horses.

The army of Connat was in front of them, filling the space between the river and the trees on both sides, champions in chariots, painted spearmen on foot around them, banners rippling out in the breeze. He saw Mingor looking enthusiastic, and Allel looking reluctant, and Cethern of Lagin afoot, his face full of grief and fury. Conal fumbled blindly behind him for a spear. His hand met empty space. He turned his head to look, and the chariot bounced over a rut in the road. The pain was everything and everywhere and all of the world for a time, so that it was a moment before he realized that his eyes were fixed on three empty slots where the spears should have been.

He stared at the emptiness for a moment, then started to laugh. He was racked with laughter, as with the pain, which it exacerbated. Emer looked at him, frowning over her scarf. He could not stop laughing. He had his sword, but he could barely stand. Would they wait for him to climb out of the chariot to challenge them? The waves of laughter fought the waves of pain, and Conal fought both of them for mastery. Emer drew the chariot to a halt, facing the army of Connat.

"Enemies of my people," he said, forcing his voice steady by will alone. "I challenge you. I am Conal ap Amagien, of Edar, Conal the Victor, and I hold this ford against whoever will stand." A wild, high giggle escaped him on the last word.

Mingor stepped forward, and Conal realized that unlike Darag, he could not fight anyone who came against him. If he killed Mingor or Allel, it would set a bloodfeud between himself and Emer, and he could not risk that. Allel, perhaps moved by the same thought, put a restraining hand on Mingor's shoulder. Cethern pushed his way forward to stand by Allel's chariot.

The pain came swelling up again so that Conal could not hear what they said, and he knew only that there was a silence he was expected to reply into. "This ford is held against you," he repeated. He drew his sword.

"You are in no fit state to fight," Allel said, "Go back, Victor. You will die to no purpose."

"Young people have not learned that life has endings," said a voice from behind. Conal did not turn to look, he did not need to. He would have recognized Inis's voice anywhere. "But I am an old man and here I am to stand beside my grandson, with my son and my granddaughter to stand with me."

Inis and Orlam came forward, supporting Conary between them.

"Ap Fathag—" Allel began.

Inis shook his head. "Weak as we are, we are all coming."

"Do you stand to fight?" Cethern asked.

"I do," Orlam said. "I will hold this ford."

"No," Allel said. "You cannot. A lawspeaker or a priest might fight to defend their home, yes, but not stand to hold a road when we must kill you at once and on purpose."

"Then you must risk that, and risk what Rathadun will make of it," Orlam said. Allel and Cethern looked troubled, and one or two of the older faces among the enemy frowned, but more looked eager and impatient.

"You can stand to fight if you insist," Allel said. "You may not hold the ford in single combat. We will all come against you. Either you are fighting folk or you are protected, you cannot be both."

"Then I will fight you, Allel ap Dallan," Conary said. His voice was cracked and feeble, but his determination showed through clearly. "Conal, will you lend me your chariot?"

"No," Conal said, speaking against the pain that was rising again. "I will rather fight to defend you."

"I have already lost one nephew to this foolishness," Conary said. Emer made a noise in her throat but said nothing. "I forbid you to fight now. There will be time when I am fallen, perhaps. Give me the chariot and your charioteer." Conal gritted his teeth against pain and frustration.

"I will fight you, Conary ap Inis," Cethern said. "I am on foot, as you see. My son and your nephew have killed my charioteer and broken my chariot. But you should know that your nephew is not dead. He swooned over my son's body and holds the ford no longer, but he lives and will recover."

"Thank you," Conary said, and swayed with the same pain that racked Conal. So Darag lived. Conal thought he was glad to hear it.

Orlam drew Conary's sword and put it in his hand. Inis handed him his shield. He took a lurching step forward toward Cethern. Cethern's sword blocked Conary's easily. Conal watched with horror-struck fascination. The wonder was that Conary could stay on his feet and avoid Cethern's blows. His sword and shield were clearly weights he could hardly lift. Yet time and again, he brought them up to block as it was needed.

"That's practice," Emer breathed admiringly as Conary staggered but stopped another high blow. Practice and something else, Conal thought as he stood and breathed, enduring. He was not sure he could do what Conary was doing. Conary brought his shield up again. He had never looked so much the king of Oriel as he did now, stooped and staggering and still undefeated.

Emer turned to look at something behind as the pain ebbed a little. "What is it?" Conal asked, holding what strength he had for when he would need it.

"Everyone's coming," she said. Her voice was awed. "Meithin and Leary and your mother and Leary's, everyone, all the fighting folk of Oriel, dragging themselves along."

Conal did not take his eyes off Conary. There was another exchange of blows. Conary feinted high and thrust low. Cethern blocked the blow with his shield and brought his own sword up fast towards Conary's belly. Conary brought his shield down to block, but too slowly. Cethern's sword went in and as Conal's pain rose high again, Conary crumpled slowly forward onto the grass.

"Do you yield, people of Oriel?" Allel was asking when Conal could hear again. "Will you give us what we ask?"

"What do you ask?" Inis asked in reply. "The Black Bull of Edar? Or our country and our homes? Is this cattle-raid or war now?"

Allel did not answer, which was answer in itself.

"Isn't this enough?" Inis asked conversationally. He turned to Conal and waved his arm in cheerful inquiry. "Don't you think this is enough?"

Conal remembered a dream, or something like a dream. He raised his hands and his voice as the pain flowed strong again. "Isn't this enough, Rhianna?" he addressed the air. "Damona, of the Judgments, have we not suffered even as the mare suffered? Bel, Lord of Moderation, who made the Wards that make us what we are, isn't this *enough*?"

The pain rose to a new crest as he shouted his defiance to the gods, and on that crest came a new wrenching. He screamed then, because his mouth was open to speak and he could not stop it. He thought the enemy might take it for a battle cry, because it was surely as loud as one.

Something heard. As the pain was at its highest, blood gushed out from Conary's fatal wound, and out of the black bloodtide came Blackie.

He thundered toward the enemy, head lowered and horns ready. It worked at Edar, Conal thought crazily, wondering which god might have thought this a good answer. Rhianna, maybe. Then, as the wrenching ebbed and his scream died away, the ground around him was covered with the shadows of champions advancing on foot. The pain ebbed and ebbed, and still they came, the shadow of an army wielding the shadows of weapons. He could recognize his own shadow, many times repeated, clustered around him and going forward. Conary's shadows rose from his fallen body, and Leary's flowed out from him, and Finca's from her, and shadows from all of those there who had borne the pain and stood ready to fight on the ninth day. More and more shadows came pressing up from behind; many of them he did not immediately recognize even as they parted around the chariot and flowed toward the army of Connat in eerie silence.

Conal raised his arms, and more shadows flowed out of him. The air around was dark with them, going forward, away from him. The army of Connat was giving way already before the army of shadows. They were back in the water, and still the shadows pursued.

"Should we go, too?" Emer asked.

The pain was still running through Conal, and he still had no spears, although most of his shadows did. "Go on," he said. Whatever he could do, he would. Emer spoke a word to the horses and they moved on, ears back uneasily.

As they went forward among the shadows, the darkness pressed around them until he could see nothing but darkness in any direction. He heard a cat growl and saw again the huge cat he had defeated on the heights of Cruachan, there among the shadows. He was standing alone on a mountaintop, stars falling all around him. Then he was in the chariot again, moving, with a rush of wings, a swirl of ravens very close, dark against darkness.

Then the shadow of the ogre Bachlach was there, his huge ax held in both hands, swinging up to strike at Conal's head.

Emer urged the horses on. Bachlach strode after them effortlessly. The pain was rising again. "I think we can outpace him," Emer said.

"He didn't have his turn," Conal said, forming the words carefully. "He survived being beheaded, and so did Darag."

"He's a god and Darag is his son," Emer said, not slackening the pace.

"How—" Conal began, but the pain, combined with the jolting of the chariot, was too much.

"I just worked it out," she said.

Bachlach's shadow was in front of them, huge and implacable, ax raised. The pain swelled up to meet him, the highest crest yet. Conal bowed his head and felt the ax-blow as mercy. The pain did not ebb, but left him entirely. His head rolled down his chest. He caught it in his right hand, laughing. It was smaller than he would have expected, about the size of the heads on the chariot, not like a living head. It must have been shrunken already.

They were still driving on through darkness. Bachlach was gone, and so was the pain. "Are you all right?" Emer asked.

"I think so," Conal said. After all, his head was safe in his hand and nothing hurt at all, which was very good. He moved a little, experimentally. He drew a deep breath. It was wonderful. "I love you," he said.

The shadows were still all around them in the dark, some of them shaped and some shapeless, all of them pressing insistently. Another swirl of ravens came out of nowhere, silently sweeping past. Then the chariot was gone and Emer was gone and he was falling through the star-shot darkness, his head clutched tight in his hand.

# — 30 —

## (ELENN)

She smiled at ap Dair, she smiled at her mother, she smiled at the Demedian king, she smiled at the wedding branches, autumn-colored now, she just smiled and smiled and waited for it to be over.

It felt as if she had kept that smile on her face every day of the four months since the black bull had come charging into camp and died at her feet. She had known at once that Ferdia was dead, though she had not understood what it meant for the war until later. She had smiled and gone on smiling, hiding everything she was feeling underneath the smile. It was surprising how much strength she found underneath. She had thought she was weak, but all the time her strength had been there, waiting for her to find it. She had always hidden her secret feelings away from her mother, but now she hid them from everyone. She was strong. It was Emer who was weak.

So Elenn waited, smiling her way through all the customary hand-kissing and congratulations of betrothal. Marriage was so familiar a ritual she could have done it in her sleep. The only thing that made this different was that the handsome young stranger standing beside her was not her new husband-to-be but his nephew, come to take his place in this ceremony and escort her back to him. Otherwise, it was all just the same, even to the dizzy speed of the proceedings. She waited, and as soon as they let her go to get her things, she hastened to tell her sister.

Emer was lying facedown on her bed in the room they shared, absolutely still. Her tangled hair spread out on the blanket. There was none of the relaxation of sleep, but she could easily have been dead. The first time Elenn had seen her like that, she had rushed to her in alarm. Now, after four months, it seemed almost normal. All the strength and independence Emer had found since she took up arms had disappeared since the battle, since Conal's death.

Elenn closed the door. "Ap Dair is back," she said to her sister's unresponsive back. "He's come straight from the ship in a tearing hurry. Urdo wants me. Wants the alliance, that is, he hasn't seen me of course. But so much the better. I am sick of men wanting me for my beauty. He will take the whole army and feed them and let them fight in his war and keep them as long as it lasts. I am betrothed to him already and we sail at sunset."

Emer rolled over slowly and sat up. Her eyes were red and the shadows under them were darker than ever. "Sunset today? Then you will get away," she said.

"Yes. I will be High Queen of Tir Tanagiri. And I will take you with me," Elenn declared. "I have been thinking about it. If Conal comes back for you, he can find you as well in Caer Tanaga as anywhere else."

In her heart, Elenn was sure Conal was dead. At the truce talks, Atha had told them he was. His mother and his father had worn their hair loose in mourning. Emer had refused to believe Atha and gone to ask Darag, who was king of Oriel now, as Elenn had always known he would be. Darag had told Emer gently that nobody had seen Conal since the battle.

It was true there was no body, but only Emer refused to believe he was dead. She had been mad, mad like Inis, talking as if she had been in the battle, when in fact everyone knew she had been back in Cruachan, not even in the camp. Since then, it was as if all the life had gone out of her. Elenn didn't understand it. It wasn't like grief as she knew grief.

More tears welled up in Emer's eyes. They both ignored them. "Have you asked Maga if I can come with you?" she asked.

"Not yet," Elenn said. "But I will, and we are leaving on the tide." Her clothes were in the chest at the foot of the bed. She could just take the whole thing. She took off her pearl circlet and dropped it in on top of them. She picked up her comb and turned it over in her fingers, then dropped that in, too. She shook off the orange bridal shawl and folded it. She would need that once more, for the actual wedding, once she met Urdo. She would wear her cloak. She could collect Beauty from the kennel master on the way, and then she would have everything. She would never come back, never. When Urdo died, she would marry someone else in Tir Tanagiri, someone she would meet there, someone she would choose herself.

"She won't let me go with you," Emer said flatly, breaking into Elenn's thoughts, which were already halfway to Tir Tanagiri.

"What makes you think that? It's a good idea. You'll be company for me, and away from here, and doing different things." All of Elenn's plans for getting away had counted on taking Emer with her. She recognized that there was an element of selfishness in this; it would be nice to have somebody familiar there with her. But even if she didn't want her, she could not leave Emer in the position she had been in herself, being forced to do what Maga wanted and knowing she had nowhere else to go.

"I know all that, and I'm grateful, really I am. But Maga won't let me go. You are bringing her an alliance. I am too valuable a piece on the gameboard for her to give up for nothing."

"You haven't asked her either," Elenn said reasonably.

Emer shrugged fiercely, showing a flash of her old fire. "I asked to go to Rathadun to train to be a priest. Ap Fial says I have the skills, and Inis said the same."

"It's twenty-one years of training," Elenn said, sitting down on her own bed.

"I know that," Emer said. "But I'd be away from here, and I'd like it and be good at it."

"Orlam says lawspeakers and priests can go anywhere," Elenn said. The idea was new to her. She'd never thought of doing anything like that. But Emer really wasn't like her at all. In some ways, it might be what her sister needed to help her get over losing Conal. She had exhausted herself day after day doing the gods' work throughout the war, after all, and never said a word about it unless you counted the babbling about axes and ravens when she came down the hill on the last day. Being an oracle-priest was something she could do where madness wouldn't even be a disadvantage. Elenn shook her head. She wanted Emer to come back to sanity, not choose madness as an escape.

"Yes. Go anywhere, have their own lives. Be useful. But Mother refused. She wants to make sure there's only one way out, the way she wants me to take. So I'm sure she won't let me go with you either, kindly as you intend it. I pleaded with her and Allel for that, and she was adamant. I'm not going through that again. I don't have the energy to spare." Emer sank down on her arms again.

"Couldn't you go anyway?" Elenn asked tentatively. "I remember Orlam saying, and maybe Inis as well, something about them taking anyone at Rathadun."

"The way they do it is that they will take a farmer's child for nothing but expect a large payment from a king's child. This means they can keep doing it. Kings' cast-out children might not be welcome anywhere," Emer said, flat despair in her voice.

"I'll ask if you can come with me, and you'll always be welcome with me," Elenn said, putting her hand on her sister's shoulder. "I'll go to ask now while she's with other people."

"Is Urdo ap Avren here?" Emer asked, her voice muffled.

Elenn almost snapped, then remembered to be patient. At least with Emer, she did not have to keep smiling. "He couldn't come himself. He's in the middle of a civil war. He sent his nephew, the new king of Demedia, and his wife has come as well. She's a Jarn and wears a veil. It seems very strange. But there are lots of Jarns in Tir Tanagiri. I'll have to get used to it."

"He must be a very new king of Demedia," Emer murmured.

"He is. His father's dead and his mother's in rebellion, but Urdo trusts him." She would have a lot of new politics to learn. She could see it would be a lot of work, but she could do it. She could manage a kingdom, even a huge high kingdom. As long as she was away from Maga and had a husband who could keep alive for long enough. She could love a husband, bear him children, do everything she needed to. "It's the rebellion that Urdo needs our army for."

"Mother will be so glad to be rid of the army," Emer said.

It was true. Maga had raised the army and now they were an embarrassment. They wanted to fight someone. The Battle at the Ford was neither a victory nor a real defeat. They had run from shadows, but the shadows hadn't actually killed anyone. The only people killed in the battle were Conal and Ferdia and Corary. When the bull died at Elenn's feet and the shadows disappeared, the priests and the kings had decided the war was over. For the time being, there was peace, unless anyone did anything new to provoke more fighting. So the army hadn't been needed. They had stayed at Cruachan rumbling with discontent all summer. The allies had gone home after the patched-up peace, but when they heard that the army of Connat remained in arms, they had kept their people in arms, too, afraid Maga was about to attack someone. Allel had tried to dismiss the army, but how could you dismiss an army that wanted so badly to stay in arms and make up for the past?

"This is a wonderful solution." Elenn agreed, not saying that it was her own idea. "Sit up and put your clothes in your chest, then let's go and find Maga, then we can say goodbye and go to the boats."

Emer sat up slowly as if it were a great effort. She didn't look at her chest or pull together the clothes that were scattered about the room, but Elenn decided not to push. In any case, she didn't have anything near as many clothes as Elenn, who had all her wedding gifts. Without looking, Emer picked up her two arm-rings, which were lying on the floor beside the bed. She pushed them onto her arms. Then she lifted her chest and looked at Elenn. Elenn picked up her own chest and led the way out into the hall.

Maga was still talking to the king of Demedia, his wife, and ap Dair. "Ah, girls," she said, smiling as they came up to her. "Ap Talorgen, ap Guthrum, let me present my younger daughter."

Emer set down her chest and bowed, and the two Tanagans bowed in return. Elenn set down her own chest. Emer was staring at ap Guthrum. Elenn could understand that. It was hard not to stare. She had hair the color of muddy straw. Her veil hid most of her face, but her hands and what was visible were yellowish-pink, nearer the color of a pig than a person. Her eyes were as gray as the winter sea, yet her expressions were kind, as far as Elenn could judge over the veil. She looked at ap Talorgen, so as not to stare at his wife and saw that he was grinning at her. She smiled graciously, then turned to her mother.

"I was wondering if my sister might go with us, to make a visit and to spend some time with me in Caer Tanaga," Elenn said boldly.

Maga frowned. Ap Dair looked thoughtful. Ap Guthrum blinked. Ap Talorgen smiled. "I don't see why not, if your parents don't mind," he said. "There will be room on the ship."

Maga smiled as ap Talorgen turned to her, but shook her head decisively. "I need Emer here," she said. "She hasn't been well, and she is to be married soon."

Emer raised her head and looked at Elenn. Her eyes held a mixture of defiance and pleading.

"Just for a few months, perhaps?" ap Guthrum said. "The winter climate in the south can be good for recovery from illness." Elenn was right, she *was* kind.

"It just isn't possible," Maga said with regretful finality. Emer's face was full of resigned despair. Elenn wasn't afraid that her sister would outright kill herself. She was no coward. But she might throw herself to the front of any fight that offered itself. Or, worse, she might just stop eating. Elenn had been coaxing her sister to eat as it was.

"We've packed her clothes," Elenn said. "She could be back in the spring."

But Maga knew as well as she did that if Emer got away, she'd never come back. She just shook her head. "It's touching to see how much you love your sister, but you will need to give all your love to your husband now," she said.

Elenn wanted to draw herself up to full height and demand to know how much love Maga gave Allel—how, after everything, Maga dared lecture her about love and marriage. But she held her smile. Arguing that way with Maga didn't achieve anything. Indeed, she knew she had lost and Maga had won. She looked at Emer with regret. She couldn't do anything else. She had to save herself, even if that was all she could do.

"Who does the younger ap Allel marry?" ap Talorgen asked.

"Lew ap Ross of Anlar," Maga said. She sounded proud, as if she expected ap Talorgen to congratulate her on her alliances. He just looked blank, as if he had never heard of Anlar. Emer said nothing, just stood there looking miserable. "Her sweetheart was killed in the fighting," Maga continued, still smiling, clearly feeling she needed to explain why Emer looked so sad.

"He is not dead," Emer said. "He is falling through the falling stars, but he will find his way home."

Ap Dair leaned forward, clearly fascinated. "The falling stars?" he asked.

Emer looked at him with contempt. "You find my mother's lies inspiring now. You turn your back on true poetry," she said.

"She's mad," ap Dair said, recoiling.

"Recovering from madness," Maga said. She turned to Elenn. "Are you ready to go? The army are boarding the boats already."

"I only need my dog," Elenn said, her chin high and her eyes meeting Maga's.

"Shall we walk out to the kennels, then?" Maga asked. Ap Talorgen smiled and picked up Elenn's chest, easily, as if it were light. Maga led the way out of the hall and they all trailed after her.

Ap Dair walked beside Elenn. "You are more beautiful than ever," he said. "It's strange. When I first saw you, I thought you were very beautiful. When everyone was dying for love of you, I sang that you were the most beautiful woman on the island. But there is something in your face now that makes my memories of you seem shallow. Urdo will be proud of you."

Elenn looked at him silently for a moment. She couldn't think of any possible response. Telling him to drop dead would have been satisfying, but she might need him again. "Thank you for helping to arrange this marriage," she said.

Allel was waiting at the kennels, Beauty with him. She was waiting patiently; even when she saw Elenn, she only gave a little whine and did not rush to her. She was almost full-grown now, her head nearly on a height with Elenn's when she was standing. The kennel master had trained her very well.

Allel had something folded in his arms. "This is a gift for your husband," he said, bowing and handing it to Elenn. It was leather, tanned and supple, folded over on itself. Emer gave a little gasp. It took Elenn a moment longer to realize what he was giving her, and then she had to suppress a shudder. It was the hide of the black bull, the bull that had been Maga's pretext for the war. It was a magnificent gift, and a terrible insult to Maga to give it to Elenn to take away. She looked up at her father, who was smiling. He wanted what was best for her, but he was usually so weak, compared to their mother.

She searched for something to say. "It must have been tanned by someone who knew all the charms well to have it ready so soon."

"I did it all myself," Allel said.

Elenn risked a glance at Maga, who was smiling unreadably. There would be storms ahead.

"Will you come with me to the ship?" she asked generally.

After she had embraced her family on the strand, she went up the little gangplank onto the rocking ship. Ap Talorgen put the leather into her chest with her other belongings. She stood with the chest on one side and Beauty on her other side, her hand resting on her dog's head. Maga and Allel stood together in something that looked like united amity from the distance the boat gave. Emer raised her hand in farewell. Elenn waved back. She wondered if Emer was mad. She hadn't gone mad because of grief herself, but she had always had a body. With Ferdia she had even had a head. She would not think of that, would never think of that again if she could help it. Poor Ferdia, too good, too honorable, to live.

The sun was setting behind the hills of Tir Isarnagiri and the boat slipped gently away from the shore. She waved one last time, then turned her back on her home and her family and stared out over the rose-gold water toward her hopes for the future. She knew that Urdo would spend one night with her and be off to war. She was used to that. She was more concerned with the work she had never yet done, the administration of his forts and organization of his supplies. She would learn. Beauty stood silently beside her, her warmth and solidity a comfort. Though ap Talorgen and ap Guthrum tried to make her more comfortable, Elenn stood still and straight as a figurehead through the night, her smile carefully on her lips, her eyes fixed hopefully before her.

# —31—

## (EMER)

Queen of Anlar sounds good, does it not?" Allel asked pleadingly.

Emer said nothing, as she had said nothing all the time her father had been with her. She submitted to allow her father to arrange the folds of the bridal orange overdress one more time. She wondered if the color looked as bad on her as it did on Elenn.

"Not quite as good, perhaps, as High Queen of Tir Tanagiri, but good enough. And Fialdun is a strongly built fortress, and Anlar is a strong ally of ours." He gestured to the Vincan tapestry that covered one of the walls of the dusty little room Lew had given her.

"At least I'll be away from you and Maga," she muttered, unable to keep silent any longer.

Allel patted her shoulder. "I'm so glad you're being sensible at last, if you can call a marriage half a month after the Feast of the Mother sensible. The branches will be bare twigs and you'll both freeze your toes off."

"None of it is sensible, or my choice," Emer said. "I'm getting married because Maga was making my life unendurable and she carefully left me no other options."

"Conal is dead," Allel said. "It's nine months since the battle, and nobody has seen any sign of him."

"Do you think I'd be marrying Lew if I didn't know that?" Emer asked, turning on her father with bitter anger. "He's falling through the falling stars, and that may be the road to death, or he may be falling forever. His name is written in my heart. I know I need to go on from there, to live my life without him. But the way I would choose to go on isn't this—there are other things I could do, things I would do better. I am a person, a human being. Father, look at me. It isn't too late even now. Let me go. She refused to let me go with Elenn, or to go to Rathadun, and she has had me too carefully guarded for me to get away. Nobody is guarding me now in this hour before the wedding. Turn your back and I will go out of the dun and down to the harbor. I won't disgrace you by joining with your enemies; I'll leave Tir Isarnagiri to find some life fit for myself far away in Narlahena or Lossia or Sifacia." For a moment she almost believed it might yet be possible.

Allel frowned petulantly. "Or on the moon," he said. "Do you call living as a mercenary champion in some strange land a fit life for a king's daughter?" He and Maga were still at feud over which of them now held the kingship, with Maga swearing she could not renounce it and had been beaten by a trick, but Emer was undoubtedly still a king's daughter. There was no getting away from that.

"A fitter life than what you and Maga would give me," Emer said. She turned her copper and bronze arm-ring with the fingers of her other hand. If Conal had lived she would have been able to escape no matter how closely guarded she was. She had been so tired, so very tired all the time since the battle; everything exhausted her. She would lie on her bed and weep, and sometimes even weeping took too much effort, so she would just lie there. Caring about anything at all was difficult. For the last few days she had felt a little better. It was almost as though there had been something holding her down that was now gone. She wondered what it might have been. She had thought it was grief, but she had not stopped grieving and yet the weight of not caring had lifted.

There was a scratch at the door. "Come in," Allel called heartily. Emer could tell how relieved he would be to get rid of her.

"You can't have it both ways," she said, almost hoping someone would overhear her. "You can't tell yourself it's all alright and at the same time feel guilty about it."

Allel turned his head away and did not reply.

It was the oracle-priest ap Fial who came in. "Not long before sunset," he said.

"I'll leave you two together," Allel said.

"Oh no, stay," Emer said, feeling cruel. She turned to ap Fial eagerly. "Could my mother have cursed me?" she asked.

Allel shuddered. "I'll see you soon," he said, and took a step towards the door.

"Never under the Hawthorn Knowledge," ap Fial replied, ignoring Allel, his eyes going distant as he answered the question. "Though parents sometimes do set a curse on their children to protect them."

"Not the Hawthorn Knowledge," Emer answered. Allel left, still smiling nervously. There had been times when Emer had understood the enjoyment Inis got out of being mad, and now she almost wanted to give way to it. "I've known all that for years, you taught me it yourself— remember the mother who set a curse that her son could be killed only by a green boar with no ears, and then he told his best friend and then quarreled with him? I always wondered how his friend managed to get the boar to stand still to be dyed."

"Stop babbling, Lady," ap Fial said. "I am here to bless your womb for marriage."

The form of address stopped her for a moment. Ap Fial usually called her "child," and she was a charioteer, a champion and not a lady, wasn't she? How could she have agreed to this marriage at all? Could Maga really have cursed her?

"I know why you're here," Emer said. "But could Maga have cursed me with helplessness for the last nine months? I have had no energy to do anything."

"She might have if she had your blood and hair. There is a charm for that to the Stormcrow. But it should not work unless you had the displeasure of the gods, which I know you do not, or unless part of your soul was outside the world, which it might have been. Now I must bless you."

"I did not seek this marriage."

"Nor did I force it on you. I am here in Anlar for the same reason you are, to get away from your mother. I've spoken to Lew, and I'll be staying with you."

"That's wonderful," Emer said. Maybe it wouldn't be too bad after all. She would have ap Fial with her, and he was a friend. Lew had a smile like Conal's. And she had already tentatively worked out a way of reorganizing Fialdun, except that everywhere in her old plan were little holes in the shape of Conal. She wouldn't weep, not now, not again. Bachlach had struck off his head. She would love him forever, but she had to make some kind of life without him. She put her hand up to her scar and rubbed it with her knuckles.

Ap Fial raised his hands to invoke Mother Breda and begin the blessing.

At sunset, Allel came back to lead her out of the hall.

Lew was smiling. The people holding the bare branches were smiling. The mud underfoot was frozen hard as iron, and was almost as cold as iron. Emer could not smile. She knew if she tried she wouldn't be able to hold back the tears. So she walked out gravely, enduring the smiles and the little sentimental sighs and the look on Lew's face as if they were minor wounds she could not stop for in battle. She could even bear it when she saw that one of Lew's branch-bearers was Amagien. Why not? He was Lew's brother, after all. She bowed to him gravely, and he bowed back, hand on heart. She would have had Amagien at her wedding in any case.

The thought was almost too much for her. She held back the tears. She had driven the chariot for nine days at the Battle of the Ford. Nobody here knew that, unless Amagien had discovered it, but she let the knowledge of it strengthen her as she danced the marriage measure with Lew, treading down the branches and at last taking both his hands and making her vows in a clear voice before the gods and the assembled people. She had said she would do this. At least she would get away from Maga.

Lew held Emer's arm as if he thought she might still escape. She looked at him. He was still smiling. He did not know how reluctant she had been to marry him, and he would never know. He was a good man, if a weak king, and Conal's uncle. She would be the best wife she could be to him.

The hall had been swept and the dogs chased away. The place was lit with many candles and full of the scent of roast boar. Amagien was playing the harp. Everyone was making wedding-night jokes, which Lew returned. He kept hold of Emer's arm as he drew her through the crowds. There were a few familiar faces from her last visit, and a few of Maga's entourage, including ap Dair, but most of those in the crowds were strangers to Emer.

Lew led her out in the first dance, whirling her among the confusion. It was a northern dance, danced in couples, not a southern dance with chains the way they danced in Connat. Emer hoped she wasn't too clumsy at it. The exercise made her feel better in a way, but also almost tired. Lying on the bed and weeping for nine months had got her out of condition. She would be able to practice the chariot again here. The stables were good, she remembered, as Lew turned her in his arms. She would make friends with the stable-master as soon as she had the chance.

After the dance Lew again kept her arm. He seemed to know where he was going, and she had no plans so she let him draw her after him. After a while they paused between two alcoves. Maga and Allel were sitting together to their right. Maga was dressed magnificently in primrose yellow, and wearing all her gold. She smiled at Lew as if he were a new possession. He would not be, Emer swore silently; she would not guide him towards her mother's policy but rather away from it. Emer bowed as coldly and as formally to her parents as she possibly could.

In the alcove opposite sat Atha and Darag, equally resplendent, both of them wearing red and silver. Atha had one breast bared to nurse a new baby. Emer had never thought she could be so pleased to see Darag.

"I didn't know they were here," she said in surprise.

"They wanted to come," Lew replied. "I didn't see any harm in it when Atha suggested it; they are one of my oldest alliances. Though ap Ranien, who is one of my councillors and whom you must meet soon, said it might annoy Maga."

"It might," Emer said. "But annoying Maga is not the worst thing. And it was very good of them to come when Atha must have given birth so recently."

"A nursing mother is lucky at a wedding, yes, but at this time of year they are quite plentiful," Lew said, laughing.

"I was thinking of their making the journey with the baby," Emer said. "But shall we go and greet them?"

She did not wait for Lew to agree but guided him towards Darag's alcove. "My blessings on your bed," Atha said as they approached. "Four children and a fortunate beginning."

Lew laughed and bowed, though all of them knew he had had a daughter already, who was dead. Atha began to joke with him, drawing him a little aside.

Darag put out a hand to Emer. "How are you?" he asked.

She had seen him when they had been patching up a truce after the battle. He was the only person she would trust to tell her that nobody was hiding Conal from her. She had fallen on the hillside in Cruachan, near the cave; why hadn't he? She had been very close to madness then and Darag had looked ravaged. He looked healthier now, but years older than the boy she had known.

"I am better than I was," she said starkly. "You, too?"

Darag bit his lip. "May I claim a lucky dance with the bride?" he asked Lew.

Lew was beaming at something Atha had said. It was going to be hard to live with a man whose smiles made her want to cry. "Yes, go, dance with the King of Oriel," he said, patting Emer gently on the hand. She managed to smile at him as she went. His eyes met hers as he was cooing over the baby.

Darag led her into the dance. He seemed to know the steps. "We would have given you our protection," he said quietly. "Not only for Conal's sake but for your own. We know how much we owe to you."

"My mother kept me far too closely guarded for me to consider escaping to Oriel," Emer said.

"We would still give you our protection," Darag said, his voice barely audible even to her.

Emer sighed. "I am no oath-breaker," she said. "Lew is not whom I would have freely chosen, as you know, but he is not a bad man, and there is work to do here. I have given my oath. I am married. It is too late. Besides, it would mean war with Connat, and you have probably had enough of that already."

"Oriel and I owe you a debt we can never repay," Darag said, looking more distressed than ever. "War with Connat and Anlar both would not be too high a price."

Emer shook her head. She and Darag knew what war meant. "We can be friends," Emer said. "That's all I think we can do for each other now."

"If Conal had lived—"

"Everything would have been different," Emer interrupted harshly.

"I had only just learned to like him," Darag said. "That makes my loss of him very great."

Emer could hardly keep control of herself when she heard this and thought of how Conal and Darag had hated each other. But Darag seemed sincere. "I was—he was—" She broke off. "It is the worst thing that could happen," she said.

"Not the worst thing," Darag said, very low. "You didn't kill him yourself."

"Oh, Darag," she said, full of sympathy she did not know how to express.

The dance was ending. Darag squeezed her hand and let it go, and then they bowed to each other. People she barely knew were pressing up to take their lucky dances with the bride. Then the outer door opened with a thump, and a blast of icy air came into the hall, blowing out a few of the candles and making people laugh and shiver. Emer turned to the door. This was her hall now, and disturbances were her responsibility, even if she had not yet taken up the keys.

Inis stood in the doorway, tall but stooping over the burden he carried, his multicolored priest's shawl blowing loose over his shoulders. The burden looked like a body, wrapped in dark cloth. It was dripping water.

Amagien had stopped playing in the middle of a phrase, and the voices that had not hushed already seemed loud and false in the spreading silence. Emer found herself taking a few steps towards the door, without having intended to.

"Ap Fathag?" she asked tentatively, trying not to make it sound like a question.

There was a moment then when she both knew and didn't know, as the wrapping fell away from his face. Then for an instant she thought it was Conal's body he carried, drowned somehow, for his eyes were closed and water ran from his hair. She thought she heard someone screaming very high and far away. Then Inis lowered the body and she kept moving forward, so that she was kneeling before Conal when he opened his eyes and looked up into her face and said her name.

# —32—

## (FERDIA)

Beneath the world, Ferdia does not yet know he is dead. He has come through the rain of stars, through the fire, through the narrow gates, past their guardians, who ignored him. Now he walks downward, which seems to be the thing to do. His wounds are visible but no longer bleeding. He has no idea how he came to be here. The walls are packed earth, making a narrow corridor. He passes a three-headed dog, which reminds him of something he has already forgotten. It raises its heads to watch him walk by, then settles them down again on its paws.

He hears the lamenting around several corners, breaking the stillness. When he comes up to them at the dark landing place, he knows he is down among the dead, and wonders how he came here.

The dead do not talk as they wait, though many remember how to weep. There is no recognition in their eyes. They stand in the darkness, all together, but each alone.

When the boat comes slipping silently down to the landing, Ferdia, always polite, is pushed to the back as the dead push forward in desperate, urgent spasm, as if time could have meaning here.

The hooded boatman reaches with his pole, pushing the dead aside, choosing the ones he will carry. This trip is for those who were killed by Darag. There are enough of them to fill the boat.

Up in the sunlight, Darag knows it and weeps. The tears reach Ferdia as a thin thread of regret. He remembers his name and his death. The boat slips downstream, crowded with lamenting souls of those who fought and lost forever.

Ferdia stares into the darkness, remembering spears, one thrown over glittering water, one thrown in a sunlit field. His best friend, his dear enemy, his broken heart. It is his lost future he mourns most. His life, his hopes, his father's kingdom, thrown away with nothing in exchange.

The boat comes at last to shore. Ferdia stands alone before the dark throne in the pillared hall, a shadow among shadows. The Lord of the Dead and his Bride look at him sadly, and judge as they must.

When he has given back his name, the sinews of his life and station, all he has been and done, his thin moth soul goes on to rebirth, wailing in the wind.

There is not, in this case, very much left at all.